New Ecological Realisms

Speculative Realism

Series Editor: Graham Harman

Editorial Advisory Board
Jane Bennett, Levi Bryant, Patricia Clough, Iain Hamilton Grant, Myra Hird,
Adrian Johnston, Eileen A. Joy

Books available

Forthcoming books

Visit the Speculative Realism website at: edinburghuniversitypress.com/series-
speculative-realism.html

New Ecological Realisms

Post-Apocalyptic Fiction and Contemporary Theory

Monika Kaup

EDINBURGH
University Press

Edinburgh University Press is one of the leading university presses in
the UK. We publish academic books and journals in our selected subject
areas across the humanities and social sciences, combining cutting-edge
scholarship with high editorial and production values to produce academic
works of lasting importance. For more information visit our website:
edinburghuniversitypress.com

Edinburgh University Press Ltd
The Tun – Holyrood Road
12(2f) Jackson's Entry
Edinburgh EH8 8PJ

Typeset in 11/13 Adobe Sabon by
Servis Filmsetting Ltd, Stockport, Cheshire

A CIP record for this book is available from the British Library

ISBN 978 1 4744 8309 4 (hardback)
ISBN 978 1 4744 8311 7 (webready PDF)
ISBN 978 1 4744 8310 0 (paperback)
ISBN 978 1 4744 8312 4 (epub)

Contents

for Bob

and for twenty years of home schooling

to the memory of my father†

Series Editor's Preface

Monika Kaup's *New Ecological Realisms: Post-Apocalyptic Fiction and Contemporary Theory* is a welcome addition to this series, covering a wide range of intellectual ground and drawing unexpected connections on nearly every page. The latter chapters of the book explore in detail some original connections between one or more philosophers and an author of contemporary post-apocalyptic fiction. Chapter 2 pairs two luminaries for perhaps the first time: Bruno Latour and Margaret Atwood. In Chapter 3, it is autopoiesis theorists Humberto Maturana and Francisco Varela dancing with the Portuguese literary lion José Saramago. Chapter 4 brings the prolific German philosopher Markus Gabriel on to the stage with science fiction superstar Octavia Butler. Finally, Chapter 5 employs the phenomenologies of Alphonso Lingis and Jean-Luc Marion to explore the dismal human collapse in Cormac McCarthy's *The Road*. In this Preface I will leave these delicacies to the reader's exploration, and focus instead on Kaup's Chapter 1, which sets forth her general thesis.

Kaup lets us know early on that the philosophical authors in the preceding paragraph were not chosen at random. In this book she is less interested in object-oriented ontology and the various new materialisms than in what she calls 'context-based realism', which she uses as a synonym for 'ecological realism' as found in the title of this book. While that description is obviously correct as concerns Latourian actor-network theory and Gabriel's ontology of fields of sense (which was first published in this very series), Kaup makes a more daring gamble in reading Maturana, Varela,

Marion and Lingis in this way.[1] This is particularly true of the two Chilean authors (namely, Maturana and Varela) whose theory of autopoiesis entails a degree of *closure* by which any cell is cut off from the remainder of reality. One of Kaup's major resources along her chosen path is a work of analytic philosophy: *Retrieving Realism*, by Hubert Dreyfus and Charles Taylor.[2] These authors too seek a context-based realism, for which they find the rudiments already at hand in the phenomenological notions of embodiment and embeddedness.

Kaup contends vigorously that the recent ontological return is not just 'the latest fad of white academic culture'. Along with providing a necessary response to the increasingly evident deficiencies of constructivism, there are at least two external forces pushing philosophy back in the direction of realism. Perhaps the most obvious of the two is climate change, which simply cannot be understood as a linguistic or textual phenomenon. The other important external force, as Kaup sees it, is neuroscience. It is one thing to express one's awareness that the human mind is not some pristine *cogito* sitting in a worldless vacuum, but quite another to come to grips with the emerging sciences of the mind. Indeed, the part of philosophy that deals with such questions as the relation between mind and brain is one of the subfields undergoing a tremendous boom in recent years. This is true not only of the expected roster of hardcore analytic philosophers, but also of phenomenologists such as Shaun Gallagher and Evan Thompson, as well as of the more Hegelian-leaning Adrian Johnston and Catherine Malabou.[3]

Yet the humanities face an immediate problem when asked to take realism seriously. Philosophical realism has largely been monopolised by various forms of scientism that treat the hard sciences as severe and demanding authorities, while the humanistic disciplines have been dismissed as a sort of cake-decorating refuge for frail aesthetes who fear the rigours of mathematics. In

[1] See Markus Gabriel, *Fields of Sense: A New Realist Ontology* (Edinburgh: Edinburgh University Press, 2014).

[2] Hubert Dreyfus and Charles Taylor, *Retrieving Realism* (Cambridge, MA: Harvard University Press, 2015).

[3] Shaun Gallagher, *Action and Interaction* (Oxford: Oxford University Press, 2020); Evan Thompson, *Mind in Life: Biology, Phenomenology, and the Sciences of Mind* (Cambridge, MA: Belknap Press of Harvard University Press, 2010); Adrian Johnston and Catherine Malabou, *Self and Emotional Life: Philosophy, Psychoanalysis, and Neuroscience* (New York: Columbia University Press, 2013).

self-defence, the humanists have proclaimed the human sphere as being somehow irreducible to the findings of natural science; phenomenology is typical in this regard. But hardcore neuroscientific approaches, such as those of Patricia and Paul Churchland, or Thomas Metzinger, do not shy away from encroaching on the traditional terrain of the humanities.[4] And even if the latter can take comfort from the arguments of David Chalmers and Thomas Nagel that consciousness remains not fully assimilable by the hard sciences, the humanities continue to cede the inanimate world to those who experiment and calculate for a living.[5] There is always a Heidegger to cry out that 'science does not think', yet this seems increasingly feeble in a contemporary world that owes many of its most intriguing innovations to science and technology.[6]

Here, Kaup finds an unusually good ally in Gabriel, who is one of the finest examples of how one can be a realist philosopher without being committed to naturalism. For Gabriel, famously, 'the world does not exist'.[7] By this he does not mean that everything is a mere illusion. Instead, his claim is that there is nothing like a universal whole that could be adequately described by some fundamental domain of knowledge. Things exist and true statements are made only relative to some 'field of sense', and the field of sense of natural science is not deeper or more adequate than those of the Las Vegas Strip or *War and Peace*. Borrowing a term from Dreyfus and Taylor, Kaup refers to Gabriel's theory as a form of 'contact realism', meaning that we are always already in contact with reality and need not waste time on pseudo-problems about how the mind can ever gain access to the real. Kaup also reads Lingis and Marion as 'contact realists', which is her way of linking them back to the more obviously contextual Gabriel and Latour.

---

[4] Patricia Churchland, *Neurophilosophy: Toward a Unified Science of the Mind-Brain* (Cambridge, MA: Bradford, 1989); Paul Churchland, *Scientific Realism and the Plasticity of Mind* (Cambridge: Cambridge University Press, 1985); Thomas Metzinger, *Being No One: The Self-Model Theory of Subjectivity* (Cambridge, MA: Bradford, 2004).

[5] David Chalmers, *The Conscious Mind: In Search of a Fundamental Theory* (Oxford: Oxford University Press, 1997); Thomas Nagel, 'What is it Like to be a Bat?', *The Philosophical Review*, 83.4 (1974), pp. 435–50.

[6] Martin Heidegger, *What is Called Thinking?*, trans. J. G. Gray (New York: Harper, 1968), p. 8.

[7] Markus Gabriel, *Why the World Does Not Exist*, trans. G. Moss (Cambridge: Polity, 2015).

This is one possible strategy for dealing with the crisis of the humanities. Another is the theme of 'emergence', which grants autonomous reality to things at levels more complex than the micro-structures typically privileged by physics.[8] In response to the possible worry that this entails a sloppy half-realism that lacks the critical potential to dismiss mere phantoms and fairies from our world, Kaup 'rejects the absolute dichotomy between human fabrication and reality', a claim strongly endorsed by Latour. For the same reason, she distances herself from Quentin Meillassoux's programme of mathematical access to a real world preceding consciousness.[9] Like Latour, she wants to do justice to such social fabrications as 'speed bumps and race', and not just 'hurricanes or earthquakes'. At the same time, Kaup also has good reasons for not hopping on the New Materialist bandwagon. As she concisely puts it: 'Phenomena that can be classified as material make up a very small portion of the objects of study in the humanities.' This rejection of materialism in favour of a context-based realism may turn out to be the most provocative and controversial aspect of Kaup's book. Time will tell.

Having established this sophisticated and colourful philosophical groundwork, Kaup has already prepared us for her fascinating interpretations of post-apocalyptic fiction. As she sees it, the main difference between this new literature and the older tradition of apocalyptic literature is its shift from models of sudden apocalypse (nuclear holocaust, alien invasions) to more gradual breakdowns of civilised order. This means that the post-apocalyptic genre is in some sense ecological. Either society breaks down step by step and ends up in cannibalism, or the boundary between human beings on one side and the animal and robotic kingdoms on the other is slowly eroded, or other assumptions of civilised life are degraded or transformed in ways that demonstrate the modern *cogito*'s entanglement with its environs. In Kaup's demonstration of this point, the various literary case studies she considers are a rare feast.

What stands out most for me about this book is its simultaneous philosophical and literary sophistication. When reading *New*

---

[8] Here Kaup cites Manuel DeLanda and Graham Harman, *The Rise of Realism* (Cambridge: Polity, 2017).

[9] Quentin Meillassoux, *After Finitude: An Essay on the Necessity of Contingency*, trans. R. Brassier (London: Continuum, 2008).

Ecological Realisms, I am reminded of the very best academic conferences I have ever attended, with new names and fresh ideas adrift in the air, and plenty of benevolent companionship with vigorous give-and-take. Kaup does not just challenge the sometimes imperious status of science, which is merely what one expects professors of the humanities to do. She is also willing to challenge the positions of such influential schools as New Materialism, Object-Oriented Ontology and Speculative Realism. Kaup is a critical fellow traveller of the sort that everyone badly needs but seldom finds.

Graham Harman
Long Beach, California
September 2020

Acknowledgements

Like many books, this study is indebted to many – friends, colleagues, as well as institutions. I would like to thank all those who have contributed time and effort during the various stages in which it developed, especially Markus Gabriel, Celia Lowe, Amos Nascimento, Michael Rosenthal and Sabine Willke. Jason Wirth made something happen in Latourian terms when he put me in touch with Markus Gabriel. Invaluable, too, were conversations with students in two graduate courses I taught on new realisms after postmodernism in 2015 and in 2019, especially with Jenny van Houdt and Phil Savage, whose interest in new realism carried on to a reading group on the topic.

A year-long sabbatical leave, awarded by the College of Arts and Sciences at the University of Washington, was indispensable because it enabled me to write the bulk of the manuscript. I am also happy to acknowledge support from the University of Washington's Royalty Research Fund for a research fellowship, which made it possible for me to finish it. I am grateful to the two anonymous reviewers for their incisive and generous comments on my manuscript. Finally, I thank Carol Macdonald, my editor at Edinburgh University Press, and my series editor, Graham Harman, for their guidance and support throughout.

Most important of all, my deepest thanks go to Bob Mugerauer, whose intellectual companionship and loving support have been essential to this project from its gestation to its completion.

Last but not least, I gratefully acknowledge Oxford University Press for permission to publish, in revised and expanded form, material from 'Antinomies of the Twenty-First-Century Neobaroque:

Cormac McCarthy and Demian Schopf', which appeared in *The Oxford Handbook of the Baroque*, ed. John D. Lyons (Oxford: Oxford University Press, 2019), 149–84.

Introduction

What comes after poststructuralism? This book is about an ongoing intellectual shift in the humanities and the humanistic social sciences in the wake of postmodernism and poststructuralism: the recovery of the real, and of realism. After decades of debate over the social and linguistic construction of everything, the problem of the real that postmodernism and poststructuralism had dismissed as naive is back on the intellectual agenda. For more than a decade now, we have been experiencing a so-called ontological turn in critical theory, a move towards questions of 'what there is', 'what is the case' and 'how things are presented or given': problems of being, existence, reality, world.

This shift constitutes a marked change of direction – even a reversal – from earlier turns in the twentieth century: most importantly, the so-called 'linguistic turn' towards the centrality of language and discourse. Coined by Richard Rorty, the linguistic turn is the name given to linguist and founder of structuralism Ferdinand de Saussure's discovery that language is not a transparent medium reflecting reality but a system through which a simulated reality is constructed in the differential code of language. In this view, language and discourse do not represent things 'as they are': on the contrary, known reality is the effect of language and discourse.

In the text-based disciplines of literary studies, the rise of theory in the 1970s set in motion a related turn, the so-called 'hermeneutics of suspicion', a phrase coined by Paul Ricoeur to capture the combative critical sensibilities of Marx, Nietzsche and Freud and the critical schools founded by them.[1] Such symptomatic reading is a mode of interpretation that assumes that a text's real meaning is not manifest in what it explicitly states or knows, but in what is unstated or concealed beneath the surface.[2] Hence it is the critic's task to 'wrest meaning' from a 'resisting text' (Best and Marcus 5); instead of listening to what the text says, the critic seeks to unmask the truth hidden beneath its surface by way of ideology critique. The linguistic turn refers to an intellectual paradigm shift. The hermeneutics of suspicion is a mode of textual analysis. Both have worked in tandem to redirect focus away from the given reality and the stated truth of the artwork to critiques of the hidden construction of meaning through language, culture and ideology as dominant concerns in literary and cultural studies since the 1970s.

At the outset of this study, which showcases a specific trend in the rehabilitation of ontology that I call new ecological realisms, it is important to acknowledge that the turn to language, culture and ideology has been enormously generative. As Stacy Alaimo and Susan Hekman observe, it 'has fostered complex analyses of the interconnections between power, knowledge, subjectivity, and language' (Alaimo and Hekman 1). The arrival of structuralism in the 1960s prompted a revolution in knowledge that shifted the focus from consciousness, human experience, action and interaction, and social reality to abstract (discursive and social) structures and formations. Structuralism displaced thinkers such as Hannah Arendt, whose study *The Human Condition* defended the claim that through action we are born into subjectivity (see Arendt 175–81). Structuralism gave way to so-called poststructuralism – not a movement of its own, but offering distinct avenues of critique of structuralism's weaknesses. While structuralism and poststructuralism rightly delegitimised naive concepts of the real, of individualism and anthropocentric humanism, they have led to some disabling generalisations that turn large areas of reality (art, religion, everyday practice, lived experience, embodied understanding, embedded action, hybrid, ecological networks of humans and non-humans) into marionettes of abstract structures by deploying monolithic causality. If the default response to literary works is to reduce them to puppets dominated by the same predictable roster of omnipotent abstract forces ('society, knowledge, power-slash-discourse' [Latour, 'Critique' 155]), what is the point of analysing them in the first place? Analyses of this type have a pre-scripted, even canned quality, a sign that they have exhausted their possibilities. The inadequacies of such pieces are the target of Bruno Latour's much-cited 2004 essay, 'Why Has Critique Run Out of Steam?'

Postmodernism is a term that refers to artistic expressions (in architecture, literature and so on) of the constructivist outlook that demystifies the real as the effect of linguistic and other mediation (see Nicol). It is distinct from poststructuralism, which names a theory of 'the relationships between human beings, the world, and the practices of making and reproducing meanings' (Belsey 5). Examining the complex relationships between postmodernism, poststructuralism and related outlooks is beyond the scope of this study; for our purposes, it will suffice to note that postmodernism overlaps with poststructuralism in emphasising the corrosive effects of language and other systems of signification on meaning, identity and other cultural phenomena falsely assumed to be stable and determinate. It is to refer to this shared stance that this study uses the terms postmodernism and poststructuralism interchangeably.

Over the last decades, resistance has been building against the erasure of the real at the hands of postmodern and other types of constructivisms.[3] Contemporary theory has returned to the drawing board to renegotiate the basic opposition between realism and constructivism, objectivism and solipsism, materialism and idealism. After 2006, the year in which Quentin Meillassoux's *After Finitude: An Essay on the Necessity of Contingency* was published in the French original, a significant number of new movements appeared under various umbrella terms: 'speculative realism' was inaugurated at a 2007 workshop meeting of four philosophers (Quentin Meillassoux, Graham Harman, Iain Hamilton Grant, Ray Brassier); since then it has enlisted new followers (Steven Shaviro) even as the original group disbanded.[4] Other currents developed independently: 'object-oriented ontology' (Graham Harman, Ian Bogost, Timothy Morton, Levi Bryant et al.), 'new materialisms' and 'feminist materialisms' (Diana Coole and Samantha Frost, Stacy Alaimo, Jane Bennett, Karen Barad et al.). Although there are some significant overlaps and cross-affiliations, these movements and their individual members do not pursue a coherent intellectual goal. They are united not by common solutions, but by a shared problematic: the search for new ontologies after constructivism, whether these are new materialisms, new realisms, object-oriented ontologies, or other varieties, such as an ontology of knowledge (Markus Gabriel's project in *Transcendental Ontology*). As Gabriel explains, '*our thoughts about the way the world is are themselves a way the world is*' (*Transcendental Ontology* xii).

Speculative realists were energised by Meillassoux's influential polemic against so-called 'correlationism', as he describes the 'philosophy of human access' after Kant. Kant's exclusion of things-in-themselves from human knowledge redefined modern philosophy as epistemology, limiting it to investigations of the forms and categories of human knowledge. With Kant's Copernican Revolution in knowledge focusing on human conditions of access to things rather than things-in-themselves, epistemology displaced ontology from its traditional rank as first philosophy. But there are other influences and earlier beginnings than Meillassoux's landmark study: for several of these scholars, including new materialists such as Jane Bennett, Bruno Latour's actor-network theory and his concept of the actant have been influential. Replacing the human-centred notion of agency and action, actants include non-humans. Further eliminating the idea of isolated agents, actants are pictured as embedded in a web of relationships: an actant is defined as who or what 'mak[es] someone do something' and who or what is 'made to act by many others' (Latour, *Reassembling* 58, 46) Although coming from a different intellectual background, Karen Barad's agential realism, for example, which studies 'intra-action' between human observers and observed matter, humans and non-humans, is deeply compatible with Latour's actor-network theory.

But the panorama of new ontologies is even more extensive: in fact, I have not yet named three of the four representatives of new ontologies that this study considers: Chilean neuroscientists and phenomenologists Humberto Maturana and Francisco Varela's theories of autopoiesis and enactivism, German philosopher Markus Gabriel's new ontology of fields of sense, and new phenomenologies after poststructuralism (Jean-Luc Marion's phenomenology of givenness and Alphonso Lingis's phenomenology of passionate identification). My fourth representative is Bruno Latour. In addition to actor-network theory, the related concept of the factish will be discussed. Both are associated with an ontology that Latour calls compositionism, which shifts from dismantling false beliefs to reassembling world.

My focus will be on new realisms rather than materialisms or object ontologies, for reasons to be explained below. Within the broader movement of the ontological turn after postmodernism and poststructuralism, my point of intervention is to orient myself towards a new realism of complex and embedded wholes, actor-networks and ecologies, rather than a realism of isolated parts and things. The four new realist theories assembled here all elaborate what – using the language of systems theory[5] – I call holistic or 'contextual' realisms, or realisms of organised wholes. All four theories posit that reality is not found by decomposing things into elementary parts, but by describing patterns, or mapping the way things are organised into ordered ensembles, constellations and configurations.

I explore applications of these ideas through close readings of recent post-apocalyptic fiction (Margaret Atwood's *MaddAddam* series, Cormac McCarthy's *The Road*, Octavia Butler's *Parable* series and José Saramago's *Blindness*) that depicts human experience and action after the destruction of modern civilisation. As a crisis narrative about the end of an entire world, apocalyptic thinking is ontological. What is more, like the new realist theories selected here, it embeds a contextual or systems vision of the real. Apocalypse is a way that the (entire) world is. It is not about depicting individuals or isolated things, but about picturing contexts. Apocalypse is a field of sense (Markus Gabriel) in which individuals and things appear. While apocalyptic narrative is about getting ready for the coming end of the world, post-apocalyptic fiction is about crawling out of the rubble and remaking world and society from within the wasteland of ruins. The 'oddly hopeful' (Irr 170) quality that characterises post-apocalyptic fictions of survival and world-making parallels the revisionary bent of new realist theories after poststructuralism. Just as new realisms revision old realisms, so post-apocalyptic fiction recreates the world after its apocalyptic destruction. The title of this study – *New Ecological Realisms* – not only describes the context-orientation of the new realist ontologies: it also speaks to the ecological concerns of contemporary post-apocalyptic fiction.

As a literary scholar, I believe that the production of concepts and rubrics of analysis is not reserved to critical theory. Compelling concepts are as likely to emerge from literary works – if one cares to listen. I aim to show that the genre of apocalyptic narrative also puts forward – is predicated on – a contextual model of the real. This, therefore, is a comparative study exploring the proposition, urged by new realist theories as well as by post-apocalyptic fiction, that grasping reality is about mapping worlds and exploring contexts, rather than about making a collection of everything that there is. I hope to show that, just as new realist theory can illuminate post-apocalyptic literature, post-apocalyptic literature also embeds new theories of the real. This is a comparative study pairing contemporary theory with post-apocalyptic fiction. To fully appreciate the achievements of both genres, this book begins with a general survey discussing the fundamentals of its concerns and ideas (Chapter 1). Next follow four in-depth chapters, which respectively introduce the four new realist theories selected (Chapters 2–5). The expository Chapter 1 presents a larger general picture of the subject of this study. Its purpose is to establish a framework for the examination of specific theorists and post- apocalyptic novels in the four subsequent case studies. Yet its organisation is different from that of the chapters that follow: Chapters 2 to 5 each pair one theory (or theorist) with one post-apocalyptic novel (or series of novels) with which they share close affinities. Chapter 1, on the other hand, considers new realist theories and post-apocalyptic fiction separately, on their own terms, in two consecutive sections. By placing theory side-by-side with literature, the four core chapters demonstrate the striking points of convergence and agreement between them. These are all the more illuminating since beforehand, the survey-oriented Chapter 1 clarifies the distinct contributions of new realist theories and post-apocalyptic fiction separately.

Since I have already said a lot about new realism, no further summary of its principal concerns and contributions – which will be unfolded more fully in the first half of Chapter 1 – is needed here. Instead, let me outline the main points of the introductory review of post- apocalyptic fiction offered in Chapter 1's second half ('Post-Apocalyptic Fiction: Living on Beyond the World-End'). Here, I establish the distinctive contribution of literature to the new context-based realisms showcased in this study. What does literature know? What are the singular traits of post-apocalyptic narrative as a literary ontology? Apocalyptic thinking is inherently ontological: it is about the world as a whole. What is at stake in apocalyptic upheaval is more than the ruin of things or the death of individuals: it is the annihilation of the world as such. In envisioning the destruction of the world, apocalyptic thinking reveals the core essence of the world. I argue that apocalyptic narrative is a literary variety of a 'systems' vision of the real that demonstrates the irreducibility of integrated wholes. According to Frank Kermode's classic account of the analogy between apocalypse and literary fiction, apocalyptic thinking makes a two-step affirmation of finitude. First, apocalypse envisions a future that is closed, headed for a predetermined end. Second, at the level of literary form, apocalyptic narratives are 'end-determined fictions' that illustrate the retrospective creation of meaning in narratives. The prophesied end of the world of apocalyptic narratives is a prototype of such closure – a fulfilling ending – required by all narratives to create coherence and meaning. Further unpacking the dual temporality of narrative, Paul Ricoeur contends that the gist of narrative is the act of configuration or emplotment: plot is the 'intelligible whole' that is superimposed on time as linear flow. This hermeneutic structure of narrative is a 'non-chronological' element that works against the chronicity of time. I contend that what I call 'world-endist emplotment' is the first of two key features defining apocalyptic ontology: unlike the propositional form of theory, narrative form enacts – or emplots – the systems theoretical insight that 'the whole is greater than the sum of its parts'.

The second distinguishing feature is what Catherine Keller calls apocalyptic narrative's 'script of binary time': apocalyptic worlds are organised around two distinct times and worlds straddling a revolutionary – and violent – break. The present world is coming to a catastrophic end, which clears the way for the emergence of another world that is radically dissimilar. This split composition hinging on a revolutionary break defines the two sub-varieties of apocalyptic narrative: whereas apocalyptic narrative proper is set on the near side of the cataclysm, post-apocalyptic narrative is situated on the far side, in its aftermath. Apocalyptic narratives are fictions of world-destruction. Post-apocalyptic narratives are fictions of world-remaking after the world-end. As narratives of survival amid the ruins depicting indeterminate new beginnings after the world-end, I argue, post-apocalyptic narratives belong to the paradigm shift also enacted by new realisms after postmodernism: like the latter, they revision the real. Unlike the earlier Cold War era variety, contemporary post-apocalyptic fiction envisions a 'slow' apocalypse of environmental and public health disasters rather than the 'fast' apocalypse of atomic holocaust. Further, distinct from sci-fi fantasy such as *Star Wars*, contemporary post-apocalyptic fiction is animated by a speculative realism of its own that extrapolates the disastrous consequences of present developments.

As noted above, to showcase affinities between these seemingly unrelated genres of new realism and post-apocalyptic fiction, the specific chapters following the overview in Chapter 1 pair one theory with one post-apocalyptic novel (or series of novels) whose concerns, I demonstrate, are particularly compatible. In brief, the pairings are: Bruno Latour's actor-network theory and Margaret Atwood's *MaddAddam* series (Chapter 2); Humbert Maturana and Francisco Varela's theories of autopoiesis and enactivism and José Saramago's *Blindness* (Chapter 3); Markus Gabriel's fields of sense ontology and Octavia Butler's *Parable* series (Chapter 4); Jean-Luc Marion's and Alphonso Lingis's new phenomenologies and Cormac McCarthy's *The Road* (Chapter 5).

Chapter 2, 'The New Realism of the Factish and the Political Ecology of Humans and Non-Humans: Bruno Latour and Margaret Atwood's *MaddAddam* Trilogy', places Latour's actor-network theory side-by-side with Atwood's *MaddAddam* trilogy. Independent of but closely paralleling Latour's call to overcome what he calls the modern constitution, the *MaddAddam* trilogy pictures the formation of a cross-species ecology of humans and non-humans. In Atwood's speculative near-future scenario of post-apocalyptic America, almost all humans have been exterminated in a bioterrorist attack by Crake, a geneticist, to save the warming planet from total ecological collapse. Stripped of the modern technologies that enable humans to exploit nature, scattered survivors are stranded on the climate-changed and polluted planet that they have manufactured. An artificial species of peaceful humanoids, the Crakers, has been bioengineered to take their place.

Published on the fiftieth anniversary of the discovery of DNA, the *MaddAddam* trilogy focuses on genetics and bioengineering. Critiquing genetic determinism, it envisions the autonomous ontogeny and cultural history of artificial species that have gone feral after the cataclysm, in particular the Crakers, as they defy their genetic programmes and develop independent purposive behaviour. Falsifying old realist notions of intrinsic nature, the Crakers' unplanned development is traced to their embedding in an emergent post-apocalyptic order after the world-end, echoing the claims of Latour's networks ontology. Atwood's artificial species are supreme instances of Latour's hybrids, artefacts of laboratory experimentation who, in the uncontrolled environment of post-apocalyptic history, acquire autonomous modes of existence. Factishes that are fabricated yet nonetheless real, these bioengineered creatures undergo an ontological transformation to become full-fledged actants. After the ecological collapse, humans can no longer subject nature to their will; the old deterministic view of nature as machine is demolished by manufactured beings developing free will like humans. In the third volume, *MaddAddam*, these join forces with the surviving humans to form a trans-species collective, embarking on an unprecedented biological and cultural evolution that interconnects natural and artificial species. The specifically ecological critique of modernity formulated by Latour also underpins the *MaddAddam* trilogy. By casting it in the form of post-apocalyptic narrative, Atwood introduces an element of temporal finitude that the straightforward propositional form of Latour's theory lacks. Set in a post-collapse future separated by an irreversible break from the modern world as we know it, Atwood's ecological order is given a speculative facticity that theoretical discourse cannot provide.

Chapter 3, 'The Ontology of Knowledge as the Enaction of Mind and World: Humberto Maturana and Francisco Varela's Autopoietic Theory and José Saramago's *Blindness*', focuses on a new realist ontology of knowledge. It argues that Maturana and Varela's concept of knowledge as embodied action is also the crux of Saramago's *Blindness*. An anti-representational theory of knowledge, the Santiago theory's pivotal insight is that all knowledge is primarily about worlds, and about world-making. Far from involving a pre-given observer representing a pre-existing reality, cognition or knowledge, is about the co-constitution of minds and worlds in the process of living. Pairing Maturana and Varela's theories with Saramago's novel brings to light striking parallels with regard to their shared rejection of the representational paradigm and their corresponding articulation of an ontological approach to knowledge. They complement each other: the propositional form of enactivist theory sets out a clear argument. For its part, the 'endism' structuring Saramago's post-apocalyptic script provides a stage for its ontology of knowledge to be acted out in narrative time.

Saramago's novel depicts the apocalyptic collapse of a city (the implicit microcosm of the world) in the wake of a fantastic epidemic of white-blindness. The events in *Blindness* enact the age-old Western metaphor of knowledge ('insight') as vision. Deprived of vision, the newly white-blind are stripped of access to the privileged position of the Cartesian disembodied observer. The apocalyptic plague of white-blindness demolishes the old realist fiction of the Cartesian detached observer and the modern representational paradigm that arose out of it. Saramago asks: What is the phenomenology of blind perception? Saramago's answer parallels two key claims formulated by Maturana and Varela: first, blind perception is immersed in its embodiment. Blind minds are 'embodied minds' in Maturana and Varela's sense, minds thrown back on the sensorimotor apparatus of their bodies, which has been reduced from five to four senses. Given its obvious deficiencies, blind perception clearly falls short of an objective 'reflection' of external reality. The central challenge confronting the blind survivors is the task of reconstituting their entire world from the ground up, a process in which, as Varela et al. contend, 'minds and worlds arise together' (Varela et al. 177). Second, the newly white-blind protagonists in Saramago's *Blindness* learn that to be blind means to be post-individual. Unlike the sighted, the blind cannot survive as autonomous individuals. Their survival is dependent on what Maturana and Varela call social coupling within self-organising collectives. They discover that lost vision can be replaced by collaborative social action: 'to organise oneself is, in a way, to begin to have eyes' (*Blindness* 296). It is not as isolated individuals but as a symbiotic collective that the white-blind are able to reclaim their humanity.

From the new realism of artefacts (Chapter 2) and the new ontology of knowledge (Chapter 3), Chapter 4, 'Apocalypse as Field of Sense: Markus Gabriel's Ontology of Fields of Sense and Octavia Butler's *Parable* Series', turns to the problem of existence as such. As Gabriel contends, existence is not an intrinsic property of things or isolated objects, but is relational: existence is defined as 'the fact that something appears in a context' (*Fields of Sense* 158). The claims of fields of sense ontology are shown to underlie Butler's *Parable* series, which, like Gabriel, makes organised contexts of meaning the touchstone of the real. The *Parable* series is organised around the life of Lauren Oya Olamina, who, after her displacement following the apocalyptic destruction of her suburban Los Angeles community, becomes a spiritual leader who founds a post-apocalyptic religion named Earthseed. Butler's post-apocalyptic survivor narrative is framed as a spiritual quest: the elements of spirituality that elsewhere figure in the background (the religious references to God, pilgrims and prophets in *The Road*; Atwood's green religion, the God's Gardeners) move centre stage.

Earthseed is a metaphysic of survival founded on the facticity of catastrophe: its maxim is 'God is Change.' A metaphysic of contingency emerging from the experience of disaster, it turns the devastating fact of destruction into a positive principle on which to found post-apocalyptic survival. The earthseed metaphor names the mobile logic of homelessness and displacement governing survival in the post-apocalyptic world: like plants, which survive by seeding themselves far from home, growing roots only to disperse again, so post-apocalyptic refugees must embrace a nomadic existence alternating between 'roots' and 'routes'. Earthseed is an ecological belief system that situates humans within an interconnected biocentric frame, thereby instituting the loss of human domination of nature in the post-apocalyptic world. Gabriel's ontology of fields of sense sheds light on the rationale underpinning Lauren's reconceptualisation of God. Apocalypse is the field that reorganises the things that appear within it. Butler shows that this field-dependence of objects also holds true for the most sublime phenomenon of all: the figure of God and the divine. Apocalyptic destruction forces Lauren to abandon the classic notion of God as unchanging being. In the post-apocalypse, God is no longer absolute in the sense of existing without cause. How God appears is relative to the post-apocalyptic world in which he appears. Lauren's notion of the relativity of God is revolutionary. It not only dethrones the biblical God, it also overthrows traditional notions of the divine as the realm of perfection in general. Field of sense ontology states the demise of 'old realist' notions of objects and metaphysics in propositional form. By demoting God to a reduced force subject to the laws of the post-apocalyptic world in which s/he appears, the *Parable* series stages them in the narrative form of apocalyptic 'endism'.

Chapter 5, 'New Phenomenologies after Poststructuralism (Jean-Luc Marion and Alphonso Lingis) and Cormac McCarthy's *The Road*', concentrates on the implications of new realism for the concept of the (human) self. The finitude of apocalyptic thinking and the post-apocalyptic script of living on after the world-end call for new models of selfhood that can account for radical breaks and transformations. Conversely, Marion's phenomenology of givenness models a post-individual and decentred self that arises in response to an overpowering event. The unnamed protagonist of McCarthy's *The Road* has been given a terrible responsibility: to raise his son, born shortly after an unnamed cataclysm that has destroyed almost all life on earth, with the exception of some scattered humans. With the sun permanently obscured, the survivors are stranded on a dying planet without renewable food sources. *The Road* is set in an entropic world where the future of life as such is in question. Making their way south in search of a warmer climate, father and son traverse the post-apocalyptic wasteland while living in constant fear of marauding gangs of warlords who practise slavery and cannibalism. The darkest of all the post-apocalyptic novels discussed here, *The Road* is a perfect match for the phenomenologies of Marion and Lingis that examine first-personal experience after the exhaustion of postmodernist and poststructuralist constructs of the subject.

Marion's phenomenology of givenness is best equipped to conceptualise first-personal experience in the post-apocalyptic condition. Marion contends that the successor to the subject is a reduced self that he names 'the gifted', a term that identifies the figure that arises from its response to the world to which it is given over (givenness). The new self that emerges is a non- autonomous self, a recipient first – 'a me *to whom*' the given is gifted – then an agent. Depending on the response by the receiver, phenomena arise, as well as the new self whose nature is defined by this dynamic (the gifted). Marion pictures a call-and-response structure whose circular organisation expresses the holistic outlook of his phenomenology. Givenness has primacy, but it is manifest only in the response it is met with. On the other hand, the response that phenomenalises the call is secondary. In other words, the organised ensemble of givenness is the ontological base unit of call and response, not the individual self. Unlike Althusser, who contends that the realm of first-personal experience is the domain of ideology, for Marion, the gifted's response is intrinsically free, in that it cannot be determined by outside forces but is governed by rules internal to the receiver. She or he may even opt to reject the call, as does the boy's mother in *The Road*, who commits suicide rather than accept the horrific burden of post-apocalyptic parenting.

For Marion, the notion of being gifted includes a darker dimension of 'what befalls' me. As such, givenness expresses the horrific condition that has been inflicted on the survivor-protagonists of post-apocalyptic fiction. The father's response in *The Road* is to embrace the responsibility for his son with passionate commitment, expressed in a mantra ('I am a father'), which also exemplifies Lingis's claims that self arises from, and peaks in, impassioned states. This passionate identification marks the birth of the man's new post-apocalyptic self, a new 'gifted', a different person than the childless man he was before the cataclysm, who has disappeared along with the world that has been annihilated. Chapter 5's analysis of post-apocalyptic identity as a creative response to survival after the world-end can also be extended to similar situations elsewhere in contemporary post-apocalyptic fiction, such as Atwood's *Oryx and Crake*, where the lone survivor, Jimmy, renames himself 'Snowman' to mark the irreversible discontinuity between his lost former self and his new existence as the last human on earth.

Notes

1. According to Ricoeur, the hermeneutics of suspicion differs from traditional hermeneutics in its attitude towards the text it explicates. 'Animated by faith and a willingness to listen', the hermeneutics of Heidegger and Gadamer – which Ricoeur calls the hermeneutics of belief – 'uncovers what wishes to be uncovered' (Kaplan 21; Simms 47). In contrast, the hermeneutics of suspicion is 'animated by mistrust and skepticism' and 'uncovers what wishes to remain hidden' (Kaplan 21; Simms 47).

2. Ricoeur's account of symptomatic reading has been the touchstone for ongoing efforts to revision critical sensibilities and methods of reading in literary studies since the early 2000s. Central expressions of the critique of symptomatic reading can be found in Stephen Best and Sharon Marcus, 'Surface Reading: An Introduction', and Rita Felski, *Uses of Literature* and *The Limits of Critique*. In addition to 'surface reading' and Felski's 'postcritical reading', further alternatives for moving beyond the impasse of symptomatic reading have been proposed, such as Heather Love's 'thin description' concentrating on empirical methods. Others are sceptical that the critique of critique is likely to have any effect: for David Shumway, 'the fundamental conflict between the text as object of critique and the text as bearer of knowledge or wisdom cannot be overcome within the humanities' (Shumway 21). I agree with Shumway's point. This study is broadly aligned with efforts to prioritise a 'listening' attitude towards the literary text.

3. In Karen Barad's words, 'Language has been granted too much power. The linguistic turn, the semiotic turn, the interpretative turn, the cultural turn: it seems that at every turn lately every "thing" – even materiality – is turned into a matter of language or some other form of cultural representation' ('Posthumanist Performativity' 120).

Critiques of the excesses of poststructuralism began to appear as early as the 1970s, increasing in the decades after. One landmark is the collection *Beyond Poststructuralism* (1996), which contains an essay by John Searle, a vocal critic of the fallacies of Derrida and his followers since the 1970s.

4. For accounts of this movement, see Gratton; Shaviro; and Harman, *Speculative Realism* (a 2018 survey by one of its participant founders).

5. My account of systems theory throughout this study is indebted to Capra, *The Web of Life*, and Capra and Luisi, *The Systems View of Life: A Unifying Vision*. These works offer the clearest, most comprehensive, systematic and detailed account of the rise of systems thinking and all its varieties in the twentieth century.

1

New Ecological Realisms and Post-Apocalyptic Fiction

To fully appreciate the distinct contributions of the two genres compared here, this study begins by offering a general overview. To this end, this chapter takes a broad sweep through the fundamental concerns and ideas of new ecological realisms and post-apocalyptic fiction respectively. I begin with the former and then turn to the latter.

The overview of new realism in the first half of this chapter is not a systematic account of the ontological turn: such works have been becoming available for specific subgroupings of the field, for example Peter Gratton's *Speculative Realism: Problems and Prospects* (2014) and, most recently, Graham Harman's *Speculative Realism: An Introduction* (2018) and *Object-Oriented Ontology: A New Theory of Everything* (2018). Designed to provide a frame of reference for the context-oriented approach to the real advocated here, this survey will proceed in two steps. The first three sections ('Finding a Path through the Ontological Turn', 'Old Realism, New Realisms', 'Realism or Materialism?') examine the recovery of the real after the exhaustion of constructivism and offer an in-depth review of principal concepts and positions central to the debate about new ontologies as they have developed independently of one another. The following section ('New Ecological Realisms') offers a synthetic presentation of the principal characteristics of the approach and the specific contribution of this study, which is double: first, to identify and systematically introduce a unique class of new ontologies – context-based realisms – that merits wider recognition as a distinct rubric. Secondly, and to this end, this study makes visible hidden correspondences between theories that have not been considered together before. The section

'New Ecological Realisms' concludes the theory overview. The following and last section, 'Post-Apocalyptic Fiction: Living on Beyond the World-End', shifts focus from theory to literature, turning to a general overview of the main characteristics and concerns of contemporary post-apocalyptic literature.

Finding a Path through the Ontological Turn

To appreciate the momentum of the shift in critical theory currently underway, it is useful to draw a larger map of the panorama of burgeoning new ontologies. Charles Taylor and Hubert Dreyfus's co-authored volume *Retrieving Realism* (2015) is an important contribution by two renowned figures in contemporary philosophy. Their defence of the need to reconfigure realism is original and illuminates this study's focus on contextual realisms. To illustrate the slipperiness of what is intended by 'retrieving realism', at the outset it is instructive to juxtapose Dreyfus and Taylor's account to Meillassoux's speculative realism. Their mixed relation illuminates the vast disparity of efforts to recover the real. To begin with, there is close agreement on the identification of the problem. The approach that Dreyfus and Taylor label 'mediational epistemology' and that they set out to challenge is the familiar disengaged stance of the detached observer. Confronting an external world that she must find access to, the observer is here, but the world is 'out there'. The '"only through" structure' of finding access, which the distant observer doesn't have, 'justifies the term "mediational"' (Dreyfus and Taylor 10): in the view they seek to topple, some tool is always needed to mediate knowledge of the world, a function successively performed by Descartes' clear and distinct ideas, Kant's logical forms, and language after the linguistic turn. This epistemology is the same that Meillassoux attacks as 'correlationalism'.[1] Like 'mediational epistemology', correlationism is a term that likewise denotes the mediational structure of human access to reality.

Given their agreement on the initial dilemma, their disagreement on remedies is all the more striking. Dreyfus and Taylor and Meillassoux march off in opposite directions. The former, writing from a phenomenological standpoint, advocate for the primordiality of an embedded and embodied knowing that is always already immersed in and engaged in the world. On Dreyfus and Taylor's account, there is no escaping embeddedness by dismissing it as correlationism. Meillassoux, on the other hand, who defends a return to the pre-critical philosophy of Cartesian metaphysics, rejects phenomenology as the most extreme form of the outlook he disclaims as correlationism, because it focuses entirely on human experience. Meillassoux, in other words, attacks the standpoint advocated by Dreyfus and Taylor as the last stand of the misguided 'correlationists'. Conversely, Dreyfus and Taylor would consider Meillassoux's neo-Cartesian agenda a relapse into mind–world dualism, one of the features they reject as 'mediationalism'. (Dreyfus and Taylor, whose study appeared a decade after Meillassoux's, neither engage with speculative realism in general nor with Meillassoux specifically.) How is it possible for both to be participants in the recovery of the real – as they are? As we shall see, the decisive point is whether or not mental and social phenomena are considered part of the domain of the real. It is vital to be aware of these discrepancies at the outset, for they show the importance of mapping the specific path that this study plots through the maze of the ontological turn.

In Europe, beyond Meillassoux and the movement he helped generate (speculative realism), Maurizio Ferraris (*Introduction to New Realism*, 2015) and Jocelyn Benoist (*Elemente einer realistischen Philosophie* [*Elements of a Realist Philosophy*], 2014) are two further representatives of an extensive debate about retrieving and revisioning realism.[2] An excellent sampling of these efforts is found in the collection *Der Neue Realismus* (*New Realism*, 2014), edited by Markus Gabriel. For Gabriel, new realism does not refer to a unified doctrine; new realism is nothing but 'a name for a debate' about reconfiguring realism (Gabriel, 'Introduction' 16). As Gabriel notes, he and Ferraris collaborated in coining the term 'new realism' to designate the change in course in contemporary European philosophy away from the dominance of postmodern anti-realism. Each went on to elaborate his own position; this study will consider the most significant contribution, Gabriel's ontology of fields of sense. Running parallel to speculative realism, whose advocates are based in France, England and the US, Gabriel's new realism groups together exchanges among a distinct set of thinkers engaging in a corresponding ontological turn after postmodernism.

More recently, the revival of realism by philosophers in the continental tradition has been assessed in *The Rise of Realism* (2017), a study co-authored by Manuel DeLanda, the recognised philosopher and Deleuzian, and Graham Harman, the founder of object-oriented ontology. This work offers further insights into key features of the post-postmodernist turn to ontology. At first sight, this collaboration may seem odd, given DeLanda's Deleuzian background. Nonetheless, it produces the proposition that a realist ontology must be based on 'individual objects' (DeLanda and Harman 75).[3] Placing objects at the centre of the 'furniture of the world' (49), Harman and DeLanda rule out what they label 'reified generalities' as valid historical actors. As DeLanda affirms: 'All reified generalities (not just the Cat in general, but also the State, the Market, Power, Resistance, Labor, Capital) must be replaced' (55). This is an important point for our purposes: such monolithic abstractions typically figure as the hidden ultimate reality in constructivist explanations. Such rejection of reified generalities is also found in other new realist contributions. As we shall see in Chapter 2, in proposing an immanent approach to the social, Latour similarly rejects reified abstractions, most importantly 'society as a whole'.

Differences between DeLanda and Harman arise over the criteria determining the identity of objects: for Harman, objects are defined by their autonomous reality 'apart from any relation to anything' (DeLanda and Harman 75). In contrast, DeLanda's ontology is process-oriented and evolutionary: individual objects are 'historical entities' (76) that have been generated and maintain their identity through time, which encompasses transformations through alternate states that are not actualised. DeLanda cites a popular example for such arguments, the liquidity of water. Water remains water even though it starts to boil at 100° Celsius and begins to freeze at 0° Celsius. In the liquid state, the frozen and gas states of water are non-manifested dispositions. Nonetheless, these virtual capacities are equally part of the identity of water as any other enduring property, such as water's molecular composition, H_2O (66). Integrating Deleuzian assemblage theory, DeLanda contends that as dynamic, changing entities, individual objects always possess two dimensions, their 'actual properties and virtual dispositions' (85). DeLanda fully develops his realist ontology in *Assemblage Theory* (2016), to which we shall return when we consider the problem of materialism vs. realism.

Far from being limited to arcane academic debates, the rehabilitation of realism also bears on current social and political issues. In fact, long before the rise of a broader academic trend, realism had been taken up by critics of colour. As Paula Moya observes, minority literature has been bogged down by fruitless debates over authenticity and essentialism vs. constructivism. For decades, writers of colour have been eager to reclaim identity and lived experience as valid frameworks of knowledge. Yet this has been challenged by postmodern critiques that debunk the reality of experience as naive and uncritical and dismiss any talk of identity as essentialist, citing its social and discursive construction. In the postmodern view, whatever is socially constructed cannot be real. Race does not exist at the level of genetics, therefore it is fictitious. However, Moya counters, this does nothing to 'explain why some people experience feelings of racial self-hatred, while others feel a sense of racial superiority' (Moya, 'Reclaiming Identity' 68). No less important, in addition to exposing the deficiencies of constructivism, race also illustrates the limits of materialism. As Michael Hames-Garcia affirms, race is 'irreducible to simple physical criteria' such as genetics, skin colour and so on (Hames-Garcia 313). Any persuasive account of race must navigate between the twin temptations of sceptical constructivism on the one hand and reductionist materialism on the other. Race is an emergent phenomenon that only operates at a specific scale. Building on the materiality of the skin, it shows itself in the immaterial realms of culture and identity, as well as in social action, where its presence is undeniable: in the US, 'walking while black' can cost someone their life. Fabricated entities can have real effects, a phenomenon that is also explored by Latour's actor-network theory.

As we shall see, the rejection of the reality of everyday experience, mind and cultural constructs as 'illusive' is a cornerstone of the old regime of realism that is renounced by the new realist theories selected here. 'Old realism' is reductionist materialism, premised on the exclusion of mental and social phenomena from reality. Separating what is unreal from what is 'real' defines 'old realism'. Instead of determining whether things are real or constructed, new realism asks: Where are things real? How do things become real that might initially have been constructed or unconstructed? As will become clear, Latour's concept of the 'factish' (a neologism composed from 'fact' and 'fetish') presents a compelling answer to this problem. Factishes are a special class of actants, hybrid things or beliefs that start out as fabrications and acquire an autonomous mode of existence, in other words, the status of 'reality' or justified belief. Race is an excellent example of a factish – constructed yet all too real. To overcome the standoff between identity politics and postmodern constructivism, Moya and Satya Mohanty defend what they call a 'postpositivist realism' as a new approach to reclaiming identity and experience as valid knowledge. Moya and Mohanty's new ontology of identity, as it were (the phrase is mine), demonstrates that the ontological turn cannot be dismissed as the latest fad of white academic culture. It responds to the inadequacy of constructivist doctrine, which cuts across cultural divides such as race and gender. The exhaustion of the constructivist paradigm has registered across the breadth of humanistic and social fields of study.

Literary studies in particular has been seeing an increasing number of denunciations of the shortcomings of the constructivist consensus and corresponding proposals for alternatives. Rita Felski has called for a 'postcritical reading' to replace the hermeneutics of suspicion. Taking up Latour's critique of critique in her *Uses of Literature* (2008) and *The Limits of Critique* (2015), Felski elaborates ways in which criticism might endorse literature as a genuine source of knowledge instead of reducing it to an object of knowledge. Instead of 'looking behind the text – for its hidden causes, determining conditions, and noxious motives', Felski suggests, literary scholars might place themselves 'in front of the text, reflecting on what it unfurls, calls forth, makes possible' (*Limits of Critique* 12). Critics need to recognise the 'text's status as co-actor' (*Limits of Critique* 12). Felski's watch phrase, 'What does literature know?' (*Uses of Literature* 77), captures my interest in post-apocalyptic literature as a distinctive source of knowledge.

In addition, this study is inspired by Derek Attridge's defence of the singularity of literature. For Attridge, against literature's instrumentalisation by forms of reading that impose a pre-existing critical agenda, critics must affirm the singularity of the literary artwork. As Attridge contends, the '*singularity* of the artwork is not simply a matter of difference from other works (what I term "uniqueness"), but a transformative difference, a difference, that is to say, that involves the irruption of *otherness* or *alterity* into the cultural field' (Attridge 136). This study likewise explores – to adapt Attridge – the singularity of post-apocalyptic literature as a distinct ontology. It contends that apocalyptic thinking does more than simply illustrate the claims of new realist theories. Seeking to fulfil Felski's and Attridge's injunctions to take literary form seriously, this analysis maintains that apocalyptic thinking cannot be

process takes place through a history of structural coupling with the world and with other organisms in the course of which they also bring forth themselves. 'Mind and world arise together in enaction' (Varela et al. 177). As Varela et al. write,

> We propose as a name the term *enactive* to emphasise the growing conviction that cognition is not the representation of a pregiven world by a pregiven mind but is rather the enactment of a world and a mind on the basis of a history of the variety of actions that a being in the world performs. The enactive approach takes seriously, then, the philosophical critique of the idea that the mind is a mirror of nature but goes further by addressing this issue from within the heartland of science. (9)

Enactivism and autopoiesis (literally: 'self-making') are varieties of self-organisation theory, which in turn is a branch of systems theory. A new outlook developed in twentieth-century science, systems thinking rejects mechanical reductionism and adopts a networks view of the world. Systems theory is one of the principal tributaries of the context-based realist ontologies presented in this study. Self-organisation (or self-assembly) describes the spontaneous emergence of new organised structures. The notion of 'self' refers to the process of endogenous (self-)generation from the interaction of component parts, free of external determination (Capra and Luisi 145).

Because readers usually encounter Maturana and Varela in a different setting – posthumanism – some explanatory comments are warranted here. The concept of self-organisation describes self-organising and self-reproducing processes in non-organic systems such as hurricanes or heat convection. In contrast, autopoiesis focuses on what makes living systems special: the capacity for self-maintenance in addition to self-generation. A cautionary note: the systems theoretical concept of self-organisation must be carefully distinguished from 'any naïve conception of autonomy as the absolute self-sufficiency of a substantial subject' (Clarke and Hansen, 'Introduction' 7). Self-organisation cannot be conflated with liberal individualism. Liberal individualism is a social expression of the mechanistic outlook: the assertion of self in competition with others. The processes of self-organisation and autopoiesis are relational. That is to say, they are conditional on 'environmental entanglement' (Clarke and Hansen, 'Introduction'

7), on constant exchanges with what lies outside the system's boundary (see also Capra and Luisi). In short, unlike much neuroscience, neurophenomenology is a non-reductionist account of consciousness. Maturana and Varela's contribution demonstrates that the search for new realisms surpassing both postmodern constructivism on the one hand as well as materialist reductionism on the other can be a collaborative venture between the natural sciences and humanistic disciplines. It is heartening to be able to count on strategic allies among scientists.

What do we mean when we talk about realism? In any debate over realism, the stakes are high: what counts as 'real' is synonymous with what counts as knowledge as such. Realism is associated with the conventional definition of knowledge as true belief, as opposed to mere belief or opinion. Among the multiple definitions of 'real' listed in the *OED*, the first specifies 'having an objective existence; actually existing physically as a thing, substantial; not imaginary'.[5] A second entry, pertaining to philosophical usage, defines 'real' as 'designating whatever is regarded as having an existence in fact and not merely in appearance, thought, or language, or as having an absolute and necessary, in contrast to a merely contingent, existence'.[6] Under 'realism', the *OED* offers 'the doctrine that matter as the object of perception has real existence (*natural realism*) and is neither reducible to universal mind or spirit nor dependent on a perceiving agent'.[7] As these entries show, real and realism are defined in opposition to what is imaginary, fictitious, subjective. The *OED* entries register a hidden contradiction inherent in the modern concept of realism: on the surface, realism seems a neutral and non-exclusive term for 'what there is' or what exists, irrespective of any particular class of things. But in fact, the meaning of realism is restricted, exclusive to a privileged class of objects: things that exist in nature, in the cosmos, in material reality, as, for example, apples, chairs, horses, soap bubbles, meteors, the sun, genes, microbes, molecules and, last but not least, climate change. In contrast, entities that are non-material, especially entities belonging to the realm of the mind – such as deities or memories – are not real, since they do not exist outside the mind. Modern realism is essentially reductive materialism or naturalism.

Mind-independence is probably the most important attribute of modern realism. In his contribution to *Der Neue Realismus*, for example, John Searle introduces his argument by rehearsing this familiar claim: 'By realism in this context I intend the view that there is a reality that is completely independent of our representations' (Searle 292). Since the rise of modern science, realism has been identified with scientific objectivity and the belief in the existence of a so-called external world posited as independent of the human mind. Thus, realism is inseparable from the modern dichotomy that separates the external world of objects and the inner world of the mind. As Thomas Nagel explains, the modern mind–body problem 'is a direct result of the concept of objective physical reality' that drove the scientific revolution of the seventeenth century. Galileo and Descartes 'made the crucial conceptual division by proposing that physical science should provide a mathematically precise quantitative description of an external reality extended in space and time' (Nagel, *Mind and Cosmos* 36). It was essential to exclude mind from the realm of reality and the domain of science. Yet it is evident that this solution is inadequate: like spatiotemporal entities, our minds are part of reality. And what about mental and social phenomena such as religion, marriage, mythology, love, art, language, money, government, private property? As John Searle words the dilemma: 'How can we account for our social and mental existence in the realm of brute physical facts?' (Searle, *Making the Social World* ix). Or, as Nagel states the predicament, 'consciousness is the most conspicuous obstacle to a comprehensive naturalism that relies only on the resources of physical science' (*Mind and Cosmos* 36). Contrary to the claims of naturalism, not everything that exists is in nature. Therefore, a more comprehensive account of reality must be found that includes mind and mental phenomena.

It is easy to see why this notion of a reality without mind would constitute a serious problem for the humanities. Since their rise in the nineteenth century, the humanities have been in a defensive position because of the monopoly of the so-called hard sciences on realism. Thwarted by positivism, the humanities most recently responded by seeking refuge in constructivism. It has now become clear that this has been a self-defeating strategy. The much-touted crisis of the humanities is in part self-inflicted and due to negligence – the neglect of what is its core mission: to consider humanistic phenomena on their own terms. If my goal is to explain how contemporary literature, art and culture are ultimately constructed by neoliberalism, I am not establishing their singularity; I am explaining it away. I am effectively making a case for phasing out the humanities as an academic field and for outsourcing the study of literature and culture to, say, economics elective courses on the cultural symptoms of late capitalism. This leaves the task of humanistic study unattended to: Why are there fields that we recognise as literature, culture and art? Why should we continue to study them with methodologies distinct from economics, biology, computer science and engineering? What are the characteristics that make humanistic phenomena singular and irreducible?

A response to the failure of constructivism, new realism searches for alternatives to both constructivism and materialist reductionism. Exposing constructivism's hidden handicap, new realists note that it is predicated on the acceptance of the naturalist concept of the real. Instead of debunking social constructs, it is vital to reclaim the notion of the real. Instead of exposing the constructedness of mind-dependent phenomena such as art, literature, religion or culture, new realism proposes to establish the singular reality that obtains for such phenomena. As Latour suggests, we need to move beyond critique to recompose the humanities (Latour, 'Compositionist Manifesto'; see also Felski, 'Introduction'). Compositionism, as advocated by Latour, upholds the principle of irreduction, the idea that 'no object is inherently reducible or irreducible to any other' (Harman, *Prince of Networks* 14). Instead of unmaking worlds by debunking fallacious beliefs, compositionism concentrates on 'gathering' or assembling worlds (Latour, 'Matters of Concern' 170). Constructivists of the hermeneutics of suspicion variety are what DeLanda terms macro-reductionists. They practise what Harman similarly calls 'overmining': subsuming something under a higher-level entity (e.g. neoliberalism) by claiming that it is nothing but its local manifestation. According to Harman, there are 'two basic ways to get rid of objects in philosophy: reducing them downward to their pieces, or reducing them upward to their effects' (DeLanda and Harman 81). In other words, to be recognised as having an 'autonomous reality', a phenomenon must be 'irreducible *upwards*' as well as 'irreducible downwards' (Harman, *Quadruple Object* 16).

Harman and DeLanda concur that, in drawing up a realist ontology, the first task is to devise a means of blocking both undermining ('micro-reductionism') as well as overmining (or 'macro-reductionism') (*Assemblage Theory* 9). Applied to our present concerns, an entity classified as 'literary' or 'artistic' must be shown – to invoke the slogan of gestalt psychology – to form a whole that is 'more than the sum of its parts'. It must have what DeLanda, borrowing a concept from systems theory, calls emergent properties, that is to say, 'properties of a whole caused by the interactions between its parts' (*Assemblage Theory* 9). These properties are not inherent in any of the constituent parts; they only appear at the higher level of the new organised ensemble (Capra and Luisi 154–5). The notion of emergence derives from systems theory, to which we will have occasion to refer throughout, as well as in Chapter 3 on Maturana and Varela.

Emergence is everywhere, occurring at all scales and in all classes of reality. One example is temperature, 'central to thermodynamics', but 'meaningless at the level of individual atoms' (Capra 28). Another is taste: the taste of sugar is 'not present in the carbon, hydrogen, and oxygen atoms that constitute its components' (Capra 28). Or take the psychology of mobs, which illustrates the dynamics of emergence in the social world; it, too, is a property of the higher-order crowd that only arises from the interaction of its members, without being present in any of them. What might be the emergent properties of literary entities that make them irreducible? A simple example: Ezra Pound's Imagist poem 'In a Station of the Metro' (1913) is composed of only two lines: 'The apparition of these faces in the crowd; / Petals on a wet, black bough.'[8] The simple act of arranging these two sentence fragments in the form of verse instead of prose transforms them into an organised ensemble that we call the lyric. As a result of being interlinked in this new unity, an immaterial qualitative shift occurs through which the words and phrases acquire new meanings – emergent properties – that they did not have before. No words were added. Yet something new appears that cannot be reduced to the quantitative act of fitting two phrases together. It is this qualitative something that makes Pound's poem 'irreducible downward'. For the same reason, Pound's poem is also 'irreducible upward', blocking macro-reductionism to reified generalities such as Fordist mass production – even though the movement towards economy and efficiency characterising the machine age may have influenced the rise of modernist minimalist aesthetics such as Imagism. Would anyone deny that temperature or taste are real because they not present at the atomic level? Of course not. Mob psychology might also survive a reductionist challenge, since the destructiveness of mobs is regularly on display in the news. But literature? The gestalt of the lyric? Art? Religion? Meaning?

Markus Gabriel offers the boldest programmatic statement of new realism's ambitious goal of reasserting the unique ontology of humanistic phenomena. As Gabriel explains,

> The crux of New Realism may be discerned in the fact that it is not premised on equating indisputable reality, which is traditionally identified with realist positions, with the 'external world' or with 'nature'. While there may be good reasons for defending some varieties of naturalism, the debate on New Realism affirms that one need not be a naturalist to be a realist. ('Introduction' 9–10)

In other words, ontologies affirming the singular reality pertaining to the diverse spectrum of humanistic phenomena – consciousness, poetry, mythology – aim for nothing less than a reconquest of sorts of the concept of the real. This study borrows Gabriel's paired concepts of old realism and new realism as convenient labels to identify the reconstructed realisms after poststructuralism examined here. On Gabriel's account, new realism is a term that stakes out a debate rather than referring to a particular doctrine (such his own ontology of fields of sense). The sole prerequisite is a commitment to working out a non-reductionist account of the real.

Old realism is restricted to spatiotemporal things. New realism, as understood in this study, is committed to a pluralistic concept of the real that recognises the manifold existents outside of the domain of the natural sciences. For this reason, Gabriel's ontology of fields of sense rejects the 'old realist' notion of reality as a unified overall totality: '*the* world does not exist' (*Why the World* 78; my emphasis). As Gabriel affirms, the notion that there is one single true and complete description of the world as it is in itself belongs to metaphysics, the branch of traditional philosophy equivalent to ontology before Kant's critical turn. In Gabriel's view, contemporary ontology must give up the ideal of an absolute, unified reality that can be grasped by a theory of absolutely everything. Rejecting ontological monism, Gabriel defends ontological pluralism: 'there exist an infinite number of fields of sense' (*Why the World* 78).

To illustrate Gabriel's claims (which we will examine more closely in Chapter 4): something can show itself in different fields. For example, the soup can on my kitchen table appears as a soup can in my kitchen, whereas in the field of subatomic physics it appears as a swirl of subatomic particles that are actually 'wave-like patterns of probabilities' (Capra and Luisi 72). In New York

City's MOMA, the soup can appears as an artwork by Andy Warhol. In neither of these cases has the soup can been 'constructed' in a way that must be distinguished from a presumed soup can in-itself that is categorically inaccessible to human perception. To Gabriel, in all three cases, the soup can shows itself as it really is in itself. As Gabriel contends, 'appearances are as real as it gets' (*Fields of Sense* 168), a point evidenced by the phenomenon of emergence at higher scales of reality as atoms congeal into soup cans that gather in artistic assemblages to form an artwork. In other words, the soup can's appearance in the form of subatomic particles in the quantum physics lab is not its real essence, in contrast to its illusory incarnations in my kitchen and in MOMA. The objects studied by natural science are only one manifestation of reality. To claim otherwise would be to 'undermine' the kitchen world as well as the world of art. As Gabriel asserts, the world is much larger than the scientific universe; there are many things that do not appear there. The universe is merely 'an ontological province' of the world (*Warum es die Welt* 41). This is because there are no pre-given objects independent of fields. As Gabriel maintains, 'fields ground objects' (*Fields of Sense* 167): the soup can appears in my kitchen but not in the world of subatomic physics; subatomic particles appear in the atomic world but not in the art museum. Once the context is established, there is a clear answer as to what counts as real. If reality appears inherent in certain objects (soup cans, atoms or artworks), this is only because of – to adapt Heidegger – the forgetting of context.

The idea that reality is open-ended and plural can be further clarified from another angle. Like Gabriel, Dreyfus and Taylor defend what they call 'plural realism' (Dreyfus and Taylor 148ff.). However, they arrive at this conclusion by way of a totally different path – by retrieving what they call the unmediated 'contact' perspective of an embedded realism. On their view, no matter which critical method we endorse as scholars or scientists, 'we are always and inevitably thinking within … taken-as-there frameworks' that we cannot justify (20). We simply take them for granted: 'You know because you're there' (22). To illustrate this point: like the scientist in the lab, the postmodern critic in the lecture hall produces knowledge by identifying problems, invoking principles, giving reasons. But in order to get to their academic workplaces, the scientist and the scholar must move through the world, leave home, make their way to campus and walk to class. Their grasp of reality during these activities is pre-reflective, unquestioned, taken for granted. To demand justification that we are in contact with reality during these everyday transactions – as we do in the lecture hall – would be absurd: we just know because we are there. In everyday experience, reality does not refer to objects that we dissect from above: reality is all around us, and we are immersed in it. Having realised this, 'one awakens to an unproblematic realism with respect to the world' (Dreyfus and Taylor 131). Such primordial realism – which Dreyfus and Taylor term 'contact realism' – presupposes 'an embodied agent, embedded in a society, and at grips with the world' (91).

Dreyfus and Taylor contend that reality is necessarily plural because it must comprise the unquestioned knowledge that obtains in such everyday experience. More assertively, they insist that 'engaged experience is primordial and the disengaged mode is derivative from the engaged one' (133). Reflective knowledge of any kind is an island of solid ground, so to speak, in the sea of unquestioned knowledge that humans navigate in the course of their lives. So long as this is understood,

> *pluralist robust realism* can avoid *reductive realism*, which holds that science explains all modes of being, and *scientific realism*, which holds that there is only one way in which the universe is carved up into kinds so that every user of such terms must be referring to what our natural-kind terms refer to. (Dreyfus and Taylor 160)

Dreyfus and Taylor's work does not figure among the four new realist theories selected here. Yet their notion of contact realism of embedded knowledge helps elucidate an important thread of this study. It is a forceful defence of so-called common-sense realism, which grants pre-reflective access to everyday reality, against the stigma of naivety. Dreyfus and Taylor build on the phenomenology of Heidegger and Merleau-Ponty and on Wittgenstein. As we shall see, the new phenonemologies of Marion and Lingis as well as Maturana and Varela's neurophenomenology are varieties of such 'contact' realisms as outlined by Dreyfus and Taylor.

A plural realism that admits the singular realities of phenomena at all scales – natural, social, artistic and mental – however, might entail different problems of its own. Might it not threaten denying that phenomena such as novels or deities are manufactured, in contrast to raw entities such as water? To counter the charge of idealism, recall that new realism rejects the absolute dichotomy between human fabrication and reality. Instead, new realism affirms the entanglement of the constructed and the real. Many things are born as constructs and then acquire efficacy to produce real-world effects: they become real. Outside of raw facts such as hurricanes or earthquakes, this is also true of speed bumps, a physical artefact, and of race, a social artefact. New realism therefore posits an inclusive rather than an exclusive relation between constructs and facts. This point is set forth by Latour's concept of the factish, which as noted above describes a unique class of actants. It will figure centrally in the third chapter on Latour and Margaret Atwood's *MaddAddam* trilogy, and merits a brief preview here.

As Latour rightly observes, all human accomplishments, not just religion and art but also technology and science, are artefacts of human activity. Scientific facts and religious beliefs, which 'old' realism – not Latour's term but useful to elucidate his point – sets apart as knowledge vs. naive belief, are actually brought into existence – become real – by means of the same procedure. On Latour's account, this procedure advances in two phases. The first phase is fabrication: religious idols are fabricated by the community of believers, who collectively invest an object (a stone, an effigy) with supernatural qualities. Likewise, scientific facts are fabricated 'in our laboratories with our colleagues, our instruments, and our hands' (Latour, *Factish Gods* 18). These analogies are due to the fact that as disciplinary fields, religion and science can be modelled as assemblages constituted by three essential components. Each must possess a domain of proper phenomena (the supernatural and the natural respectively), a community of practitioners (the congregation or the scientific community), and technologies or instruments that allow the community of practitioners to interact with the phenomena that belong to its respective domain (sacred objects and beliefs or subatomic particles) (see DeLanda, *Assemblage Theory* 88). In the second phase of Latour's factish production, the construct enters the world and becomes an actant – that is to say, an autonomous force endowed with real-world effects. 'If human agency is restored' to both scientific facts and religious beliefs, Latour concludes, 'the belief that was to be shattered disappears, along with the shattering fact. We enter a world that we had never left, except in dreams – the dreams of reason – a world where arguments and actions are everywhere *facilitated*, *permitted*, and *afforded* by factishes' (*Pandora's Hope*

274). A key principle of the new realist ontologies considered here, Latour's factish thus ignores old realism's puzzle, 'Is it real or constructed?', to tackle a new mystery: 'How is it real?', 'Where is it real?' and 'How does it become real?'

As noted above, old realism is materialism or naturalism, the notion that matter is the ultimate layer of reality, which can be analysed with the methods of the natural sciences. Here is where Meillassoux's influential polemics directed against Kant's methodological scepticism falls short. Correlationism, as we saw earlier, is Meillassoux's name for the post-Kantian doctrine of the inaccessibility of things-in-themselves outside of 'the correlation between thinking and being' (Meillassoux 5). Issuing a clarion call for a return to the absolute real, independent of the human observer, Meillassoux's brilliant philosophical manifesto was a landmark declaration of the exhaustion of the constructivist paradigm. However, Meillassoux's proposal for overcoming what he calls the philosophy of human access, a synonymous term referring to modern philosophy from Kant to the present (including its two branches of continental and analytic philosophy), leads to what this analysis considers unacceptable consequences. It results in his endorsement of the naturalist notion of reality as independent of the mental realm. As he declares, 'we are in consciousness or language as in a transparent cage. Everything is outside, yet it is impossible to get out' (Meillassoux 6). But this is an outdated view. According to Noë's enactivist account of the mind,

> You are not your brain. We are not locked up in a prison of our own ideas and sensations. The phenomenon of consciousness, like that of life itself, is a world-involving dynamic process. We are already at home in the environment. We are out of our heads. (*Out of Our Heads* xiii)

As we shall see in Chapter 3, contemporary neurophenomenology overcomes the dual threat of idealism and materialism.

Meillassoux aims to recuperate metaphysics, the ontology of the absolute without correlation of the pre-critical thinkers – he provocatively dubs it 'the *great outdoors*' (7) – for our time. He concedes that this must proceed via speculative thought – hence, speculative realism. The speculative path to the overcoming of finitude – the epistemological limits of human knowledge – routes through the existence of fossil remains of the early history of earth before the emergence of life. Meillassoux contends that Kant is wrong because there are events in the early history of earth, before the appearance of humans, that we know for certain are true. Fossils are material evidence of such 'ancestrality' – a time 'anterior to the emergence of the human species' (10). Meillassoux's model is Descartes, and he forcefully reinscribes Cartesian subject–object dualism. Because he is intent on purifying reality of mediation by thought, Meillassoux's speculative realism runs counter to the aims of this study, which, as stated, are to reject old realism's reduction of realism to materialism, and to affirm the singular reality of mental phenomena.

Meillassoux's *After Finitude* is symptomatic of the shortcomings of the dominant tenor of speculative realism. Ray Brassier, for example, makes an argument for thinking beyond finitude that complements Meillassoux's. Unlike Meillassoux, who goes backwards in evolutionary time, to challenge correlationism Brassier fast-forwards in evolutionary time, to the coming solar apocalypse and the certain extinction of life on earth. For Brassier, 'extinction is a symptom of the *posteriority*, which is the direct counterpart to . . . ancestrality'. As he explains, the 'posteriority of extinction indexes a physical annihilation which no amount of chronological tinkering can transform into a correlate "for us"' (Brassier 229). The speculative realist intent on recovering the in-itself, the Cartesian world without mind – the *'world without spectators'* (Gabriel, *Why the World* 7), a reality from which the human spectator has been edited out – is misguided. The justified rejection of postmodern constructivism, and the parallel welcome critique of anthropocentric humanism, have caused some speculative realists to lapse into the opposite extreme – a relapse into materialist reductionism. To guard against backsliding into idealism, many of these theorists, including some new materialists, have thrown out the baby (understanding humans) with the bathwater (anthropocentrism as well as radical constructivism).

In *The Ends of the World*, Déborah Danowski and Eduardo Viveiros de Castro take up Meillassoux's and Brassier's critique of correlationism in the context of their study of contemporary environmental apocalypticism that envisions the catastrophic ends of climate change. Noting parallels between the contemporary boom in apocalyptic visions of the end of the world and speculative realism's metaphysical speculations about ancestrality and the solar apocalypse, they discern a shared trope that opposes the world to humankind as 'radically *other*, not-ours' (Danowski and Viveiros de Castro 26). For example, apocalyptic scenarios of the extinction of human life on earth – the 'world without us' (21) – show striking resemblances to Meillassoux's notion of nature as a 'glacial wasteland' (Danowski and Viveiros de Castro 35), cold and indifferent to humans.

In Danowski and Viveiros de Castro's account, speculative realism's quest for the real aims at death rather than life. At the simplest level, this evidences age-old correspondences between mythology (such as apocalyptic narrative) and metaphysics, showing a deep kinship between philosophy and literature that also informs this study. But beneath the superficial parallel lurks a deeper dissonance. Anthropogenic climate change, Danowski and Viveiros de Castro astutely observe, renders speculative realism's reflections on 'radical exteriority' (35) or 'Being as external to thought' (32) obsolete. 'When we displace the problematic of anti-correlationism to the "ecological" plane of the sublunar', they write,

> we can see the irony of our current predicament as that of a catastrophic *terrestrial objectification of the correlation*. That is, the fact that human thought, materialized as a giant technological machine of planetary impact, effectively and destructively *correlates the world*, burying the arche-fossils of the remote past under thick layers of anthropogenic soil – concrete, plastic, tarmac . . . rich with what will be the anthropofossils of a future perhaps not so far away. (36)

In Meillassoux's metaphor, the Anthropocene is literally eroding the 'great outdoors' through its geologic objectification of correlationism. Danowski and Viveiros de Castro's insights further support this study's proposal to recast the real as inclusive of the worlds fabricated by humans.

Realism or Materialism?

This brings us to the problem of materialism. No matter how one might twist and turn the issue, it is simply the case that the bulk of the phenomena of humanistic study are not material, but non-material.[9] The meanings of literary texts, the meanings of patterns of culture, consciousness, experience, the lifeworld, history, political action, religion, ethics – all these are non-physical (social or mental) phenomena. Phenomena that can be classified as material make up a very small portion of the objects of study in the humanities. It is instructive to look back to the early debates about the method and objects of humanistic study as the qualitative understanding of meanings rather than quantitative explanation of physical objects by general laws.[10] As Gabriel observes, at the centre of the humanities is *Geist* (a German term denoting meaning, idea or spirit), which gave its name to the German term for the humanities, *Geisteswissenschaften* (literally, science of the mind). As Gabriel explains, 'spirit in this context does not merely refer to something mental or subjective; rather, it designates the hermeneutic dimension of human understanding' (*Warum es die Welt* 173). To attend to the distinctive ontology of mental and social phenomena does not require pretending that these exist in a vacuum. It simply means to take them seriously, on their own terms, which includes tracing connections and interactions with phenomena in other fields. This said, I agree with Gabriel's judgment that 'it is essential to rehabilitate spirit' (*Warum es die Welt* 173).

At the beginning of the twenty-first century, the humanities have come a long way since the days of Hegel's *The Phenomenology of Spirit*, which upholds consciousness as the highest form of reality from which all other manifest forms of reality, including matter, emanate. We now know that non-material meanings are deeply entangled with material things. For example, it matters whether literature is composed on paper, typewriters, computers, is circulated in print or in digital form; cultural rituals involve physical objects of all stripes. Consciousness arises immanently from the neural network of the brain that is embedded in the living body, and so on. But human language, experience, consciousness cannot be naturalised without destroying the emergent qualitative properties that make them what they are. This is why it is misleading to claim that 'we are walking, talking minerals', a statement attributed to the Russian geochemist Vladimir Vernadsky, the developer of a theory of the biosphere to describe the layer of life surrounding earth (Margulis and Sagan, *What Is Life?* 49; see also Bennett 10). This assertion is a classic example of 'undermining' (Harman). Human bodies may be composed of minerals, but the essential properties that make us human – including those needed to become authors of books and participants in debates on new materialisms – do not exist at the scale of geology. It is essential to underscore the 'irreducibility of conscious experience to the physical' (Nagel, *Mind and Cosmos* 68). Thus, love may be traceable to specific patterns of biochemistry in the brain, but as a mental state it is not reducible to it. As the phenomenologist Brian Treanor observes in his critical review of speculative realism and new materialisms, this 'sort of realism is committed to radically flattening out the differences between humans and other entities' (Treanor 63).

Although I have learned much from various forms of new materialisms, I therefore endorse realism rather than materialism: unlike materialism, realism is not limited by the exclusion of mental phenomena. To justify this decision, and to further buttress the argument for new embedded realisms endorsed here, it is helpful to consider some of the key proponents and propositions of new materialisms. DeLanda's Deleuze-inspired assemblage theory, which I consider the most sophisticated of the new materialist theories, is a good place to begin. As DeLanda explains his view,

> Assemblage theory operates within a realist ontology. Realists have a harder task than philosophers with other ontological commitments because it is not enough to state one's position: we must in addition specify what the contents of an autonomous world are, or at least, what should *not* be included among its contents. Many religious people, for example, are realists about transcendent spaces and entities, like heaven and hell, angels and demons. But a materialist philosopher can only be realist about *immanent* entities, that is, entities that may not subsist without some connection to a material or energetic substratum. And while it may be simple for a materialist to get rid of angelic or demonic creatures, there are other forms of transcendence that are far more difficult to remove. (*Assemblage Theory* 138–9)

As can be seen in this passage, DeLanda defends assemblage theory both as a realist ontology and what he calls a materialist social ontology. Nonetheless, his commitment to materialism forces him to reject entities that do not possess traces of 'a material or energetic substratum'. As I am arguing here, humanistic study needs to be unapologetic about the reality of non-material entities that make up its principal concern. This is why this study engages, but does not focally consider, new materialist ontologies.

As many proponents of new materialism affirm, new materialism no longer subscribes to the old view of matter as passive and inert that was characteristic of Newtonian science and the seventeenth-century mechanical universe. Matter is newly seen as active and creative, capable of producing independent effects. As Prigogine and Stengers explain in *Order Out of Chaos*, the so-called 'new science' in the twentieth century that broke with the deterministic idea of a timeless, changeless universe led to 'a new view of matter in which matter is no longer the passive substance described in the mechanistic world view but is associated with spontaneous activity' (9). According to Capra and Luisi, the new view of matter as an actant was developed simultaneously in several scientific fields that proved intransigent to the mechanistic Cartesian paradigm:[11] quantum physics, which discovered that at the subatomic level, the isolated solid objects of classic Newtonian physics do not exist; organismic biology, which showed that organic matter spontaneously combines to form higher-level structures; the new science of ecology, which recognised that in phenomena such as food chains or ecosystems, organisms are bound together in trans-species constellations that form functional wholes. A fourth field to challenge the mechanistic paradigm was Gestalt psychology, which claims that perception in living organisms operates through irreducible perceptual patterns ('Gestalt'). As Capra and Luisi explain, developments in these four disciplines ran parallel. Jointly they pioneered so-called systems thinking, a fundamental reorientation of science towards a holistic view of nature emphasising relationships, connectedness, context and the spontaneous immanent emergence of ever more complex entities. Later in the twentieth century these insights were developed further in the science of complex dynamical systems, such as complexity theory and the theory of self-organisation. In Capra's definition, 'self-organization is the spontaneous emergence of new structures and new forms of behavior in open systems far from equilibrium, characterized by internal feedback loops and described mathematically by nonlinear equations' (85).

Contemporary new materialisms liberally draw on these fields, riding on the coat tails of twentieth-century innovations in the natural sciences to popularise this new view of active matter. For example, Karen Barad's 'agential realism' builds on quantum theory, specifically the work of Nils Bohr. Bohr resolved the paradox that electrons show themselves as particles in some experimental situations and as waves in others (Capra and Luisi 71). Bohr's notion of complementarity postulates that 'the particle picture and the wave picture [are] two complementary descriptions of the same reality, each of them only partly correct and having a limited range of application' (71–2). As Barad observes, Bohr's insight challenged the foundations of the mechanistic outlook 'that takes "things" as ontologically basic entities' (Barad, 'Posthumanist Performativity' 131). According to quantum theory, 'at the subatomic level, matter does not exist with certainty at definite places, but rather shows "tendencies to exist", and atomic events do not occur with certainty at definite times and in definite ways, but rather show "tendencies to exist"' (Capra and Luisi 72). In other words, reality is not limited to the actual; it also includes virtual tendencies that are not actualised. This insight also figures centrally in the materialist philosophy of Deleuze and Guattari, who express it in the notion of virtuality. As DeLanda eludicates this point: 'the "virtual is not opposed to the real but to the actual . . . Indeed, the virtual must be defined as strictly a part of the real object – *as though the object had one part of itself in the virtual into which it is plunged as though into an objective dimension*"' (Deleuze qtd in *Assemblage Theory* 109).

In a dramatic shift, the discovery by subatomic physics 'of the dual aspect of matter and of the fundamental role of probability has demolished the classical notion of solid objects' (Capra and Luisi 72). Equally important, quantum theory also dissolved the classical scientific notion of the detached observer: 'The crucial feature of quantum theory is that the observer is not only necessary to observe the properties of an atomic phenomenon but is also necessary to bring these properties about' (Capra and Luisi 74). This discovery, expressed in Heisenberg's uncertainty principle, serves as the basis for Barad's notion of 'intra-action' between human observers and observed phenomena. Barad explains that she coined the term to describe the ontological interdependency between observing and observed systems 'in contrast to the usual "interaction", which presumes the prior existence of independent entities or relata' ('Posthumanist Performativity' 133; *Meeting the Universe Halfway* 139).[12] In Barad's view, 'a specific intra-action . . . enacts an *agential cut* (in contrast to the Cartesian cut – an inherent distinction – between subject and object) effecting a separation between "subject" and "object." That is, the agential cut enacts a *local* resolution *within* the phenomenon of the inherent ontological indeterminacy' ('Posthumanist Performativity' 133). This allows us to conclude that '"we" are not outside observers of the world. Nor are we simply located at particular places *in* the world; rather, we are part *of* the world in its ongoing intra-activity' ('Posthumanist Performativity' 146).

Although there is nothing wrong with these claims in principle, there is a problem with the reasoning that equates the reality of subatomic physics with the macroscopic reality of the human social world. Barad confuses ontological scales of existence that should be carefully distinguished. For if quantum physics opened up a view on to the strange reality of the atomic world that contradicts the fundamental laws of solid matter applying at the macroscopic and planetary levels of the universe, it follows that the bizarre properties of matter that appear at the subatomic scale are absent at these higher scales. For if they weren't, Bohr would not have been awarded the Nobel Prize for describing them – they would have been as familiar as our living rooms. Passing over the vast scalar difference between the atomic and the human social worlds, Barad simply extends the situated insights of quantum theory to settle the conflict between scientific realist and postmodern constructivist outlooks. In Barad's view, 'agential realism is an account of techno-scientific and other practices that takes feminist, antiracist, poststructuralist, queer, Marxist, science studies, and scientific insights seriously, building specifically on important insights from Nils Bohr, Judith Butler, Michel Foucault, Donna Haraway, Vicki Kirby, Joseph Rouse, and others' ('Posthumanist Performativity' 129). It is misleading to draw simple analogies between atoms and humans as if they existed on the same level.

In Barad's opinion, intra-action, coined to describe the unique characteristics of subatomic matter, also holds the key to human discursive practices:

> On an agential realist account, *discursive practices are specific material (re)configurings of the world through which local determinations of boundaries, properties, and meanings are differentially enacted. That is, discursive practices are ongoing agential intra-actions of the world through which local determinacy is enacted within the phenomena produced.* ('Posthumanist Performativity' 138; see also *Meeting the Universe Halfway* 148)

Similarly, intra-action also explains human embodiment:

> All bodies, not merely 'human' bodies, come to matter through the world's iterative intra-activity – its performativity. This is true not

> only of the surface or contours of the body but also of the body in the fullness of its physicality, including the very 'atoms' of its being. Bodies are not objects with inherent boundaries and properties; they are material-discursive phenomena. 'Human' bodies are not inherently different from 'nonhuman' ones. ('Posthumanist Performativity' 141; see also *Meeting the Universe Halfway* 151–2)

Barad appears to be waving intra-action as a magic wand to reconcile what has been separated by the intellectual history of the past five centuries: language and body, nature and culture, humans and non-humans, Marxian economic materialism and naturalist materialism – the list goes on. Like a Hegel in reverse, she enthrones the particular – the ontology of atomic matter – as the new absolute: 'In summary, the universe is agential intra-activity in its becoming' ('Posthumanist Performativity' 135). It is odd to see this lapse into reductionist universalism in a scholar who originally entered the debate by building on one of the revolutionary theories of the twentieth century, demonstrating the 'irreducibility' principle, as it were, for ontologies of matter at different scales of reality. Fortunately, there is another way forward, as I will explain.

New materialisms tend to be a variety of blends of Deleuze, Latour, Spinoza, the above-mentioned four twentieth-century fields (organismic biology, quantum theory, ecology and Gestalt theory) that challenged the mechanistic paradigm, and their subsequent developments. Jane Bennett's notion of 'vibrant matter' or 'vital materialism', for example, builds on Hans Driesch (organismic biology), Latour (non-human actants), Spinoza (*conatus*), Deleuze and DeLanda (immanence and assemblages), Vernadsky (ecological geology), evolutionary theory, as well as contemporary complexity theory, which plots the virtual trajectories – so-called attractors – of complex systems. Indeed, Bennett adopts as her title the programmatic shift of metaphors of the so-called new science: the change from the Cartesian model of matter as machine (determined and quantifiable) to a new picture of matter as active and unpredictable. As Capra describes this change: 'Instead of being a machine, nature at large turns out to be more like human nature – unpredictable, sensitive to the surrounding world, influenced by small fluctuations' (Capra 193).

Bennett tracks active, creative matter – 'irreducible to matter as extension in space' (Bennett 80) – at multiple scales from non-organic systems (hurricanes and blackouts) to living tissue and organisms (stem cells, worms) to multi-species ecological constellations. Her study 'theorize[s] a vitality intrinsic to materiality as such', aiming 'to detach materiality from the figures of passive, mechanistic, or divinely infused substance' (xiii). For Bennett, the notion of 'vitality' describes 'the capacity of things – edibles, commodities, storms, metals – not only to impede or block the will and designs of humans but also to act as quasi-agents or forces with trajectories, propensities, or tendencies of their own' (viii). Bennett's vision is close to Latour's in seeking to replace the modern dichotomy of passive nature vs. free humans by envisioning a new political ecology of humans and non-humans. In accordance with self-organisation theory, Bennett outlines a nested hierarchy of organised systems-within-systems. In contrast to Barad, Bennett is attentive to scale, carefully describing the irreducible properties and laws operating at each level, which disappear if one ascends or descends the scale. In other words, what Bennett calls '*thing power*' (20) is shown to assume different phenotypes as the focus progresses from lower chemical and molecular to more complex biological and ecological levels.

That said, in making her point about the paradigm shift from the old materialism of determined things to the new materialism of vibrant matter, Bennett eventually overstates her case. In 'A Life of Metal', a chapter on geology, she announces that she will turn her 'attention explicitly to the figure of life to see just how far it can be pulled away from its mooring in the physiological and organic. Does life only make sense as one side of a life–matter binary, or is there such a thing as a mineral or metallic life?' (53). Next she performs a series of rhetorical sleights-of-hands that conflate the activity of metallic matter with life as such, drawing on Deleuze and building on Vernadsky's speculative notion of 'living matter as a geological force' that was cited above (Margulis, *What is Life?* 49; Capra and Luisi 67; see Bennett 11, 61). References to 'material vitality' and 'metallic *vitality*' are used interchangeably with 'impersonal life' and 'a life of metal' (Bennett 61, 59). It is certainly true that we can no longer categorically separate living from non-living entities. As we now know, in evolutionary history life emerged immanently from non-life (see Margulis, *What is Life?*). But it is one thing to recognise the inseparability of the organic and the non-organic, and quite another to equate them.

To conclude this critical review of the claims of new materialisms, it is ironic that perhaps the most vivid illustration of Bennett's new materialist notion of vibrant matter comes from quantum theory, one of the few fields of systems thinking that Bennett does not engage with. The so-called 'quantum effect' describes the 'fundamental "restlessness" of matter that is characteristic of the atomic world': the smaller the area a particle is confined to, 'the faster [it] will "jiggle around" in it' (see Capra and Luisi 75). In the atomic world, matter is pictured 'not at all as passive and inert but as being in a continuous dancing and vibrating motion whose rhythmic patterns are determined by the molecular, atomic, and nuclear configurations' (75). As Capra and Luisi insist, the dynamic essence of subatomic matter has no analogy in the macroscopic world. Its discovery unleashed a technological revolution, atomic energy and atomic weapons, which – more than anything else – establishes the role of matter as a powerful actant.

New Ecological Realisms

We have now arrived at the point where we can offer a systematic exposition of the approach and contribution of this study. As I have argued, constructivism plays into the hands of the dominant reductionist realism that consigns humanistic fields to a second-rank status as an academic discipline. The ontological turn now underway is essential to the welfare of the humanities in the STEM research university of the future. To meet the challenge resulting from recent advances in the STEM fields, including insights into the neurobiology of the brain, the microbiology of living beings, computing and artificial intelligence, and so on, the humanities need to redouble their efforts to re-establish the singular ontology of their field as distinct from that of the natural sciences. First and foremost, this requires mounting a strong defence of the irreducibility of humanistic objects of study. As stated, this concerns speculative and imaginary expression in particular: mythology, fantastic literature, as well as conspiracy theories. All these are non-material entities, yet they have real effects. Therefore, materialist ontologies of any type – including 'new materialisms' – will not do: materialisms require the rejection of phenomena incompatible with a materialist outlook, however liberally conceived – including the new materialist view of matter-as-actant. For humanistic ontologies, the emphasis shifts to a different question: Which qualities and properties do literature, culture, mythology and so on exhibit that do not exist in other fields or at other scales of existence?

In Felski's words, 'What does literature know?' (Felski, *Uses of Literature* 77).

The four new realist ontologies considered here all subscribe to a realism of organised wholes rather than a realism of isolated things and objects. What they have in common is a shift of focus from seeing pieces and isolated entities to a focus on organised patterns and relationships. As Markus Gabriel phrases it: the world is neither a collection of objects nor a collection of facts. Existence is 'the fact that something appears in a context' (Gabriel, 'Why the World'). Gabriel introduces the notion of fields of sense to express the hermeneutic dimension of contexts as meaningful wholes. Next, Latour's actor-network theory is a networks ontology. There are individual actants, yet these are not understood as isolated entities. Actants are always embedded in alliances; they are nodes in an extended actor-network. In the actor-network, action is not autonomous, but borrowed, influenced, afforded, translated and distributed (Latour, *Reassembling* 46). For their part, Maturana and Varela's theories of autopoiesis and enactivism formulate a non-representational ontology of knowledge. The concepts of autopoiesis and enactivism express the co-constitution of living organisms and their environments. Instead of disengaged minds representing pre-existing external worlds, minds and worlds are brought forth – enacted – together in the process of living. Finally, Marion's and Lingis's new phenomenologies of givenness and passionate identification are contact ontologies of everyday experience in Dreyfus and Taylor's sense. They map the interactions of embodied humans who are embedded in a social context and engaged in the world. Reality is not in front of them to be analysed dispassionately; reality is all around them, and they are always already immersed in it. Importantly, Maturana and Varela's, Marion's and Lingis's theories are also post-individualist phenomenologies. Phenomenology is often charged with individualism, a charge that is not applicable to any of the theories discussed here. Marion pictures a reduced self, a self 'unto whom' things are given, and who, in receiving the gift, is transformed into a figure Marion names 'the gifted'. 'The gifted' is a term that describes the self that comes after the Cartesian and the poststructuralist subjects. As noted earlier, Maturana and Varela emphasise the constitutive circularity that binds together mind and world into a functional unit. '*All doing is knowing, and all knowing is doing*' (Maturana and Varela, *Tree of Knowledge* 26).

Latour's actor-network ontology, Gabriel's new realist ontology of fields of sense, Maturana and Varela's non-representational ontology of knowledge, and Marion's and Lingis's new 'contact' phenomenologies share one important feature: they all abandon the mechanistic paradigm, the outlook that defines 'old' realism. In the mechanistic view, the world is a collection of isolated objects. Reality can be determined by reducing things to their smallest parts (mechanistic reduction), or by making a complete inventory of everything there is (metaphysics). It assumes that there is an ultimate layer of reality 'behind' phenomena, which can be reached by reductionist decomposition or by abstraction to absolute laws. Mechanism is a reductionist realism, privileging matter, the phenomena of the natural sciences. Mechanism was invented by physicists, and it has produced stunning results in a variety of other disciplines over the past centuries, including modern microbiology and genetics. But it encountered its limits in the life sciences, the social sciences and, last but not least, the humanities, by failing to grasp problems not amenable to the mechanical-reductionist outlook. Non-material entities cannot be quantified, counted or measured. But it does not follow that non-material entities are not real: they are. Instead of being dissected, they must be described or mapped. The source of the trouble is an inadequate concept of the real. To establish the irreducible reality of humanistic phenomena, we need to reconceptualise the real.

Latour, Gabriel, Maturana and Varela, and Marion and Lingis all endorse a holistic, contextual, systems-oriented, ecological and embedded realism. In the account of systems theory, one of the main tributaries of the rise of contextual realism in the past century,

> the great shock of twentieth-century science has been that living systems cannot be understood by analysis. The properties of the parts are not intrinsic properties, but can be understood only within the context of the larger whole. Thus the relationship between the parts and the whole has been reversed. In the systems approach, the properties of the parts can be understood only from the organization of the whole. Accordingly, systems thinking does not concentrate on basic building blocks, but rather on basic principles of organization. Systems thinking is 'contextual', which is the opposite of analytical thinking. Analysis means taking something apart in order to understand it; systems thinking means putting it into the context of a larger whole. (Capra and Luisi 66)

As Capra and Luisi explain, 'systems thinking means a shift of perception from material objects and structures to the nonmaterial processes and patterns of organization' (Capra and Luisi 79). In the mechanistic outlook, the base ontological units are objects. In the networks outlook, the base ontological units are not isolated objects, but organised wholes, such as systems (like autopoiesis and enactivism), organised ensembles (Marion's givenness), networks (Latour) or fields of sense (Gabriel). The difference between these two paradigms of the real is not absolute, but a 'figure/ground shift' of perspective (Capra and Luisi 83). In the mechanical-reductionist view, autonomous objects are primary and relationships secondary. In the systems view, relationships – qualitative patterns – are primary and objects secondary (Capra and Luisi 81). Like systems theory, Gabriel's notion of 'fields of sense' posits organised contexts as touchstones of the real. Fields are real, not objects. As Gabriel maintains, existence is 'not a property of individuals, but rather of fields of sense' (*Fields of Sense* 65). Similarly, Latour's position is accurately characterised as a 'realism of relations' (Harman, *Prince of Networks* 75). Actants never act alone; they are always embedded in a web of relationships and effects that facilitate, influence, deflect, frustrate or amplify their course of action.

The framework of interconnectedness also explains why Maturana and Varela's neurophenomenology and Marion's phenomenology of givenness can be classified as post-individual: rather than pre-existing its relations, the self is brought forth through them. As Marion contends, givenness has primacy because it comes first. At the centre is not the self, but the world in which the self is embedded. In Marion's words, 'at the center stands no "subject", but a gifted, he whose function consists in receiving what is immeasurably given to him, and whose privilege is confined to the fact that he is himself received from what he receives' (*Being Given* 322). Contextual realisms reject classical concepts of the real such as objects, elementary parts, collections of things, the antithesis between appearance and (ultimate) reality, and the dichotomy between reality and construction. Their place is taken by a new relational set of concepts: relationships, pattern, organisation, factishes, systems scale, emergent properties, fields and so on.

The new realist ontologies constellated here come from a great variety of backgrounds – sociology of science and technology

(Latour), neuroscience and phenomenology (Maturana and Varela), continental philosophy (Gabriel), phenomenology (Marion, Lingis). Some have become very familiar outside their immediate fields (Latour), others less so (Marion). Some ontologies are recent (Gabriel), while others began to take shape in the 1970s, 1980s and 1990s (autopoiesis and enactivism). For his part, Latour has been developing actor-network theory since the 1980s but did not publish a definitive statement until 2005 in *Reassembling the Social: An Introduction to Actor-Network Theory*. The publication of Marion's work occurred in the late 1990s and 2000s, while Lingis's work coincided with the proliferation of new realisms and new materialisms and made an appearance in Graham Harman's work (see *Guerrilla Metaphysics* 59–70). Some of the selected theories have not previously been related to the ontological turn and the rubric of new realism (Maturana and Varela, Marion). And while Latour inspired many self-identified new realists and new materialists, his work predates the explosion of new ontologies since the millennial turn, as do Maturana and Varela's Santiago theories of knowledge as autopoiesis and enaction. My decision to retrieve these slightly older works whose roots go back to the heyday of constructivism is due to the persuasiveness of their contextual or systems approach to the real.

Just as the selected theories did not emerge from a common source, they have never been discussed together. Outside their respective core fields, some have been considered under a different rubric: as noted earlier, autopoiesis and enactivism have been explored through the concept of posthumanism (see Hayles, Wolfe). The Santiago theory's appeal to posthumanism is a result of its biocentrism, which does not categorically set humans apart from other organisms. By gathering these four theories together under the rubric 'new ecological realisms', I hope to achieve two main goals: first, to promote the category of contextual or ecological realisms as a distinct rubric, and second, to bring to light correspondences between important theories that have gone unnoticed. Although the concept is not new,[13] the idea of a holistic, contextual or 'systems' realism has not received the attention it deserves. This becomes clear if we consider how natural it is to think of realism in connection with objects, as illustrated in the *OED* definition of 'real' quoted earlier.

Highlighting hidden affinities between theories is the more valuable the more distant they are commonly assumed to be. Gabriel, modern systems theorists and Maturana and Varela make parallel claims, although at first glance they seem nothing alike, the latter being neuroscientists, the former an expert on German Idealism. Phenomenology, in turn, was founded on the rejection of subject–object dualism. By introducing what Dreyfus and Taylor call a contact realism of embedded knowledge, phenomenology became one of the earliest advocates of contextual realism in the twentieth century. That with the rise of systems thinking following close on its heels, these two context-based – albeit very different – approaches flourished side by side shows how powerful its impulse actually is.

A comment on terminology is perhaps in order here. In describing what I call new ecological ontologies, I use a series of terms – contextual or context-based, holistic, embedded, ecological, relational, networks, systems thinking – interchangeably. There are slight differences of meaning among them: holistic suggests integrated or functional wholes, while networks suggest looser assemblages. Networks are non-linear: they go 'in all directions' (Capra and Luisi 95). The networks model comes to the fore in Latour's actor-network approach. Describing interconnections among different species and their environments, the concept of ecology conceptualises the most complex class of wholes (Capra and Luisi 341ff.). Ecology has very specific connotations with environmentalism. What makes new realisms not only contextual but also ecological is that they reconnect the human cultural world with the natural environment, both living and non-living, by undoing what Latour calls the modern constitution. Indeed, Latour's new realism is overtly ecological in the environmental sense. Nature no longer exists; and current environmental thinking, in Timothy Morton's pithy phrase, must be recast as 'ecology without nature'. To adapt Meillassoux's metaphor, new realism takes us out of the prisonhouse of the mind, not to postulate a Great Wilderness that has disappeared, but to picture our place in the nature-cultural collectives into which humans have transformed the planet.

The notion of embeddedness appears in all four new realist theories selected here. While its meaning undergoes slight shifts, it expresses contextual realism's opposition to anatomising. As discussed earlier, the pre-reflective knowledge of common-sense realism examined by Dreyfus and Taylor is embedded. This phenomenological idea of embeddedness also appears in Marion's phenomenology of givenness: the self is not the source of experience, but emerges from the shock of the given, and its response to what befalls it. Finally, such primordial embeddedness also underpins the autopoietic notion of 'structural coupling' between organism and environment through recurrent interactions. A second dimension of embeddedness denotes the idea of nested structures: systems that are integrated into higher-level systems and that are themselves composed of smaller systems. Embeddedness in this sense expresses a systems approach to scale that stresses irreducible differences between higher- and lower-scale levels. (As discussed, descending to lower-scale entities does not amount to breaking up wholes into elementary pieces.) Embeddedness as a scalar phenomenon is key to systems thinking: as Capra and Luisi explain, 'throughout the living world we find systems nesting within larger systems. Cells are parts of tissues; tissues are parts of organs, organs parts of organisms; and living organisms are parts of ecosystems and social systems' (Capra and Luisi 80). Likewise, scalar embeddedness is also a feature of Gabriel's fields of sense ontology: every field of sense can appear in another field of sense. For Gabriel, nested structures are open-ended; the world as a unified totality does not exist. The terms enumerated above will take centre stage at different moments of this study. I am using them interchangeably to describe the overall shift to prioritising connectedness over isolated objects.

I conclude this synthetic presentation of the approach and contribution of this study by returning to the earlier discussion of objects, with the aim of accounting for differences with object-oriented ontology, which is not treated here but with which the new context-oriented realism I espouse overlaps in important ways. Object-oriented ontology sees itself as one participant strand in the larger movement of speculative realism, but its origins predate the latter, going back to the 1990s, and first appearing in print in Harman's debut book *Tool-Being* (2002).[14] Its common misrepresentation as an offspring of speculative realism is a retrospective misconstruction of the 2007 gathering of the four original speculative realists that inaugurated the eponymous movement, in preparation for which its name was coined as a 'necessary compromise' (Harman, *Speculative Realism* 2) to unite four very different philosophical projects, of which object-oriented ontology was one.

Object-oriented ontology (OOO) mounts a strong defence of

objects from a shared concern to fend off human-access thinking (Harman's term for correlationism). It therefore approaches objects with a keen eye for their irreducibility to, and partial withdrawal/disclosure from, any relation. According to Harman,

> Objects need not be natural, simple, or indestructible. Instead, objects will be defined only by their autonomous reality. They must be autonomous in two separate directions: emerging as something over and above their pieces, while also partly withholding themselves from relations with other entities. (*Quadruple Object* 19)

In the figure/ground shift from seeing objects to seeing relationships as primary adopted by this study, OOO thus occupies the opposite side of the aisle. For OOO's principal proponents, Harman and Morton, the commitment to realism requires a repudiation of the primacy of relationism. In Harman's account, the existence of pre-given objects is primary: 'Real objects, apart from any relation to anything, are the ultimate stuff of the cosmos' (DeLanda and Harman 75). Yet OOO cannot be faulted for relapsing into mechanism: OOO's objects are always understood in relation to other objects: 'These relations are the very carpentry of things, the joint and glue that hold the universe together' (Harman, *Guerrilla Metaphysics* 20). OOO self-identifies as a kind of extended phenomenology of everything including humans that puts 'object-object relations on the same footing as subject-object relations' (Harman, *Quadruple Object* 140). Further concurring with the aims of this study, OOO also posits the reality of non-material mental and social objects, joining Latour and other new realists in rejecting materialism (DeLanda and Harman 3), for precisely the same reason as does this study: materialism 'reduce[s] the subject–object relations to the object–object relation of the brain' (Harman, *Quadruple Object* 140). Harman's objects thus comprise not merely material entities such as raindrops, snowflakes, helicopters or mountains; they also include mental and social phenomena. As Harman jests, the philosophical movement of speculative realism is something he helped construct, yet it is now real in the sense of being independent of its founders, who may resign from it or die 'without exterminating this intellectual trend' (Harman, 'Object-Oriented Philosophy' 189).

OOO's careful parsing of the complex ways in which objects are withdrawn in various object–person as well as object–object encounters is nevertheless troubled by the 'forgetting of context', on whose specification, as argued above, the very act of naming objects is premised. In *Hyperobjects*, Morton similarly states that the essence of objects is what is withheld from relations: 'hyper-objects are not simply mental (or otherwise ideal) constructs, but are real entities whose primordial reality is withdrawn from humans' (Morton 15). The problem is, as subatomic physics has demonstrated, that at the subatomic level there are no discernible objects at all. As discussed above, subatomic particles are 'not "things", but . . . interconnections among things' (Capra and Luisi 72). In the atomic world, solid objects dissolve into a web of virtual tendencies. If this is the case, the claims of object-oriented ontology cannot be true in the axiomatic way that they are stated, and need to be framed by qualifications of scale or context.

At the most general level, this analysis defends the networks approach to realism because it holds the key to solving the problem of complexity. As the evolutionary and organismic biologists Richard Lewontin and Richard Levins maintain, it is 'no exaggeration to claim that complexity is the central scientific problem of our time' (Lewontin and Levins 65). Complex problems such as ecology, public health, food security and poverty have persistently evaded reductionist solutions. While it has sponsored spectacular successes in science, scientific reductionism, Lewontin and Levins note, has encountered 'dramatic failures in attempts to deal with more complex systems' (297).

> It is a recognition that the long traditions of reductionist science, so successful in the past, are increasingly inadequate to cope with the systems we are now trying to understand and influence. The great errors and failings of attempts to apply science to matters of urgent concern have come from posing problems too narrowly, too linearly, too statically. Infectious disease did not disappear as was predicted thirty or forty years ago. Pesticides increase pest problems, antibiotics create new pathogens, hospitals are foci of infection. Food aid may increase hunger. The straightening and 'taming' of rivers increase floods [*sic*]. Economic development does not necessarily lead to equitable, just societies. (149)

Such unexpected and counterproductive effects of interventions 'directed at solving a particular problem' (106) demonstrate the actual interconnectedness of life. Organisms and ecosystems are very different from the artificial systems of engineering such as machines. They require a shift from seeing parts to seeing wholes and interconnections. As Lewontin and Levins point out, 'we cannot conceive of a membrane or a liver or even DNA by itself' (188).

Like Capra and Luisi, Lewontin and Levins reject mechanistic reductionism. Unlike the former, Lewontin and Levins defend a dialectical approach to complex dynamic systems that corrects systems theory's premise of harmony and self-balance. They caution that interrelatedness is not necessarily benevolent, as suggested in notions such as homeostasis (Lewontin and Levins 116). In ecosystems, for example, 'predator and prey are not "one" until the last stages of digestion' (107). It is therefore essential not to obscure conflicts among opposing forces within systems. Lewontin and Levins insist on considering the qualitative differences between different kinds of wholes: the unities that are organisms are very different from ecosystems and societies. On this point, they are in agreement with Maturana and Varela, who maintain that higher-level systems, including human and animal societies, are not autopoietic. As we shall see, the dark side of interconnectedness illustrated by predator–prey dynamics is a core concern in contemporary post-apocalyptic fiction. We will have occasion to revisit this conflict between cooperative and competitive aspects of ecological and social systems throughout this study. With this, we now turn to the distinct contributions of post-apocalyptic fiction in the second half of this overview.

Post-Apocalyptic Fiction: Living on Beyond the World-End

This study showcases a context-based approach to realism, positing that reality is about mapping worlds rather than about making a collection of everything there is. It argues that such new ecological realisms represent a promising escape from the intellectual impasse that results from the postmodern insight into the social and linguistic construction of the world that humans inhabit. If it is universalised, radical constructivism leads to unacceptable consequences, denying the distinctive status of non-linguistic phenomena and undermining the notion of the real as such: 'there is nothing outside the text'. This study proposes that literature constitutes an important alternative source of such new ontologies of organised wholes. Specifically, this is true of a particular literary genre, post-apocalyptic fiction, which depicts human experience and survival after the destruction of modern civilisation, and whose distinctive contribution we will now consider.

As a crisis narrative positing the end of an entire world, apocalyptic thinking asks about the very condition of what constitutes world (non-material ideas and values, as well as facts and material objects). Because it envisions destruction at a planetary or cosmic scale, apocalyptic narrative shares the ontological bent of new ecological realisms after poststructuralism. Like the latter, apocalyptic thinking offers a contextual or systems vision of the real, concentrating on organised contexts in which things appear, rather than isolated things and parts. Apocalypse is a way the entire world is. It is the field of sense (Markus Gabriel) in which things appear in a certain way. Apocalyptic thinking highlights the Heideggerian point of the primordiality of being over knowledge: to exist is to be – always already – in a world. World is what is easily overlooked because it is too familiar. The apocalyptic destruction of the world renders explicit what has been taken for granted; apocalypse works as Heidegger's broken tool does at the local scale of the everyday lifeworld. By positing the annihilation of the world and the need for its renewal, apocalyptic thinking defamiliarises world as an organising pattern of relationships. By destroying the world, apocalyptic thinking reveals the core essence of the order of the world. It lays bare the constitutive principles of the meaningful world as the space in which humans dwell and understand things, including its social, political and economic structures.

Following Elena Gomel, Caren Irr, Heather Hicks, James Berger, Teresa Heffernan and Peter Szendy, I distinguish between two basic varieties of apocalyptic thinking, apocalyptic and post-apocalyptic narratives. Whereas apocalyptic narrative is about getting ready for the coming end of the world, post-apocalyptic narrative is about crawling out of the rubble and remaking the world from within the wasteland of ruins. In contrast to apocalypse, which narrates the coming end of time and of the world, contemporary post-apocalyptic narratives are 'oddly hopeful works' (Irr 170). They are about what happens next, when history starts up again and survivors remake the world in the aftermath of catastrophe. Apocalyptic narratives are fictions of world-destruction. Post-apocalyptic narratives are fictions of world-remaking after the world-end. Apocalypse insists that there is no future. Post-apocalypse, in contrast, speculates about new tomorrows after the end. For this reason, these two sub-genres are governed by distinct temporalities, a distinction that this study seeks to develop more clearly. Yet even though post-apocalyptic fiction envisions new beginnings after the world-end, it is nonetheless premised on catastrophe as the formative break that wipes the slate clean, establishing the conditions into which its survivor-protagonists are thrown.

This study proposes that there is a close affinity between new ecological realisms after poststructuralism and contemporary post-apocalyptic fiction: both revision the real. The attribute 'contemporary' refers to a burst of new post-apocalyptic narratives appearing since the late 1990s and after the millennial turn, which are focused on a distinct set of concerns that distinguish them from earlier Cold War era post-apocalyptic fiction.[15] The works we will be considering are Margaret Atwood's *MaddAddam* series, whose three volumes are *Oryx and Crake* (2003), *The Year of the Flood* (2009) and *MaddAddam* (2013); Cormac McCarthy's *The Road* (2006); Jose Saramago's *Blindness* (1995); and Octavia Butler's *Parable* series, in two volumes, *Parable of the Sower* (1993) and *Parable of the Talents* (1998). All are narratives of survival set in the immediate aftermath of a cataclysm. Shipwrecked on the post-apocalyptic wasteland of ruins, their survivor-protagonists set about the task of remaking the world at all levels of existence. These range from short-term concerns of supplying basic needs such as food and shelter by scavenging, to long-term and more complex concerns such as inventing alternative forms of community and value. This study suggests that, in their respective media, new ecological realist theories and post-apocalyptic literature envision new, sustainable concepts of the real and of world that depart from existing paradigms that have exhausted their explanatory power. Furthermore, in so doing, it establishes how the characteristics of apocalyptic form are constitutive of the context-based ontology it articulates. This analysis will show that, just as new realist theories can illuminate post-apocalyptic fiction, post-apocalyptic fiction also embeds new ecological concepts of the real.

Of the several existing studies of contemporary post-apocalyptic fiction, only one, Danowski and Viveiros de Castro's *The Ends of the World*, considers these works in relation to post-postmodern theories.[16] As noted in the section 'Old Realism, New Realisms' above, Danowski and Viveiros de Castro offer original reflections on the consequences that dwelling on an environmentally damaged planet might entail for philosophers and writers. In an age when humans have become geological agents, they ask, what kind of 'thought' and 'mythology' are 'adequate to our times' (Danowski and Viveiros de Castro 113)? Given the predicament of climate change, in Danowski and Viveiros de Castro's view, Meillassoux's and Brassier's speculative return to Cartesian realism, or an observer-independent reality, seems oddly out-of-date. For the Anthropocene can be understood as the 'catastrophic *terrestrial objectification* of the correlation' (36). An objectivist approach that writes humans out of the picture of the non-human world now faces a steeper challenge than ever. Indeed, this was Dipesh Chakrabarty's original point in arguing that climate change spells 'the collapse of the age-old humanist distinction between natural history and human history' (Chakrabarty 201). We therefore need an integrated ontology capable of thinking the irreversible inter-connections between the realms of humans and non-humans. This final section of this synoptic Chapter 1 showcases the contributions of post-apocalyptic fiction to this end.

Apocalyptic thinking is a defining trait of the contemporary. For decades, we have been living in the age of a 'doom boom'.[17] As Peter Szendy observes, ever since 'Hiroshima and Nagasaki, when it first became evident that human beings had acquired the power to destroy life on earth, and to destroy it in a spectacular and rapid manner, apocalyptic thoughts and images have increasingly proliferated' (Szendy ix). Monica Germanà and Aris Mousoutzanis echo this assessment:

> Haunted by the joint specters of historical events (Hiroshima, the Holocaust, Chernobyl, 9/11) and anxieties about humankind's future (sustainability, global warming, terrorism), apocalyptic responses have proliferated both in the forms of narrative (dystopian fiction, disaster movie, and trauma literature) and wider cultural manifestations of eschatological belief. (Germanà and Mousoutzanis 1–2)

This development registers – to adapt Hegel – the contemporary ascent of humans to the status of world-apocalyptic superpower, rivalling the old superpowers, God and Nature. Yet conceptually, the idea that the modern world is headed for disaster is a contradiction in terms. The resurgence of apocalyptic thinking in the twentieth century marks a major shift in the conceptualisation of modernity. Any study of contemporary apocalyptic thinking must therefore first consider the formative role of apocalypse in the history of modernity.

As Reinhard Koselleck explains, the concept of modernity first emerged in opposition to the Christian temporality of apocalypse. Until well into the sixteenth century, Europeans lived in the temporality of Christian eschatology, which is to say that they lived in constant expectation of the End of the World, even as the End of the World was constantly deferred (Koselleck 6). Europeans became modern at the moment they stopped believing in the Christian doctrine of the Final Days. Koselleck defines modernity (in German, *Neuzeit*, literally 'new time') as the result of an increasing divergence between past and future: upheavals such as the scientific revolution and European overseas expansionism drove a wedge between the space of experience (*Erfahrungshorizont*) and the horizon of expectation (*Erwartungshorizont*). According to Koselleck, '*Neuzeit* is first understood as a *neue Zeit* from the time that expectations have distanced themselves evermore from all previous experience' (276). 'From that time on, the space of experience was no longer limited by the horizon of expectations . . . It became a rule that all previous experience might not count against the possible otherness of the future. The future would be different from the past, and better, to boot' (280). At the rise of modernity, then, the Christian end of the world recedes to the status of what Koselleck terms a 'future past', a future rendered obsolete by the indeterminate future of change that takes the place of apocalypse on Europe's horizon of expectation.

Apocalyptic narrative is a narrative about time. More precisely, as both Koselleck and Frank Kermode affirm, it is about the temporality of a future that is closed because its events are as familiar as they are certain to arrive. Modernity marks the moment when the finitude of biblical apocalypse is replaced by a secular future that is both open and unknown – a 'future not inferable from experience' (Koselleck 282). The Enlightenment idea of progress, the secular future of the modern outlook, is categorically different from the closed future of Christian eschatology. In the closed future of religious apocalypse, there is no creativity, no change and no agency (human or non-human) other than that of God's will. According to the modern concept of the future as undetermined, this is not a future at all.

That said, the claim that modernity arose as an anti-apocalyptic temporality has been complicated by recent accounts (such as John Hall's) of the persistence of apocalyptic thinking in modern European culture. A range of movements from post-Enlightenment political ideologies such as the Jacobins in Revolutionary France to the violent revolutions in Russia and China to the Third Reich of Nazi Germany exemplify the so-called revolutionary or 'secular apocalyptic' (Hall 132).[18] They blend eschatological expectations of violent utopian renewal with modern secular political struggles. The Jacobin Reign of Terror set the paradigm for such sacred revolutionary violence: the 'violent utopian pursuit of [a] new sacred civic order' (119). As Hall notes, such 'violent fundamentalism is distinctly modern' (110).

The term apocalypse derives from a Greek root that means 'to uncover, disclose'.[19] Its literal meaning, 'disclosure of knowledge', or the unveiling of ultimate truths, names its characteristic blending of futurity and certainty. As Lois Zamora notes, apocalypse 'is eschatological in nature ... it is concerned with final things' (Zamora 10). In their studies of apocalyptic patterns in twentieth-century fiction, Zamora and David Leigh both identify the closed future of a determinate end as the organising principle of apocalyptic narrative. According to Zamora, the apocalyptist 'sees the future breaking into the present, and this world being replaced by a new world under God's aegis' (11). Conversely, Leigh explains that apocalypse 'is a genre of revelatory literature with a narrative framework, in which a revelation is mediated by an otherworldly being to a human recipient, disclosing a transcendent reality which is both temporal, insofar as it envisages eschatological salvation, and spatial, insofar as it involves another, supernatural world' (Reddish qtd in Leigh 5).

The events of Revelation, narrated by John the Apostle, are – to modify Koselleck's term – futures past, in a second and paradoxical sense, insofar as, despite their futurity, they are accomplished fact, the fulfilment of a divine plan. Even though they have yet to unfold on earth, the precise sequence of events is fixed, as revealed in John's prophetic narrative. In the Book of Revelation, the apocalyptic events that produce the violent end of the present age and inaugurate a timeless age of redemption are unleashed by the opening of a book, the scroll of seven seals. As Catherine Keller notes, with the breaking of each seal, a new chapter in the unfolding world-destruction opens: 'the first four correspond to the four horses of the apocalypse' and the 'tribulations unfold and worsen according to a pattern of sevens' (Keller 3). Far from mirroring reality, the divine text engenders earthly reality, which obeys the written plot. The book is the manifestation of God's purpose; that the heavenly script it contains is the prime cause of apocalyptic world history attests to the temporal structure of predetermination.

Unlike modern chronological time, apocalyptic temporality is teleological as well as eschatological, a time lived in expectation of an approaching utopian end realm. As Frank Kermode has observed, teleology, the sense of an approaching end, is a quality that apocalypse shares with narrative as such. Narrative cannot help but be teleological. Its overt orientation towards an overall purposive design makes apocalypse the epitome of narrative as such: apocalyptic narratives are 'end-determined fictions' (Kermode 6). Apocalypse is 'analogous to literary fictions, by means of which we impose . . . [meaningful] patterns on historical time' (35). Kermode's analogy between apocalypse and literary narrative posits that, like apocalypse, narrative in general is driven by the sense of an ending: closure. Closure is the structuring device that establishes narrative meaning. Or, as Peter Brooks insists, 'the ultimate determinants of meaning lie *at the end*' (Brooks 52). In narrative, meaning is established retrospectively, from the viewpoint of the ending: 'the telling is always *in terms of* the impending end' (52). In short, apocalyptic finitude is the mirror of narrative closure.[20]

For a better understanding of the relation between narrative and temporality, Paul Ricoeur returns to Sartre's distinction between living and telling. Stories have a determinate ending; life does not. For Sartre, because of its retrospective nature, narrative distorts the experience of life, which is by definition open-ended. Countering Sartre, in *Time and Narrative* Ricoeur argues that, far from misconstruing lived experience, narrative captures its essence, a claim that he explains by introducing the concept of 'narrative identity' (*Time and Narrative* vol. 3, 244). Human lives unfold as we look back to the past to understand who we are.[21] Retrospection, and the backward-looking imposition of closure, are prerequisites for establishing meaningful order, which can only be seen from the end point (*Time and Narrative* vol. 1, 67). Thus, although narration proceeds chronologically, this order is a non-chronological dimension that works against the chronicity of time. The gist of narrative is the act of 'configuration', which links together disparate events and organises them into an 'intelligible whole' (*Time and Narrative* vol. 1, 65). This is a logical structure that is superimposed on time as linear flow, yet it is only 'by virtue of' such composition that 'something counts as a beginning, middle, or end' (38). The bottom line is that such hermeneutic structures do not pre-exist narrative, but are produced by it, more specifically by the narrative act of configuration that is emplotment.

Kermode's and Ricoeur's insights into the crucial role of form in narrative connect to the earlier discussion of realism vs. materialism. They also shore up this study's argument that we need a more capacious concept of the real that embraces – instead of denying – form. While literary form has material aspects – such as print, digital or other kinds of writing surfaces – its gist is non-material. Form is an organised pattern of meaning, an intelligible whole, a hermeneutic configuration. As a configuration of relationships, form is irreducible. As Capra points out, it cannot be quantified or broken down into smallest parts; it must be described or mapped. In other words, context is primary.

These insights into the irreducible realism of organised forms pertain not just to narrative as such; they are also borne out by the debate over literary realism specifically. In his influential 1957 study *The Rise of the Novel*, Ian Watt stresses that novel realism hinges on form. The novel's version of realism 'does not reside in the kind of life it presents, but in the way it presents it' (Watt 11). Though indebted to the rise of scientific empiricism and of modern rational and secular forms of knowledge, the novel was born through formal innovation and stylistic experimentation. As Watt maintains, novelistic realism differs from referential realism: it is based on a self-conscious 'skepticism about language', about the fact that 'words did not all stand for real objects, or did not stand for them in the same way' (27, 28). According to Watt, the mode of imitating reality developed by the new genre that came to be known as 'the novel' in the eighteenth century is an innovative 'narrative method' (34). Novel realism, writes Watt, is analogous to the procedures of a 'jury in a court of law' (31). As in science, truth-telling is central to trials. Yet in contrast to science, juridical truth cannot be a 'view from nowhere': it cannot dispense with the observer and narrative. Juridical realism, and by Watt's lights, novel realism, hinges on a 'view from somewhere'; it presupposes a world that includes the human observer.

Rethinking Watt's argument about the novel's formal realism in his 1987 study *The Origins of the English Novel, 1600–1740*, Michael McKeon specifies the novel's characteristic mode of simulating authenticity. He argues that the novel invented a new category of truth – verisimilitude, or believable truth – that is self-consciously distinct from that of modern science. In Catherine Gallagher's summary of McKeon's argument, the novel's standard of truth is less strict and more capacious – 'truth conceived as mimetic simulation' (Gallagher), as the term's literal meaning ('truth-likeness') suggests. According to McKeon, 'the widespread acceptance of verisimilitude as a form of truth, rather than a form of lying, founded the novel as a genre' (Gallagher 341). As Gallagher notes, this 'also created the category of fiction' (341).

This brings us to our central question: What are the unique features of apocalyptic thinking as a literary – or, more specifically, narrative – ontology? Narrative is a special class of holistic ontology due to its singular nature, which – as shown by Kermode and Ricoeur – is emplotment. The singularity of apocalyptic ontology – to adapt Derek Attridge – is defined by what I call its 'world-endist emplotment'. Thus, apocalyptic ontology does more than simply illustrate the claims of new realist theories after constructivism, Unlike the straightforward propositional form of theory relying on direct statements and logical conclusions, the ontology of apocalyptic form is enacted – or emplotted – rather than stated.

If this is the case for apocalyptic narrative, what about the variety of post-apocalyptic fiction, which as noted earlier does not envision the coming world-destruction, but speculates about new beginnings after the world-end? How does narrating an open-ended post-apocalyptic future relate to the claims just stated? As narratives, such stories about survival in the aftermath of apocalypse are governed by the same laws of narrative configuration just described. While the 'end-determined' nature is epitomised by apocalypse proper, both varieties of apocalyptic narrative are organised by a dual-time structure, which interlinks two levels of time through retrospective or prospective devices of comparing 'before' and 'after', as I explain next.

In addition to world-endist emplotment, there is a second feature that characterises the singularity of apocalyptic ontology. As the theologian Catherine Keller explains, apocalyptic thinking is defined by a 'script of binary time, a before and an after' (90). Apocalyptic worlds are organised around two distinct times and worlds straddling a radical – and violent – break. The first, the world of the here-and-now, is approaching a catastrophic end, giving way to another world that it is 'discontinuous with' it (93). Whereas apocalyptic narrative proper is set on the near side of the divide, post-apocalyptic narrative takes place on the far side, in the future to come. This split composition pivoting on a revolutionary break defines both sub-varieties of the apocalyptic. The violent upheaval exposes the ontological order of the world, as in Heidegger's broken tool analysis, but on a planetary scale. Thus, rather than abstractly describing reality, as narrative of world-destruction and world-remaking, apocalypse stages ontological transformation.

Having discussed the formal structure of the apocalyptic, we now move on to considering the particulars of its contemporary revival. In reading for 'new realisms' in recent post-apocalyptic fiction, I take my cue from Fredric Jameson's provocative suggestion that 'the historical novel of the future (which is to say of our own present) will necessarily be Science- Fictional inasmuch as it will have to include questions about the fate of our social system, which has become a second nature' (Jameson, *Antinomies* 298). 'To read the present as history', he contends, 'will mean adopting a Science-Fictional perspective of some kind' (*Antinomies* 298). In accordance with Jameson's claim, the revival of apocalyptic thinking in twentieth- and twenty-first-century literature and culture is premised on a variety of realism that one might – to capture resonances with new realist theory – term a speculative-realist impulse. I am here referring to the cognitive function of realism as imparting truthful knowledge about the world.

Christian apocalypse is based on religious prophecy. In contrast, Cold War and environmental apocalyptic thinking are based on rational prediction and scientific prognosis.[22] The difference is crucial. It is a shift from a prophesied future to a secular forecast, even as both are projections of global destruction. An example of scientific apocalypse is the prognosis of the heat death of the universe in the coming solar apocalypse 4.5 billion years from now. In studies of twentieth-century apocalyptic fiction, the differences between religious and scientific apocalypse are sometimes elided. The emergence of apocalypse as a paradigm for the modern is not synonymous with a revival of the narrative of Christian apocalypse, as, for example, Leigh suggests in stating that 'modern fiction texts used the apocalyptic tradition as found in the book of Revelation and other classic works dealing with the end of the world' (xi).

There are, as usual, important exceptions. Leigh's claim does apply to contemporary Christian fundamentalist revivals of biblical apocalypse such as Tim LaHaye's sixteen-volume *Left Behind* series (1995–2007). It is also valid for some works of twentieth-century fiction, such as Gabriel García Márquez's *One Hundred Years of Solitude*. As Lois Zamora has shown, García Marquez's iconic novel of the Latin American Boom is narrated in the prophetic mode of Revelation from an apocalyptic vantage point after the end of human history. Its narrator, Melquíades, is the keeper of the archive of the history of Macondo, which comprises two scales, the secular history of Colombia and of the Buendía clan and the sacred history of the cosmos. In Melquíades's room, it is always March and always Monday, evidence of the fact that like John the Apostle, his narrative discloses knowledge from an other-worldly location beyond time. Melquíades's narrative progresses in a spiralling movement, going both forwards and backwards in time, alternating between retrospection and prophecy. Haunted by an original curse, Macondo is predestined to be annihilated in a future cataclysm that is approaching relentlessly as history moves forward. 'The end of the apocalyptic manuscript and the end of time coincide' (Zamora 28). The curse that dooms the Buendías, incest, is modelled on biblical original sin, a burden that future generations, like the descendants of Adam and Eve, are powerless to escape. García Márquez often remarked that solitude is the opposite of solidarity. The eponymous one hundred years of soli-tude that the Buendías live out from their origin to their destruc-tion is a pre-appointed span of time: *'The first of the line is tied to a tree and the last is being eaten by the ants'* (García Márquez 420).

While both foretell the future, religious prophecy works dif-ferently than scientific prognosis. As Koselleck observes, while 'prophecy transgressed the bounds of calculable experience, prog-nosis remained within the dimensions of the political situation' (Koselleck 13). The 'wrath of the biblical hurricane' that erases Macondo from the face of the earth is a good example. It illustrates that the future of mytho-religious prophecy is beyond calculable experience (García Márquez 422). The cataclysmic wind arrives because, as the novel's last sentence reads, 'races condemned to one hundred years of solitude did not have a second opportunity on earth' (422). Aureliano only learns about his and his family's inevitable fate at the moment he manages to decipher Melquíades's parchments, when the apocalypse is already upon him. There was nothing in his or his relatives' lived experience that could have led them to expect this ending; future destiny, revealed in writing, breaks into lived experience as alien force. It is the irruption of the marvellous into the lifeworld of human experience. In other words, Macondo's apocalyptic destruction is part of the magical realism of García Marquez's iconic novel.

Macondo's mythical apocalypse may serve as a contrasting foil against which to define the calculable cataclysms of the contemporary post-apocalyptic fiction considered here. The near-future cataclysms envisioned by Atwood, Saramago, Butler and McCarthy are based on a risk analysis, calculable rationally by way of prognostication. As Ulrich Beck has argued, the multiplication of various technological and environmental hazards has reconfigured modernity, leading to the rise of a 'risk society' focused on risk management. The speculative realism of contemporary post-apocalyptic fiction discussed here follows the logic of calculating such man- made risk scenarios. Risk is communicated through various types of narrative. As Ursula Heise notes, 'apocalyptic narrative, in this secular sense, can appropriately be understood as a form of risk perception' (Heise 141). Contemporary post-apocalyptic fiction manifests risk awareness through the critical extrapolation of hazardous current technological, environmental, economic and political trends. In an interview, Octavia Butler invokes Robert Heinlein's 'three categories of science-fiction stories: the "what-if" category; the "only-if" category; and the "if-this-goes-on" category' as a frame of reference for her *Parable* series: 'I liked the idea. So this is definitely an if-this-goes-on story' (Canavan, 'Butler's Lost Parables' n.p.). Both Butler and Atwood stress that their post-apocalyptic works are speculative fictions relating the catastrophic consequences of present developments. As Atwood insists, '*Oryx and Crake* is speculative fiction, not a science fiction proper', which she views as a type of fantasy. 'It contains no intergalactic space travel, no teleportation, no Martians . . . The *what if* of *Oryx and Crake* is simply, *What if we continue down the road we're already on?*' ('Writing *Oryx and Crake*' 285).

Contemporary apocalyptic literature's role as a cultural expression of the risk society maps neatly on to Jameson's hypothesis mentioned earlier, concerning the science fictional emplotment of what he refers to as 'the historical novel of the future (which is to say of our own present)'. Both observations concern the problematic of the contemporary, which is the topic of Theodore Martin's recent study of contemporary fiction. How do you periodise the contemporary? Unfinished by definition, and quintessentially unspecific as a deictic shifter (like 'now'), 'the contemporary' presents a challenge to historical thinking. As Martin asks, 'how do you critique a present situation that is already in the process of changing' (Martin 17)? Martin looks to the much-noted boom of genre fiction in contemporary literature for an answer. He conjectures that genre revivals, such as post-apocalyptic narrative, 'allow us to narrate what counts as contemporary' (9) by linking it back to familiar historical features. The salient point for our purposes is the temporal oscillation between two levels of time, the pre-collapse present and the post-collapse future.

Apocalyptic narrative ties present developments to projected futures, as was noted earlier in Keller's concept of 'the script of binary time'. The shift from religious to speculative-realist frameworks, furthermore, goes hand in hand with another important difference, a corresponding change from absolute certainty to approximate knowledge. Divine knowledge is absolute. Modern science (which serious science fiction and related speculative fiction look to as a standard) generally provides less than complete certainty, that is to say, statistical approximations (see Capra and Luisi 82). If in the twenty-first century the future is no longer entirely open and undetermined as Enlightenment optimism suggested, neither has it reverted to the completely predetermined and closed future of the religious apocalyptic, as some radical doomsters might claim. In the contemporary period governed by climate change, the future appears in the form of various risk scenarios, ranging from better to worse, contingent on preventive action taken – or not taken – now. Whether or not the unfinished nature of 'now' will end up being apocalyptic is causally hardwired to present human intervention. As Frederick Buell has argued in his revealingly titled *From Apocalypse to Way of Life*, contemporary risk-based apocalyptic narratives have shrunk the genre-specific distance between pre-apocalyptic present and post-collapse future. This is because the coming catastrophe is the direct result of human actions taken in the present, rather than predetermined by divine decree as payment for original sin. For this reason, speculative-realist ('if-this-goes-on') fiction, such as Butler's or Atwood's, 'represent crisis as a present reality, not just a future nightmare' (Buell 274).

The idea of risk narrative allows us to revisit the foregoing discussion of literary verisimilitude. From this angle, post-apocalyptic fiction's speculative realism appears as a fresh and creative permutation of the characteristic truth-likeness of the novel invented in the eighteenth century. In disclosing our own reality as a 'swollen present' carrying the virtual seeds of yet-to-be-actualised developments, post-apocalyptic fiction has adapted the novel's formal realism to the demands of depicting the world in the age of the Anthropocene. Truth-likeness, or believable truth – the unique standard of novel realism, where fiction becomes a higher form of truth-telling – can thus be appreciated in a new futurist form, a new artistic achievement tailored to the needs of our own time.

Atwood's juxtaposition between fantasy and speculative fiction speaks to a wider genre debate in SF studies about the difference between 'serious' science fiction with scientific aspirations, whose modern instances are H. G. Wells or Philip K. Dick, and futuristic fairy tales along the lines of *Star Wars*. In his foundational study *Metamorphoses of Science Fiction*, Darko Suvin defines SF as 'the *literature of cognitive estrangement*' (Suvin 4). Suvin's two-pronged definition of SF as a mode of defamiliarisation on the one hand and as a mode of cognition on the other delimits the genre from both realist and historical novels as well as from fantasy. Suvin writes: 'Estrangement differentiates SF from the "realistic" literary mainstream extending from the eighteenth century into the twentieth. Cognition differentiates it not only from myth, but also from the (folk) fairy tale and the fantasy' (8). While he defends science fiction against its dismissal as fantasy, in substance Suvin's claim corresponds to Atwood's position. This claim also extends to twenty-first-century post-apocalyptic novels more generally. As Hicks observes, as 'a subset of science fiction, post-apocalyptic fiction also tends to extrapolate from a set of verifiable premises about the likely effects of contagion, radiation, global warming, or other current threats, in order to imagine the future' (Hicks, *Post-Apocalyptic Novel* 26).

The post-apocalyptic works considered in this study fall under Suvin's category of cognitive estrangement. For this reason, I have selected José Saramago's *Blindness*, for example, which depicts the outbreak of a plague of hyper-contagious white-blindness.

Blindness has a fantastic element, but it functions as a tool of defamiliarisation, to outline a realistic apocalyptic scenario, an epidemiological catastrophe of global dimensions and its aftermath, one of the key themes of contemporary post-apocalyptic narrative. On the other hand, Bruce Sterling's post-apocalyptic novel *Distraction* (1998), for example, fails to fulfil the condition of extrapolation from verifiable premises. *Distraction* cobbles together too many unlikely disasters in a fantastic scenario of a post-apocalyptic US in 2044 that borders on the absurd: a bankrupt government in a permanent state of emergency that nonetheless prepares for war with the Netherlands, the US air force setting up roadblocks to shake down citizens for funds, the overnight collapse of the economy as a result of the Chinese publication of English-language intellectual property online, and the invention of a mind-altering agent that produces bicameral minds that can do two things at once.

For slightly different reasons, the same verdict applies to outré fantasy such as Colson Whitehead's post-apocalyptic novel *Zone One* (2011), set in the aftermath of a zombie apocalypse. Whitehead imagines a plague that turns humans into cannibal zombies. Its protagonist Mark Spitz is part of an armed sweeper team tasked with the elimination of the remaining 'skels' (zombies) from a walled-off area in lower Manhattan, known as Zone One, to prepare it for future human resettlement. Most of the human survivors suffer from 'PASD, or Post-Apocalyptic Stress Disorder' (Whitehead 54), as a result of survival in the 'wasteland' teeming with zombies since the initial outbreak.[23] A concept coined during the drive to reconstitute human society from scattered safe zones – an effort that fails in the end when the camps are overrun by zombie hordes – PASD names the precarity of life in the post-apocalyptic condition more generally. Nonetheless, in *Zone One*, the fantastic device of a zombie apocalypse serves as a means to evoke horror and serial combat of the action-adventure type rather than the critical extrapolation of real-world trends.[24]

In contrast, as Chapter 3 will examine further, the fantastic device of a contagious plague of white-blindness in *Blindness* functions less to evoke the thrill of horror, than to debunk the logic of dehumanisation that reduces the infected to the status of animals and abject Others. It also troubles the Western association of vision (sight) with knowledge (insight). For all these reasons, it falls on the side of probability rather than improbability. Overall, outbreaks of plague form a major plot device in contemporary post-apocalyptic fiction. In addition to Saramago's white-blindness and Whitehead's zombie plague, these include the bioengineered lethal virus disguised as a wonder drug in Atwood's *MaddAddam* trilogy. To give another example, in Kevin Brockmeier's *Brief History of the Dead* (2006), the world population has been wiped out by a virus spread by Coca Cola.[25] But in depicting the victims' afterlives in a City of the Dead, the plot veers off into fantasy. In short, it all depends on whether or not the premises and function of these near-futurist plagues are primarily rational or fantastic.

One additional point about the characteristics of contemporary speculative-realist apocalypticism remains to be made. When twentieth- and twenty-first-century fiction recovers the apocalyptic temporality of the closed future, the mood switches from utopian associations with hope to dystopian associations with fear. Religious apocalypse is about the triumph of good over evil. The fall of Babylon and the destruction of the beast manifest the victory of justice that, as Keller puts it, ends 'the age of captivity to evil' and inaugurates 'the age of redemption' (Keller 90). Rather than spelling out hopes for salvation, however, speculative-realist visions of the world-end are tragic.[26] The imminent destruction is a threat, not the prelude to the fulfilment of a sacred vision. In *Archaeologies of the Future*, Fredric Jameson takes note of this phenomenon in proposing to add apocalypse as a fourth 'term or generic category' to the existing concepts of utopia, dystopia and anti-utopia:

> we probably need another term to characterize the increasingly popular visions of total destruction and of the extinction of life on Earth which seem more plausible than the Utopian vision of the new Jerusalem but also rather different from the various catastrophes (including the old ban-the-bomb anxieties of the 1950s) prefigured in the critical dystopias. The term apocalyptic may serve to differentiate this narrative genre from the anti-Utopias as well. (199)

Jameson endorses Suvin's claim that utopia is a 'socio-economic sub-genre' of the 'broader literary form' of SF (xiv), defined as the literature of cognitive estrangement (see Suvin 61).[27] In Suvin's view, the genre-defining cognitive estrangement of SF hinges on the narrative dominance of a 'strange newness, a *novum*' (Suvin 4). Instances of this *'fictional "novum" (novelty, innovation) validated by cognitive logic'* (63) may range from voyages to strange and distant places to time-travelling to social or technological innovations. In SF, the new and unorthodox future that replaced millennial expectations at the rise of modernity finds its fictional expression in Suvin's *novum*. As Jameson observes, in the apocalyptic the modern temporality of novelty and change turns from hopeful to fearful. This means that the science-fictional *novum* as such becomes a threat (see Suvin 208ff.; Jameson, *Archaeologies* 189).

The tragic apocalyptic shaping the post-apocalyptic novels considered here forms part of the twentieth-century darkening of the modern form of utopia from fulfilment of hope to nightmarish scenarios of oppression. In picturing destruction on a global scale, apocalypse is the most extreme variety of modern dystopias depicting the disastrous consequences of present developments. As stated in the quotation above, the tragic apocalyptic also differs from anti-utopias such as Orwell's *1984*, which denounce twentieth-century political utopias as totalitarian (see Jameson, *Archaeologies* 200–2). In *1984*, the protagonist, Winston Smith, the last defender of individual freedom, dies, but history goes on under the totalitarian rule of Big Brother. In apocalyptic fiction, when the hero dies, the world ends. The difference between apocalypse and dystopia is similar to that between apocalypse and tragedy. In apocalypse, as Kermode puts it, 'the earthly runs to a stop' so that 'henceforth "time shall be no more"' (Kermode 89). In tragedy, the crisis neither stops time nor does it end succession: 'the world goes forward in the hands of the exhausted survivors' (82). Apocalypse surpasses both tragedy and dystopia in its total, all-encompassing scope of destruction.

Having discussed the singularity of narrative apocalyptic ontology that sets it apart from abstract theory, and having explored its adaptation in contemporary fiction, we now turn to a closer examination of the two basic types of apocalyptic and post-apocalyptic narrative. As crisis narratives depicting the destruction of an entire world, apocalyptic and post-apocalyptic stories are both planetary in scale. Beyond the world-historical magnitude of the cataclysm, however, they can be clearly distinguished from each other from a narratological perspective. Apocalyptic and post-apocalyptic narratives are governed by different temporalities. In apocalyptic genres, the catastrophic event is 'in-story'. Szendy offers a neat formula of apocalyptic cinema that is also valid for word-based narratives: *'the end of the world is the end of the movie'* (Szendy

2). Conversely, if the catastrophe occurs prior to the events narrated, or at their very beginning, the narrative is post-apocalyptic. Szendy presents a definition that is worth reproducing at length:

> The genre of apocalyptic cinema is closely related to, yet distinct from, a similar genre primarily known as post-apocalyptic cinema, which concentrates on survivors of a catastrophic event struggling to reestablish a livable society. In order to be classified as an apocalyptic film, the event threatening the extinction of humanity has to be presented within the story. If this catastrophe occurs prior to the events depicted on the screen, the film is post-apocalyptic. Naturally, there can be a blurring of the lines of these two genres, and a number of pictures that can legitimately be labelled as both. (Mitchell qtd in Szendy 52)

This taxonomy hinging on the opposite placement of the catastrophe at the end versus prior to – or at the beginning of – the narrative works well for all practical purposes. It also helps explain the contrary mood of these two varieties: post-apocalyptic narratives are 'oddly hopeful' because they look forward towards a new future opening up after the horror of destruction. As Irr explains, 'the subjects of the post-apocalyptic novel convey an intense need for new modes of survival and the reproduction of the social unit. These are oddly hopeful works; they typically devote less of their narrative energy to horror than to the slow crawl out of the wreckage and toward signs of other survivors' (Irr 169–70). In contrast, gloom sets the mood in apocalyptic narratives of the tragic type. The close of *One Hundred Years of Solitude* illustrates this point: gloom descends as portents and signs of the imminent end time proliferate. Although it borrows the biblical topos of the supernatural annihilation of earthly history, García Márquez's magical realist apocalypse is shorn of any utopian or millennial expectations.

In his often-cited study *After the End: Representations of Apocalypse*, James Berger points to the staple utopian end realm of apocalyptic narrative as evidence that the post-apocalyptic is not separate from, but part of apocalyptic thinking. As he contends,

> In nearly every apocalyptic presentation, something remains *after the end*. In the New Testament Revelation, the new heaven and earth and New Jerusalem descend. In modern science fiction accounts, a world as urban dystopia or desert wasteland survives. Very seldom – as in

Mary Shelley's *The Last Man* or Gore Vidal's *Kalki* – does the end of the narrative coincide with the end of the world. Something is left over, and that world after the world, the *post-apocalypse*, is usually the true object of the apocalyptic writer's concern. The end itself, the moment of cataclysm, is only part of the point of apocalyptic writing. The apocalypse as eschaton is just as importantly the vehicle for clearing away the world as it is and making possible the post-apocalyptic paradise or wasteland. (Berger 5–6)

Countering Berger, this study reserves the notion of post-apocalypse for an unpredictable new beginning after the end, the opening of a new chapter in history. It understands the apocalypse not merely as a violent break, but as a rupture that also resets the clock. What happens next cannot be known or prophesied in advance. This is an issue distinct from the risk-based ('if-this-goes-on') continuities between pre-collapse worlds and their catastrophic ends discussed earlier. Anything that appears in the *eschaton*, the final events of the divine plan, is part of the predetermined future of apocalyptic narrative, not what happens next. As a future that is certain, it belongs to the *telos* of the apocalyptic narrative plot. Whereas apocalyptic futures are closed and deterministic, post-apocalyptic developments are open and indeterminate. In the unfolding world of post-apocalypse, the future is once again uncertain, and uncertainty results from spontaneous activity and its (unplanned) consequences.

Seeking to update Kermode, Berger contends that the 'visions of the End that Frank Kermode analyzed in terms of a sense of an ending have increasingly given way to visions of after the end [*sic*], and the apocalyptic sensibilities both of religion and of modernism have shifted toward a sense of post-apocalypse' (Berger xiii). Berger's examination of the post- apocalyptic as 'aftermaths or remainders' (xii) of apocalypse allows him to read contemporary American culture as post-apocalyptic, bearing the traumatic traces of historical events that are portrayed apocalyptically – the Holocaust, Vietnam, the upheavals of the 1960s, slavery. Most of the works and cultural expressions he examines – including Reaganism, Thomas Pynchon's *Vineland* and Toni Morrison's *Beloved*, third-generation Holocaust memoirs, Derrida's writing on the Holocaust, talk shows, disaster films – are not science fictional. Essentially, Berger assimilates apocalypse to the phenomenon of trauma: as he remarks, post-apocalyptic discourse demands 'saying the unsayable' (Berger xx); apocalyptic moments leave traumatic traces, remainders and symptoms that post-apocalyptic narratives, as trauma narratives, 'work through' to either repress or come to terms with. Following Berger, Gomel similarly contends that post- apocalypse is not clearly delimited from apocalypse, but is a narrative processing the traumatic remainders of disaster. For Gomel, 'postapocalypse seems to be concerned not with the sharp moment of death but rather with the interminable duration of dying. If the apocalypse promises glorious rebirth, postapocalypse is enmeshed in the backward-looking narrative of trauma' (408).

In reserving the notion of the post-apocalyptic for unforeseeable new beginnings after the world-end, this study does not claim that the traumatic post-apocalyptic posited by Berger and Gomel is irrelevant to the study of post-apocalyptic literature as understood here. The melancholic reflections on apocalyptic ruin and the extinction of natural life in McCarthy's *The Road*, for example, can be read as trauma narrative. However, Berger's approach of broadening apocalyptic to trauma narrative diminishes the planetary scale and finitude of apocalypse. *The Road*'s setting, too, is post-apocalyptic America, which shows that Berger's post-apocalyptic America is figurative, whereas McCarthy's is literal. That said, Berger's study appeared in 1999, before the most recent burst of post-apocalyptic fiction after the millennial turn, of which Octavia Butler's *Parable* series, published in the mid-1990s, was a rare harbinger.

For different reasons, my notion of the post-apocalyptic also differs from those of Teresa Heffernan and Elizabeth Rosen. In Heffernan's view, post-apocalyptic culture is characterised by the loss of the sense of a meaningful ending and of the revelation of ultimate truths connected to apocalypse. As she argues in her study *Post-Apocalyptic Culture: Modernism, Postmodernism and the Twentieth-Century Novel*, this describes the twentieth century. Twentieth-century culture is post-apocalyptic insofar as the grand narratives that used to organise and give meaning to the world have been unsettled. Heffernan traces post-apocalyptic thinking in eight canonical modernist and postmodernist novels by writers from William Faulkner and E. M. Forster to Salman Rushdie, Angela Carter and Toni Morrison. In so doing, she assimilates the notion of the post-apocalyptic to the postmodern idea of the dismantling of master narratives and the rejection of closure, an approach also taken by Elizabeth Rosen's *Apocalyptic Transformation:*

Apocalypse and the Postmodern Imagination, which explores the clash between apocalyptic narrative and postmodernism. For both Heffernan and Rosen, the meaning of the prefix post- in post-apocalyptic is not temporal ('after') – the time after the end of the world – but epistemological ('against'). In other words, the post-apocalyptic refers to the anti-apocalyptic. A distinct variety of the post-apocalyptic, theirs is a form of epistemological scepticism, the dismantling of the apocalyptic paradigm as a hermeneutic paradigm.

In contrast to the nuclear holocausts characteristic of Cold War post-apocalyptic fiction, the contemporary post-apocalyptic works selected here are set in the aftermath of environmental catastrophes such as climate change, mass extinctions, energy crises, resource depletion, pollution and public health disasters such as pandemic diseases and lethal plagues.[28] They describe a shift from one type of man-made planetary destruction, the 'instantaneous apocalypse' of atomic holocausts, to another, the 'slow apocalypse' of environmental catastrophe. That the genre of post-apocalyptic fiction has attracted writers of international standing demonstrates the urgency of these concerns (see Hicks, *Post-Apocalyptic Novel* 6). Both types belong to the tragic apocalyptic, warning humans of their imminent self- and world- destruction unless they change course. As Claire Colebrook notes, since the end of the Cold War, crisis awareness has persisted and even strengthened, whereas 'the sudden nuclear annihilation of the cold war [is] perhaps the only potential extinction threat that has abated' (Colebrook 40). Thus, the prominent concerns of the 'burst' of new post-apocalyptic narratives that have appeared since 2000, as Caren Irr observes, have been 'themes of environmental, technological, and/or epidemiological catastrophe' (Irr 169).[29]

Indeed, as Frederick Buell has shown, environmental apocalypticism emerged much earlier. The founding works of the post-war environmental movement in the 1960s and 1970s by Rachel Carson, Paul Ehrlich and the Club of Rome employed apocalyptic rhetoric to conceptualise the environmental crisis as an 'imminent, world-ending catastrophe' (Buell, 'Global Warming' 262). According to Buell, the conservative debunking of environmentalism as 'no future' doomsterism has led to important transformations in environmentalist discourse. More sober than their predecessors, contemporary eco-apocalyptic fiction depicts a slowed catastrophe, exploring crisis as an ongoing phenomenon and 'as a place in which people presently dwell' (Buell, 'Global Warming' 277). Buell's characterisation fits the post-apocalyptic novels discussed here, which this analysis modifies to stress the compatibility of crisis-as-a-way-of-life scenarios with apocalyptic world-end scripts.

To clarify the unique characteristics of contemporary post-apocalyptic fiction, a brief comparison with Cold War post-apocalyptic novels depicting the threat of nuclear annihilation is helpful. My examples, Walter Miller's *A Canticle for Leibowitz* (1960) and Russell Hoban's *Riddley Walker* (1980), are both set millennia after a nuclear holocaust has wiped out modern civilisation.[30] Society has regressed to medieval (*Canticle*) and primitive (*Riddley Walker*) levels of development. Both novels envision modern science and technology as a threat: Are technology and science to blame for global destruction? Does the path of scientific and technological development inevitably end in catastrophe? To answer these questions, both novels trace post-collapse efforts to regain the advanced levels of scientific and technological development before the nuclear holocaust.

In the post-apocalyptic society of *Riddley Walker*, the post-collapse legend of 'Eusa', a mythical representation of the nuclear holocaust and its aftermath, warns against the dangers of technology. Nonetheless, eventually different groups manage to reconstruct lost modern technologies, succeeding in rediscovering gunpowder. Realising that the recovery of nuclear power is only a question of time, the protagonist exiles himself from the re-modernising society headed once more for global self-destruction. *Canticle for Leibowitz* tells an analogous story that spans two millennia after the destruction of twentieth-century civilisation in a nuclear war, known as the 'Flame Deluge'. After a purge of scientific documents and scientists in the immediate aftermath ('the simplification'), the monks of the Order of Leibowitz devote themselves to 'booklegging' and the secret preservation of scientific knowledge and manuscripts in a remote abbey in the American Southwest. Centred on the Abbey, *Canticle*'s account of post-apocalyptic history progresses in three stages that allegorise three epochs of world history: a pre-scientific age of faith and myth, a modern age of scientific and technological revolutions, and the contemporary era of space travel and weapons of mass destruction. Like twentieth-century civilisation, its far-future successor ends up being annihilated in a nuclear war. Both *Riddley Walker* and *A Canticle for Leibowitz* subscribe to a grim historical determinism by which technological modernisation is inevitably lurching down the path to global nuclear destruction. Despite being given a second chance on earth after a twentieth-century nuclear cataclysm (unlike the residents of Macondo), post-apocalyptic history lapses into a repetition of apocalyptic narrative. Both novels are reminiscent of deterministic rise-and-fall theories of civilisations in the mould of Spengler's *Decline of the West*, in which early stages of creation and growth give way to final stages of development that end in self-destruction. The logic of repetition compulsion underpinning Miller's and Hoban's Cold War post-apocalyptic narratives cautions against nuclear technology and perhaps technology as such. Although set in the distant future, these far-future societies replicate the flaws of twentieth-century civilisation.

In contrast, a striking characteristic of the post-collapse world in twenty-first-century post-apocalyptic fiction is the disappearance, or permanent destruction, of large modern systems – the state and government, the market economy, industry, urban civilisation, mass communication, mass transportation, the military and so on. McCarthy's *The Road* is emblematic of this point. The two survivor-protagonists traverse the post-apocalyptic landscape by walking on former state roads; the road is there, but the state has vanished: 'there's not any more states' (*The Road* 43). Unlike the post-apocalyptic survivors in *A Canticle for Leibowitz* and *Riddley Walker*, recent post-apocalyptic narratives tend not to reconstruct ruined modern technologies.[31] The systems and institutions that empowered humans to destroy the planet remain defunct. This is symptomatic of the revisionary impulse of the most recent iterations of the genre. After the end of the world as we know it, the survivor-protagonists of contemporary post-apocalyptic narratives build another world and future, rather than re-establishing the old. Concretely, this means that contemporary post-apocalyptic narratives endorse the slogan 'small is beautiful'. They imagine small, self-sustaining collectives that make do in low-tech environments. The spirit of localism and low-tech post-apocalyptic world-making is best expressed in the slogan of a novel that – for several reasons – is not considered here, James Howard Kunstler's *World Made by Hand* (2008): 'a world made by hand . . . one stone at a time' (Kunstler 142).[32]

More abstractly, the apocalypse marks a genuine bifurcation point, after which the post-apocalyptic historical process branches off in a new, unscripted direction. This process is described in the systems theoretical concept of emergence, which depicts the spontaneous arising of novel phenomena that did not exist before in self-organising processes. In the boldest fictional post-apocalyptic scenarios, the new social organisation that emerges spontaneously in processes of self-organisation is not modern, but what Bruno Latour calls non-modern. This is the case in Atwood's *MaddAddam* trilogy, which speculates about an unplanned biological and cultural evolution in which human survivors band together with non-humans in a trans-species collective.

Post-apocalyptic fiction after the turn of the millennium is often referred to as near-future post-apocalyptic fiction. Its plots are set in the immediate aftermath of collapse, with their starting points ranging from the proverbial 'morning after' to weeks or a few years after the cataclysm, and narrated time covers no more than a few months, years, at most a decade or two. Their *courte durée* perspective, as it were, limits attention to the immediate tasks of survival and of constructing a livable world on the wreckage of the old. The longer the elapsed time span between the catastrophic event and new post-apocalyptic developments, the more the emphasis shifts away from immediate survival and reconstruction to a retrospective critique of post-apocalyptic history. The heroism and optimism of new beginnings typical of the *courte durée* give way to the critical-reflective – even dystopian – stance of the distant vantage point of the post-apocalyptic *longue durée*. Examples of the *longue durée* variety, *Riddley Walker* and *A Canticle for Leibowitz* illustrate this point. In contrast, the events in Atwood's *Oryx and Crake* begin only a few weeks after Crake's bioterrorist extermination of almost all of humanity by means of an artificial plague. McCarthy's *The Road* is set about a decade after an unspecified cataclysm that has caused the permanent obscuring of the sun, leading to the extinction of almost all life except humans. The action of Saramago's *Blindness* begins on the day of the outbreak of a mysterious and devastating pandemic of white-blindness.

These observations shed further light on the hybrid make-up of Butler's *Parable* series. Not coincidentally, the *Parable* series pioneered the climate change concerns of post-millennial fiction, an early instance of diminishing Cold War era fears of the 'fast apocalypse' of Mutually Assured Destruction. Butler's series forms an intermediate link between the *courte durée* and the *longue durée* varieties of post-apocalyptic fiction: it combines both types. The first volume, *Parable of the Sower*, is an instance of the 'morning after' variety, opening with the destruction of Lauren Oya Olamina's neighbourhood. The second volume, *Parable of the Talents*, has features of the dystopian *longue durée* type, including the dynamics of re-modernisation also found in *Riddley Walker* and *A Canticle for Leibowitz*, as we shall discuss in more detail in Chapter 4.

Heather Hicks insightfully traces post-apocalyptic fictions of survival to the lineage of the Robinson Crusoe archetype. According to Hicks, they explore the predicament of the shipwrecked lone survivor stranded in an unfamiliar world, who 'goes about salvaging and rebuilding his existence, scrap by scrap' (Hicks, *Post-Apocalyptic Novel* 2). Typically, post-apocalyptic fiction features 'ragged bands of survivors; demolished urban environments surrounded by depleted countryside; defunct technologies; desperate scavenging; poignant yearning for a lost civilization, often signified by the written word; and extreme violence, including cannibalism, enacted by roving gangs of outlaws' (6). Yet the travails of the post-apocalyptic castaway play out at a planetary scale: 'the story of a single shipwrecked man has been transformed into the story of a wrecked world' (1).

As Timothy Clark argues in *Ecocriticism on the Edge*, the transition from local scales of human activity to higher planetary scales presents challenges of readability and representation. It requires a 'global imaginary' (Clark 16). The destructive effects of anthropogenic change at the scale of the planet, such as climate change, may be too vast and too complex to represent in a non-reductionist manner. Any such attempt can only be limited and approximate. One might point out that for literary narrative to confront the problem of scale is merely to catch up with developments in modern science, which has long wrestled with producing knowledge about phenomena that are too vast, too small, or too complex to know with certainty.

Similarly engaging scale and organised complexity, Timothy Morton coined the term 'hyperobject' to describe ecology in general and climate change in particular. He draws on object-oriented ontology to conceptualise the quintessential elusiveness of this phenomenon for human observers. As a thing that is 'massively distributed in time and space relative to humans' (*Hyperobjects* 1), climate change is real but, like 'icebergs' glimpsed from a ship

(19), withdrawn from humans in its full extension. Climate change is a hyperobject because it is 'nonlocal': any 'local manifestation of a hyperobject is not directly the hyperobject' (19). In addition to scale, climate change's withdrawal from human observation is due to non-linearity, or 'phasing' (69–80). Ecological systems, such as the butterfly effect discovered by the meteorologist Lorenz (71), are non-linear systems that contain multiple feedback loops; 'any disturbance will not be limited to a single effect but is likely to spread out in ever-widening patterns' (Capra and Luisi 354). At bifurcation points, non-linear systems may branch off into new states, at which point they become unpredictable. Naturally, Morton maintains, the system continues to exist, even though it disappears from human view into unpredictable trajectories. Perhaps inspired by Lorenz, who baptised these trajectories 'strange attractors', Morton captures the uncanny and disorienting character of ecosystems, which elude human ideas of stability and order, in the felicitous notion of 'dark ecology'.

To return to the post-apocalyptic Crusoe, and to modify Hicks's point: the man-made planetary destruction that sets post-apocalyptic survivor narratives into motion tends to turn them against the ideological grain of the Crusoe archetype. Rather than a civilisational ideal to be reclaimed, the best contemporary post-apocalyptic novels confront the lost modern civilisation as a flawed structure best left behind. In the spirit of radical renewal, the novels by Atwood, Saramago, Butler and McCarthy considered here construct new, unfamiliar – even non-modern – post-apocalyptic futures and communities.

I conclude by addressing the intense moralism of post-apocalyptic fiction. In near-future post-apocalyptic fiction, the post-collapse reversion to scarcity prompts two opposite responses: for one, the 'bad guys' among the human survivors revert to predators. In the absence of political and legal institutions, some regress to a Hobbesian 'natural state of war', where individuals fight each other to the death. They band together in marauding gangs of warlords engaging in slavery and cannibalism. As Hobbes posited, lawless existence is lived in continual fear and danger of violent death. One characteristic feature of contemporary post-apocalyptic fiction is extreme physical violence. The most stressful aspect of the post-apocalyptic world is insecurity. For the survivors, worse than the chance of death from starvation or exposure is the risk of violent death, enslavement and rape at the hands of murderous marauders who have degenerated to savages. Irr suggests that such violence 'results . . . from the common condition of scarcity . . . Terror then derives not so much from specific events or ideas as from proximity to the other person's or group's perpetual hunger' (Irr 171). The two protagonists in McCarthy's *The Road*, a father and his young son, live in constant terror of being captured by road agents, who keep other humans as livestock to be eaten. In Saramago's *Blindness*, as the spread of a contagious white-blindness brings about the collapse of social order into anarchy, a gang of blind thugs preys on the helpless blind, extorting valuables and sex. A novel not considered here, Marcel Theroux's *Far North* is set in a post-apocalyptic Siberia, which is flooded with refugees from the climate-ravaged south. A transnational gang of slave traders prey on them, driving their captives across hundreds of miles to forced labour camps. Such horrific scenarios of degeneration suggest that modern machines are the precise equivalent of human labour. Replacing human labour with machines and technology, the process of industrialisation led to the recession of slavery and forced labour. Conversely, when machines and technology become defunct in the global apocalypse and survivors revert to primitive economies, human slavery returns from the shadows to the centre of social life.

The protagonists of contemporary post-apocalyptic fiction are defined against this background. Post-apocalyptic fiction retains the moral fervour of apocalyptic thinking that divides humans into 'bad guys' who are damned and 'good guys' who have been saved. Irr points out the intense interest of twenty-first-century post-apocalyptic fiction in 'collective life' and efforts to refound the social unit via 'new sustainable' groups that are 'nomadic, flexible' and small (Irr 169, 171, 172). The strong emphasis on values stems from the apocalyptic in both its utopian and tragic forms. The reversion from anonymous modern society to face-to-face communities is illustrated by Saramago's *Blindness*: the white-blind's field of social interaction shrinks to what lies within earshot. As Irr notes,

> the uniformly small size of these visions of primitive communism lends an anarchic, even libertarian, flavor to twenty-first-century accounts of the social revolution. No states or state functionaries ever seem to survive environmental or epidemiological crisis, and communication networks also disappear when the technologies that enable them collapse. (Irr 171–2)

In McCarthy's *The Road*, the alternative social unit comprises the father and son dyad. Crucially, the collective is inseparable from the values it is founded on: they stand for not eating people and a passionate commitment to life, defying human savagery and the impending extinction of life on earth. As I will discuss in Chapter 5, the world created by the man and his son is a counter-wasteland, the antithesis of the human savagery of the road agents. This world is created by various practices, including storytelling, everyday practices of making-do, and a particular style of collectivity. Similarly, Butler's protagonist Lauren Olamina gathers together a collective around a post-apocalyptic religion that Lauren invents in response to the experience of disaster: God is Change. As will be shown in the chapters that follow, the novels discussed picture new collectives that abandon the principles of competition and domination for the values of cooperation and ecology: a trans-species ecological collective of human survivors and artificial species (Atwood); an organised society of the blind (Saramago); a post-apocalyptic religion built on loss and uprootedness (Butler); and a post-apocalyptic self founded on passionate commitment (McCarthy).

Notes

1. An important qualification of this point must be made concerning Descartes' position. While Dreyfus and Taylor reject Descartes' philosophy as 'mediational', Meillassoux seeks to return to the Cartesian doctrine of a reality without mind.

2. Ferraris's *Introduction to New Realism* is a slightly revised and expanded version of the earlier *Manifesto of New Realism* (2012). The French original of Benoist's study was titled *Élements de philosophie réaliste: Réflexions sur ce que l'on a.*

3. DeLanda and Harman's co-authored study is framed as a dialogue on a series of topics. The respective contributions of each author are clearly identified.

4. Notably, the ontological turn in contemporary critical theory aligns with a corresponding trend in contemporary fiction, so-called neo-realism. Postmodern fiction, which put into practice the anti-realist premises of postmodern critical theory, is no longer the dominant contemporary literary style. According to Robert Rebein, neo-realism is not 'a monolithic realism, but rather . . . a number of different, at times overlapping, realisms, all of them making use of a common

core of techniques and exhibiting the same belief in the power of language to accurately represent life "as it really is"' (Rebein 30). Notably, the rehabilitation of realist writing in the 1980s and 1990s was the work of creative writers moving against the grain of the then-dominant constructivist critical doctrine (Shechner 35). On contemporary neo-realist fiction, see Versluys, Rebein, Claviez, Leypoldt, Fluck and Shechner. Contemporary post-apocalyptic fiction is part of this neo-realist trend in fiction. Its post-apocalyptic scenarios presume an unquestioned, taken-for-granted contact with reality.

5. *OED* s.v. 'real', *adj.* A.I.1.a.

6. *OED* s.v. 'real', *adj.* A.I.1.b.

7. *OED* s.v. 'realism', *n.* I.1.A.

8. Ezra Pound, 'In a Station of the Metro', in *Modernism: An Anthology*, ed. Lawrence Rainey (Oxford: Blackwell, 2005), 43.

9. When material things appear in humanistic contexts, they usually do so in actor-network constellations. This point is demonstrated by 'thing theory', introduced in Bill Brown's edited collection *Things* (2004) and his monograph *A Sense of Things: The Object Matter of American Literature* (2003). The latter study examines the proliferation of things in the literary imagination of late nineteenth- and early twentieth-century American writers. *Things* traces the circulation of things as they affect humans and as humans are affected by them – as commodities, possessions, in 'the magic by which objects become values, fetishes, idols, and totems' ('Thing Theory' 5). Thing theory aligns with Latour's point that the modern dichotomy between free human agents and determined matter is misleading. As Brown observes, 'in fact the world is full of "quasi-objects" and "quasi-subjects", a term [Latour] borrows from Michel Serres' (12).

10. On the original debate in the nineteenth century about method in the human sciences and anti- positivist responses (the Romantic legacy, Wilhelm Dilthey and so on), see also Polkinghorne 20ff.

11. My account of these scientific developments here and throughout is indebted to Capra, *The Web of Life* and Capra and Luisi, *The Systems View of Life: A Unifying Vision*, which offers a comprehensive and systematic account of the rise of systems thinking.

12. Published a year after *Meeting the Universe Halfway* (2007), 'Posthumanist Performativity' (2008) presents the essentials of Barad's theory of 'agential realism'.

13. Jocelyn Benoist, for example, makes contextuality a centrepiece of his realist ontology (*Elemente einer realistischen Philosophie*).

14. As Graham Harman writes, the 'term "object-oriented ontology" apparently dates to some notes I made in 1997, though the prehistory of this approach stems from 1991–2, in the course of a graduate student's early efforts to make sense of Heidegger's famous tool-analysis' (*Speculative Realism* 91).

15. This study considers post-apocalyptic fiction in a realistic vein that directly engages with the political issues of the day related to the threat of planetary annihilation. Beckett's influential contemporary play *Endgame*, for example, has also been read as apocalyptic for placing its characters in a dead world after an unspecified catastrophe, which may or may not be a nuclear apocalypse. I am not considering works such as *Endgame*: Beckett's minimalist, stripped-down style makes any potential thematic references too elusive to pursue for present purposes.

16. A fascinating text discussed by Danowski and Viveiros de Castro, Davi Kopenawa and Bruce Albert's collaborative work *The Falling Sky: Words of a Yanomami Shaman* (2013) offers an indigenous Amazonian cosmopolitical (cosmos cannot be detached from politics) critique of Western greed and ecological ignorance, tracing its deepest causes to the exploitative anthropocentric cosmovision of modern culture. *The Falling Sky* does so by employing the genre of apocalyptic narrative, but substitutes an Amazonian apocalyptic tradition for the Western apocalyptic script. Danowski and Viveiros de Castro show that the Yanomami 'have never been modern' in Latour's sense. What Westerners call 'nature' – in contrast to 'society' – the Yanomami experience as a cosmopolitan arena, a 'society of societies'. Brian Willems's *Speculative Realism and Science Fiction* also connects contemporary ontologies after postmodernism with literature, but this study does not focus on apocalyptic form.

17. I borrow this phrase from Michael Ruse, 'The Doom Boom'.

18. Its ramifications extend beyond Europe, including the rise of anti-colonial millennarian movements among native peoples around the world, such as the Ghost Dance among Plains Indians, the Cargo Cults of the South Sea, or the millenarian creed of the Canadian Métis prophet Louis Riel. A characteristic trait of these movements is religious syncretism, blending native and Christian elements. Hall contends that secular and religious apocalyptic movements combine the sacred and the secular in much the same way: 'Developments of terrorism, revolution, guerrilla warfare, and anticolonial struggle have consolidated what may be called "secular-sacred" apocalyptic struggle as a dominant feature of modern insurgency' (146).

19. See *OED*, s.v. 'apocalypse', *n.*
20. Not coincidentally, narrative closure was one of the major targets of postmodern fiction. That postmodern anti-realism draws on the dismantling of narrative closure underscores the centrality of the ending to the determination of narrative meaning, and more generally supports the argument about the singularity of narrative ontology put forward here.
21. The role of narrative as a 'powerful and basic tool for thinking' has recently been taken up in the new field of cognitive narratology (Herman, 'Stories' 163). Herman considers narrative's ability to impose closure as a major tool for imposing order on the chaotic stream of experience. 'In coming to a conclusion, tellings mark even the most painful or disturbing experiences as endurable because finite' (173). While pursuing this angle lies beyond the scope of this study, it suggests that Kermode's and Ricoeur's concerns with the organising powers of narrative have lost none of their appeal.
22. As noted earlier, I am referring to a channel of the modern apocalyptic distinct from the revolutionary political apocalyptic described by Hall. The revolutionary apocalyptic is utopian; it pursues violent upheaval as the means to bring about a new visionary order. In contrast, Cold War and environmental apocalyptic are tragic, seeking to avert the violent cataclysm.
23. On *Zone One*, see Hoborek, and Hicks, *The Post-Apocalyptic Novel in the Twenty-First Century*, 105–36.
24. My assessment of *Zone One* differs from Martin's, who reads survival after the zombie apocalypse as a metaphor for the tedious routines of contemporary work (see Martin 161–94).
25. Laura Byrd, a Coca Cola employee and scientist posted on a research mission in Antarctica, is the only human survivor, as a result of the contingency that she doesn't like Coke.
26. This point is also expressed in the distinction between tragic and comic modes of apocalypse, which is 'shaped by a frame of acceptance' (see Garrard 95).
27. This makes Thomas More's *Utopia*, for example, an early work of SF.
28. A detailed taxonomy of post-Second World War apocalyptic fiction, Heather Hicks's valuable survey article 'Apocalyptic Fiction, 1950–2015' provides a rich account of sub-varieties emerging at various historical moments, such as 'postmodern mutations' (1960s), 'the feminist apocalypse' (1970s) and 'the American apocalypse' (1980s).
29. Echoing this point, Adam Trexler notes that 'there is no shortage

of novels that use climate change to envisage an end-of-the-world scenario' (Trexler 79).

30. On *A Canticle for Leibowitz* and *Riddley Walker*, see Pavelich and Abberley.

31. An exception is Emily St John Mandel's *Station Eleven*, which depicts the collapse of modern civilisation, the death of most humans, and the reversion to a pre-technological age after the outbreak of a deadly virus, the 'Georgia flu'. It ends with signs of a slow recovery of modern technology, the sight of a town lit by electric light. Nonetheless, *Station Eleven* likewise portrays a decentralised post-collapse lifestyle of small isolated communities in low-tech environments.

32. In addition to Kunstler's novel and Mandel's *Station Eleven*, another instance of this trend in contemporary speculative post-apocalyptic fiction is Jim Crace's *The Pesthouse* (2007). Like McCarthy's and Atwood's narratives, Kunstler's and Crace's novels are set in near-future post-apocalyptic America and present devolutionary scenarios of reversion to various levels of pre-technological development. In *World Made by Hand*, set 'sometime in the not-distant-future' (cover blurb), life has been scaled back to small towns after the end of oil supplies and long-distance travel, the collapse of the global economy and mass media, and the collapse of government at the federal and state levels after the destruction of Washington, DC, and Los Angeles by terrorist nuclear bombs. Large cities have become uninhabitable, as have many coastal areas as a result of global warming. Vulnerable without antibiotics and modern medicine, the population has been decimated by a series of epidemics. But the severing of long-distance communications is seen to have positive effects, in revitalising community life, which had lapsed 'in the old days, when television and all the other bygone diversions held people hostage in their homes' (Kunstler 208).

The Pesthouse presents a grimmer scenario: an unspecified event has plunged America into a new Dark Age of hostility to technology and idolatry, characterised by the horrors of religious superstition and persecution, including the demonisation of metalwork. Masses of refugees stream to the East Coast to emigrate, along highways teeming with bands of criminals. The narrative begins after the outbreak of a plague ('the flux') that kills all the residents of Ferrytown, a station on the migrant trail, except for two survivors. Strangers thrown together by catastrophe in the eponymous pesthouse, Margaret, a local, and Franklin, a migrant, join the stream of refugees. *The Pesthouse* also envisions a return to the local in response to the collapse of large-scale modern systems: with an orphaned baby they have adopted, Margaret and Franklin return to homestead in the pesthouse.

The most optimistic of contemporary post-apocalyptic novels, *World Made by Hand* celebrates the revitalisation of local self-government. Machine-age technologies yield to sustainable and self-sufficient economies based on farming and local trade. 'We believe in the future', declares one character: unlike 'the world we've left behind', it is 'a world made by hand' (Kunstler 142). Both Kunstler's and Crace's novels exemplify the return to face-to-face communities characteristic of contemporary post-apocalyptic fiction. Yet unlike Atwood's, Saramago's, McCarthy's and Butler's works, they are formulaic compositions less worthy of in-depth readings.

2

The New Realism of the Factish and the Political Ecology of Humans and Non-Humans: Bruno Latour and Margaret Atwood's *MaddAddam* Trilogy

This chapter explores the sociologist of science Bruno Latour's attempt to revision Enlightenment modernity and its constitutive dualisms by replacing it with an integrated ecological model that transcends the segregated realms of society vs. nature, humans vs. non-humans, facts vs. values, science vs. humanities/social sciences. I begin with Latour because, of all the new realist theories considered here, his programmatic focus on dissolving what he calls the 'modern constitution' founded on the separation of so-called nature (the realm of non-humans) from so-called society (the domain of humans), and the related Cartesian dualism of world vs. mind, arguably makes him the closest ally of the post-apocalyptic fiction discussed here. As explained in Chapter 1, post-apocalyptic fiction is about remaking the world after the catastrophic collapse of modern society. Similarly, Latour's work, as Rita Felski has observed, is about 'making rather than unmaking' ('Introduction' 221), about rebuilding the world from the ruins of the dualistic modern regime. Just as post-apocalyptic fiction shifts focus from world-destruction to world-recreation, Latour's aim is to move beyond dismantling the 'modern constitution' towards reassembling the world. Latour's imperative is what he calls 'composition', a concept by which he means the gathering of members of both realms, humans and non-humans, into a common world, one single 'collective'.

Latour pursues his objective through two distinct types of studies, an 'anthropology of the moderns', which is more theory-oriented and speculative, and actor-network theory (ANT), which is an empirical research method devised for practising science beyond the modern dualist settlement. The common goal to be achieved through both tracks is nothing less than the abolition of the dichotomy between the 'two cultures' of the natural sciences and the social sciences/humanities, the modern schism dividing the scientific from the political and religious spheres that was established at the rise of modern science. Latour describes the modern dichotomy of the 'two cultures' in *We Have Never Been Modern* as follows: 'the representation of non-humans belongs to science, but science is not allowed to appeal to politics; the representation of citizens belongs to politics, but politics is not allowed to have any relation to the nonhumans produced and mobilized by science and technology' (28). Further, *'the modern Constitution allows the expanded proliferation of the hybrids whose existence, whose very possibility, it denies'* (34).

Latour's research programme is to trace hybrid actor-networks that cross the segregated realms of nature and society, showing that the dualist modern settlement is belied by the existence – indeed, the continuous expansion – of hybrids that weave across these divided realms. His objective is to demonstrate that the modern convention of separating nature 'out there' from human mind and society 'in here' had imploded by the end of the twentieth century. Latour's claim that 'pure' nature no longer exists describes the condition of the Anthropocene: on the climate-changed planet, nature as such (as an autonomous realm beyond the reach of humans) has been destroyed by anthropogenic climate change. There is no more 'wilderness': as Brian McKibben observes, 'by changing the weather, we make every spot on earth man made and artificial. We have deprived nature of its independence, and that is fatal to its meaning. Nature's independence *is* its meaning; without it there is nothing but us' (McKibben 50). This state of affairs is named by Latour's concept of 'nature-culture' (*We Have Never* 41). According to Dipesh Chakrabarty, the Anthropocene invalidates the modern separation of natural history from human history (Chakrabarty 201).

In the place of the dualist segregation of natural vs. social worlds, objects vs. subjects, Latour posits an aggregate of a multiplicity of hybrid actor-networks. In *Reassembling the Social: An Introduction to Actor-Network Theory*, Latour words his call to arms as follows: 'After nature, it is society that has to go. If not, we will never be able to collect the collective' (*Reassembling* 164). According to Latour, the collective (a term substituted for the tainted word 'society') that is to succeed the modern dualist constitution is no longer modern: 'As soon as we direct our attention simultaneously to the work of purification and the work of hybridization, we immediately stop being wholly modern, and our future begins to change' (11). But neither does the new collective embrace the postmodern or revert to the premodern: it is simply non-modern: 'A nonmodern is anyone who takes simultaneously into account the moderns' Constitution and the populations of hybrids that that constitution allows to proliferate' (47). Latour espouses a new ontology that prioritises relationships, interconnections and networks, that is to say, an ecological realism, or a networks ontology.

I pair Latour with Margaret Atwood's near-future science fiction trilogy *MaddAddam* because, as I will argue, there is a stunning correspondence between Latour's project of convening an ecological collective of humans and non-humans to replace the modern dichotomy of society vs. nature and Atwood's trilogy. As discussed, recent post-apocalyptic fiction depicts human experience and action (in conjunction with non-humans) after a cataclysm that has extinguished most of the human race and destroyed late capitalist civilisation and its institutions and technologies. The ecological collapse strips humans of their modern technologies, and hence of domination over the rest of nature, thereby expelling humans from their age-old place in nature as a 'kingdom within a kingdom', as Spinoza put it (*Ethics* III, Introduction). Indeed, by depicting *tabula rasa* scenarios of precarious human survival in neo-primitive situations, post-apocalyptic literature offers a speculative record of human experience after the destruction of fossil-fuelled modern civilisation. However, and as Atwood's trilogy makes plain, the apocalypse does not spell the end of the Anthropocene as such, for the anthropogenic changes to earth's ecosystems are irreversible. What it does instead is to demote humans to the status of one species among many that they had occupied before advanced technologies made them their master. In the absence of the modern technologies that have been transforming earth's geology and climate since the beginning of the industrial revolution, humans are shipwrecked on the climate-changed and polluted planet – which McKibben dubs 'Eaarth' to signal its contamination in contrast to 'Earth' – that they have manufactured. Like Latour, Atwood's trilogy embraces an ecological standpoint, whose basic unit, the ecosystem, is defined as 'a community of different species in a particular area, interacting with its nonliving, or abiotic, environment (air, minerals, water, sunlight, and so on) and with its living, or biotic environment (with other members of the community)' (Capra and Luisi 342). The basic principle of ecology is interdependence: a shift of perspective from isolated individuals or species to their mutual dependence within a larger whole (Capra and Luisi 353). But while Latour's formulations are abstract, Atwood's fictional world pictures in concrete detail the destructive consequences of human activity in what Latour calls the hybrid actor-networks that make up the planet.

Among contemporary post-apocalyptic fiction, Atwood's trilogy stands out in that it goes beyond common post-apocalyptic scenarios of last-man survivor narratives after the near-extinction of the human race, by depicting the beginning of a new cycle of biological evolution and cultural history. In principle, this is because Atwood focuses on genetics and bioengineering: *Oryx and Crake* was 'published on the fiftieth anniversary of James D. Watson and Francis Crick's discovery of DNA and in the same year that the entire human genome was sequenced' (Howells 163). The three volumes of the *MaddAddam* trilogy, *Oryx and Crake* (2003), *The Year of the Flood* (2009) and *MaddAddam* (2013), progressively trace the dawning of an ecological new order after the near-total annihilation of humankind at the hands of a bioscientist and lone-wolf bioterrorist, Crake. In a desperate attempt to head off the impending environmental collapse of the planet as a result of ruthless corporate-capitalist exploitation, Glenn, alias Crake, destroys humankind in a grand utopian scheme of purification by 'making it new': Crake designs the Crakers, a transgenic breed of humanoids to take the place of humans, while killing humans off with a hyper-infectious lethal virus secretly distributed in the form of aphrodisiac pharmaceuticals. The Crakers are a gentle but hardy, non-competitive and non-hierarchical, collectivist breed of vegetarians designed for ecological coexistence on a warming and environmentally degraded planet. But Atwood offers us not only Crake's planned extinction (the violent end of the anthropogenic evolutionary history we know), but unplanned biological evolution after extinction, the autonomous natural and cultural history that emerges from the ruins of fossil-fuelled modern civilisation. In this future moving forward after the collapse of the Anthropocene, humans and non-humans band together in an ecological transspecies collective for the purpose of inter-species collective survival, coexistence and even interbreeding.

I argue that Atwood presents a science fictional articulation of Latour's vision, gathering an ecological collective that folds humans and non-humans together under a new constitution that is radically non-modern, demolishing the dichotomy of the 'two cultures'. Indeed, the modern spheres of society and nature are defunct and cannot be resurrected: the surviving humans (about twenty individuals in the third volume) are too few to re-establish 'society'. As for nature, there is little organic left in the fictional world of the *MaddAddam* trilogy: transgenic animal splices fabricated by corporate bioengineering have escaped their cages and laboratories, gone feral, and begun to change natural ecosystems. No trace is left of the concept of wilderness as 'untamed' nature (Garrard 67). In Atwood's post-apocalyptic wilderness, going into the wild no longer holds the promise of an escape from civilisation. Instead, entering the 'great outdoors' on Atwood's Eaarth brings encounters with creatures that are artefacts of human civilisation. But these animals no longer obey their designers' genetic programs. In Timothy Morton's terms, the *MaddAddam* trilogy articulates a dark ecological vision. Pleading for an 'ecology without nature', Morton urges ecological thought to embrace the weirdness, uncanniness, monstrosity or 'strange strangeness' of environments: 'environments are made up of strange strangers' (*Ecological Thought* 46). Atwood's collective of organic and artificial species epitomises Morton's uncanny ecology. Ecology is derived from Greek *oikos* ('household'), suggesting continuities with the familiar domestic sphere. However, in Atwood's non-modern 'Eaarth household', the atmosphere of domestic familiarity is dispelled by the intrusion of transgenic creatures at once familiar ('like' pigs, dogs, sheep) and utterly alien.

Atwood's trilogy offers a daring and speculative vision of the future autonomous biological evolution – and, as I will show, cultural history – of artificial species, first and foremost Crake's peaceful humanoids, but also the less salutary transgenic hybrids of pre-apocalyptic corporate experimentation, such as Pigoons ('smart pigs' from splices with human cortical tissue), wolvogs (vicious wolf/dog splices deceptively designed as camouflaged domestication), liobams (experimental lion/sheep splices) and bobkitten (artificial predators to control rabbit pests). When Jimmy, the lone human survivor and focaliser of narration in *Oryx and Crake*, goes to scavenge for food and supplies among the ruined urban wasteland, he finds himself targeted as potential prey by a hunting party of enterprising Pigoons, as eager to taste human flesh as Jimmy is to kill Pigoons for processing into pork and bacon. Atwood's transgenic species are supreme instances of the 'population of hybrids' that, as Latour maintains, the modern Constitution of the dualist nature/society doctrine at once 'rejects and allows to proliferate' (*We Have Never* 47). Both natural – real, living beings – and social – artefacts fabricated by humans working in modern bioscience and bioengineering – the Crakers, Pigoons and other splices cannot come home in either of the moderns' two houses, nature or society. They have been produced in what Latour calls the 'unthinkable nonplace' (96), the no-man's land between the natural and social worlds, by the hidden hybrid networks crossing these segregated domains. Indeed, the question Atwood asks in the *MaddAddam* trilogy is the same that Isabelle Stengers poses in *Cosmopolitics I*, which, with a nod to Latour's work, explores an 'ecology of practices' via a new alliance between the natural and social sciences. Stengers' question is: What happens when our scientific factishes enter history and acquire autonomous modes of existence? A Latourian term that will be explored more fully below, 'factish' identifies the particular types of hybrid beings that are both constructed (by successful experimentation in scientific laboratories) and real (autonomous forces with an independent life in the 'external' world, not mere fictions). A specifically ecological critique of modernity implicit in Atwood's novels corresponds closely to a critique of that kind elaborated in Latour's writings. Atwood and Latour have closely comparable – specifically bio-centric, post/humanist – views of desirable alternatives to various modern conceptions and practices.

At the same time, I argue that the *MaddAddam* trilogy also stands apart from Latour's formulations of a new ecological ontology of nature-culture. Like other post-apocalyptic fiction discussed here, Atwood employs the tools of post-apocalyptic fiction to picture near-future scenarios of post-collapse survival. The singularity of post-apocalyptic literature – to adapt Derek Attridge's term – consists in literature's unique mode of access to speculative realism. Fictional (in the sense of literary) worlds differ from theoretical ontologies in their media-specific make-up: what fiction says about worlds and worlding is always cast in the mould of the particular, a specific narrative about a specific event and place. These are irreducible to conceptual abstraction.

Furthermore, as explained in the previous chapter, apocalyptic thinking is defined by what Catherine Keller calls 'the script of binary time, a before and an after' (Keller 90). It is organised around two distinct times and worlds straddling a radical break: the present time (and world) that is 'running out', and the 'coming time' (and world), 'discontinuous with it', which 'succeed[s] it' (Keller 93). Therefore, the world-endism of Atwood's apocalyptic thinking urges the temporal irreversibility of ontological transformation more forcefully than Latour. The Otherness of the recomposed world of the post-apocalypse in the *MaddAddam* trilogy is sharply outlined by the apocalyptic 'barrier of time' (Jameson, *Archaeologies* 85). As I will show in the following, Atwood's and Latour's new ecological ontologies converge in three major areas, which I will discuss in turn: the pharmacological instability of artificial species, or the factishes of modern bioengineering (the focus of *Oryx and Crake*); the replacement of the modern fact vs. value dichotomy with what Latour calls 'matters of concern' (the emphasis in *The Year of the Flood*); and the formation of an ecological collective of humans and non-humans (the concern of *MaddAddam*).

Bruno Latour's Networks Ontology

Through a series of studies over several decades, including *We Have Never Been Modern* (1993), *Pandora's Hope: Essays on the Reality of Science Studies* (1999), *Politics of Nature: How to Bring the Sciences into Democracy* (2004), *Reassembling the Social: An Introduction to Actor-Network Theory* (2005) and *On the Modern Cult of the Factish Gods* (2010), Latour has called for a reconceptualisation of modernity beyond once-definitive dualisms (nature/society, subject/object, mind/matter, humans/ non-humans), a product of the dichotomy of the 'two cultures' and of the arch-modern logic of 'rupture'. At the same time, he has urged the recognition of the actual results of modernisation – 'the proliferation of hybrids' of these domains (*We Have Never* 1). Modernity, according to Latour, is defined by a fundamental paradox: while, in the wake of Galileo, Descartes and Kant, it has insisted on the conceptual segregation of pure realms of nature/non-humans and society/humans in theory, in practice it has sponsored the very expansion of hybrids across the segregated realms of nature vs. society, technology/science vs. politics that it overtly denies. Furthermore, writes Latour, this internal contradiction between these two concurrent activities is actively suppressed: 'there shall exist a total separation between the work of hybrids and the work of purification' (*We Have Never* 31). In other words, in addition to instituting a double divide – between nature and society, and between the overt affirmation of purification and the covert practice of hybridisation – the third move (or 'guarantee') of Enlightenment modernity is to cloak its internal contradictions in silence.

Throughout his extensive and distinguished career, Latour's programme has been to expose Enlightenment modernity's hidden contradictions and to seek an alternative, non-dissociative way of thinking the modern as a hybridising practice beyond the logic of dualisms and pure realms. The target of Latour's critique is the division between Science (with a capital S) and the humanities/social sciences, which obscures the actual interconnectedness between so-called objective facts and subjective values, reality and politics, humans and non-humans, mind and world, and which aids and abets a 'science fundamentalism' that denies the reality of anything outside of what can be measured and quantified. By the late twentieth century, and after successive cycles of techno-logical innovation, the 'massive expansion of hybrids' produced in modernity's hidden networks across the pure realms of humans and non-humans 'has saturated the constitutional framework of the moderns' (*We Have Never* 62, 51). This population of hybrids, which Latour (following Michel Serres) calls 'quasi-objects, quasi-subjects' (51), and 'whose proliferation the moderns cannot explain' (73), has become an insurmountable challenge: it 'has exploded modern temporality along with its constitution' (73). Latour's watchwords in combating the logic of dualism and puri-fication are 'to hybridise' and 'to ecologise', that is to say, to think contextually and relationally. In Latour's revisionary account of modernity, the 'work of mediation becomes the very centre of the double power, natural and social. The networks come out of hiding' (139).

In theorising a convergence between traditional science and the social sciences/humanities, Latour is closely allied with the philosopher of science Isabelle Stengers.[1] Stengers' popular book, co-authored with Nobel Prize winner and chemist Ilya Prigogine, *Order Out of Chaos: Man's New Dialogue with Nature* (1979; 1984), takes stock of this shift. The science of complex dynamic systems, to which Prigogine's research on dissipative structures made a definitive contribution, shattered the atemporal view of the domain of classical Newtonian science as the 'timeless' and universal as opposed to the time-oriented and culture-specific phenomena studied by the social sciences and humanities. As Stengers and Prigogine write in the Introduction to *Order Out of Chaos*: 'We are becoming more and more conscious of the fact that on all levels, from elementary particles to cosmology, randomness and irreversibility play an ever-increasing role. *Science is rediscovering time*. It is this conceptual revolution that this book seeks to describe' (xxviii). Notably, what Stengers and Prigogine (in the French title of their book, *La Nouvelle Alliance*) call the 'new alliance' between the natural sciences and social sciences/humanities is not the result of the social sciences/humanities becoming more quantitative and mathematised – quite the opposite. As Fritjof Capra put it, 'instead of being a machine, nature at large turns out to be more like human nature – unpredictable, sensitive to the surrounding world, influenced by small fluctuations' (Capra 193).

Latour pursues his effort of rethinking modernity in two parallel but interconnected sets of works. The first set is more theoretical than empirical, and it is aimed at reconceptualising modernity via an 'anthropology of the moderns'. It includes *We Have Never Been Modern, Politics of Nature* and *On the Modern Cult of the Factish Gods*. (Latour returned to this effort on a grand scale in his most recent book, *An Inquiry into Modes of Existence: An Anthropology of the Moderns* [2013].)[2] By borrowing from anthropology techniques of writing culture, Latour anatomises the internal contradictions of dominant modernity's 'Modern Constitution' or the 'Modernist Settlement'. He goes on to draft what he calls an alternative 'nonmodern constitution' that, in the place of the dualist modern settlement, envisions an alternative collective that gathers together both humans and non-humans, which he variously refers to as the 'parliament of things' (in *We Have Never Been Modern*) or a 'political ecology' (in *The Politics of Nature*). As is obvious from the wording, these are blueprints for a common world or collective that replaces the divide between 'external' nature, the domain of mute things-in-themselves, and society, the domain of the association of free subjects. Latour's new collective of humans and non-humans starts from the occluded site of Enlightenment modernity, the 'unthinkable nonplace' (*We Have Never* 96) of mediation between the poles of nature and society where the networks have been carrying out their work of producing hybrids.

It is for this reason that, as Graham Harman observes, Latour envisions a new kind of realism, which is why his work is of primary importance for this project: it is not that Latour is a constructivist, let alone postmodern, as he is sometimes charged with being.[3] Rather, Latour merely discards the classic, scientific, anatomising realism of isolated parts, modelling a new realism that takes into account interactions between internals and externals, parts and wholes – 'a realism of relations' (Harman, *Prince of Networks* 75). Paralleling Markus Gabriel's work examined in Chapter 4, Latour can be thought of as formulating both a negative ontology (the critique of modernity) as well as a positive ontology (non-modern ecological alternatives to modern practices and beliefs). Latour's positive ontology hinges on the principle of composition, or of reassembling the world, a vision that he articulates in his 'Attempt at a "Compositionist Manifesto"'. As he states there, 'while critics still believe that there is too much belief and too many things standing in the way of reality, compositionists believe that there are enough ruins and that everything has to be reassembled piece by piece' (Latour, 'Compositionist Manifesto' 476). Equally important, analogous to Gabriel's tenet that the world (in the sense of unified totality) does not exist, Latour cautions that 'this common world that has to be built . . . will never make a whole' (474).

The second strand of Latour's analysis is actor-network theory (ANT). Emerging from a series of empirical studies in science and technology published in the 1970s and 1980s, actor-network theory culminated in the 2005 definitive statement in *Reassembling the Social: An Introduction to Actor-Network Theory*. Like Latour's theoretical studies on the 'anthropology of the moderns', actor-network theory hinges on the insight that we must let go of the dichotomy of nature vs. society. *Reassembling the Social* approaches this task by focusing on the society/subject pole of the Great Divide, and by providing an empirical research methodology rather than a theoretical explanation as given in *We Have Never Been Modern*. For Latour, the social is not a separate realm, the macrocosmic 'context' or 'hidden structure' that frames events and human actions. Instead, the social is nothing but a (theoretically) unlimited network of associations and assemblages. Recovering the dynamic meaning of 'social' as 'to associate', Latour proposes what he calls 'actor-network theory' as a 'sociology of associations' that offers an alternative to the 'sociology of the social': rather than an invisible frame in which events happen, the social is nothing but 'a *type of connection* between things that are not themselves social' (*Reassembling* 5), an ongoing heterogeneous network created by multiple actors, human and non-human. As Harman has pointed out, a premise of Latour's work is the principle of 'irreduction': the refusal to divide reality into a world of surface phenomena or appearances and an underlying but hidden reality, with the latter figuring as the absent cause that produces the former.[4] Instead, Latour places phenomena of all types (cultural, scientific, economic, religious, political and so on) on one single, connected plane, a flat ontology, without deciding in advance what the paths of cause and effect are.

Though an empirical research method, the conceptual abstraction of *Reassembling the Social* is substantial. As Latour explains, to perform an actor-network analysis is not 'to glide like an angel' gazing down at the social world from above, but 'to trudge like an ant' on the ground, tracing even the 'tiniest connections' between things (*Reassembling* 25). (This insect is a fortuitous homonym of ANT, the acronym of actor-network theory.) Latour urges the adoption of a deliberately myopic perspective, making no pre-judgements about causality by abstracting to pre-established social formations. Tracing an actor-network means following an actor or actant – who can be either human or non-human – and mapping the resulting heterogeneous network of connections he or she is making. An actant is defined as someone 'who 'mak[es] someone do something' (58) and as 'what is made to act by many others' (46). Emerging as it does from the society pole of the modern nature/society divide, actor-network theory centrally features the reconceptualisation of the core characteristic of the social – the agency of the free human subject. Whereas anthropocentric modern humanism attributes agency (as well as speech) exclusively to humans, viewing nature as passive and mute, actor-network theory flattens the asymmetry between humans and non-humans (both things and animals). Latour writes that a superficially helpful but misleading way of introducing actor-network theory would be to say that it is 'sociology extended to non-humans' (109). Like humans, non-humans can be actants, that is to say, beings endowed with the capacity to transform reality. Further, in contrast to critical sociology, whose framework of 'social explanation' envisions few abstract causes (power, capitalism, the state, empire and so on) that generate a mass of local effects, a good ANT study multiplies the number of 'strong' local actants – that is to say, mediators that actively translate, mongrelise, transform, rather than mere intermediaries that 'just sit there' and passively transmit and transport external or global forces (128). The strength of traditional sociology, Latour suggests, is 'saying *substantive* things about what the social world is made of . . . where the ingredients are known. But that doesn't work where things are changing fast . . . New topics, that's what you need ANT for' (142).

The remainder of this section will probe further into specific Latourian concepts that are particularly relevant to demonstrating the centrality of Latour's work to the problem of this study, the emergence of new ecological realisms after poststructuralism. If there is a first among Latour's many innovative ideas, it is the concept of the actor-network. As stated, Latour defines actors as mediators, beings that make a difference: 'An intermediary . . . is what transports meaning or force without transformation: defining its inputs is enough to define its outputs . . . Mediators transform, translate, distort and modify the meaning or the elements they are supposed to carry' (*Reassembling* 39). The distinction between active mediators and passive intermediaries (placeholders, puppets moved by an external force) replaces the modern dualism of mind vs. matter, subject vs. object; in short, the distinction between humans and non-humans. Unpredictable, self-generated action is no longer reserved for humans to the exclusion of animals and things, but is distributed across all realms of beings. Latour compares the distinction between mediators and intermediaries to the Deleuzian distinction between creative virtuality and preformed potentiality. In an imaginary dialogue with a student that constitutes the middle section of *Reassembling the Social*, Latour writes:

> 'What can I do with ANT?' . . . [N]o structuralist explanation. The two are completely incompatible. Either you have actors who realize potentialities and thus are not actors at all, or you describe actors who are rendering virtualities actual (this is Deleuze's parlance by the way) and which require specific texts. (155)

To repeat: intermediaries are no actors at all. In other words, Latour's loosening of the dichotomy between humans/society and non-humans/nature is accompanied by a tightening of the definition of agency, now principally available to all beings. For example, the concept of mediator (and the dichotomy between mediator and intermediary) is first introduced in *We Have Never Been Modern*: the hybrids whose proliferation in the hidden networks between the poles of nature and society Latour discusses are such actors, or mediators. This is why Latour also calls them 'quasi-objects, quasi-subjects'. Hybrids are what they are, primarily not because they may look like aliens (half-human, half-thing) – even if that may be the case sometimes, as we shall see in our Latourian reading of Atwood's *MaddAddam* trilogy. They are hybrids because, beginning as natural objects or artefacts, they transgress the boundary from intermediary to full-fledged mediator: 'They become mediators – that is, actors endowed with the capacity to translate what they transport, to redefine it, redeploy it, and also to betray it. The serfs have become free citizens once more' (*We Have Never* 81). In short, hybrids are beings that shift their mode of existence: from dependent or passive to independent. More precisely, this study reads the make-up of hybrids – 'half object and half subject' (117) – as a dynamic process of transformation – from object to subject. Hybrids that begin as artefacts (like Atwood's artificial species) pass from being constructed (literally, made by humans) to becoming 'real'.

Non-humans (objects, things, animals) are included among the population of actors, beings 'that make others do something'. *Reassembling the Social* draws on research on animal societies across the scale of macro-organisms, from ants to baboons, as well as to the role of innovation in the history of technology, where 'tools . . . have been turned . . . into mediators that triggered the evolution of modern man' (*Reassembling* 81). For this reason, actor-network theory 'uses the technical term *actant*' (54) which it borrows from narrative theory: '*any thing* that does modify a state of affairs by making a difference is an actor – or, if it does not have a figuration yet, an actant' (71). Action must be clearly distinguished from figuration (a term designating the form of actants, whether an individual, a collective or an abstract being): 'if agency is one thing, its *figuration* is another' (53). According to Latour, abstract actants ('the invisible hand of the market') are no more real than individuals, they just have a different figuration, '*ideo*- instead of anthropomorphic' (53).

A key feature of actor-network theory is the non-autonomous and non-originary nature of agency. Latour explains: 'An "actor" in the hyphenated expression actor-network is not the source of an action but the moving target of a vast array of entities swarming toward it' (*Reassembling* 46). Action is not autonomous, but 'borrowed, distributed, suggested, influenced, dominated, betrayed, translated. If an actor is said to be an actor-network, it first of all is to underline that it represents the major source of uncertainty about the origin of action' (46). The point about distributed agency refers to the fact that no actant acts alone. It is connected to a network or collective (an actor-network). If there seems to be a contradiction between the idea of distributed agency and the distinction between mediator and intermediary, it is only superficial. Latour's notion of agency is profoundly dialectical, at once 'making do' and being 'being made to do': on the one hand, an actant is someone who makes others do something (a mediator). On the other, she or he is in turn also the recipient of action, made to act by others. This is the meaning of the hyphen in actor-network: 'Action is *overtaken*' (45) because many other agents are present when individual actants act, and action, human or otherwise, is always refracted by other forces. Thus, action should be viewed as a 'node' or a 'knot' (44). Action is always an actor-network. In fact, one can think of actor-networks as examples of, or a theoretical model for, self-organisation in complex dynamical systems, a topic we will turn to in the next chapter. Self-organising systems are able to generate their own form and order through exchanges between insides and outsides, system and environment.

A related point concerns the inability to separate actants from attachments: by virtue of being actor-networks, actants are never isolated, but well-connected. Latour insists that we deconstruct the metaphor of marionettes as synonymous with passivity and manipulation by external forces and the equation: far from inhibiting agency, attachment facilitates it, as in the phrase of 'networking' and being 'well-connected'. Latour explains:

What's wrong with the word [actor] is not that it is often limited to humans – this limit we have learned to encroach upon – but that it always designates a *source* of initiative or a starting point ... [W]e are now interested in mediators making other mediators do things. 'Making do' is not the same as 'causing' or 'doing': there exists at the heart of it a duplication, a dislocation, a translation that modifies at once the whole argument. It was impossible before to connect an actor to what made it act, without being accused of 'dominating', 'limiting', or 'enslaving' it. This is no longer the case. The more *attachments* it has, the more it exists. (*Reassembling* 216–17)

Here we also see one reason why Latour has elected the myopia of an ant as the mascot, as it were, of ANT. Seeing very little one step at a time, her task is to follow the actant and trace the network, painstakingly establishing connectors and connections.

As a way of distinguishing ANT from the 'sociology of the social', Latour writes that doing actor-network theory is about 'learning how to feed off uncertainties', instead of deciding in advance what the 'furniture of the world' (*Reassembling* 115) is composed of. The first part of *Reassembling the Social* is organised around examining five major uncertainties, four of which are the nature of groups, actions, objects and facts, most of which have been discussed in the foregoing account. The fifth describes an ANT study:

A good ANT account is a narrative or a description or a proposition where all the actors *do something* and don't just sit there. Instead of simply transporting effects without transforming them, each of the points in the text may become a bifurcation, an event, or the origin of a new translation. As soon as actors are treated not as intermediaries but as mediators, they render the movement of the social visible to the reader. (128)

Latour takes care to point out that 'feeding off uncertainties' does not make his work postmodern. Postmodernism is a theory of representation. In contrast, actor-network theory describes how actants associate with other actants by 'making them do', and by 'being made to do', things in the world. Actor-network theory is therefore ontological, not epistemological. It is about the enacting of worlds, bringing forth worlds by doing. According to Latour, the postmodern critique of representation only registers the crisis of the modern and its dichotomies (such as external world vs. word), without overcoming it: 'Instead of moving on to empirical studies of the networks that give meaning to the work of purification it denounces, postmodernism rejects all empirical work as illusory and deceptively scientistic' (*We Have Never* 46).[5] Latour places his ontology in relation to Heidegger's: it continues Heidegger's project of undoing the forgetting of being in Western metaphysics. But whereas Heidegger dismissed technology from originary thinking as *Gestell*, 'pure instrumental mastery' (*We Have Never* 66), Latour considers modern science and technology as the centre of his work: 'Who has forgotten Being? ... Look around you: scientific objects are circulating simultaneously as subjects objects and discourse. Networks are full of being' (66). The focus on technology is a concern he shares with Margaret Atwood, as we shall see in the next section.

I conclude this discussion of Latour's work with what I see as his second major contribution to the debate over what comes after poststructuralism: a critique of the modern method of critique, the related phenomenon of constructivism, and his concept of the factish. His remarks lead to the heart of the science wars over what constitutes 'scientific reality', but they are equally relevant to the culture wars over political correctness in the humanities and social sciences. Latour coins the term 'factish' to name his revision of the core modern dichotomy between scientific facts and non-scientific, 'mere' belief (*doxa*), and the separation of facts and values, dating back to Galileo, who banned value from science. On Latour's account, construction does not entail the absence of reality: instead, construction and reality are successive stages of the same process by which human constructs (factishes) become real forces in the world. To an English-speaking audience, Latour presented this problematic in a compelling way in his influential 2004 article, 'Why Has Critique Run Out of Steam? From Matters of Fact to Matters of Concern'. The central target of that essay was the hierarchy between the 'knowing' modern critic and scientist and the naive believer, whose cherished beliefs of folk philosophy the critic debunks.[6] Latour argues that critique has become too cheap: given that there are now reductive positivists who dismiss the reality of anything other than, say, genes, conspiracy theorists who attribute 9/11 to a CIA plot, and creationists who deny evolution, modern critique needs to be refurbished. Supposedly, scientific facts are 'strong' objects that are thought to 'speak for themselves'. Fetishes (a term designating unquestioned belief), in contrast, are 'weak' objects thought to be fabricated, the result of a false projection of agency on the part of the human believer. But as Latour contends, the dichotomy between facts (autonomous agents) and fetishes (fictions, creatures and instruments of human beliefs) is a false one: like fetishes, 'facts are fabricated ... Whereas we fabricate them in our laboratories with our colleagues, our instruments, and our hands, facts are supposed to become, by some magical effect of reversal, something that no one has ever fabricated before' (*Factish Gods* 18).

Isabelle Stengers offers a helpful clarification of this point. According to Stengers, there is a difference between 'raw, empirical, neutral' facts 'independent of us', such as an earthquake or a falling tree (*Cosmopolitics I* 49), and experimental facts. The latter emerge not from 'nature' but from 'a reality staged in the laboratory' (67). In contrast to raw facts such as earthquakes,

> the experimental 'fact' reflects the singularity of the history in which it was produced. At the core of this history is that facts have value only if they can be recognized as being able to obligate practitioners to agree on their interpretation. And the practitioner who represents this fact, and claims to speak in its name, can do so only if she has first satisfied the strict obligations that will determine the value of what she proposes. (49–50)

For Stengers, it is such constraints – instituted by humans – that distinguish experimental scientific facts: the twin notions of requirements (addressed to the experimental fact) and obligations (to be fulfilled by the scientist). Similarly, Latour demonstrates in his work on Pasteur's microbiology that the reality of the laboratory is not 'nature', but an artificial nature, nature staged to create scientific phenomena according to new procedures invented for just that purpose. These ensure that their existence is witnessed by authorised spokespersons, scientists, who represent these phenomena to the human public at large by taking testimony from natural forces that are mute as well as invisible. However, as Latour explains, the difference between experimental facts and natural facts was erased, while the difference between facts and human artefacts was purified. Indeed, in her philosophy of modern science *Cosmopolitics I* and *II* (surveying developments from the rise of Newtonian mechanics to the emergence of complexity theory and the science of self-organisation at mid-twentieth century), Stengers adopts Latour's term, factish, to describe the particular beings that are constructed through successful experimentation in the laboratory.

In other words, the difference between scientific facts and unquestioned beliefs (which Latour dubs 'fetishes') is not that facts are real and beliefs are constructions. As Latour explains, '"Fetish" and "fact" can be traced to the same root. The *fact* is that which is fabricated and not fabricated . . . But the *fetish* too is that which is fabricated and not fabricated' (*Pandora's Hope* 272). Latour argues that both are artefacts that are felt to be real, that is to say, to be autonomous forces in the 'real' world – world-making actants – for parallel reasons: they have successfully undergone a previous phase of human construction, according to the particular – and very different – protocols of modern science on the one hand, and various religious and secular beliefs on the other. In other words,

> if we add to the facts their fabrication in the laboratory, and if we add to the fetishes their explicit and reflexive fabrication by their makers . . . [what appears] in their stead is . . . what I call the factish . . . But if human agency is restored in *both* cases, the belief that was to be shattered disappears, along with the shattering fact. We enter a world that we had never left, except in dreams – the dreams of reason – a world where arguments and actions are everywhere facilitated, permitted, and afforded by *factishes*. (273–4)

Thus, 'it is *because* it is constructed that [the factish] is so very real, so autonomous, so independent of our own hands' (275). In this way, Latour has changed the question: we are no longer engaged in stale discussions over the 'social construction' of everything. Nor are we in a sterile debate over realism vs. constructivism, adjudicating a false dichotomy (Is it real? Is it constructed?) for the purpose of explaining away naive beliefs and putting in their place the facts of science (and other objects of modern critique). Instead, we are facing a different and more interesting question, the question of affordance: What are the successful practices that are required for artefacts, scientific or not, to become real? What happens when scientific factishes enter history and acquire autonomous modes of existence?

Latour's solution to the impasse of modern critique is to direct the critic to a new task: composing non-modern ecological alternatives to modern practices: 'The critic is not the one who debunks, but the one who assembles' ('Critique' 171).[7] One such reconfiguration – important for our purposes because of its relevance for Atwood's *Oryx and Crake* and *The Year of the Flood* – is 'matters of concern', a concept that Latour suggests as a replacement for the flawed notions of facts and values: 'the critical mind, if it is to be relevant again, is to be found in the cultivation . . . of a realism dealing with what I will call *matters of concern*, not *matters of fact*' ('Critique' 157). The problem with these notions is an unquestioned hierarchy that prioritises facts over values: 'values always come too late' (*Politics of Nature* 97), after 'facts' have 'marked' their 'territory' (97). Appeals to facts come with pre-established notions of what counts as 'externalities' – factors that are irrelevant and can legitimately be ignored – that subsequent appeals to value are powerless to question. In fact, tackling the problem of value is one of the prime motives behind Latour's proposal for a new holistic realism:

> Reality is not defined by matters of fact. Matters of fact are not all that is given in experience. Matters of fact are only very partial and, I would argue, very polemical, very political renderings of matters of concern, and only a subset of what could also be called *states of affairs*. ('Critique' 157)

The inspiration for the new task of assembling matters of concern is, once again, Heidegger, in this case the late Heidegger's concept of thing as a gathering of world, developed specifically to counter the modern scientific concept of thing as 'object'. The collective to be gathered (in Latour as in Heidegger) is one that includes humans as well as non-humans – the parliament of things, or political ecology.

This problem is elucidated in more detail in *Politics of Nature*, which focuses on outlining a 'political ecology' to replace the modern division of nature vs. society. Latour maintains that the fact vs. value distinction actually bundles a number of distinct, overlapping activities that need to be unpacked. First, 'facts' and 'values' each contain a demand about something to be 'taken into account' (*Politics of Nature* 109): in the case of facts, it is the 'requirement of external reality' (as in the statement 'facts are there whether we like it or not' [104]). In the case of values, it is the 'requirement of *prior* consultation' (expressed, for example, in the declaration 'there's an ethical problem here!' [106]). In addition, 'facts' and 'values' each imply a power 'to arrange in rank order' (109): values ask us to form a hierarchy among legitimate priorities; facts prompt us to establish closure in any given case. Having broken the fact/value distinction into these four distinct demands, Latour suggests that they can be rearranged in a new order. The old distinction between facts and values is exchanged for what he calls a 'new separation of powers', the 'power to take into account' and the 'power to arrange in rank order' (109). The new dispensation cuts across the old distinction of nature vs. society by placing 'natural' facts and 'social' values on an equal footing, without granting 'facts' undue priority. It is worth quoting a longer excerpt that summarises the argument:

> We distinguish two other *powers*: *the power to take into account, and the power to put in order*. The first power is going to retain from facts the requirements of perplexity, and from values the requirement of consultation. The second is going to recuperate from values the requirement of hierarchy, and from facts the requirement of institution. In place of the impossible distinction between facts and values, we are thus going to have *two powers of representation of the collective* that are at once distinct and complementary. While the fact–value distinction appears reassuring, it did not allow us to *maintain the essential guarantees* that the new Constitution requires ... The collective no longer construes itself as a society in a single nature, for it creates a *new exteriority*, defined as the totality of what it has excluded by the power of putting in order and which obliges the power of taking into account to go back to work. The dynamics of the progressive composition of the common world thus differ as much from the politics of humans as from that of nature under the old Constitution. (*Politics of Nature* 233)

To recapitulate: the new constitution for the political ecological assembly of humans and non-humans, and the new separation of powers that it is to follow (Latour calls it a 'new bicameralism' [113]) abandons none of the ingredients of the old divisions, nature vs. society and facts vs. values. It merely institutes a level playing field, a flat ontology,[8] according to the principle of irreduction. Its advantage is that the hierarchies and the exteriorities that result from this process are no longer construed as pre-established and self-evident. They are acknowledged to be deliberate and fabricated – in other words, factishes, beings that are necessary but nonetheless man-made. As we shall see, *The Year of the Flood*, the second volume of the *MaddAddam* trilogy, explores 'matters of concern' in analogous ways to Latour's critique of facts vs. values: the novel portrays a green religion that sets itself up as a counterculture to corporate bioengineering.

Isabelle Stengers makes an important observation regarding

Latour's concept of the factish that will be relevant to the following discussion of Atwood's *MaddAddam* trilogy, and that is worth considering before turning to it next. Scientific factishes are also *pharmaka*. Borrowing Plato's reference to the sophists' use of the *pharmakon* (mediated by Derrida) as a drug that may act as a remedy or a poison, Stengers points to 'the pharmacological instability of our factishes' (*Cosmopolitics I* 32). Pharmacological instability augments the factish's constitutional slippage between fabrication and reality. Not only do factishes shift between being real and being made, it is also uncertain whether they are beneficent or maleficent. Stengers mentions the antagonism between the factish-*pharmakon* and the 'modern tradition', with 'its contempt for fetishes, its fear of the *pharmakon*' (80). The pharmacological instability derives from the same passage as the factish instability, to which it draws fresh attention: the transition of experimental facts from the places and early stages of fabrication (the laboratory) into history and the world at large. It involves a metamorphosis from dependency and fabrication (on and by a creator, the scientist in particular and human society more generally) to an autonomous mode of existence as an actor-network. The essence of Stengers' point is captured by the image of the genie out of the bottle, liberated from a controlled environment and set free in the world. As evolutionary biologists Richard Lewontin and Richard Levins explain, the problem is really a challenge for modern science, which must learn to overcome the biases of its origins in the purifying regime of the Moderns, as Latour would put it. According to Lewontin and Levins, the 'central intellectual problem of our time is that of complexity' (183).

Margaret Atwood's *MaddAddam* Trilogy

In Margaret Atwood's near-future science fiction trilogy, we find a stunning literary analogue to Latour's network ontology, including the outline of a non-modern 'political ecology' or a 'parliament of things' that takes account of the joint production of the natural and the social. The remainder of this chapter explores these parallels, while also appreciating the specifics of Atwood's literary contribution.

Atwood's trilogy is a speculative vision of a dystopian future generated in the wake of the spectacular triumph of genetics and molecular biology. The discovery of DNA in the 1950s, 'hailed as the greatest discovery in biology since Darwin's theory of evolution', placed biology, which had become 'almost negligible' at that time, once again at the frontlines of science (Capra 77). But it also inaugurated a new phase of scientific determinism: biology narrowed from studying organisms and ecosystems to studying molecules and biochemistry. Believing that they had discovered the 'alphabet of life', biologists embraced genetic determinism: DNA functions like a computer program, programming the organism, whose 'fixed essence is seen as residing in the genes' (Lewontin 10). As Richard Lewontin explains, genetic determinism assumes the 'internal self-sufficiency of DNA', which is supposed to be 'self-replicating' (11). It subscribes to 'the view that the complete blueprint of the organism and all the information necessary to specify it is contained there' (6). The organism is merely the passive product of its genes. According to Lewontin and the molecular biologist Steven Rose, the genetic programming dogma led to a revival of Descartes' metaphor of the body as a machine: the living organism is nothing but a machine reproducing and executing the program of the genes. But whereas the seventeenth-century metaphor of the machine was mechanical – the universe as a clockwork – the mid-twentieth-century metaphor of the machine was informational – organisms as genetic computers. Indeed, the comparison of DNA to 'information' that could be 'copied' was related to the simultaneity of advances in computer science with the growth of molecular biology. As Rose explains, the 'information-theory metaphor' was enshrined into the founding document of Watson and Crick's famous 1953 *Nature* paper: Crick 'has called this the "Central Dogma" of molecular biology, a one-way flow of information: / DNA → RNA → protein / . . . once "information" has passed into the protein it *cannot get out again*' (Rose 120).

The genetic programming doctrine in turn gave rise to what Rose calls the fashionable ideology of ultra-Darwinism (176). As Richard Dawkins, one of its prime spokespersons and author of *The Selfish Gene*, proclaims: 'We are survival machines – robot vehicles blindly programmed to preserve these selfish molecules known as genes' (qtd in Rose 1). The irony is that biological determinism had been dominant until the Second World War, when the 'revulsion' against Nazi uses of biological theories led to its replacement with 'environmentalist explanation of social fact' (Lewontin 16). Nonetheless, within two decades after 1945, 'genetic explanations again came to dominate' (Lewontin 16). But more importantly, as Lewontin explains, the genetic programming dogma is simply wrong because it is bad biology:

> If we had the complete DNA sequence of an organism and unlimited computational power, we could not compute the organism, because the organism does not compute itself from genes ... There exists, and has existed for a long time, a large body of evidence that demonstrates that the ontogeny of an organism is the consequence of a unique interaction between the genes it carries, the temporal sequence of external environments through which it passes during its life, and random events of molecular interactions within individual cells. It is these interactions that must be incorporated into any proper account of how an organism is formed. (17–18)

Or, as Capra puts it, while 'biologists know the precise structure of a few genes, they know very little about the ways in which genes communicate and cooperate in the development of an organism. In other words, they know the alphabet of the genetic code but have almost no idea of its syntax' (Capra 78). But neither is there cause to replace genetic determinism with environmental determinism. Deterministic explanation as a whole needs to be discarded. As Lewontin maintains, 'the organism ... bears a significant mark of random processes ... The metaphor of computation is just a trendy form of Descartes' metaphor of the machine. Like any metaphor, it catches some aspect of the truth but leads us astray if we take it too seriously' (Lewontin 38).

Margaret Atwood is known for insisting that she writes speculative fiction, not science fiction, which she views as a type of fantasy: *Oryx and Crake* 'contains no intergalactic space travel, no teleportation, no Martians ... Every novel begins with a *what if* and then sets forth its axioms. The *what if* of *Oryx and Crake* is simply, *What if we continue down the road we're already on?*' ('Writing *Oryx and Crake*' 285–6).[9] The quibble over terms aside, in making this point Atwood effectively subscribes to Darko Suvin's influential claim that science fiction produces an effect of '*cognitive estrangement*', defamiliarising our familiar existing society (Suvin 4). Following Suvin's postulate in his recent study, *Archaeologies of the Future: The Desire Called Utopia and Other Fictions*, Fredric Jameson reinforces this point by stating that the 'proper function' of utopia/dystopia (which, like Suvin, he considers to be sub-categories of science fiction) is critical: it lies in 'critical negativity, that is in their function to demystify their opposite numbers' (*Archaeologies* 211). Jameson insists that the political significance of the utopian genre is not the imagination of blueprints for various types of 'perfect society' (72), but simply this encouragement to envision alternatives to the status quo. In Jameson's view, SF does not focus on supplying new prescriptive ideals, but rather envisions the 'future as disruption' (211):

> Disruption is, then, the name for a new discursive strategy, and Utopia is the form such disruption necessarily takes . . . For it is the very principle of the radical break as such, its possibility, which is reinforced by the Utopian form, which insists that its radical difference is possible and that a break is necessary. The Utopian form itself is the answer to the universal ideological conviction that no alternative is possible, that there is no alternative to the system. But it asserts this by forcing us to think the break itself, and not by offering a more traditional picture of what things would be like after the break. (231–2)

Likewise, Atwood's speculative fiction as a mode of apocalyptic warning via the extrapolation of destructive trends in the 'road we're on' is a good instance of Jameson's 'radical break or secession of Utopia from political possibilities as well as from reality itself' (*Archaeologies* 232).

To fill in the picture of Atwood's 'road' to disaster: one lane – as it were – on Atwood's road to perdition is the genetic programming dogma. This defines the views of Crake as well as the genetic scientists and bioengineers in the compounds, the gated company towns of rival pharmaceutical and bioengineering corporations in Atwood's *MaddAddam* trilogy. Top salaries are paid to geneticists for coming up with the boldest ideas for DNA recombinations to create artificial new species that can perform any predetermined task: for example, fabricating transgenic pigs that grow replacement organs for humans (named Pigoons because their torsos are bloated like balloons with stockpiled organs ready for harvesting). All that matters is the 'information' stored in the genes, which the bioengineers tinker with; the finished organism counts for nothing, as the latter is supposedly nothing but a replicant of the former. Even closer to Jameson, the other lane on Atwood's road to catastrophe is deregulated capitalism. For Jameson, SF's characteristic 'future as disruption' challenges the 'universal belief' that there is no alternative to capitalism, that 'the historic alternatives to capitalism have been proven unviable' (*Archaeologies* xii). In the pre-apocalyptic world destroyed by Crake's genocidal act of bioterrorism, rival corporations are dividing up global markets and resources among themselves. The state has disappeared, along with any democratic check on corporate exploitation that would protect consumers and citizens and prevent the coming global environmental collapse. Pharmaceutical companies (named HelthWyzer in neo-Orwellian newspeak) actually manufacture new diseases that they introduce into the population disguised as vitamin supplements, and which they subsequently cure with another set of drugs, thus multiplying their profits. Hypermodern technology coexists with extreme inequality, and modern society has reverted to a caste society. A gulf separates the haves (the residents of the fortified corporate compounds) from the have-nots, who inhabit the 'pleeblands', slums rife with crime and environmental and economic hazards. Collectively, the compounds are protected by private armies, the CorpsSeCorps (Corporate Security Corporation). Having taken the place of national armed forces, the CorpsSeCorps double as a secret security service, tracking and murdering any dissenters and opponents to the ruling order.

Each of the three volumes of the *MaddAddam* trilogy is organised by a dual-time structure that transforms the binary time of apocalypse into a narrative strategy.[10] Narration alternates between the post-apocalyptic present, focalised through a human survivor – different individuals in each volume – and the 'time before' the cataclysm, presented through that same focaliser's memories (and second-hand reconstructions) of the pre-apocalyptic past. As Jameson notes, the SF genre turns on a temporal 'double inscription' (*Archaeologies* 101), a historical schism; it straddles a 'barrier of time' (85). This is the radical break of systemic change, the Event of the historical 'transition' (87). In addition to their dual-time logic, the trilogy's three volumes are constructed in ever-widening circles that extend outwards in scope and forwards in time from the knowledge standpoint established in *Oryx and Crake*, with each volume revealing new information about the central mystery of the annihilation of the human race and of modern civilisation.

The first two volumes (*Oryx and Crake* and *The Year of the Flood*) cover the events of the apocalypse and their prehistory from the contrasting perspectives of gender (male vs. female), scale (individual vs. collective), class (elite vs. non-elite) and politics (mainstream vs. counterculture). The third volume, *MaddAddam*, continues the history of post-apocalyptic life, departing from the moment of the joint ending of the first two volumes, Jimmy's discovery of three other human survivors and the ensuing dramatic events. While the first two volumes cover the immediate aftermath of the collapse, the subject of *MaddAddam* is the intermediate ecological posthuman future after the annihilation of the trilogy's Babylon, fossil-fuelled modern civilisation. The developments in *MaddAddam* mark a key point of bifurcation towards a new post-apocalyptic order.

Oryx and Crake: The Pharmacological Instability of the Factishes of the Modern Biosciences

The major revelation of *Oryx and Crake* is the fact of the cataclysm, its bioterrorist cause, Crake's authorship, as well as his reasons and methods. We learn that the focaliser, Jimmy, has been deliberately immunised against the pandemic unleashed by his ex-friend Crake. Jimmy has been left alive (albeit without his knowledge and consent) to take care of the Crakers in the immediate aftermath of the apocalypse. On introducing himself to the Crakers, Jimmy renames himself Snowman to mark the irreversible discontinuity between his lost former life in human society and his new existence as the last human on earth among artificial species and the ruins of the modern techno-capitalist world. 'He no longer wanted to be Jimmy . . . He needed to exist only in the present, without guilt, without expectation. As the Crakers did' (*Oryx and Crake* 349). The narrative set in the post-apocalyptic present depicts Snowman going about his daily routine as guardian of the Crakers, living on the seashore near the Crakers' new habitat in a former park.

The *novum* – the 'strange newness' on which SF centres (Suvin 4) – of *Oryx and Crake*, genetically engineered living beings, are artefacts of modern science. But now that the entire modern world that produced them, including its machines, laboratories, factories and scientist-creators, is dead, the creatures have gone feral. The challenge Jimmy faces, and the substance of the learning experience as his new post-apocalyptic self, Snowman, is to understand and coexist with them. Snowman's clumsy helplessness and his dependence on the Crakers for part of his food vividly portrays the deposition of humans from their status of masters of nature. Unlike

Jimmy's pre-apocalyptic world, Snowman's post-apocalyptic world is organised by an 'ecological' ontology: no member of this world is allowed to forget that the first principle of ecology is the mutual dependence of beings within a larger network, through feedback cycles and other flows. Humans can no longer submit nature to their will. Atwood's apocalyptic ontology, which pivots on revolutionary breaks that unmake the world to remake it as another that is radically different, thus dramatically enacts an ontological transformation that Latour's theory can only describe abstractly.

As Snowman reflects while walking in the urban wasteland of the compounds, where exotic splices contend with native plants in overgrowing the debris: 'The whole world is now one vast uncontrolled experiment – the way it always was, Crake would have said – and the doctrine of unintended consequences is in full spate' (*Oryx and Crake* 228). Snowman's comment identifies the central mystery of *Oryx and Crake* and Atwood's trilogy as a whole – the pharmacological instability of the factishes of modern bioengineering. Not only are these creatures all genetic hybrids of different natural species. As importantly, they are also hybrids at a categorical level: they straddle the boundary of the duality between object and subject, determination and agency.

As Latour explains, the modern dichotomy of nature vs. society posits that beings are either constructed (which means they are weak and illusory) or not (which means they are facts and real), and that they are either determined machines (nature) or unpredictable and free agents (humans). The Crakers and the other transgenic animals and plants are neither. They are factishes, or cyborgs (Donna Haraway): they are both fabricated and real, both determined and autonomous. More precisely, they undergo an ontological transformation, from determination and domination towards autonomy. Because they veer off the set path of linear cause–effect where they began, they are *pharmaka*, unpredictable beings who escape the determination of their creation and their scientist-creators. *Oryx and Crake* stages the instability at this bifurcation point from determination to indeterminacy. The ontogeny of organisms is not predetermined by their genes: it is the result of the historical process of living. The self-organising process of ontogeny is the focus of autopoietic theory and the theory of enactivism, which we will turn to in the next chapter. Having been programmed, the Crakers develop independent purposive behaviour. Or, in the language of actor-network theory, they become actants: non-humans that are considered to be passive intermediaries, they assert themselves as full-fledged mediators. It is no accident that the scientific disciplines at issue in Atwood's fiction are the biosciences and bioengineering. It is the complexity of living beings that is most likely to destabilise the segregated realms of the modern constitution. As learning systems, organisms are a very different part of 'nature' than inorganic entities. This is illustrated by the difference between kicking a stone and kicking a dog: the stone will react according to the universal laws of Newtonian physics, whereas the dog will respond according to internal rules that result from its ontogenic development (Capra and Luisi 136).

The Crakers are programmed to be gentle and cooperative, incapable of violence, domination and exploitation of any kind – economic, environmental or sexual. This is Crake's solution for the hyperviolent and exploitative society that he and Jimmy grew up in, and which cost his father's life. When Jimmy joins Crake at the Paradice project, Crake explains the genetic design of the Crakers (while keeping their deeper purpose a secret). In order to create a more perfect being than humans,

> what had been altered was nothing less than the ancient primate brain. Gone were the destructive features, the features responsible for the world's current illnesses. For instance, racism – or, as they referred to it in Paradice, pseudospeciation – had been eliminated . . . merely by switching the bonding mechanism: the Paradice people simply did not register skin colour. Hierarchy could not exist among them, because they lacked the neural complexes that would have created it. Since they were neither hunters nor agriculturalists hungry for land, there was no territoriality: the king-of-the-castle hard-wiring that had plagued humanity had, in them, been unwired. They ate nothing but leaves and grass and roots and a berry or two; thus their foods were plentiful and always available. Their sexuality was not a constant torment to them, not a cloud of turbulent hormones: they came into heat at regular intervals, as did most mammals other than man.
>
> In fact, as there would never be anything for these people to inherit, there would be no family trees, no marriages, and no divorces. They were perfectly adjusted to their habitat, so they would never have to create houses or tools or weapons, or, for that matter, clothing. They would have no need to invent any harmful symbolisms, such as kingdoms, icons, gods, or money. (*Oryx and Crake* 305)

Humans do not live in balance with their environment, which is the reason for the coming environmental collapse. In contrast, the Crakers are programmed to live in equilibrium with their environment. In addition to being vegetarians, eating mostly grass, leaves and roots, they are also caecotrophs, with DNA borrowed from rabbits, who reingest their own waste to fully process plant nutrients, such as cellulose and vitamins (*Oryx and Crake* 158). As Crake explains, this 'boiled down to eating your own shit' (159). 'Any objections to the process were purely aesthetic', which is to say, irrelevant (159). By eating what they excrete, the Crakers minimise a key feature of organisms, which, as Lewontin elaborates, is that 'they are in a constant process of altering their environment' (55).

> Every species, not only *Homo sapiens*, is in the process of destroying its own environment by using resources that are in short supply and transforming them into a form that cannot be used again by the individuals of the species. Food is turned into poisonous waste products by every metabolizing cell. (Lewontin 55)

In evolutionary biology, this paradox that air and food are transformed into unusable waste is known as the Red Queen hypothesis: like the chess queen in *Through the Looking Glass*, to survive, organisms have to 'keep running just to stay in the same place' (Lewontin 58) because their own activities are changing the conditions of their environment. By eating their own waste, the genetically altered Crakers slow down the Red Queen dynamism significantly. The human overconsumption of resources is eliminated. Crake elucidates his motive: 'As a species we're in deep trouble, worse than anyone's saying . . . we're running out of space-time. Demand for resources has exceeded supply for decades in marginal geopolitical areas, hence the famines and droughts; but very soon, demand is going to exceed supply *for everyone*' (*Oryx and Crake* 295). In high school, Jimmy and Crake learn about the apocalyptic fires and floods that detail the extent of environmental degradation: rising sea levels have pushed the eastern coast of the US inland, drowning the cities of Boston and New York; Florida and Texas have been turned into deserts, the Everglades burned (63). By the year of Crake's apocalypse, the US north-east has acquired a tropical climate, with the corresponding heat, humidity and afternoon thunderstorms that Jimmy and all other survivors have to weather without air conditioning.

Engineered to survive in the polluted post-apocalyptic environment, the Crakers have 'UV-resistant skin, a built-in insect repellant' and 'immunity from microbes' (304). Because they will have to do without modern medicine, they are equipped with an organic self-healing mechanism by way of purring, like cats, at ultrasound frequencies 'used on bone fractures and skin lesions' (156). The male Crakers' urine contains chemicals that are deterrents against animal and other transgenic predators such as wolvogs. In a twice-daily ritual, the men gather to urinate in a circle around their village, demarcating 'an invisible line that marks their territory' (154). The 'ring of pee' is an invisible fence around their domain, keeping invaders out but also keeping the Crakers in. Unlike humans, the Crakers live in small groups on a small footprint, and they are designed not to outgrow it. As Crake explains, '*Homo sapiens sapiens* was not hard-wired to individuate other people in numbers above two hundred, the size of the primal tribe' (343). To keep populations small as well as to eliminate sexual violence, reproduction and sexuality have been thoroughly redesigned. Craker women go into heat only every three years, which triggers a blue discoloration of the abdomen and buttocks and the release of pheromones, with the help of DNA from baboons and octopus, to which the males respond with a similar discoloration of the genitals. A group mating follows for which the woman chooses four males, the offspring of which is adopted as the child of the entire tribe. Because the male and female Crakers are sexually aroused strictly by the release of chemicals, 'there's no more unrequited love' and 'no more thwarted lust': 'No more prostitution, no sexual abuse of children, no haggling over the price, no pimps, no sex slaves. No more rape' (165). Paternity becomes indeterminate, and in any case, it 'no longer matters who the father of the inevitable child may be, since there's no more property to inherit, no father–son loyalty required for war' (165). The Crakers are also faster-maturing and have shorter lifespans than humans. Adolescents at the age of four, they are programmed to drop dead, suddenly and without suffering, at the age of thirty. Here, Crake has reversed the evolutionary trend of 'neoteny', the theory that more highly evolved organisms tend to mature more slowly (Lewontin 13). As Crake comments, with humans 'too much time' is 'wasted in childrearing' (*Oryx and Crake* 158). The Crakers' external appearance is one of supernatural beauty, like 'statues', nude without a trace of self-consciousness, with perfect proportions, luminous green eyes from jellyfish genes, and varying between all available skin colours 'from deepest black to whitest white' (102, 100). The only features that Crake had not been able to control are their dreaming and their singing. At every step, the Crakers may break into song, a supernatural sound, as if 'crystals are singing' or 'ferns unscrolling' (105). Singing and dreaming are the only Craker traits that Crake learns he was unsuccessful with during his lifetime: '*We're hard wired for dreams . . . We're hard wired for singing.* Singing and dreams were entwined' (352).

Crake's utopian bio-technological fix to the dystopian present has two parts or stages: one is about death – the bioterrorist annihilation of humans – whereas the other is about life, their replacement with bioengineered Crakers. As Crake comments: 'They were inextricably linked – the Pill and the Project. The Pill would put a stop to haphazard reproduction, the Project would replace it with a superior method. They were two stages of a single plan' (304). Only the first project, the BlyssPluss pill, meets with significant success (although there are some important exceptions). Crake's idea of introducing a lethal supervirus through a pill marketed as an all-in-one wonder drug – promising to be mind-altering aphrodisiac, birth control pill and rejuvenation agent – is ingenious. It certainly seems to prove his point about the weakness of humans lying in the lack of control of *ratio* over the animal part in *animal rationale*. 'We're hormone robots, anyway, only we're faulty ones' (166) is Crake's opinion of humans. Lewontin and Levins put the matter less reductively: human ecology 'is a convergence of biological and social processes in which our biology has become socialized, but for that is no less biological' (162).

Crake is a classic lone wolf terrorist (or saviour of the planet, depending on one's viewpoint). However, his method is not entirely original. For one, he appropriates his idea from HelthWyzer's secret corporate programme of manufacturing and spreading new diseases, or 'hostile bioforms' (211), among the pleebland population. This is an instance of institutionalised corruption. Crake's second influence, the MaddAddamites, are located in the pleeblands rather than the compounds. They are an underground bioterrorist group who organise via a computer game website named Extinctathon, '[m]onitored by MaddAddam. *Adam named the living animals, MaddAddam named the dead ones. Do you want to play?*' (214). The members' codenames reference extinct animals (Crake is Glenn's Extinctathon codename, for the red-necked Australian crake). The MaddAddamites are bioengineers who design artificial bioforms that attack corporate targets, such as asphalt-eating microbes and pesticide-resistant pests for genetically modified coffee. Crake tracks them down and employs them as hired brains or 'code serfs' for the Craker project in his Paradice unit.

In alternating chapters, the second retrospective narrative reconstructs Jimmy's biography in the pre-apocalyptic past. It proceeds chronologically from a sheltered childhood in the compounds as the son of a bioengineer involved in the Pigoon project at OrganInc, to his adolescent friendship with Glenn (the future Crake) – a 'numbers guy' unlike Jimmy, who is a 'word guy' – at another compound (HelthWyzer). Growing up in a culture that glamorises violence and exploitative sexuality, Jimmy and Glenn illegally consume violent computer games and entertainment for adults, such as Blood and Roses, a game in which players pit documents of civilisation against acts of mass murder ('one *Mona Lisa* equaled Bergen Belsen' [79]), or BrainFrizz, an entertainment that features live executions. Watching HottTotts, a global porn site, together, they are introduced to eight-year-old Oryx, a Third World child sold into slavery by her impoverished family, whose image leaves a deep impression on both youngsters. Both Crake and Jimmy fall in love with Oryx, who is later recruited in person by Crake for his Paradice project. Beautiful, inscrutable and self-possessed, Oryx is the only woman whom the hyper-rational and egotistical Crake comes close to loving. Jimmy, a hedonist and chronic womaniser, comes to worship her. After college, he is reunited with Crake when he is hired at Crake's Paradice project, where the Crakers have been bioengineered. Betrayed by Crake, and after shooting Crake in revenge for his killing Oryx – thus probably carrying out Crake's own plans for his suicide – Jimmy waits out the apocalypse in the quarantined Paradice Dome.

Like everyone with any influence in the world of the compounds, Crake is a dyed-in-the-wool biological reductionist and genetic determinist. As a partisan of the genetic programming dogma, he is also a prototypical modern purifier in Latour's sense.[11] In the Paradice project, the 'two cultures' of science and humanities are strictly separated, and the latter are slated for elimination in the design of the Crakers. In engineering his utopian eco-friendly humanoids, Crake is determined to destroy traits that have been considered the crowning achievement of human civilisation – art and religion.

> *Watch out for art*, Crake used to say. *As soon as they start doing art, we're in trouble.* Symbolic thinking of any kind would signal downfall, in Crake's view. Next they'd be inventing idols, and funerals, and grave gods, and the afterlife, and sin, and Linear B, and kings, and then slavery and war. (*Oryx and Crake* 361)

In his disdain for 'idols', Crake takes the classic position of the modern iconoclast. Smashing the fetishes of art and religion in the name of modern science and rationality, Crake embodies the modern repudiation of non-naturalist knowledge. In Latour's apt phrase, the modern constitution is founded on the 'crossed-out God': 'no one is truly modern who does not agree to keep God from interfering with Natural Law as well as with the laws of the Republic' (*We Have Never* 33). But as Latour demonstrates, the iconoclasts are not exempt from having naive beliefs of their own. This is confirmed by developments after Crake's death. A paragon of the scientific anti-fetishist, in the place of the religion and art that he debunks, Crake simply puts another creed that he, the reductive positivist, embraces uncritically – genetics. The Crakers are designed to have a diminished capacity for abstract thought, only a simple vocabulary, and no writing. 'It was one of Crake's rules that no name could be chosen for which a physical equivalent . . . could not be demonstrated. No unicorns, no griffins, no manticores or basilisk' (*Oryx and Crake* 7). They are supposed to be incapable of knowing about their own mortality, the ex-static being-toward-death that Heidegger in *Being and Time* posits as the principle that distinguishes human existence from that of animals. Indeed, it is Crake's intention to reduce the Crakers' existence to that of animals, so that they will never develop the tools to master nature through artefacts, either symbolic or technological.

Jimmy and Crake are opposites, and their contrasting careers speak volumes about the segregation between the 'two cultures' of the modern constitution that the two friends respectively represent.[12] Indeed, *Oryx and Crake* is Atwood's savage parody of the social impoverishment that results from the combined triumph of reductive scientism and economic materialism. The liberal arts college that Jimmy attends, Martha Graham Academy, is a low-status, underfunded institution bordering the pleebland slums. Its curriculum is utilitarian, focused on producing graduates 'with employable skills' in service jobs (*Oryx and Crake* 188). Jimmy has no illusions about his future employment options: 'window dressing was what he'd be doing, at best – decorating the cold, hard, numerical world in flossy 2-D verbiage' (188). Indeed, his postgraduate jobs are in advertising, working as a word 'serf' (198), the last of which is at Crake's Paradice project. In contrast, the bioengineering school that recruits Crake, Watson–Crick Institute – the equivalent of Harvard, 'before it got drowned' (173) – offers luxurious top-flight amenities. Its nickname is 'Asperger's U' because of the high percentage of autistic geniuses (193).

Through its central protagonists Jimmy and Crake, *Oryx and Crake* sets up a personification of the dichotomy of reason vs. feeling and facts vs. values that, as Latour maintains, is the root of the modern dilemma. In this matter, too, Atwood's apocalyptic world-endism urges the problem more forcefully than Latour's theory, whose propositional form lacks the eschatological script of 'if this goes on'. Crake has above-average intelligence, is absorbed by his projects, is egocentric, and lacks empathy and social skills. Unsentimental and cynical, Crake debunks feelings in the classic manner of the scientific iconoclast: 'Falling in love, although it resulted in altered body chemistry and was therefore real, was a hormonally induced delusional state' (193). Without much inner torment, Crake kills his mother and future stepfather Uncle Pete, for betraying his father's planned whistleblowing on HelthWyzer's toxic vitamins, which led to his father's assassination, which was covered up as suicide by falling from a pleebland overpass. Testing early versions of his BlyssPlus pill on them, he reports watching his mother dissolve as being 'impressive', like 'putt[ing] salt on a slug' (177). Although Crake annihilates the human race to save the planet, and thus acts ethically, he never questions the scientific fact vs. culture-as-fetish dichotomy and the doctrine of genetic determinism.

Jimmy is a 'neurotypical', 'a person minus the genius gene', according to Watson–Crick jargon (194). He is also empathetic, sociable and popular with women. A gifted performer since his teens, he copes with his dysfunctional family by staging impromptu performances in high school, impersonating 'Evil Dad' and 'Righteous Mom' (60). But his values are strongly influenced by his mother, who becomes a conscientious objector to the system and defects to a global underground resistance movement while Jimmy is in high school. A bioengineer on Jimmy's father's research team at the OrganInc Pigoon project, Jimmy's mother turns against genetic engineering as unethical: 'You're interfering with the building blocks of life. It's immoral. It's . . . sacrilegious' (57). In contrast, Jimmy's father defends the received view that science is value-neutral: 'It's just proteins . . . There is nothing sacred about cells and tissue' (57). Jimmy's conscience is formed by the values of his dissident mother (see Bosco 167). (Incidentally, Crake's conscience is similarly formed by the values of his ethical bioscientist father.) Before her public execution for treason (which Jimmy is made to watch on TV), Jimmy's mother addresses her last words to her son, secretly alluding to Jimmy's pet raccoon-skunk: '*Goodbye. Remember Killer. I love you. Don't let me down*' (258). Shipwrecked in the post-apocalyptic world, Jimmy-Snowman turns to language and his memory of words as a strategy for survival. '"Hang on to the words", he tells himself. The odd words, the old words, the rare ones. *Valance. Norn. Serendipity. Pibroch. Lubricious*' (68).

True to the modern constitution and in line with the genetic reductionism of Watson– Crick, Crake brackets off anything from his design of the Crakers that smacks of the traditional realm of the humanities – the non-quantifiable and the unpredictable. But already, while still in the artificial 'uterus' of the Paradice Dome, the Crakers give evidence of overflowing the limits of Crake's design. Contrary to Crake's assertion that 'that stuff's been edited out', Oryx, the Crakers' first teacher, reports that they started asking questions about who made them, and that she told them the truth: 'I said it was Crake' (311). In appointing – without the latter's knowledge and consent – his friend, Jimmy, the humanist and aficionado of language and art, to the task of teacher and guardian of the Crakers in the post-apocalyptic period, Crake takes a definitive – if unwitting – step towards undermining his own plans.[13] Responding to the Crakers' insistent questions about their origins, Snowman invents a fictional mythology for them, in which Crake and Oryx are deified: Crake created the Crakers, the 'Children of Crake'. Oryx created the animals, the 'Children of Oryx'. Animals are sacred, which is why it is wrong to eat them. The Children of Oryx 'hatched out of an egg' when they were born (the Paradice Dome), and Snowman was to lead them out of the egg to their new home on the seashore. Jimmy fabricates a colourful origin story for the Crakers to make sense of the post-apocalyptic wasteland they are stranded in. The ruined objects littering the environment are remnants of 'the chaos' that Oryx and Crake destroyed: 'And then Oryx said to Crake: *Let us get rid of the chaos. And so Crake took* the chaos, and he poured it away . . . And this is how Crake did the Great Rearrangement and made the Great Emptiness' (103). Drawing on his humanist training, Jimmy reintroduces the same cultural artefacts – religion (the 'crossed-out God'), narrative and symbolic thinking – that Crake thought he had 'edited out' of the Craker genome. As Snowman reflects, '[t]he Crake they're praising is his fabrication, a fabrication not unmixed with spite: Crake was against the notion of God, or of gods of any kind, and would surely be disgusted by the spectacle of his own deification' (103–4).

If Snowman supplies the basic coordinates, the Crakers are quick to take the lead in fabricating their new cult. As he observes, 'Crake thought that he'd done away with all that, eliminated what he called the G-spot in the brain. *God is a cluster of neurons*, he'd maintained . . . They're up to something, though, something Crake didn't anticipate: they're conversing with the invisible, they've developed reverence' (157). On returning late from his scavenging trip in the ruined compounds, Snowman finds that they have made an idol of him in his absence: the Crakers are 'sitting in a semi-circle around a grotesque-looking figure, a scarecrow-like effigy', to which some are chanting and crooning, while others are making percussion (360). When he shows himself to them, their explanation is: 'We have made a picture of you, to help us send out our voices to you' (361). Defying their genetic program, the artificial creatures of Crake's Brave New World have thus reinvented the category of supernatural objects, the fetish, which their modern iconoclast-creator had wanted to eradicate.

In conclusion, the lessons of *Oryx and Crake* are twofold: the first concerns the non-modern realism of the factish. The novel resonates with Latour's point that the dichotomy of facts and fetishes separating the 'real' objects of science from the 'imaginary' objects of culture and religion is a false one. Facts are not the opposite of naive beliefs or 'fetishes'. Knowledge cannot be segregated from belief. Reality is not the opposite of construction. The trap that Crake has fallen into is what Latour has so aptly named 'the modern cult of the factish gods': fancying himself the debunker of naive belief in art and religion, Crake has only made a cult of science. A science fundamentalist, he is exposed as a naive fetishist of the 'Genome God'. But his reductionist beliefs are in flagrant conflict with his actual practice as a genetic engineer, the production of hybrid organisms that borrow traits from both humans and non-humans.

The second lesson follows from the first, and concerns Stengers' point about the pharmacological instability of scientific factishes. This instability is again related to an ontological problem, but one of a different type: the difference between the controlled environment of the laboratory and nature outside the laboratory. Like all scientific artefacts, the Crakers undergo an ontological transformation as they leave the laboratory of the Paradice Dome and enter the history and reality of the post-apocalyptic world at large. In the process, they acquire an autonomous mode of existence as actants: they stop being intermediaries (marionettes controlled by others) and become full-fledged mediators. Not only does Crake think of the Crakers as instruments of his will, so does Jimmy: 'These people were like blank pages, he could write whatever he wanted on them' (349). By deconstructing the modern constitution, *Oryx and Crake* reveals the uncanny face of ecology 'after nature'. Morton's comment on the ecocritical outlook of Mary Shelley's *Frankenstein* also extends to *Oryx and Crake*: Atwood's novel is dark-ecological, as Morton notes (referring to *Frankenstein*), 'not because it compels us to care for a pre-existing notion of nature, but because it questions the very idea of nature' (*Ecology without Nature* 194). Bioengineered to take the place of extinct humans in Crake's design for post-apocalyptic ecological succession, the Crakers forcefully display the stubborn uncanniness of living beings. Animals, Morton suggests, should be called '*strange stranger[s]*' (*Ecological Thought* 41). The Crakers are even stranger than thought possible in Crake's wildest imagination.

But it is not until Jimmy wakes up in the post-apocalyptic 'hereafter' that the truth of the Crakers' non-predictability is 'revealed' to him. By then, it is too late. Atwood makes excellent use of the temporal finitude of the apocalyptic script: through the dual-time structure of juxtaposing post-apocalyptic present with the memory of the pre-apocalyptic past, she presents the contrasting worlds of modernity (doomed and lost) and non-modern future after the end of modern history, like opposite wings of a painting by Hieronymous Bosch. Jimmy's time travel from the pre-apocalyptic into the post-apocalyptic world resembles that of John of Patmos in Revelation, as he is lifted into the heavenly throne room and taken on 'a tour of the end things' (Keller 3). The difference is that John returns to earth to tell the tale, whereas Snowman cannot come back. Shipwrecked in the post-apocalyptic time, Snowman's narrative is but a soliloquy. The discontinuity between

Jimmy's anthropocentric modern world and Snowman's actual non-modern ecological world stands out all the more clearly. *Oryx and Crake* ends with Snowman's discovery of three other human survivors on the beach after he returns to the Crakers from a scavenging trip.

The problem of the pharmacological instability of factishes returns us to the question of ecology, that is to say (as Lewontin and Levins observe), 'the rich interconnectedness of the world' that manifests itself by way of 'unexpected, often counterproductive effects of interventions directed at a particular problem' (106). As actants in an ecological setting, the Crakers are nodes in a complex web of other actants: they are not isolated, but '*well-attached*', as Latour puts it (*Reassembling* 218). Some of the bonds connect them to their human creators (Crake and Snowman), but others connect them to non-humans, things and other organic and artificial species in the post-apocalyptic world. The question of gathering the ecological collective of humans and non-humans after the end of the Anthropocene becomes the central issue of *MaddAddam*, which we will explore in the last section of this chapter.

The Year of the Flood:
Shifting from Matters of Fact to Matters of Concern

The second volume, *The Year of the Flood*, covers the same period as *Oryx and Crake* in both the post-apocalyptic present and the retrospective past-time narratives. Like two parallel lines meeting, *The Year of the Flood* ends on the same scene of encounter between Jimmy and the three other human survivors, to which it adds further participants. But in place of Jimmy's solitary and masculine perspective, *The Year of the Flood* shifts the focalisation to women, as well as widening from the individual to a collective experience. *The Year of the Flood* programmatically shifts perspective, as it relocates narration to the opposite pole of the social spectrum. Narration and focalisation leave the world of genetic and informational science, of power, of corporate compounds, of males and of lone individuals, to enter life on various social margins, the most critical of which is the religious counterculture of the God's Gardeners.

There are two focalisers: Toby, a middle-aged woman, and Ren, who is in her twenties like Jimmy, and who in fact dated him at

HelthWyzer high school. Whereas *Oryx and Crake* is set in the elite compounds, *The Year of the Flood* is set in the pleeblands. And whereas the first volume is constructed around the rivalry between two male friends, one a genius scientist, the other a humanist, the second volume follows the story of the God's Gardeners, a green religion founded by Adam One. Countercultural separatists who have delinked from the real-world dystopia of unchecked capitalism, the Gardeners have returned to moral values. An apocalyptic sect, they see the catastrophe coming, and have changed course to live by a set of anti-materialistic religious, ecological and communitarian principles to prepare themselves for the coming environmental collapse, which they call 'the waterless flood'. Although the apocalypse that happens is not the one they expected, a substantial number of the Gardeners survive as a result of their preparations.

Both Toby and Ren belong to the Gardeners: Ren enters as a child when her mother Lucerne runs away from her husband in the compounds to live with Zeb, a Gardener 'Adam'. Toby joins as an adult, becoming Pilar's successor as 'Eve Six' and the Gardeners' herbalist, healer and beekeeper after Pilar's death. Orphaned during her college years by HelthWyzer, which murders her mother with a disease-inducing drug and drives her father into ruin and suicide, Toby is rescued by the Gardeners from Blanco, a pleebland crime lord. As with Jimmy in *Oryx and Crake*, the retrospective narrative chronologically follows Toby's and Ren's pre-apocalypse biographies through their memories. The present-time narrative covers Toby's and Ren's survival in the eponymous 'year of the flood': Ren survives locked in a quarantine room in Scales and Tails, a pleebland strip club, until she is rescued by Amanda, an artist, tough former 'pleebrat' (child of the pleeblands) and Ren's friend from Gardener days. Subsequently, Amanda and Ren are attacked by three armed psychopaths who succeed in abducting Amanda, but Ren escapes and finds refuge with Toby at the AnooYoo health spa, where Toby has weathered the apocalypse, her place of work since she had to leave the Gardeners for fear of Blanco's revenge. On their way to rescue Amanda from her captors, Toby and Ren discover a small group of human survivors living in a cobb house in the Arboretum, including some former Gardeners and some former bioengineers from Crake's Paradice team. Amanda's rescue occurs in the closing scene on the beach, which is where the parallel storylines of the first two volumes of the *MaddAddam* trilogy are joined. The three human survivors Jimmy stumbles upon are revealed to be two 'Painballers' (ex-convicts and veterans of a gladiator game whose survivors become empathy-less predators) and Amanda (Blanco has since been killed).

In juxtaposing the bioscientific setting of *Oryx and Crake* to the eco-religious setting of *The Year of the Flood*, Atwood places on the agenda the dichotomies of knowledge vs. belief and scientific facts vs. ethical values. As we have seen, the modern split also structures the rivalry between the scientist Crake and the humanist Jimmy. But just as *Oryx and Crake* probes science, *The Year of the Flood* is a focal investigation of 'value'. That this is also a contest between two utopian ideals is suggested through naming: Crake's Paradice project claims the same territory of perfection as Adam One's EdenCliff Rooftop Garden, the God's Gardeners' first home. Atwood stages a contest between the two rival master narratives of science and religion. Like *Oryx and Crake*, *The Year of the Flood* challenges the paradigmatic separation of facts and values, and the notion of a value-free science. It enacts Latour's suggestion of replacing the problematic dichotomy between facts and values by moving from matters of fact to matters of concern. The matters of concern at issue have been presented in *Oryx and Crake*: the catastrophic consequences of the toxic mix of deregulated capitalism and biogenetic determinism that results in the near-destruction of the planet and the annihilation of the human race.

Atwood's eco-Doomsday scenario transposes Latour's claim that the positivistic realism that brackets off value as 'externalities' is inadequate: scientific facts are not independent of what humans do (since they make them in the first place), and therefore not independent of moral value. But Atwood's apocalyptic rhetoric of no-future and world-end raises the stakes to a pitch inaccessible to theory. As Capra writes, agreeing with Jimmy's mother's objections to genetic engineering: 'Although much of the detailed research may not depend on the scientist's value system, the larger paradigm within which this research is pursued will never be value free. Scientists, therefore, are responsible for their research not only intellectually but also morally' (Capra 11). An example illustrating the entanglements of facts and values is the difference between statistical means and statistical medians. As Lewontin and Levins note, 'whereas it is often claimed that statistical techniques are ways of letting the objective data speak for itself, all the real work is done by the *a priori* decisions imported into the analysis' (Lewontin and Levins 68). Both methods are factually correct, yet they yield very different results. 'There is, then, no single "correct" measure of average density or wealth either in ecology or in political economy. The question is: What side are you on?' (Lewontin and Levins 74). Like Latour, Lewontin and Levins (as well as Stengers), Atwood is after a more holistic, relational realism, a non-reductive realism beyond the modern mechanism of purification.

The Year of the Flood brings back religion, the 'crossed-out God' of the modern constitution. Does this mean that Atwood is suggesting a reversion to the dark ages, exchanging Crake's science fundamentalism for a religious fundamentalism? The answer is no: the God's Gardeners are not a traditional monotheistic religion, but a new green religious cult. They do not 'find religion': they fabricate it. Like Earthseed, the post-apocalyptic green religion in Butler's *Parable* series that we will consider in Chapter 4, the Gardeners' cult is an artefact, cobbled together from various sources, including Christianity, the ecological movement, as well as science, modern cosmology and evolution. The God's Gardeners don't simply advocate a 'return to religious values'; they espouse an enlightened quest for a solution to the urgent matters of concern posed by the predations of unregulated capitalism and genetic engineering. As complementary sides of a bifocal panel, *Oryx and Crake* and *The Year of the Flood* stage what Latour calls 'iconoclash': 'iconoclash aims at suspending iconoclastic gestures' (*On the Modern Cult* x). The new 'reverence for the images of science' (*On the Modern Cult* 71) is denounced by a green cult that debunks the false gods that the compound world worships. In this way, the entrenched roles of fact-oriented iconoclast vs. value-oriented idolater are overturned: because people now believe in genetic determinism in the same way that they used to believe in God, there is again need for demystification. Only this time the iconoclasts are those who embrace (ecological) values, and the idolaters are modern.

That the Gardeners' project is an enlightened and ethical one (not anti-rational obscurantism) is borne out by the fact that many Gardeners are former scientists and doctors, refugees from the compounds and defectors from the corporations. This is the case with Pilar, Toby's teacher at the Gardeners and a member of the Gardener leadership, the so-called 'Adams' and 'Eves'. Pilar was a bioscientist on the same HelthWyzer research team as Crake's father before his murder for threatening to expose their secret poison pharmaceuticals programme. Pilar lists the number of oncologists, internists, eye surgeons and gynaecologists among the members (*Year of the Flood* 105). No doctor or scientist 'with any shred of the old medical ethic left in them' (105) is still at the corporations; they are either dead or have joined an underground group such as the Gardeners. Through their decentralised social organisation of small collectives (such as the EdenCliff Rooftop Garden) and their associated 'truffle cells' (underground contacts in the compound world), they stay well-informed about external events. (The truffle for EdenCliff is Glenn at HelthWyzer, the teenage son of Pilar's assassinated colleague, who as we learn discovers the truth about his father's death at the same time as Pilar.) This is why, although focalisation is lodged in the countercultural margins in *The Year of the Flood*, the second volume of the *MaddAddam* trilogy confirms and deepens the portrait of corporate devastation of the globe in *Oryx and Crake*. As Pilar insists, 'those Corporation pills are the food of the dead . . . It's not only a rule of faith among us, it's a matter of certainty' (105).

The God's Gardeners embrace a holistic ecological worldview known as deep ecology, a term coined by Norwegian Arne Naess.[14] Unlike anthropocentric 'shallow' ecology, deep ecology 'does not separate humans . . . from the natural environment. It sees the world not as a collection of isolated objects, but as a network of phenomena that are fundamentally interconnected and interdependent. Ultimately, deep ecological awareness is spiritual or religious awareness' (Capra 7). As Adam One reflects,

> why do we think that everything on Earth belongs to us, while in reality we belong to Everything? We have betrayed the trust of the Animals, and defiled our sacred task of stewardship. God's commandment to 'replenish the Earth' did not mean that we should fill it to overflowing with ourselves, thus wiping out everything else. How many other Species have we already annihilated? (*Year of the Flood* 52–3)

The Gardeners live by a ritual calendar of festivals like Christians, except that these feasts and their saints are 'green': for example, 'The Feast of Adam and All Primates', 'The Feast of Saint Euell of Wild Foods', 'The Feast of Saint Dian, Martyr' (for Dian Fossey). Each of the fourteen sections in *The Year of the Flood* begins with a sermon by Adam One on a subject related to a specific festival, which serves as a systematic introduction to the principles of the

Gardeners' beliefs. (The quotation above comes from the sermon on 'The Feast of Adam and All Primates'.) Spatially, the EdenCliff Rooftop Garden is a classic utopian enclave, just like Crake's Paradice project. The Gardeners live segregated in this enclave from what they call the 'exfernal world' (312). Like Thomas More's utopia surrounded by a moat, EdenCliff Gardens is an 'imaginary enclave within real social space' (Jameson, *Archaeologies* 15).

Far from opposing science, the Gardeners embrace it. This links them closely to the 'great environmental apocalyptics' of the 1960s and 1970s (Rachel Carson, Paul Ehrlich and so on) examined by Frederick Buell. The Gardeners' deep ecological outlook is founded on scientific insight into the reductive approach to nature as the cause of the coming environmental collapse. Adam One's sermons blend value and scientific fact: for instance, the sermon on 'The Feast of Adam and All Primates' concludes with a reference to the 'knots of DNA and RNA that tie us to our many fellow creatures' (*Year of the Flood* 53). Significantly, it is the scientific prognosis of the looming environmental catastrophe that motivates the Gardeners' embrace of religious apocalyptic thinking. As Toby learns upon joining the Gardeners, a 'massive die-off of the human race was impending, due to overpopulation and wickedness, but the Gardeners exempted themselves: they intended to float above the Waterless Flood, with the aid of the food they were stashing away in the hidden storeplaces they called Ararats' (47). This is why the end they anticipate is not like Armageddon, but a 'slow apocalypse' they call 'the waterless flood'. As Adam One proclaims,

> For the Waterless Flood is coming, in which all buying and selling will cease, and we will find ourselves thrown back upon our own resources, in the midst of God's bounteous Garden. (126)

> Take comfort in the thought that this history will soon be swept away by the Waterless Flood. Nothing will remain of the Exfernal World but decaying wood and rusting metal implements; and over these the Kudzu and other vines will climb; and Birds and Animals will nest in them, as we are told in the Human Words of God: 'They shall be left together unto the Fowls of the mountains, and to the Beasts of the Earth; and the Fowls shall summer upon them, and all the Beasts of the Earth shall winter upon them.' For all works of man shall be as words written on water. (312)

But unlike the biblical apocalypse preordained by a divine plan, the waterless flood is a catastrophe fabricated by humans. The Gardeners are very clear that they have invented their green cult, and that it is a counterfactish to the factish of the environmental crisis.

Though a human artefact, the ecological catastrophe is no less certain than its biblical antecedent. The damaged planet is slouching towards its Last Day. As is evident in the passage quoted above, the voice of Adam One is modelled on the biblical apocalyptic narrator. Like John of Patmos, Adam One's vision depicts events at the end of time,

> when the corrupt world of the present will be supplanted by a new and transcendent realm. From a point ostensibly beyond the end of time, the apocalyptist surveys the whole of human history, focusing on its cataclysmic end. For him, the future is past: He states God's plan for the completion of history, alternately in the prophetic future, then as accomplished fact. (Zamora 2)

The Gardeners adopt key features of the Book of Revelation, including its moral dualism which envisions the coming of a 'redeemed future' (Keller 90) after the annihilation of the corporate Babylon. And like the early Christians of John's time, they are dissenters who face persecution.

The Gardeners' preparation for the final events of the waterless flood is not just spiritual; it is a sustainable way of life that is built on a set of ecological everyday practices. These are linked to the annual ritual calendar of green saints' days and festivals. The Gardeners are vegetarians, beekeepers and avid recyclers who harvest and eat wild plants and fungi as well as growing their own food. This is also part of their school curriculum: Gardener children take classes in 'organic botanics' and participate in 'gleaning' expeditions into the pleeblands to scavenge among dumpsters. The recycling ethos extends to burial practices: burial for deceased Gardeners is a practice called 'composting', whereby the human body is returned to nature. When Toby's mentor Pilar dies, she is composted in a park and an elderberry shrub is planted on her grave, so that Pilar's spirit can pass into the elderberry tree. They practise organic medicine (Pilar's speciality, and after her, Toby's) by growing medicinal mushrooms and cultivating maggots to train on infected wounds to prevent gangrene. Some of the mushrooms are *pharmaka*, drugs for palliative and visionary use in small doses, poisonous in large doses. Others (the 'death angel') are lethal, and reserved for emergencies (*Year of the Flood* 101). Maggots are treated not as vermin, but as symbiots of humans. In the post-apocalyptic period, Toby saves Jimmy's life by treating his infected foot with maggot therapy. Maggots harvested from carcasses are also food during hard times: 'just think of them as land shrimp' (328). In wedding biblical apocalypticism to scientific insight and an ecological lifestyle, the Gardeners practise what Latour envisions as a 'new separation of powers', the responsibility of 'taking into account' and 'arranging in rank order' 'matters of concern' from across the spectrum of the former notions of facts and values.

Among the Gardeners' beliefs, consisting of anti-capitalism and non-anthropocentric deep ecology, another needs to be mentioned that could be identified as either vitalism or panpsychism. While both trends are part of the rebellion against modern scientific mechanism (Descartes' idea that nature is a machine), these concepts are not identical. Vitalism, which posits that 'some non-physical entity, force, or field must be added to the laws of physics and chemistry to understand life' (Capra 25), flourished in the nineteenth and early twentieth centuries through philosophies such as Bergson's *élan vital*.[15] Capra argues that vitalism does 'not really go beyond the Cartesian paradigm . . . [but] merely add[s] a nonphysical entity as the designer . . . Thus the Cartesian split of mind and body led to both mechanism and vitalism' (26). Vitalism is part of a wider current of panpsychism, the belief that 'mind is a fundamental feature of the world which exists throughout the universe'.[16] As Steven Shaviro explains, from 'the pre-Socratics, on through Spinoza and Leibniz, and down to William James and Alfred North Whitehead, panpsychism is a recurring underground motif in the history of Western thought' (Shaviro 86). The idea of nature as living being, in which humans are not the only beings that possess mind, is also part of the green religion of the Gardeners. The main representative of this idea is Pilar. As Toby recalls, when apprenticing her in her expertise of herbalist and healer,

> Pilar took Toby down to the dank cellars below the Buenavista Condos and showed her where the mushrooms were grown. Bees and mushrooms went together, said Pilar: the bees were on good terms with the unseen world, being the messengers to the dead. She tossed that crazed little factoid off as if it was something everyone knew . . . Mushrooms

were the roses in the garden of that unseen world, because the real mushroom plant was underground. The part you could see – what most people called a mushroom – was just a brief apparition. A cloud flower. (*Year of the Flood* 100)

Pilar also passes on her bee lore: 'A bee in the house means a visit from a stranger, and if you kill the bee, the visit will not be a good one. If the beekeeper dies, the bees must be told, or they will swarm and fly away' (99). After Pilar's death, Toby brings them this news as well as the news that she will now be their 'new Eve Six' (181). In the third novel, *MaddAddam*, Toby goes to consult with the spirit of the dead Pilar at the elderberry bush, where she has a vision of a Pigoon farrow.

Even though the apocalypse that actually happens is not the ecological collapse that the Gardeners had expected, many Gardeners manage to survive. As Adam One concludes,

For the Waterless Flood has swept over us – not as a vast hurricane, not as a barrage of comets, not as a cloud of poisonous gasses. No: as we suspected for so long, it is a plague – a plague that infects no Species but our own, and that will leave all other Creatures untouched. Our cities are darkened, our lines of communication are no more. The blight and ruin of our Garden is now mirrored by the blight and ruin that have emptied the streets below. We need not fear discovery now: our old enemies cannot pursue us, occupied as they must be by the hideous torments of their own bodily dissolution, if they are not already dead. (*Year of the Flood* 424)

True to the script of Revelation, the Gardeners' survival as a small collective is ironically due to the fact that they have been facing finitude at the largest scale. But in contrast to the salvation of the devout in Revelation, the practices that end up saving them are secular: their environmentally sustainable practices.

That said, the twenty-five years of Gardener history narrated in *The Year of the Flood* also chronicle internal dissension. Atwood confronts the problematic dimensions of utopianism, the drive to purity and conformity, by depicting the break-up of the Gardeners in Year 18 of the ritual calendar, seven years before Crake's apocalypse, and three years before the destruction of EdenCliff Garden by the CorpsSeCorps and the official banning and persecution of the remnants of the cult. Adam One's half-brother

Zeb breaks away to form his own group – none other than the MaddAddamites who run Extinctathon. Zeb pulls up the website for Toby shortly after the schism: 'EXTINCTATHON. *Monitored by MaddAddam. Adam named the living animals, MaddAddam named the dead ones. Do you want to play?*' (268). Zeb becomes MaddAddam when he decides to break with Adam One's pacifism and embrace bioterrorist strategies to bring down the corporate system.

In addition to the surprise encounter on the seashore in the final scene, where Toby and Ren chance upon Jimmy as Jimmy stumbles on to Amanda and the Painballers, this is another moment where the two parallel narratives of *Oryx and Crake* and *The Year of the Flood* converge at one point, for Crake also pulls up this website to go to. In narratological terms, both are 'nodes' in what Christoph Bode terms a 'future narrative'. Future narratives are defined as multilinear narratives that maintain an open future, in contrast to 'past narratives', whose temporal flow from beginning to end is linear (Bode and Dietrich 16–17). The difference between future and past narratives is not genre: future narratives exist in literature and other media such as film, especially and including computer simulation and computer games. A node is a point of bifurcation, a point of choice and of contingency, where at least two different possibilities are realised. Bode's goal is to provide a narrative theory of the type of non-linear narration that has long existed, but that has only come into full visibility with the advent of new electronic media. A future narrative in Bode's sense, the *MaddAddam* trilogy has several such nodes that arise from the networked design of its science fictional world, where the same events are narrated multiple times and are seen to take different directions. The MaddAddam website is the most paradigmatic of these in the first two volumes of the trilogy. The prompt '*Do you want to play?*' is a paradigmatic node: Zeb's 'click' on the prompt realises one course of events, as do those of each of the other Grandmasters of the Extinctathon game; additional clicks are Toby's and Jimmy's. The most momentous click of all is, of course, Crake's, which inspires the Paradice project. Indeed, the non-linear 'nodal' narrative organisation of the trilogy constitutes a significant modification of its apocalyptic script, contravening apocalyptic teleology. In part, this is because Atwood's novels are post-apocalyptic fiction, which focuses on remaking world after the world-end, and reopening the future after the end of history. As such, the trilogy is in keeping with its Latourian goal of demolishing the modern dichotomy of the 'two cultures' and of gathering a new collective of humans and non-humans, a subject to which I now turn.

MaddAddam: Gathering the Ecological Collective of Humans and Non-Humans

This last section returns to the subject of the human loss of control over the artefacts of modern science and technology and Stengers' question of what happens when scientific factishes leave the laboratory to enter history and acquire autonomous modes of existence. As Toby, the focaliser in *MaddAddam*, reflects, 'speculations about what the end of the world would be like after human control of it ended had been – long ago, briefly – a queasy form of entertainment' (*MaddAddam* 32). But now the end of anthropocentric history has arrived. *MaddAddam* picks up the narrative of events as history starts up again. There is a new post-apocalyptic Alpha out of Omega and the world is remade through an unplanned biological as well as cultural evolution. But in contrast to New Jerusalem, in the redeemed future of Atwood's 'New Eaarth' humans are no longer at the helm of creation.

MaddAddam follows the same dual-time structure as *Oryx and Crake* and *The Year of the Flood*, but the narrative moves even further away from the corporate world that caused the collapse, and towards new and unpredictable developments. Jimmy and Crake, central to the events of *Oryx and Crake*, become completely marginal. The narrative picks up at the end of the first two volumes, the nodal event of the encounter on the seashore, and advances from there. In the battle with the Painballers, Amanda is rescued, but the Painballers escape due to the intervention of the innocent Crakers. Present-time narration then narrows to the daily life of the small collective of about twenty human survivors at the cobb house: this includes several of Crake's Paradice team under their former Extinctathon Grandmaster names, both men (Ivory Bill, Manatee, Zunzuncito, Beluga) and women (White Sedge, Tamaraw, Swift Fox, Lotis Blue); Zeb and his group of MaddAddamite bioterrorists (Shackleton, Crozier, Katuro, Rebecca); as well as Toby, Amanda, Ren and Jimmy. Subsisting by farming, including the herding of Mo'Hairs (hybrid lambs spliced to grow human hair in all colours) for milk, and scavenging in the urban wasteland, life in the human collective is focused on 'making-do' in the post-apocalyptic world, including the formation of romantic couplings, one of which is Toby and Zeb.

In *MaddAddam*, the continuing threat posed by the Painballers provides the occasion for the central conflict whose resolution produces the formation of a new ecological collective between humans and non-humans. This alliance, furthermore, is neither initiated nor dominated by humans. It is an actor-network that unites Crakers, Pigoons and humans as actants of equal power. In tracking the defeat of the Painballers, Atwood's fictional networks ontology describes the rearrangement of post-apocalyptic survivors (both human and non-human) in a post-apocalyptic web of associations that is singular and specific to a particular task. Bigger than food chains or cycles, it is something like a trans-species settlement in the artificial wilderness on New Eaarth. This coalition begins to form as the Crakers are settled next to the cobb house after the Painballers' escape. With Jimmy unconscious, the Crakers appoint Toby as their new chief mythologist for their daily ritual storytelling sessions. Beginning to self-direct their learning as they replace Jimmy with Toby, their interest also shifts from Crake to Zeb: 'We know the story of Crake. We know it many times. Now tell us the story of Zeb, Oh Toby' (*MaddAddam* 54). In this way, Zeb becomes the culture hero of the past-oriented narrative in *MaddAddam*, figuring as Crake's and Adam One's counterpart in this role, in which the latter had served in *Oryx and Crake* and *The Year of the Flood* respectively. Zeb is a trickster survivor and digital-urban cowboy of sorts, and it is fully appropriate that his character completes the triad, alongside Crake (bioscience) and Adam One (green religion).

The cobb house collective of humans and Crakers is the initial (and more primitive) stage of an expanding post-apocalyptic trans-species ecology in *MaddAddam*. The cobb house is not a post-apocalyptic pastoral retreat for humans. As an inter-species ecology, it is also more radical and extensive than the ecological alliance between Jimmy and the Crakers in *Oryx and Crake*. In housing together ex-bioengineers from the Paradice project and the Crakers, the cobb house throws together two groups that are radically segregated in the modern constitution: biological arte-facts and their makers. In point of fact, this is initially a cause of consternation among the MaddAddamites, who at first resist cohabitation with the Crakers precisely because of the ontological difference between creatures and their creators. At the beginning, there are demeaning comments such as 'I hope Crake's Frankenpeople aren't moving in with us' (*MaddAddam* 19), showing that the MaddAddamites objectify the Crakers as 'things' and are reluctant to accept their humanity. As artificial beings, the Crakers are disqualified from membership in society, the domain of humans with free will.

But as the MaddAddamites come to realise, in the emerging non-modern world after Crake's destruction of bio-capitalist Babylon, Crake's laws are suspended. Anthropocentrism is defunct. And although they soon come to warm to what Morton calls new dark-ecological modes of association, they never suspend their view of the Crakers as constructs. They engage in long dinner table discussions of the Crakers' genetic design:

> Ivory Bill, Manatee, Tamaraw, and Zunzuncito have cleared their plates and are deep into a discussion of epigenetics. How much of Craker behavior is inherited, how much is cultural? Do they even have what you could call a culture, separate from the expression of their genes? Or are they more like ants? What about the singing? Granted, it must be some form of communication, but is it territorial, like the singing of birds, or might it be termed art? Surely not the latter, says Ivory Bill. Crake couldn't account for it and didn't like it, says Tamaraw, but the team hadn't been able to eliminate it without producing affectless individuals who never went into heat and didn't last long. (*MaddAddam* 139)

Like Crake, the MaddAddamites take the typical attitude of scientific iconoclasts who are 'in the know' about the genetic reality behind phenomenal appearance, by making ironic comments about the pros and cons of various Craker traits: Manatee praises 'the built-in insect repellent: genius'. Zunzuncito agrees: 'And the woman who can't say no. That color-coded hormonal thing, you have to admire it' (43). Throughout, the MaddAddamites posture as artificers of the Crakers who stress the Crakers' status as products bioengineered in the Paradice laboratory. This is the case even as they begin to concede that the Crakers' behaviour is beginning to be unpredictable and uncanny: their 'brains are more malleable than Crake intended. They've been doing several things we did not anticipate during the construction phase' (273).

Yet, as both Latour and Stengers argue, none of this knowledge about their original genetic engineering detracts from the powerful independent mode of existence that the Crakers acquire in the post-apocalyptic reality, outside the controlled environment of the Paradice laboratory and therefore the control of their makers. As we have seen in the discussion of *Oryx and Crake*, the Crakers are hybrid non-humans who transgress the boundary from passive intermediaries (carrying out Crake's predetermined genetic design) to full-fledged mediators. Their ontogeny illustrates Latour's apt comment, 'the serfs have become citizens' (*We Have Never* 81). Surpassing Latour, Atwood's apocalyptic world-making, straddling a revolutionary break that divides time into 'before' and 'after', makes this point with singular forcefulness. On opposing wings of the same bifocal panel two versions of Crakers and other artificial species appear: the first is the bioengineered machine; the second is the non-predictable uncanny organism that it has become in the process of living. In addition, it depicts two corresponding versions of humans: the first is the bioengineer and master of nature; the second the human survivor newly embedded in reciprocal links of dependency with the artificial creatures of his own making.

MaddAddam tracks the Crakers' generation of spontaneous and creative action that far exceeds the initial stirrings of this impulse in *Oryx and Crake* (the question about their makers and the fabrication of an idol representation of Jimmy). All three volumes of the trilogy contain evidence that not only do Crakers and Pigoons become actants, but so do all the artificial species left behind among the debris of modern civilisation. Rakunks (a raccoon-skunk splice without the smell) were bred as pets; as a boy Jimmy had a pet rakunk named Killer, but after her disappearance his eco-dissident mother liberates Killer into the wild (*Oryx and Crake* 61). Jimmy observes a large population of feral rakunks in the woods in *Oryx and Crake*. Wolvogs, bred as 'BioDefences' to guard prisons (*Oryx and Crake* 205), also get loose during the apocalypse. Arch-predators, by the *MaddAddam* stage wolvogs have completely eliminated the feral rakunk population. From the rooftop of AnooYoo, Toby observes liobams in the wild:

The liobams are actual. They must be zoo animals freed by one of the more fanatical sects in those last desperate days. They don't look dangerous, although they are. The lion-sheep splice was commissioned by the Lion Isaiahists in order to force the advent of the Peacable

Kingdom. They reasoned that the only way to fulfil the lion/lamb friendship prophecy without the first eating the second would be to meld the two of them together. But the result hadn't been strictly vegetarian. (*Year of the Flood* 94)

The degree of cross-species hybridisation in Atwood's trilogy is stunning. Liobams are experimental factishes cloned at the behest of a religious cult, to make peace between natural predators (lions) and natural prey (lambs). But instead of serving as passive intermediaries of these predetermined values, the liobams betray their purpose. Toby witnesses this later on as she observes 'two liobams on the hunt' (*Year of the Flood* 238) near a flock of Mo'Hairs, whose long human hair is in bad shape. As Toby reflects,

> in advertisements, their hair had been shiny – you'd see the sheep tossing its hair, then a beautiful girl tossing a mane of the same hair. *More hair with Mo'Hair!* But they're not faring so well without their salon treatments … The purple Mo'Hair is the most jittery. Don't look like prey, Toby thinks at it. Sure enough, it's the purple one the liobams go after. They cut it out from the group and chase it for a short distance. The pathetic beast is impeded by its coiffure – it looks like a purple fright wig on legs – and the liobams quickly pull it down. (238)

Of all the artificial animals, the Mo'Hairs turn out to be among the most domesticated and least transformative in the post-apocalyptic ecosystem. They continue to serve as the instruments – intermediaries – of other beings, 'being made to do things' more than 'making others do things'. Still, they also make others do things in ways that betray their genetic purpose, so they remain actants: cloned to supply human hair for transplants (Toby had a Mo'Hair transplant to be safe from Blanco), Mo'Hairs now supply food – the cobb house collective herds them for milk, and they supply predators with meat.

In the rise of non-modern post-apocalyptic actor-networks in the *MaddAddam* trilogy, there is a wide spectrum between the emergence of indeterminacy from spontaneous purposive action (in Crakers and Pigoons) on the one hand, and from the multiple causality that is characteristic of complex dynamic systems, such as ecosystems, on the other. The organisation of ecosystems, composed of different species, consists of multiple and discontinuous feedback loops. The concept of feedback – one of the major discoveries of Norbert Wiener and cybernetics in the 1950s – implies circular causality.

> A feedback loop is a circular arrangement of causally connected elements, in which an initial cause propagates around the links of the loop, so that each element has an effect on the next, until the last 'feeds back' the effect into the first element of the cycle. The consequence of this arrangement is that the first link ('input') is affected but the last ('output'), resulting in self-regulation of the entire system, as the initial effect is modified each time it travels around the cycle. (Capra and Luisi 89)

Feedback, in other words, is the logic of self-regulating systems. This underlying loop pattern also explains the post-apocalyptic repurposing of the Mo'Hairs by both humans and liobams. Unlike linear causality, circular causality is multidirectional and interactive. Whereas linear causality separates cause from effect, in circular causality the former effect is redeployed as a new cause that in turn transforms the original cause into a new effect. Reciprocal feedback, where causation flows in both directions, is key to any actor-network. There are two types of feedback cycles: negative ('self-balancing') feedback between elements that balance each other (for example, prey/predator; blood sugar/insulin) and positive ('self-reinforcing') feedback, between elements that augment each other in potentially vicious cycles (for example, in violence). Both types are found in ecosystems. As Lewontin and Levins explain, 'the elementary pairwise interactions between species have been studied extensively. But whatever the model, the core relation is the feedback loop, negative for predator–prey relations and positive for competition and mutualism' (156). The correlation between Mo'Hairs (prey) and liobams (predators), for example, is negative feedback: the more Mo'Hairs (and rakunks) there are, the more there is to eat for the liobams (and wolvogs). But the resulting increase in liobam predators will cause a decrease in the number of their prey, which in turn will eventually also lead to the decimation of the predators. Thus, the last effect 'feeds back' into the first element of this post-apocalyptic food cycle. The causal 'loop' has closed. The circular causality of interacting feedback cycles leads to the emergence of non-linear and multiple causality in ecosystems, dubbed hyperobjects by Morton to signal their bizarre elusiveness.

As the examples discussed show, the negative feedback cycle between predators and prey is key to Atwood's speculative vision of the post-apocalyptic future after the end of anthropocentric history. This shows Atwood's unsentimental vision of ecology as a network of distinct forces whose relationships can be antagonistic as well as cooperative and harmonious. Atwood's vision is holistic in the sense that it is ecological and relational (rather than reductive) and non-anthropocentric. But *MaddAddam* is also in accordance with Lewontin and Levins, who caution against overcompensating against scientific reductionism with an excessive embrace of wholeness. Ecological interdependence does not imply benevolence. Interconnectedness does not mean that beings in an ecosystem are all 'one': 'Predator and prey are not "one" until the last stages of digestion' (Lewontin and Levins 107). Even if prey and predator balance each other in a negative feedback that stabilises the system as a whole, their relationship as parts of the whole is hostile, not harmonious.

As noted, it is the common need for defence against a threat from super-predators (the Painballers) that motivates the formation of the ecological alliance between Crakers, Pigoons and the cobb house humans. In keeping with the post-anthropocentric scenario, these predators are not animals, but degenerated humans: Painballers suffer from neurological degeneration through the destruction of their 'empathy circuits' (*MaddAddam* 144). In the chapter entitled 'Piglet', a detachment of fifty Pigoons approaches the cobb house in ordered formation, carrying a dead piglet adorned with flowers and foliage on their backs. The humans suspect an attack on their persons or their garden. But the smart pigs are seeking to form an alliance and peace treaty with the humans against a common enemy, the Painballers, who have been killing their young. This is revealed by the Crakers, who emerge as diplomats and translators between the Pigoons and the humans. These developments sound the Latourian theme of the 'parliament of things' and of 'political ecology'. An 'advance deputation of Crakers' meets the Pigoons and leads them closer, then urinates in a line to demarcate a boundary against their further advance (269). A gifted young Craker named Blackbeard, who has been befriending Toby and learning to read and write, steps forward and translates the Pigoons' business. According to Blackbeard, the Pigoons are 'Children of Oryx and Children of Crake, both' (268) and have come to propose a mutual non-aggression pact:

'It is easier for them to talk to us', says Blackbeard simply. 'And in return, if you help them to kill the three bad men, they will never again try to eat your garden. Or any of you', he adds seriously. 'Even if you are dead, they will not eat you. And they ask that you must no longer make holes in them, with blood, and cook them in a smelly bone soup, or hang them in the smoke, or fry them and then eat them. Not any more.' (270)

The Pigoons are also requesting the humans' help in shooting and killing the Painballers, as they know well the power of 'guns', or, in Blackbeard's objective correlative translation, 'sticks' that 'make holes' 'with blood com[ing] out' (270). The Pigoons leave the dead piglet behind as a gift for the humans to eat as they choose.

This moment marks a bifurcation point in the Crakers' spontaneous evolution as autonomous actants, and their passage from determination to indeterminacy. Without the Crakers' mediation and diplomacy, the inter-species coalition would not have come about. Blackbeard has performed as an inter-species translator for the Pigoons once before, but not in public. When earlier Toby goes on a meditation quest to communicate with the spirit of the dead Pilar at the elderberry bush, she has a vision of a Pigoon farrow with five piglets (*MaddAddam* 223). Toby senses that this is the form of Pilar's apparition and that the sow is the widow of the boar she shot in the AnooYoo garden. Of those present, Blackbeard is the only one who also understands the farrow's message, spreading word among the Crakers that the Pigoons 'think that [Toby] shouldn't have killed the boar, but they're forgiving [her] because maybe Oryx said [she] could' (263–4). In an astonishing twist, the bogus mythology invented by Jimmy positing Oryx and Crake as deities is validated as real. The Pigoons are really part-human, and Toby really shot the boar. How else could Blackbeard possibly know this unless Jimmy's make-believe mythology had become the actual truth? How could Blackbeard (but not the humans) understand the Pigoons, unless it was because the Crakers are transgenic splices of human with animal DNA?

Next follows the first climax of history on *MaddAddam*'s 'New Eaarth': the battle of the eco-collective with the Painballers at the Paradice Dome, which ends with their capture and the deaths of Jimmy, Adam One (who had been the Painballers' hostage), as well as some Pigoons. The eco-collective leaves the cobb house to march into battle like an army: armed humans, Pigoons, and

Blackbeard as translator. Species-related differences are made use of: Blackbeard goes as a translator, but the remainder of the Crakers stay home because of their genetic disposition for non-violence. Pig scouts and the pigs' 'odour radar' (436) locate the Painballers in the Paradice Dome; they advance, with each MaddAddamite shielded by one pig as a guard. The pigs demand that Jimmy ride on their backs because of his injury. 'We're just the infantry as far as they're concerned', thinks Zeb. 'But they're the generals' (340–1). The actual events of the battle are told retrospectively in Blackbeard's voice to the Crakers in 'The Story of the Battle', a section that marks another milestone in the autonomous cultural history of the Crakers. Here, a Craker takes control of a human cultural technique, narrative, for the first time. Blackbeard's narration adapts Craker mythology for the purposes of secular history: 'This is the Story of the Battle. It tells how Zeb and Toby and Snowman-the-Jimmy and the other two-skinned ones and the Pig Ones cleared away the bad men, just as Crake cleared away the people in the chaos to make a good and safe place for us to live' (358). Blackbeard demonstrates his skills as an inter-species mediator by actively translating concepts and events that he witnessed but that are alien to his pacific Craker mates:

> A *battle* is when some wish to clear others away, and the others want to clear them away as well. We do not have battles. We do not eat a fish. We do not eat a smelly bone. Crake made us that way. Yes, good, kind Crake. But Crake made the two-skinned ones so they could have a battle. He made the Pig Ones that way too. (360)

The second climax of post-apocalyptic history on 'New Eaarth' is the subsequent trial of the captive Painballers. Even more than the initial treaty meeting at the cobb house, this episode fictionalises Latour's 'parliament of things', where humans and non-humans (Crakers and Pigoons) are seated together as free citizens in a common political collective, something like the United Nations of different species. To this, Atwood adds another layer of meaning derived from apocalyptic thinking: the final defeat of Satan (the Painballers) and the Final Judgment. The charges against the Painballers are presented, a brief discussion ensues among the humans, then there is a vote by pebble, 'black for death, white for mercy' (369). The Pigoons 'vote collectively through their leader, with Blackbeard as their interpreter. "They all say *dead*", he tells Toby' (369–70). Following a unanimous vote for death, the Painballers are escorted to the seashore by the humans and Pigoons and shot. As Latour explains, for an ecological collective to be assembled after the demolition of the modern constitution, several impediments have to be overcome so that humans and non-humans can be seated together. The first is the redistribution of 'speech between humans and nonhumans, *while learning to be skeptical of all spokespersons*' (*Politics of Nature* 232). In the Painballers' trial, nature is no longer mute and humans are no longer the only authorised spokespersons for it, as was the case in the modern constitution. The Pigoons can communicate to the humans, through Blackbeard's translation (again, just as at the United Nations).

The second requirement is the redistribution of 'the capacity to act as a social actor' (*Politics of Nature* 232). Here, too, nature is no longer passive and excluded from political representation; instead, non-humans get the vote and acquire social agency on a par with humans. As a result, writes Latour, the 'collective as finally convened allows a *return to civil peace*' (233). This proves indeed to be the case in *MaddAddam* after the execution of the Painballers. Atwood's apocalyptic script blends the Latourian and ecological theme with the element of annihilation of evil. Finally, the Pigoons and humans go their separate ways, having reaffirmed their mutual non-aggression pact. In Blackbeard's account:

> And they said also that even though the Battle was over now, they would keep the pact they made with Toby, and with Zeb, and they would not hunt and eat any of the two-skinned ones, and they would also not dig up their garden any more. Or eat the honey of the bees. / And Toby told me the words to say to them, which were: We agree to keep the pact. None of you, or your children, or your children's children, will ever be a smelly bone in a soup. Or a ham, she added. Or a bacon. (*MaddAddam* 370)

The political ecology uniting Crakers, Pigoons and humans under a new non-modern political constitution in *MaddAddam*'s 'New Eaarth' is as important as another radical development, the fact that Crakers and humans have been interbreeding and that three women (Amanda, Ren and Swift Fox) have given birth to four hybrid babies fathered by Craker men. The last chapter, 'Book' completes this trajectory towards a posthuman future. It is the first chapter entirely narrated by Blackbeard. One subject is the accession of the Crakers to full command of the human technologies of reading and writing: Blackbeard is now the sole author of Toby's journal, having taken over from her after her death. He reports passing on literacy to the four young hybrid children so that they in turn can take over as archivists after his death, which he has learned to anticipate through Toby's instruction. The other subject is a glimpse into historical 'drift' – to adapt biologists Humberto Maturana and Francisco Varela's term to replace the concept of teleological evolution[17] – after the death of the last two central human protagonists, Toby and Zeb. Zeb sets out with a small expedition to investigate new signs of human survivors, and does not return. In response, Toby takes her leave and walks into the forest, taking her lethal mushrooms with which to commit suicide. In her honour, Swift Fox, pregnant with another hybrid of which Blackbeard is proud to report being one of the ritual 'fourfathers' (390), promises to name the child Toby if it is a girl. Blackbeard narrates these events in a journal entry entitled 'The Story of Toby', which ends as follows:

> This is the end of the story of Toby. I have written it in this Book. And I have put my name here – Blackbeard – the way Toby first showed me when I was a child. It says that I was the one who set down these words. / Thank you. / Now we will sing. (390)

The *MaddAddam* trilogy thus ends with a partially optimistic view into a posthuman future, where Crakers, and the hybrid offspring of Crakers and humans, become the protagonists of new recorded history after the coming deaths of the last natural humans.

Notes

1. As Schmidgen documents, Latour met Stengers as part of group of 'philosophers, sociologists, and humanities scholars supervised by [Michel] Serres' in the late 1980s (*Bruno Latour in Pieces* 80). The convergence of Latour's and Stengers' projects intensified in the 1990s, when both worked on redefining the relationship between science and politics beyond the dichotomy of the 'two cultures'. Latour dedicated *Politics of Nature* to Stengers for inspiring his concept of 'political ecology' with her 'cosmopolitical' approach as a philosopher of science. In return, Stengers' *Cosmopolitics I* and

Cosmopolitics II builds on key Latourian concepts, such as actants and factishes.

2. *An Inquiry into Modes of Existence* has a panoramic focus that compares the various types of truth production across the disciplines of science, law, economics, but also politics, art and religion. In this book, Latour distances himself from the empirical focus of ANT and returns to philosophy at a grander scaler than ever before (see also Tresch). The concept of 'modes of existence' aims to do nothing less than mediate across the dichotomy between words and things: 'To speak of different *modes of existence* and claim to be investigating these modes with a certain precision is thus to take a new look at the ancient division of labor between words and things, language and being' (*Inquiry* 21). However, as Schmidgen has pointed out, there are inconsistencies between *An Inquiry into Modes of Existence* and Latour's previous work, such as the use of categories that seem to coincide with those of traditional sociology criticised 'in the name of ANT' and an expansive 'tableau of modes of existence' that goes against 'all previous criticism of "big pictures"' (Schmidgen 129). For the purposes of this project, *Inquiry* is much less helpful than Latour's previous publications.

3. This charge was crystallised by the citation of Latour's work in Alan Sokal's infamous hoax article in *Social Text* and the follow-up book, *Fashionable Nonsense*, at the climax of the so-called science wars in the 1990s (see Schmidgen 109–11).

4. 'Irreductions' is the second and theoretical part of Latour's *The Pasteurization of France*. Its main motto is, 'We do not want to reduce anything to anything else' (qtd in Schmidgen 77).

5. Schmidgen explains that despite the attack on Baudrillard and Lyotard in *We Have Never Been Modern*, Lyotard's *Postmodern Condition* 'actually has many points of contact with [Latour's] own works, such as the view that science is an agonistic field or in identifying rhetoric as an important component of scientific practice' (103–4).

6. Like his anthropology of the moderns in general, Latour developed his critique of modern critique in his engagement with Michel Serres. Latour calls Serres an *'anthropologist of science'* and a practitioner of an acritical philosophy that does without a critical 'metalanguage' (Latour, 'The Enlightenment without the Critique' 93, 87). In *Conversations on Science, Culture and Time*, Serres echoes these claims, professing to 'avoid metalanguage' and practise interdisciplinary reading as a 'refusal of the separation between science and literature' (91, 50).

7. Latour has repeatedly mounted passionate defences of the arts against reductivist critical readings: 'Apart from religion, no other domain has been more bulldozed to death by critical sociology than the sociology of art. Every sculpture, painting, *haute cuisine* dish, techno rave, and novel has been explained to nothingness by the social factors "hidden behind" them' (*Reassembling* 236).

8. The term 'flat ontology' in this sense was first circulated by Manuel DeLanda in 2007 (see DeLanda and Harman 85).

9. Criticism on the *MaddAddam* trilogy engages with Atwood's adaptation of apocalypticism, and the complex of utopia/dystopia and SF. See Canavan, Howells, Hengen, Stein and Bosco.

10. This is noted by Howells for *Oryx and Crake* (172).

11. Atwood's Crake can persuasively be read alongside Mary Shelley's Frankenstein, in Stein's words, as 'classic examples of the trickster-scientist' (see Stein 143).

12. The portrait of Jimmy and Crake as representatives of the 'two cultures' is also noted by Stein (149).

13. Jimmy's humanistic subversion of Crake's reductivist genocentric agenda is also noted by Caravan (146), Howells (171) and Bosco (170).

14. This point is also made by Canavan (150).

15. Prigogine and Stengers write that 'the birth of modern science was marked by the abandonment of the vitalist inspiration and, in particular, of Aristotelian final causes' (*Order Out of Chaos* 80). Thus, the vitalist rebellion and what Isaiah Berlin called the 'Counter-Enlightenment' (*Order Out of Chaos* 80) reacts against the abyss separating the world of science from the everyday world of life, which Latour terms the modern work of purification.

16. 'Panpsychism', *Stanford Encyclopedia of Philosophy*, available at <http://plato.stanford.edu/entries/panpsychism/> (accessed 26 February 2015).

17. The actual term is 'natural drift' (Maturana and Varela, *Tree of Knowledge* 117), as Chapter 3 will explain.

3

The Ontology of Knowledge as the Enaction of Mind and World: Humberto Maturana and Francisco Varela's Autopoietic Theory and José Saramago's *Blindness*

We will propose a way of seeing cognition not as a representation of the world 'out there', but rather as an ongoing bringing forth of a world through the process of living itself.

Maturana and Varela, *The Tree of Knowledge*

An organisation, the human body is also an organised system, it lives as long as it keeps organised, and death is only the effect of a disorganisation. And how can a society of blind people organise itself in order to survive. By organising itself, to organise oneself is, in a way, to begin to have eyes.

Saramago, *Blindness*

This chapter engages with exciting new non-representationalist theories of knowledge coming out of the heart of science. It focuses on Chilean neuroscientists and phenomenologists Humberto Maturana and Francisco Varela's theory of autopoiesis, or self-making, systematically presented in *The Tree of Knowledge: The Biological Roots of Human Understanding* (1987), as well as the theory of enactivism, which Maturana's younger colleague Varela subsequently developed in collaboration with Evan Thompson and Eleanor Rosch in *The Embodied Mind: Cognitive Science and Human Experience* (1993). Autopoietic theory is nothing less than a general theory of the organisation of the living, while enactivism has a narrower focus as a theory of cognition. While they place emphasis on different aspects of a joint concept of cognition in living organisms, the close relation between autopoietic theory and the theory of enactivism justifies the use of the umbrella term 'Santiago school' to refer to both (Capra and Luisi 129; Varela,

'Early Days'). While key ideas about the circular organisation of living systems date from Maturana's thought and publications in the 1960s, the concept of autopoiesis was developed in close personal collaboration between Maturana and Varela in 1970–71 at the University of Chile in Santiago, while co-authoring the foundational essay, *Autopoiesis and Cognition: The Realization of the Living* (1973; 1980).[1]

Maturana and Varela offer a non-representational theory of knowledge that does away with the Cartesian duality of subject and object. For Maturana and Varela, cognition is not a representation that an autonomous observer makes of an independently existing external world. The central insight of the Santiago school is that, instead of reproducing a pre-existing objective reality, 'all cognition brings forth a world' (*Tree of Knowledge* 29). In making this claim, Maturana and Varela introduce a new way of thinking about knowledge: knowledge is primarily about worlds, that is to say, knowledge must be appreciated through the lens of ontology. Hence, Maturana and Varela loosen the traditional association of knowledge with epistemology that dates from the Kantian critical turn. (The term 'loosen' is appropriate because the ties with epistemology are transformed rather than cut. The new ontology that Maturana and Varela develop is 'epistemic' in the sense that the existence of an observer forms an integral part of it.) Although made independently from – and in most cases, earlier than – the other new realist theories after postmodernism considered here, their paradigm shift from epistemology to ontology clearly aligns with the parallel efforts of Bruno Latour, Markus Gabriel, Jean-Luc Marion and Alphonso Lingis. In his 1995 memoir essay, 'The Early Days of Autopoiesis', Varela states this point explicitly:

> Autopoiesis continues to be a good example of alignment with something that only today appears more clearly configured in various fields … and which I identify with the term ontological turn. That is, a progressive mutation of thought which ends the long dominance of the social space of Cartesianism … Knowing, doing, and living are not separate things … (74)

Indeed, one key assumption underlying Maturana and Varela's theory is that knowledge is action: 'All doing is knowing, and all knowing is doing' (*Tree of Knowledge* 26). In Latourian terms, the theories of autopoiesis and enactivism are 'compositionist', meaning that they are not simply about worlds, but more specifically about world-making. Knowledge is 'effective action' (29). As Varela explains in the afterword to *The Tree of Knowledge*, 'I have proposed using the term *enactive* to designate this view of knowledge, to evoke the idea that what is known is brought forth' (255). Varela introduces the concept of enactivism to highlight this new view of knowledge as 'doing' as opposed to passive representation. Varela et al. elucidate this position even more clearly in *The Embodied Mind*:

> We propose as a name the term *enactive* to emphasize the growing conviction that cognition is not the representation of a pregiven world by a pregiven mind but is rather the enactment of a world and a mind on the basis of a history of the variety of actions that a being in the world performs. The enactive approach takes seriously, then, the philosophical critique of the idea that the mind is a mirror of nature but goes further by addressing this issue from within the heartland of science. (9)

To characterise autopoietic theory and enactivism as a non-representationalist theory of knowledge is to specify the view that they reject. In contrast, calling it ontological and compositionist is to articulate the view they embrace.

Similar to Latour, the methodological spirit behind the Santiago school is hybrid, bridging the dichotomy of the 'two cultures' of the sciences and the humanities. But while they share this general attitude with Latour and Stengers, they work it out in an idiosyncratic way. One cannot underestimate the fact that Maturana and Varela are primarily scientists committed to scientific standards of knowledge. The fact that their work draws on both biology and cognitive science as well as on the humanist methodologies of phenomenology and hermeneutics is of the utmost importance to the pathbreaking originality of their ideas. Maturana and Varela identify themselves as 'phenomenologically inclined cognitive scientist[s]' (*Embodied Mind* 3). In contrast to dominant trends in cognitive science, which tend to adopt an exclusively third-personal view of the mind, Maturana and Varela insist on holding on to the central concerns of phenomenology, the study of first-personal experience and consciousness, while addressing them, as stated in the foregoing quotation, 'from within the heartland of science'. Varela coined the term 'neurophenomenology' for this hybrid approach 'to the study of consciousness that combines the disciplined examination of conscious experience with the analysis of corresponding neural patterns and processes' (Capra and Luisi 263). Maturana and Varela postulate a 'fundamental circularity in scientific method', whose roots they trace back to Hegel and the hermeneutic circle but which expands knowledge to the process of life as such (*Embodied Mind* 9).

The nineteenth-century scientific observer, Varela el al. explain, 'could be imagined as a cognizing agent who is parachuted onto the earth as an unknown, objective reality to be charted' (*Embodied Mind* 4). The Santiago theory rejects both poles of the mind/world dualism, the Cartesian fiction of the disembodied observer that the philosopher Thomas Nagel has called the 'view from nowhere' (see *Embodied Mind* 27), as well as the notion of a pre-existing external world. According to autopoietic and enactivist theory, cognition is embodied action, and the mind, following Merleau-Ponty, is the embodied mind (*Embodied Mind* 27 and *passim*). This position stems from the phenomenological tradition, which, as Varela et al. observe, was developed by Husserl, Heidegger and Merleau-Ponty specifically to overcome scientific subject/object dualism and to posit the inseparability of mind and world (4). *The Tree of Knowledge* opens with a rebuttal of the mimetic paradigm. Similarly, expressing their phenomenological outlook, Varela et al. begin *The Embodied Mind* with a reflection on the embeddedness of cognition in the circularity of an 'already-given condition':

> Minds awaken in a world. We did not design our world. We simply found ourselves with it; we awoke both to ourselves and to the world we inhabit. We come to reflect on that world as we grow and live. We reflect on a world that is not made, but found, and yet it is also our structure that enables us to reflect upon this world. Thus in reflection we find ourselves in a circle: we are in a world that seems to be there before reflection begins, but that world is not separate from us. (3)

Varela et al. clarify that *The Embodied Mind* 'is devoted to the exploration of this deep circularity' (12).

What distinguishes the theories of autopoiesis and enactivism as a contribution to the new ontologies considered here? First, they consider mind and world as a historical process, a fact that sets them apart from Latour and Gabriel, who do not. As we shall see later on, they share this approach with the phenomenologist

Jean-Luc Marion, a congruence that derives from their common phenomenological approach. But unlike Marion, Maturana and Varela are interested in emergence (in the evolutionary sense of the term), which is a unique type of creation that is self-organising. Autopoiesis is a biocentric and non-anthropocentric theory of ontogeny that spans the entire arc of life, from lower-order physiological interactions just mentioned to higher-order interactions in the social and linguistic realms of both animals and humans. The idea of emergence denotes the immanent arising of novel phenomena within a network, which result spontaneously from interactions between assembled components, without direction from outside (see Capra and Luisi 154ff.). In Maturana and Varela's view, mind is an emergent phenomenon: 'mind and world arise together in enaction' (*Embodied Mind* 177). The theory of autopoiesis set out in *The Tree of Knowledge* describes the co-constitution of organism and environment. As Maturana and Varela maintain,

> we are continuously immersed in this network of interactions, the results of which depend on history. Effective action leads to effective action: it is the cognitive circle that characterizes our becoming, as an expression of our manner of being autonomous living systems. Through this ongoing recursiveness, every world brought forth necessarily hides its origins. (*Tree of Knowledge* 241–2)

The essential feature of emergence is that it describes a process that is context-based and differential. Things don't arise in isolation, they emerge from reciprocal interactions between components of an assemblage. The notion of emergence expresses the cybernetic logic of network-based genesis. Cybernetics, and twentieth-century systems theory more generally, is the other intellectual lineage that Maturana and Varela belong to, which is why their work is also classified as second-generation or 'second wave' cybernetics (Hayles 131). Shaped by the double influence of both the phenomenological as well as the cybernetic schools, the Santiago theory embraces the basic premises of the ecological paradigm of holistic, networked thinking; it is therefore a prime exhibit of the 'new ecological realisms' after poststructuralism that form the subject of this study. Maturana and Varela offer an ecological model of knowledge that shifts the focus from parts to wholes, from isolated objects (and subjects) to a relational and dialectical view of their co-dependent arising in the process of living.

The second feature that sets Maturana and Varela apart from the other new ontologies considered here is their focus on embodiment, embodied action and embodied minds. Maturana and Varela first developed their ideas through studying the visual system in general and colour perception in particular. They maintain that colour is not a pre-given attribute of the external world; it is dependent on perceptual-cognitive processes that are biologically determined (by the organisms's sensorimotor apparatus) and culturally modified. In *The Embodied Mind*, colour perception forms the core case study of Varela's theory of cognition as embodied action.

This chapter pairs Maturana and Varela with José Saramago's *Blindness*, a novel that similarly explores the problem of vision. *Blindness* is an allegorical novel about the apocalyptic collapse of modern civilisation due to a pandemic of a strange white-blindness. The novel asks: What is the phenomenology of blind perception? How do human beings orient themselves in the world if they are suddenly deprived of vision and reduced to four of the five cardinal senses – hearing, smell, taste and touch? Saramago's answer parallels Maturana and Varela's insights: blind perception is immersed in its embodiment. The sudden loss of vision throws the newly white-blind back on the sensorimotor apparatus of their bodies, which they discover has been reduced from five to four senses. 'Embodied minds' in Maturana and Varela's sense, the white-blind are forced to acknowledge something that the sighted are at liberty to ignore: their dependence on the taken-for-granted physiological infrastructure of their species-specific embodiment. If Saramago wasn't familiar with enactivist theory, his intuition of its principles is uncanny. Perception, as philosopher and cognitive scientist Alva Noë explains, is not a movie in our heads but a 'skillful bodily activity' (*Action in Perception* 2). It is therefore best illustrated by 'a blind person tap-tapping his or her way around a cluttered space, perceiving that space by touch, not all at once, but through time, by skillful probing and movement' (*Action in Perception* 1).

In more general terms, *Blindness* literalises its critique of the Cartesian fiction of the disembodied observer by eliminating vision itself. Vision, as Descartes put it, is 'the noblest of all senses' (qtd in Jay 21). As Martin Jay has shown, visuality has been at the centre of Western philosophy from the Greeks to the present day. From Plato's parable of the cave to Bentham's panopticon, metaphors of sight (insight, enlightenment and so on) have been synonymous with knowledge. By destroying vision, the plague of white-blindness also eliminates the fiction of the Cartesian detached observer and the representational paradigm according to which the pre-existing subject faces off against a pre-existing world of objects. Actively exploring the world into which they are thrown, Saramago's blind protagonists destroy the old realist 'epistemology of the "outside spectator"' (Jay 302).

A fantastic disease that defies rational explanation, white-blindness differs from ordinary blindness in that its victims are 'living inside a luminous halo' (*Blindness* 90). Its 'luminosity' suggests that Saramago's fantastic white-blindness is more than a disability: it entails superior insight not accessible to the sighted. As I will argue, one central insight imparted by white-blindness is the revelation of being embodied minds: demolishing the fiction of worldless minds, white-blindness shows that minds are embedded in the world and co-constituted by ongoing interaction with it. By fabricating a disease that is unequivocally fictitious, *Blindness* presents an estranged perspective on mind and knowledge that encourages the suspension of ingrained beliefs. Saramago's defamiliarising idea of an infectious white-blindness destroys the representational paradigm, to explore perception not as objective reflection, but as the enaction of world. The crucial point of *Blindness* maps neatly on to that of *The Tree of Knowledge*: we do not perceive the objective space of the world, but 'live our field of vision' (*Tree of Knowledge* 23). The difference is illustrated by the so-called 'blind spot', an area on the retina where the optic nerve emerges that is not sensitive to light. If human sight was a passive camera-like recording of reality, we would have a hole in our visual field. But we don't. As Maturana and Varela put it, *'we do not see what we do not see'* (*Tree of Knowledge* 19). A central character in *Blindness* similarly concludes, 'I think we are blind, Blind but seeing, Blind people who can see, but do not see' (*Blindness* 326). Saramago's novel also demonstrates what Markus Gabriel, in a different context, specifies as the 'ontological condition' of mind (*Transcendental Ontology* ix). Among the post-apocalyptic novels discussed here, Saramago's expresses this point most forcefully because of its amputation of vision, that is to say, its blockage of the royal road to the representational paradigm.

Like Atwood's, McCarthy's and Butler's novels, Saramago's

Blindness is a post- apocalyptic survivor narrative. It tracks the apocalyptic collapse of an entire city (and the nation it is part of) and their modern social order. Saramago's pandemic blindness is the equivalent of the artificial plague in Atwood and the environmental causes of disaster in other post-apocalyptic novels. Like other post-apocalyptic novels, Saramago's contagion conducts a laboratory experiment of sorts that installs an unfamiliar 'hereafter' in place of the ruined modern world. Homeless nomads wandering the ruins of the modern city, Saramago's white-blind have to make do by hunter-gathering for basic needs such as food and shelter; they are likewise forced to reinvent social relationships and specify the values that will govern the new post-apocalyptic social order.

The newly white-blind protagonists in Saramago's *Blindness* learn that to be blind means to be post-individual. Unlike the sighted, the blind cannot survive as autonomous individuals. As in Atwood, Butler and McCarthy, a small group forms the alternative social unit, whose members in Saramago's case are the first victims of the contagion who are reunited in quarantine. I will henceforth refer to them as the Ward One collective. *Blindness* is animated by an odd optimism that runs counter to the horror it describes, a feature also characteristic of other post-Cold War post-apocalyptic novels. In the following I argue that this curious post-apocalyptic hopefulness noted by Irr can best be understood through Maturana and Varela's theories of autopoiesis and enaction. The second major insight presented in *Blindness* is that post-apocalyptic survival is dependent on what Maturana and Varela call social coupling within self-organising collectives. The members of the Ward One collective discover that vision can be substituted by collaborative social action. Through reciprocal interaction within the small group, the blind inmates manage to escape their dehumanised condition in quarantine. It is not as isolated individuals but as a symbiotic collective that the white-blind are able to reclaim their humanity and escape the asylum.

Saramago's apocalyptic world-endism, which splits history into a 'before' and a post- collapse 'hereafter', imposes a radical break that wipes the slate clean and highlights the intrinsic creativity of world-making. What better way to illustrate this than to picture blinded selves stranded on the ruins of their old world? Cut off from their familiar sighted lifeworld, the newly white-blind are reborn as new cognitive agents who must embark on an entirely new process of ontogeny, or life process from birth to death, by coming to grips with the world and coexisting with others. Everything, from daily routines to identity and society, has to be recreated. Their fitful progress reveals that world is brought forth through the interaction between newly sightless humans and their environment. Neither this new world nor its blind cognitive agents pre-exist the apocalypse. As the doctor's wife, Saramago's central protagonist, explains: 'And how can a society of blind people organise itself in order to survive. By organising itself, to organise oneself is, in a way, to begin to have eyes' (*Blindness* 296). As the final section will explore, Saramago's novel depicts the development of a society of the blind as a form of collective ontogeny.

Humberto Maturana and Francisco Varela's Autopoietic Theory and Enactivism

To recapitulate: the core insight of the Santiago theory is that all knowing is doing: knowledge or – to use the scientific term – cognition is a mode in which organisms bring forth a world. It entails not 'processing information, but specifying what counts as relevant' (*Tree of Knowledge* 253). As Fritjof Capra observes, the 'Santiago theory provides ... the first coherent scientific framework that really overcomes the Cartesian split. Mind and matter no longer appear to belong to two separate categories but are seen as representing merely different aspects, or dimensions, of the same phenomenon of life' (175). This means, first, that cognition is not an objective representation of an external reality, but neither is it a solipsistic projection of an inner one. Maturana and Varela reject both scientific representationalism and its polar opposite, the romantic and postmodern paradigm of solipsism. As they explain in *The Tree of Knowledge*, this 'is like walking on the razor's edge' between two extremes (133), which they describe as an 'epistemological Odyssey, sailing between the Scylla monster of representationism and the Charybdis whirlpool of solipsism' (253).

This section engages the core ideas of autopoiesis and enactivism, while appreciating differences between Maturana and Varela's earlier formulation and Varela et al.'s subsequent development. Autopoeisis and enactivism overlap substantially. Indeed, enactivism presupposes many of the core concepts and premises first developed in the context of autopoietic theory: the complementary categories of organisation vs. structure, structural coupling, drift, non-representationalism, cognition as interdependent or networked making, and most importantly, prioritising living organisms over non-living cognitive systems (such as computers). The following discussion will develop these ideas in the context of autopoiesis, and shift to enactivism at the end to cover where it departs from it. In *The Tree of Knowledge*, Maturana and Varela mark their differences through the device of boxed commentaries that are separated from the main text. Little cartoon figures that resemble Varela and Maturana are inserted into the margins of these boxes and serve to identify the voice that authorises the text (a few of the boxes are co-authored like the main text).

Maturana and Varela define 'autopoiesis' as the formal organisation common to all organisms, or living systems. Autopoiesis is a subset of self-organisation theory, a larger phenomenon which in turn is a subset of complexity theory, the new twentieth-century science of open or 'dissipative' systems, operating far from equilibrium. Nobel Laureate Ilya Prigogine's research on dissipative structures showed that they are able to create 'order out of chaos', thus negating both Newtonian mechanics as well as nineteenth-century thermodynamics (the law of entropy). In classical thermodynamics, the dissipation of energy is associated with waste. Prigogine's concept of dissipative structure showed that 'in open systems dissipation becomes a source of order' (Capra 89). This idea of the spontaneous emergence of organisation – self-organisation – is also the core of Maturana and Varela's theory of autopoiesis as the theory of the 'organization of the living'. As Maturana and Varela state, 'Living beings are characterized in that, literally, they are continually self-producing. We indicate this process when we call the organization that defines them an *autopoietic organization*' (*Tree of Knowledge* 43). Among the several implications of this claim, the most important is autonomy, by which they mean that living systems are products of their own organisation. The autopoietic process is endogenous, which is to to say that it is 'directed by the internal rules of the system' (Capra and Luisi 145). External influences may disturb it, but they cannot control it. Autopoietic development includes the 'creation of a boundary that specifies the domain of the networks' operations and defines the system as a unit' (Capra 98–9). Maturana and Varela define organisms as '*autonomous* unities' (*Tree of Knowledge* 47), by which they mean that they are self-bounded, self-generating and self-maintaining (see Capra 208).

The simplest example of an autopoietic unit is the living cell. As Maturana and Varela explain, 'the molecular components of a cellular autopoietic unity must be dynamically related in a network of ongoing interactions', biochemically known as 'cell metabolism' (*Tree of Knowledge* 46). In a cell, metabolism functions only because there is a boundary, the membrane that distinguishes the cell from its environment and defines it as an autonomous unit. But this boundary does not pre-exist the organism; it is itself the product of the dynamics of the cell's metabolism. Here we confront a biochemical example of the circularity and reciprocity that defines the living. As Maturana and Varela maintain, 'these are not sequential processes'; it is not that 'first there is a boundary, then a dynamics, then a boundary, and so forth' (46). The cell (the organism as a bounded entity), its organisation (the dynamics of metabolic exchange) and its environment all emerge at the same time. 'The most striking feature of an autopoietic system is that it pulls itself up by its own bootstraps and becomes distinct from its environment through its own dynamics, in such a way that both things are inseparable' (46–7). Maturana and Varela identify this unique type of organisation – autopoietic organisation – as the definition of the living: its crucial feature is that each component helps produce and transform the other components while 'maintaining the overall circularity of the network' (Capra 96). Hence the emphasis falls not on isolated parts (membranes or cellular components such as the nucleus or mitochondria) but on the processes and relations between them. It is the total set of relations and dynamics that matter and that constitute the organisation through which the organism continually 'makes itself'. Autopoiesis illustrates the notion of the emergence of irreducible wholes: the organism as a whole is more than the sum of its parts.

Maturana and Varela make an important distinction between organisation, an abstract pattern, and structure, its material embodiment: '*Organization* denotes those relations that must exist among the components of a system for it to be a member of a specific class. *Structure* denotes the components and relations that actually constitute a particular unity and make its organization real' (*Tree of Knowledge* 47). In other words, organisation identifies a particular class or type of system: '"Organization" signifies those relations that must be present in order for something to exist' (42). It refers to the inventory of the parts and their basic relations that need to be present for a system to belong to a particular class. Organisational or operational closure is a key trait of autopoietic systems that defines them as autonomous unities, but so is their 'openness'. Living systems are both structurally open (dependent on a continual exchange of matter and energy with the environment) as well as organisationally closed (and thus autonomous). As Ira Livingston observes, autopoietic systems seem to work out a simple compromise between closure and openness in a 'semipermeable membrane' (83). Cells, for example, are open in that they continually exchange energy and matter with their environment, even as they are enclosed by their membranes. This is true for all organisms, including humans: they consume food, whether this be oxygen for animals or CO_2 for plants, and they excrete waste. At the same time, they achieve homeostasis, a self-regulating mechanism that allows organisms to maintain themselves in a state of dynamic equilibrium, for example in sustaining a stable body temperature against variations in environmental conditions.

To illustrate the distinction between organisation and structure, Maturana and Varela offer the example of a toilet: a toilet organisation is defined as the abstract configuration of parts and their relationships (a system of regulation for water inflow and outflow, and so on); if these are present, the system belongs to the 'toilet' class. Organisation is non-material: it is a pattern, a form, a configuration of elements. To describe a system's organisation is to map its logic. Unlike material structure, organisation is something that cannot be counted, weighed or measured. It is this recognition of the essential role played by non-material entities that makes the Santiago theory a key player among the new ontologies after postmodernism: though flourishing a decade or more earlier, like Latour and Gabriel it rejects naturalist reductionism. For the new realist stance advocated here, non-material structures form essential parts of reality. To shift from the problem of structure to the problem of organisation, as Capra and Luisi like to point out, is to ask a new kind of question: not 'What is it made of?' but 'What is its pattern?' (see Capra and Luisi 4). It is to move from mechanistic thinking to systems thinking. To consider the example just mentioned, a toilet can be built in different ways (from plastic or ceramics) and it would still be a toilet (Maturana and Varela, *Tree of Knowledge* 47).

What distinguishes living systems such as cells from non-living systems such as toilets is that non-living systems are entities with fixed components and organisation (Capra 159). Non-living systems have been designed by an external agent: this is what simple systems such as toilets have in common with sophisticated machines such as computers. Their organisation does not develop autonomously. But there are boundary cases. To clarify the difference, Capra offers the example of the vortex funnel as a non-living system that is also dissipative (Capra 169). 'Although the structure of a living system is always a dissipative structure, not all dissipative structures are autopoietic networks' (161). Vortices occur in hurricanes as well as in bathtubs when water is drained. They are self-organising but extremely unstable 'open systems' – systems that exchange energy flow with their environments – where the dissipation of energy creates a higher-order class of system through amplification processes of positive feedback loops. Like organisms, vortices are self-generating, which is to say that they spring up spontaneously from the network of interactions of forces that include (in hurricanes) rising ocean temperatures, updrafts of warm air and wind. But in contrast to organisms, they are not self-maintaining: when the water runs out or when the hurricane hits land or the temperature drops, the vortex funnel disappears. Only living systems are autopoietic in that they are able to maintain their organisation over time and through critical instabilities.

Organisational or operational closure is perhaps the single trait of autopoietic systems that has drawn most critical attention. However, it is easily misunderstood if viewed in isolation from autopoiesis's other characteristics and taken to be synonymous with autopoiesis as such. Thus, in her otherwise illuminating discussion of Maturana and Varela, Katherine Hayles glosses the term 'organizational closure' to mean that 'living systems operate within the boundaries of an organization that closes in on itself and leaves the world on the outside' (Hayles 136). In linking operational closure to an inside/outside dichotomy, Hayles misconstrues Maturana and Varela's theory. In fact, autopoietic theory posits a reciprocal relation between organism and environment, never a dichotomous one. Hayles further equates Maturana and Varela's term with another concept that they emphatically oppose: the liberal tradition and the 'reconfigur[ation] of the liberal humanist subject' (140). In Hayles's view,

> the foundational ground for establishing the subject's autonomy and
> individuality has shifted from self-possession, with all of its implica-

tions for the imbrication of the liberal subject with industrial capitalism. Instead, these privileged attributes are based on organisational closure (the system closes on itself, by itself) or on the reflexivity of a system recursively operating on its own representations (the observer's distinctions close the system). Closure and recursivity, then, play the foundational role in autopoietic theory that self-possession played in classical liberal theory. (146)

Hayles misconstrues autopoietic theory as a refurbished version of liberal humanism. On the contrary, autopoietic theory reconstitutes humanism as biocentric and ecological humanism beyond the liberal and anthropocentric paradigm. For Maturana and Varela, there is no autonomy without *inter*dependence. There is no operational closure without structural openness. Liberal subjects have unconditional autonomy. In contrast, the autonomy of autopoietic systems is dynamic and conditional: first, they originate by way of a reciprocal co-constitution with their environments. Secondly, the survival of autopoietic unities depends on maintaining reciprocal interactions with what is outside their boundaries. If these exchanges lapse, organisms break down and die. 'Organizational closure' may be an unfortunate choice of term on Maturana and Varela's part. Its actual meaning is 'organizational stability' in the sense of an inventory of a class of systems' constituent parts in their basic relations.

The key point is that autopoietic autonomy is premised on reciprocity. Structural openness complements operational autonomy in the living system's paradoxical make-up: the organism is thus 'not cut off from its environment' (Mugerauer, 'Maturana and Varela' 160). As Maturana and Varela contend in the passage quoted above, an organism 'becomes distinct from its environment . . . in such a way that both things are *inseparable*' (*Tree of Knowledge* 46–7; my emphasis). In the terminology of the Santiago school, organisms are 'structurally coupled' to their environment. The notion of structural coupling expresses an ongoing relation of mutual exchanges. According to Maturana and Varela, '[w]e speak of structural coupling whenever there is a history of recurrent interactions leading to the structural congruence between two (or more) systems' (75). To stay alive, cells, for example, maintain continuous biochemical interactions and exchanges with the media in which they exist. But structural coupling also exists between two autopoietic unities, such as two cells, or two organs, or two organisms. This can result in symbiosis, or in the transformation of unicellular into multicellular organisms.

Having outlined key constituents, we now turn to the historical aspect of autopoiesis and enactivism. Organisms go through a life process from birth to death. History, development and growth play a role, whether this is a matter of days as in the case of some insects, months, years, decades as in humans, or centuries, as in the case of sequoia trees (*Tree of Knowledge* 85). The developmental life process of an individual organism is known as ontogeny, as distinct from phylogeny, the evolutionary history of the species to which it belongs. Maturana and Varela define ontogeny as 'the history of structural change in a unity without loss of organization in that unity' (74). For example, organisms continually replace their cells during their lifetimes, and cells continually replace their components, such as mitochondria, cell fluid and so on. In living systems, the structure and its physical components change ceaselessly even as the system preserves its abstract organisation, such that it continues to be recognisable as a cat, a wolf, a frog or a human. Ontogeny thus adds a third dimension to the complementary relation between abstract organisation and physical structure: in addition to closure (organisation) vs. openness (structure), there is also historical continuity (organisation) vs. historical change (structure).

A feature of both autopoiesis and enactivism, the mutuality of structural coupling entails yet another point. The structural congruence that exists between unities that are structurally coupled – whether this be an organism and its environment, or two or more organisms – further implies that the ontogenic changes that they undergo over time will also be coordinated. Reciprocity of structural coupling involves not only co-constitution, but also mutual transformation and development – such as co-ontogenies in structurally coupled organisms. For instance, 'all the ontogenies of the different members of an ant colony are bound together in a co-ontogenic structural drift' (*Tree of Knowledge* 186). According to Maturana and Varela, structural coupling is 'always mutual; both organism and environment undergo transformations' (102). As they explain, 'the ontogenic structural change of a living being in an environment always occurs as a structural drift congruent with the structural drift of the environment' (103).

'Drift' is the concept that Maturana and Varela propose to express historical change in ontogeny (individual development, or 'structural drift') as well as on the larger scale of phylogeny (evolution, or 'natural drift'). Like Darwin's term 'natural selection', 'natural drift' repudiates creationism. There is no higher plan or design controlling the changes that individual organisms undergo in their ontogenic transformations and that their species have travelled in the phylogenic history of their lineages over many generations. Like Richard Lewontin, Maturana and Varela deem the notion of the 'unfolding' of an 'inner program' or 'fixed essence' that these terms imply problematic (Lewontin 6, 10). As they maintain,

> evolution is a *natural* drift, a product of the conservation of autopoiesis and adaptation . . . There is no need for an outside guiding force . . . to explain the directionality of the variations in a lineage, nor is it the case that some specific quality of living beings is being optimized. Evolution is somewhat like a sculptor with wanderlust: he goes through the world collecting a thread here, a hunk of tin there, a piece of wood here, and he combines them in a way that their structure and circumstances allow . . . With no law other than the conservation of an identity and the capacity to reproduce, we have all emerged. (*Tree of Knowledge* 117)

Unlike 'evolution', 'natural drift' overtly expresses the non-teleological nature of this process, which lacks a pre-established goal or external guiding force. I dwell on this point because the idea of self-organising drift describes a key feature of the development of the white-blind in Saramago's novel.

In taking this view, Maturana and Varela substantially concur with evolutionary biologists Lewontin and Levins's critique of neo-Darwinism and related popular myths about evolution. In the phenomenon of evolution there is 'no progress or optimization of the use of the environment, but only conservation of adaptation and autopoiesis' (*Tree of Knowledge* 115). Evolution is not the 'survival of the fittest', nor does it amount to organisms finding an 'ecological niche' for themselves. Rather than an unilateral activity on the part of the organism, evolution is the co-evolution of organisms and environments that are coordinated via structural coupling. On Maturana and Varela's account, organisms and environments are embarked on a journey of co-drifting. This journey began at the origin of life on earth about 3.5 million years ago with the emergence of the first micro-organisms, and will not end until the solar apocalypse terminates the history of our entire solar system and extinguishes all life on earth in about three billion years (see *Tree of Knowledge* 34–9). As Lewontin affirms, ecological niches 'do not preexist organisms but come into existence as a consequence of the nature of the organisms themselves' (Lewontin 51). For Lewontin, the misleading metaphor of adaptation to pre-existing conditions is best replaced with that of construction: 'the actual process of evolution seems best captured by the process of *construction*' (48). Lewontin's concept of performative construction is congruent with the emphasis that autopoietic theory places on the mutual 'bringing forth' of cognitive agents and their worlds.

That said, autopoiesis is really a theory of ontogeny, or the history of organisms, rather than of evolution, or the history of species. Maturana and Varela's central concern is the homeostatic self-making and self-perpetuating of the living system within the reciprocity of its structural coupling. Nonetheless, natural drift (evolution) expresses a historical perspective that is also essential to ontogeny, but easily overlooked there because the life process involved is relatively short. Coupling is not a fixed structure, but a reciprocal dynamic. Its essence is recurrent interactions: if these interchanges lapse, coupling disappears. Conversely, at a higher ('third-order') social level, structural coupling among 'co-drifting organisms give[s] rise to a *new phenomenological* domain, which may become particularly complex when there is a nervous system' (*Tree of Knowledge* 180–1). As we shall see, the ideas of co-drifting organisms and collective ontogeny express crucial features of the emergence of a society of the blind in Saramago's novel. In *Blindness*, reciprocal interaction among a self-organising group leads to coordinated ontogenic drift of the group as a whole.

Maturana and Varela classify cells as first-order autopoietic systems. Composites of cells form metacellular organisms (plants, animals and humans), which are referred to as second-order autopoietic systems (*Tree of Knowledge* 87). Maturana and Varela cite the work of the microbiologist Lynn Margulis on the origin of metacellulars as composites of single-cell organisms (see *Tree of Knowledge* 87–8). Margulis has contributed an important insight into how the macrocosm, the world of visible higher life forms, emerged from the microcosm, the world of micro-organisms.[2] Margulis's theory, known as symbiogenesis, states that the evolution of higher life forms emerged through the symbiosis of previously independent organisms. The idea of symbiosis refers to a key problematic that also structures the post-apocalyptic developments in *Blindness*. It therefore warrants a closer look.

Like Margulis's work, Saramago's novel calls for a revisionary assessment of what Maturana and Varela call the 'natural drift' of living systems: What is the logic of evolution? Is it bloody competition, or is it symbiotic cooperation? And do these have to be mutually exclusive? Margulis discovered that the components that are found inside nucleated cells ('eukaryotes'), such as mitochondria, including the cell nucleus itself, originally constituted independent organisms, other microbes (Margulis and Sagan, *Microcosmos* 31). These bacteria were ingested but processed incompletely, and eventually came to take up residence inside the host. In this way, nucleated cells evolved out of the fusion of non-nucleated cells ('prokaryotes'). In the terminology of autopoiesis, non-nucleated cells evolved into composite unities of nucleated cells through structural coupling, by establishing a relationship of cooperation and interdependence. Margulis's notion of symbiogenesis undermines the popular myth of evolution as raw competition: nature is 'red in tooth and claw', with the alternatives of eating or being eaten. According to Margulis, this view of evolution as 'chronic bloody competition' completely misses the cooperative and symbiotic side of natural life: 'Life did not take over the globe by combat, but by networking. Life forms multiplied and complexified by co-opting others, not just by killing them' (Margulis and Sagan, *Microcosmos* 29). Moreover, microbes are also interesting for their pharmacological relationship to their metacellular hosts. As Margulis affirms, all life today remains 'embedded in a self-organizing web of bacteria' (Capra 216). From soil cultures to the digestive organs of higher organisms, bacteria populate the contemporary macrocosm in symbiotic relationships without which the latter could not survive. On the other hand, the entry of some microbes into our bodies may cause fatal disease.

To continue the parallel with Saramago, white-blindness is shown to be hyper- contagious, spreading through personal contact like an infection against which there is no immunity. Defying naturalist explanation, Saramago's fabricated plague of white-blindness posits a scenario reminiscent of the beginning of life on earth: How will the newly sightless survive? By reverting back to the Hobbesian 'state of nature' as war? Or by cooperation? *Blindness* pictures both alternatives: the former in the criminal gang of blind hoodlums who take control of the asylum, and the latter in the Ward One collective. The natural-cultural world is not deterministic, but unpredictable. Looking across the disciplinary fence between literature and science, *Blindness* thus joins the gathering chorus of non-reductivist biologists including Maturana and Varela, Margulis, and Levins and Lewontin, who critique the neo-Darwinist reductivism of modern biology. As Brian Goodwin, a Goethean biologist, writes,

> Darwinism sees the living process in terms that emphasize competition, inheritance, selfishness, and survival as the driving forces of evolution . . . But Darwinism shortchanges our biological natures. We are every bit as cooperative as we are competitive; as altruistic as we are selfish; as creative and playful as we are destructive and repetitive. (Goodwin xvi–xvii)

Goodwin's focus on morphogenesis is closely aligned with Maturana and Varela's interest in ontogeny.

The question of cooperation vs. competition brings us to the largest and most complex self-organising unities discussed by Maturana and Varela – societies, groups and collectives. These assemblages of macrocosmic organisms are termed third-order systems. It makes no categorical difference whether the populations in question happen to be ant colonies or beehives, animal societies such as herds of antelope or baboons, or human societies. All these are 'third-order systems' insofar as they are aggregates of individual organisms. Autopoietic theory is genuinely posthumanist and biocentric in proposing a theory that accommodates humans together with non-humans within a shared taxonomy. Like Latour, Maturana and Varela eliminate anthropocentrism by refusing to elevate humans into a segregated domain above the 'lower' forms of life. But the Santiago theory has a different emphasis: unlike Latour, it focuses exclusively on living organisms, and they define life's essence as non-autonomous creativity (creativity that arises from interdependence), the capacity of organisms to make and maintain themselves through a system of coordinated exchanges with their outsides. This is not creativity according to the romantic individualist paradigm, but post-individual creativity.

What kind of structural coupling binds social collectives ('third-order unities') together? *Blindness* pictures the new social order emerging in the city of the white-blind in a memorable comparison to ant colonies:

They did not find their way around, they kept very close to the buildings with their arms stretched out before them, they were constantly
bumping into each other like ants on the trail, but when this happened
no one protested, nor did they have to say anything, one of the families
moved away from the wall, advanced along the wall opposite in the
other direction, and thus they proceeded and carried on until the next
encounter. (*Blindness* 225–6)

Saramago's analogy between ants and the white-blind invites a
closer look through the lens of autopoietic theory. According to
Maturana and Varela, an important differentiation needs to be
made between colonies of social insects (ants, termites, bees and
wasps), herds of vertebrates and human groups with regard to the
'*mechanism* of structural coupling' (*Tree of Knowledge* 186) that
assembles these collectives.

So-called social insects are bound together by a 'continuous
chemical flow, called *trophallaxis*' (*Tree of Knowledge* 186).
Therefore, they only have 'chemical coupling' (186). In contrast,
social vertebrates and primates have 'social coupling'. Herds of
antelope or packs of wolves coordinate their behaviour through
reciprocal communication (gestural and vocal) such that each
individual is 'continually adjusting its position in the network
of interactions that forms the group' (192). Some vertebrate and
primate behaviour is innate (phylogenic), some is learned (ontogenic); the more sophisticated the nervous system, the more flexible the organism becomes as a learning system. Capra rehearses
the popular saying that kicking a stone is different from kicking a
dog: whereas 'the stone will *react* to the kick according to a linear
chain of cause and effect', 'the dog will *respond*' according to its
species-specific pattern of organisation (Capra 219). As autopoietic systems with a rudimentary nervous system, ants fall on the
same side of the balance sheet as dogs, although their learning is
much more limited.[3] Because vertebrates possess the faculty of
imitation, behaviours learned by individual animals also become
shared collective behaviours. The result is the appearance of the
phenomenon of collective ontogenies: 'the individual ontogenies of
all the participating organisms occur fundamentally as part of the
network of co-ontogenies' (*Tree of Knowledge* 193). In substance,
therefore, Saramago's analogy between ants and the white-blind is
misleading. Its value instead lies in picturing the apocalyptic threat
of dehumanisation that the white-blind are facing. As such, it also

provides a measure of their triumph as they succeed in remaking a livable world.

In discussing social coupling in third-order societies, Maturana and Varela make an important point about communication that nicely illustrates the non-representationalism of autopoietic theory. They contend that 'biologically, there is no "transmitted information" in communication. Communication takes place each time there is behavioral coordination in the realm of structural coupling' (*Tree of Knowledge* 196). The purpose of communication is social rather than referential. It serves not to hold the mirror up to nature, but to forge and cement unity among the organisms that are members of a group. As Maturana and Varela affirm, the 'metaphor of the tube' for communication is a false one: communication 'depends on not what is transmitted, but on what happens to the person who receives it' (196). It is a tool of social reciprocity. It is not about stating objective facts; it is about 'the right things to say', as it were, 'to make friends'. In short, communication is about making (social) worlds. It belongs to the domain of ontology. The following section on Saramago will explore how 'social coupling' characterises the linguistic and non-verbal communication among the quarantined blind internees in *Blindness*.

Maturana and Varela argue that unlike first- and second-order autopoietic systems, third-order 'social' systems, including animal and human societies, are not autopoietic in the sense of this higher unit's ability to make and maintain itself as a unit (*Tree of Knowledge* 88–9; see Capra 212). Organisms and societies are aggregates that differ greatly with regard to the autonomy of their components. The cellular components in organisms possess a minimum of autonomy. In contrast, as aggregates of human individuals, human societies have a maximum degree of autonomy. Social insects and animal societies are located at various points in between. On Maturana and Varela's view, in human systems, the whole system exists for the parts; in organisms, the parts exist for the whole: the 'organism restricts the individual creativity of its component unities . . . The human social system amplifies the individual creativity of its components, as that system exists for these components' (*Tree of Knowledge* 199). Hence societies are not super-organisms: societies that view themselves as such are totalitarian. Maturana and Varela's example is 'Sparta', which they locate in the vicinity of social insects – a coded reference to Pinochet's Chile, the totalitarian regime under whose rule

Maturana struggled to continue his work at the University of Chile, and which prompted Varela's departure for the US and later France in 1973.[4] If autopoietic theory here reveals any 'liberal' tendencies in defending democracy against authoritarianism, this same sentiment also appears in Saramago.

Blindness pits the authoritarianism of biopolitical power which quarantines the infectious blind against the democratising forces of blind self-organisation. For related reasons, Maturana has strongly objected to Niklas Luhmann's application of autopoiesis to social systems (Capra 212). According to Luhmann, abstract systems, such as law, economy, religion, art and so on, have a self-referentiality that justifies the extension of Maturana and Varela's concept of autopoiesis beyond the realm of the living, and to consider social systems under the label 'social autopoiesis'. Luhmann claims that communication in abstract social systems functions like an autopoietic network: 'Social systems use communication as their particular mode of autopoietic reproduction. Their elements are communications that are recursively produced and reproduced by a network of communications and that cannot exist outside of such a network' ('Social Systems' 3). Maturana objects that Luhmann's decision to 'place communications at the center ... excludes the human beings actually communicating' (Maturana and Poerksen 107). To speak of the autopoiesis of communication as does Luhmann is to attribute traits that are exclusive to life – the capacity for self-maintenance – to non-living social systems. Autopoietic theory describes biological life from the microscopic to the visible macroscopic forms. The large social systems created by certain organisms (humans) fall outside its scope. Unlike the actants of actor-network theory, for example, who need be neither human nor living beings, autopoietic agents must be biological. Maturana's (and, to a lesser extent, Varela's) disagreement with Luhmann's social autopoiesis is illuminating because it reveals what they are really interested in: small groups interlinked by traceable interactions – an orientation that they, not coincidentally, share with post-apocalyptic fiction.[5]

Autopoietic theory is a theory of ontogeny as reciprocal creation that, as we have seen, crucially incorporates collective ontogenies of co-drifting organisms. Significantly, however, these third-order 'social' systems are defined as small collectives. Their size or scale is limited to reciprocal structural coupling by way of face-to-face relationships of personal contact. Maturana and Varela make clear that there has to be reciprocity and that it has to be continuous without lapsing: 'any particular organism is a member of a social unity only as long as it forms part of that reciprocal social coupling' (*Tree of Knowledge* 193). In sheer numbers, they could range up to one or two hundred individuals, but not much more – a scale that encompasses animal herds. Indeed, it is precisely the small scale of face-to-face contact that affords the creativity of 'bringing forth' – enacting, in Varela et al.'s terms – worlds and minds.

Maturana and Varela's lack of interest in large and anonymous social systems – in contrast to Luhmann – is a perfect match for the parallel orientation of post-apocalyptic fiction. The sentiment of small is beautiful – or 'neotribal visions' (Irr 171) – inspires the formation of new sustainable groups everywhere in contemporary post-apocalyptic fiction. Among the novels considered here, Atwood's posthuman collective of Crakers, humans and Pigoons, Butler's Earthseed collective, McCarthy's father–son dyad and Saramago's blind collective in Ward One all fit this category. In Saramago, the amputation of vision restricts the range of social coupling to individuals within earshot. Traversing the city, the doctor's wife and her group

> crossed a square where groups of blind people entertained themselves by listening to speeches from other blind people, at first sight neither group seemed to be blind, the speakers turned their heads excitedly towards the listeners and the listeners turned their heads attentively to the speakers. They were extolling the virtues of the fundamental principles of the great organised systems, private property, a free currency market, the market economy, the stock exchange, taxation, interest, expropriation and appropriation, production, distribution, consumption, supply and demand, poverty and wealth, communication, repression and delinquency, lotteries, prisons, the penal code, the civil code, the highway code, dictionaries, the telephone directory. (*Blindness* 310–11)

In Saramago's city of the white-blind, survivors discuss the modern social systems that have been destroyed by the apocalyptic plague. That they do so in scattered in-person gatherings underscores the difference.

As the passage just quoted shows, language – more precisely, the spoken word – is of special importance to white-blind world-making. It is only in human societies that the structural coupling that generates third-order collectives is 'linguistic coupling' because it is enacted through language. As the next section will show, linguistic coupling takes us into the heart of the social dynamics of post-apocalyptic self-organisation in *Blindness*. Like animal communication, language is also social action, except that in humans, social bonding is effected by the 'linguistic coordination of actions' (*Tree of Knowledge* 209).[6] For Maturana and Varela, 'Essential to a linguistic domain is the co-ontogenic structural drift that occurs as the members of a social system live together' (209). In other words, human social systems result from the co-ontogenies forged by linguistic coupling.

Maturana and Varela defend the view that 'language is a condition *sine qua non* for the experience of what we call mind' (231). Affirming the anti-naturalist and humanistic bent of autopoiesis, they contend that 'the mind is not something that is within my brain. Consciousness and mind belong to the realm of social coupling' (234). Robinson Crusoe is offered as an illuminating example: by keeping a calendar, reading the Bible every evening and dressing for dinner, Robinson Crusoe preserved his social coupling with English society, 'where he had his human identity' (234). Maturana and Varela affirm that 'it is in language that the self, the *I*, arises' (231). This is a loaded claim, which is easily misconstrued if the emphasis is misplaced. For one, emphasis is on the process of arising rather than on the 'I' as a fixed substance, which Varela, a practising Buddhist, thinks is an illusion, and which both autopoietic theory and enactivism claim does not exist until it is 'brought forth' in the act of knowing.

The claim that self arises in language seems to echo poststructuralist claims of the Lacanian and Derridean variety. But the analogy is misleading. In fact, it means just the opposite. Here again, close attention needs to be paid to emphasis. Language, as Saussure showed, has two aspects, *langue* (language as abstract system of differential meanings) and *parole* (language as performance: speech). Bypassing speech in the wake of Saussure, structuralism theorised language as abstract structure. In contrast, and paralleling their concern with language's dimension as performative social coupling rather than abstract system, Maturana and Varela similarly view language as (social) performance, as reciprocal speech. This is clarified in the passage that follows the statement just quoted:

> it is in language that the self, the *I*, arises as the social singularity
> defined by the operational intersection in the human body of the recur-
> sive linguistic distinctions in which it is distinguished. This tells us that
> in the network of linguistic interactions in which we move, *we main-
> tain an ongoing descriptive recursion which we call the 'I.' It enables
> us to conserve our linguistic operational coherence and our adaptation
> in the domain of language.* (Tree of Knowledge 231)

This is a vital point. It warrants quoting the concluding paragraph of *The Tree of Knowledge* that summarises Maturana and
Varela's views on language:

> We humans, as humans, exist in the network of structural couplings
> that we continually weave through the permanent linguistic trophal-
> laxis of our behavior. Language was never invented by anyone only
> to take in an outside world. Therefore, it cannot be used as a tool to
> reveal that world. Rather, it is by languaging that the act of knowing,
> in the behavioral coordination which is language, brings forth a world.
> We work out our lives in a mutual linguistic coupling, not because
> language permits us to reveal ourselves but because we are constituted
> in language in a continuous becoming that we bring forth with others.
> We find ourselves in this co-ontogenic coupling, not as a preexisting
> reference nor in reference to an origin, but as an ongoing transforma-
> tion in the becoming of the linguistic world that we build with other
> human beings. (234–5)

In short, Maturana and Varela are language realists rather than
sceptical constructionists: language is world-making. Language is
enactive (actively bringing forth world).

For the Santiago school, language therefore belongs in the framework of ontology. The alienation of thought and language from
being is usually assumed to be at the root of modern philosophy
and modern theories of language, leading to methodological scepticism and concerns with epistemological conditions of access to
reality (see Gabriel, *Transcendental Ontology* vii). As the passages
above demonstrate, Maturana and Varela dispute the quintessential modern alienation of mind and language from world. Language
does not separate us from reality, it is rather the link that couples
us to the world and to others, and that we use to build habitable
worlds, make identities and form collectives. The threat of idealism so eloquently summoned by Meillassoux is beside the point.

Our social world is a world made of words: marriage, citizenship, money, or private property are objective realities created by speech acts. As John Searle has shown, language – such as declarations of war, criminal sentencing, oaths of office, baptisms or naturalisation ceremonies – plays a pivotal role in the creation and maintenance of human social institutions. For Searle, the above are acts of collective intentionality that open up a new realm of instituted social reality. This domain is objective (think about citizenship status), although it is not material like rocks or earthquakes. It is the realm of factishes (Latour). Maturana and Varela's enactive approach to language makes a similar point, though without, as noted above, undertaking an analysis of social systems.

Earlier in *The Tree of Knowledge*, Maturana and Varela challenge representationalism in a somewhat different context that is no less important than the idea of communication and language as enaction. This is their trenchant critique of the information-processing paradigm as a model for the human brain, which became dominant after the rise of cybernetics.

> [T]he nervous system does not 'pick up information' from the environment, as we often hear. On the contrary, it brings forth a world by specifying what patterns of the environment are perturbations and what changes trigger them in the organism. The popular metaphor of calling the brain an 'information-processing device' is not only ambiguous but patently wrong. (*Tree of Knowledge* 169)

According to Capra, '[s]ince the 1940s almost all of neurobiology has been shaped by this idea that the brain is an information-processing device' (Capra 265). Known as 'cognitivism', cognitive science using the computer analogy of mind is guided by 'the hypothesis that cognition – human cognition included – is the manipulation of symbols after the fashion of digital computers' (Varela el al., *Embodied Mind* 8). In a passage that merits quoting at length, Varela el al. summarise their objections:

> Instead of *representing* an independent world, [cognitive systems] *enact* a world as a domain of distinctions that is inseparable from the structure embodied by the cognitive system ... [W]e must call into question the idea that the world is pregiven and that cognition is representation. In cognitive science, this means that we must call into question that idea that information exists ready-made in the world and

that it is extracted by a cognitive system, as the cognitivist notion of an *informavore* vividly implies. (*Embodied Mind* 139–40)

In repudiating the informational paradigm of the mind, Maturana and Varela also part ways with the intellectual tradition from which they emerged – first-generation cybernetics.

Given its rejection of the 'programming' paradigm for the brain, the Santiago theory is also an excellent match for Atwood's *MaddAddam* trilogy. As a result of the apocalyptic rhetoric of world-endism and the post-apocalyptic script of a new tomorrow after the world-end, post-apocalyptic plots tend to describe their survivor-protagonists undergoing a rebirth of sorts. Shipwrecked on the ruins of their former world, they must remake their lives and their worlds from scratch. As we saw in the last chapter, Jimmy's renaming himself 'Snowman' articulates his awareness of having to embark on a new life process, a new ontogeny. The *MaddAddam* trilogy forcefully contrasts ontogenic self- and world-making with genetic determinism. Crake believes that he has 'stored' a genetic code in the Crakers' DNA that will control the development of the living organism like a computer program reading off data. But the Crakers prove this assumption false. As Lewontin and Levins maintain in an essay entitled 'Are We Programmed?', unlike computers, 'brains generate spontaneous activity' (Lewontin and Levins 56). Far from being machines, the Crakers turn out to be unpredictable creatures whose development follows the principle of structural drift. When they elaborate a mythology of their origins, the Crakers illustrate the autopoietic autonomy of living organisms. In the previous chapter, we explored this process through Latour's concept of the factish. But Maturana and Varela's notion of autopoietic ontogeny would have served equally well. Altogether, this illustrates the substantial compatibility between the theories that this study considers under the label of new ecological realisms after poststructuralism.

In *The Embodied Mind*, Varela el al. trace the genesis of the enactivist paradigm of non-representational cognition from within the heart of what was originally an informational model of mind (6). Enactivism offers a new response to the question, 'What is cognition?':

Enaction: A history of structural coupling that brings forth a world [and that works] through a network consisting of multiple levels of interconnected, sensorimotor subnetworks. (206)

As stated earlier, more than autopoiesis, whose basic tenets it shares, enactivism stresses the open-endedness of the interactions between organism and environment in the reciprocal process of 'bringing forth' minds and worlds.

We conclude this outline of the Santiago theory with a discussion of vision, a concern that Maturana and Varela share with Saramago's *Blindness*. The visual system, one of the best-researched areas of the brain (*Embodied Mind* 96), offers excellent support for the claims of autopoiesis and enactivism. In the physiology of vision, the stimuli sent by the retina do not directly reach the visual cortex, but must pass through an intermediary, the 'so-called lateral geniculate nucleus (LGN)', which is located in the thalamus (*Tree of Knowledge* 162; *Embodied Mind* 95). The thalamus is the major relay station in the brain for sensory information. Thus the LGN does not just receive retinal projections, but actually functions as a junction where signals from many parts of the body converge, of which retinal ones make up only 20 per cent.

> As is clear, the retina does not affect the brain like a telephone line that encounters a relay station at the LGN, since more than 80% of the interconnections come together at the LGN at the same time. Consequently, the retina can modulate – but not specify – the state of the neurons in the geniculate nucleus, whose state will be given by all the connections it receives from many different parts of the brain. (*Tree of Knowledge* 162; see also *Embodied Mind* 95)

Furthermore, some of the 'data' coming together at the LGN is generated internally rather than received externally like visual data, such as 'data' from the hypothalamus, which 'regulates primal drives such as hunger or sex' (Hanson 55). Maturana and Varela use the analogy of a 'hectic family discussion' at the dinner table to illustrate the chaotic convergence of sensory signals in the LGN, of which retinal stimuli constitute only one voice. Unlike computers, part of what the brain of a living observer 'sees' is the result of 'interferences' from internal perturbations, for example sexual arousal or hunger.

Perception and cognition do not operate through 'simple sequential way[s]' (*Tree of Knowledge* 162) but through interactions between co-dependent systems whose circular causality results in bringing forth a world: 'all knowing is doing as sensory-effector correlations in the realms of structural coupling in which the nervous system exists' (166). According to representational theory, observers contemplate what is recorded by the retina. But this is not how biological vision works, where perception is enacted (actively brought forth). In Maturana and Varela's maxim 'we live our field of vision' (23), the key word is 'field'. Maturana and Varela's use of the term is congruent with Gabriel's concept of 'field of sense', which he defines as the places where things appear (*Why the World* 68). In the enactive approach to biological vision, fields, not objects, are primary. We don't see individual objects in themselves; the sensorimotor biology governing our visual field determines how objects appear in it.

In *The Embodied Mind*, enactivism is developed specifically via colour perception as a case study (157ff.). According to Varela et al., just as vision is not a passive recording of retinal stimuli, the appearance of colour is not an objective function of the reflection of wavelengths of light by surfaces. Colour is not a quality of things in the world. Like vision generally, it is the product of interacting networked systems. Colour appearance has a psychophysical structure deriving from the visual system.[7] This is relevant for our present purposes: as we shall explore further in the final section of this chapter, the fantastic white-blindness pictured in Saramago's novel is described as a kind of overexposure that erases objects and colours. As the first blind man recalls, he was 'plunged into a whiteness so luminous, so total, that it swallowed up rather than absorbed, not just the colours, but the very things and beings, thus making them twice as invisible' (*Blindness* 6). Again, the affinities between Saramago and enactivism are uncanny. Long-term blindness, writes Noë, is best not imagined 'like being in the dark' because it 'is not experienced as . . . an absence' of light (*Action in Perception* 2). Instead, he suggests imagining 'that you are in a fog so dense that no matter where you turn or how you strain you only experience a homogeneous whiteness' (2). For Noë, the white-blindness scenario serves to illustrate the enactive approach to perception as something that we do rather than a movie we watch as detached spectators. In contrast to vision, 'touch is *intrinsically* active' (97). Therefore, Noë suggests, 'touch, not vision, should be our model for perception' (*Action in Perception* cover blurb).

Varela el al. build on Hurvich and Jameson's so-called opponent-process theory, according to which colour results from interactions between three distinct colour 'channels' (one achromatic and signalling brightness; the other two chromatic: red/green and yellow/blue) in the visual system, which in turn are generated by combinations of different types of receptors in the cone cells of the retina. The 'two chromatic channels are opponent: an increase in red is always gained at the expense of green and vice-versa' (*Embodied Mind* 159). Varela et al. note that the opponent-process theory explains 'the structure of color appearance by showing how it results from the differential responses of the achromatic and chromatic channels. Thus the organization of hues into mutually exclusive or antagonistic pairs reflects an underlying opponent organization' (159). In addition to this 'psychophysical' (159) structure, perceived colour is relatively independent of locally reflected light for two other reasons: first, 'the perceived color of things remains relatively constant despite large changes in the illumination' (the so-called '*approximate color constancy*'); second, 'two areas that reflect light of the same spectral composition can be seen to have different colors depending on the surroundings in which they are placed' (the so-called '*simultaneous color contrast or chromatic induction*') (160). According to Varela el al.,

> these two phenomena force us to conclude that we cannot account for our experience of color as an attribute of things in the world by appealing simply to the intensity and wavelength composition of the light reflected from an area. Instead, we need to consider the complex and only partially understood processes of cooperative comparison among multiple neuronal ensembles in the brain, which assign colors to objects according to the emergent, global states they reach given a retinal image. (160–1)

Moreover, colour is not 'perceived in isolation from other attributes, such as shape, size, texture, motion, and orientation', or, further afield, from other sense modalities such as sound (62–3). In sum,

> The visual system is never simply presented with pregiven objects. On the contrary, the determination of what and where an object is, as well as its surface boundaries, texture, and relative orientation (and hence the overall context of color as a perceived attribute), is a complex process that the visual system must continually achieve. (167)

Therefore, 'color provides a paradigm of a cognitive domain that is neither pregiven nor represented but rather experiential and enacted' (171). In short, colour perception constitutes a paradigmatic case study of the theory of cognition as embodied action.

As Varela el al. show in their discussion of the neurophysiology of colour perception, cognition is embodied because it operates through sensorimotor coupling between the visual system and the organism's environment. As Varela et al. never tire of insisting, enactivism (like autopoiesis) does not make a case for cognitive solipsism. Far from projecting self-enclosed hallucinations, vision and colour perception also respond to external physical realities such as light and its different frequencies. As they emphasise, enactivism strikes a middle path between the extremes of solipsism and objectivism (*Embodied Mind* 172): 'mind and world arise together in enaction' (177). Vision illustrates the circular causality of the mind. Maturana and Varela's foregoing remark on living one's visual field continues: 'We do not see the "colors" of the world; we live our chromatic space' (*Tree of Knowledge* 23). With this observation, I turn to Saramago's *Blindness*.

José Saramago's *Blindness*

Blindness's original title in the Portuguese, *Ensaio sobre a cegueira*, translates literally as 'essay on blindness', as if the author's intention was to write not fiction, but a scientific tract. Noting this intertextual reference to 'the scientific prose of the 18th century' and 'its studies of the perception of the blind and the deaf mute', critic Werner Thielemann conjectures that such trans-disciplinary references to the natural sciences serve to disorient the reader, and to disguise the social critique that the text actually offers (Thielemann 8). In and of itself, this is a valid point. From our present perspective, however, Saramago's intertextual reference to scientific tracts is more than a rhetorical ploy: it represents a clue that this novel is a rigorous investigation of the phenomenological and social worlds enacted by blind 'cognitive agents'. The difference is that the author conducts his investigation into blindness in the mode of fiction. Saramago's cross-disciplinary reference to science further shores up the comparative orientation of this study that pairs new realist theories with post-apocalyptic fiction.

Because the catastrophe that strikes in *Blindness* is not due to an environmental collapse proper as in McCarthy, Butler and

Atwood, but a pandemic of infectious blindness, Saramago's novel may seem a mismatch for post-apocalyptic fiction. But in fact, the events narrated in *Blindness* follow the post-apocalyptic script: the total collapse of the modern state and modern civilisation as we know it, whose survivors face the question of how to reconstitute life in the aftermath. The novel is organised into seventeen unnumbered chapters. Unlike Atwood and Butler, Saramago does not alternate between the post-apocalyptic present and (the memory of) the pre-apocalyptic past. Instead, *Blindness* follows a linear narration that moves inexorably forward without much retrospection (or prospection, for that matter) across the apocalyptic break. In its myopic focus on the here and now, the narrative mimics the way the blind are pictured orienting themselves in space, by tentatively feeling themselves forward while immersed in a white fog. Narration and focalisation are trapped in the present, limited to focusing on the events of the medical pandemic and the unfolding collapse in its wake.

In keeping with this focus on a social and public health experiment of a city going blind, *Blindness* opens *in medias res* with the scene of the first man's becoming blind as he is stopped at a light at an intersection. Signalled by the victim's desperate cry 'I am blind', the discovery of the disease is immediately followed by a phenomenological description that marks an uncanny difference from ordinary blindness: as the first blind man puts it, 'I see everything white'; 'it's as if I were caught in a mist or had fallen into a milky sea' (*Blindness* 3). Saramago uses a traditional authorial (heterodiegetic and extradiegetic) narrator. However, focalisation weaves in and out of the sighted perspective of objective narration and the subjective perception of the blind.

At the end, *Blindness* introduces a twist that to the best of my knowledge is unprecedented in post-apocalyptic fiction: the novel closes with the sudden disappearance of the disease, which is as miraculous as its onset. The white-blind survivors regain their sighted selves. Reversing the outbreak of the pandemic, the fantastic restoration of sight is signalled by the exclamation 'I can see' (322), a process that follows the exact order of the initial sequence of infection. This device of undoing the catastrophe and restoring the old world that had vanished underscores the fantastic nature of Saramago's story. Notably, it reconfigures the world-endism of apocalyptic thinking, building a bridge across the 'barrier of time' (Jameson) characteristic of the genre. Defamiliarising apocalyptic thinking's quintessential finitude, it turns the clock back from the 'time after' to the 'time before'.

The first blind man is escorted home by a stranger who comes to his rescue, but then takes advantage of the mishap to steal his car; the Good Samaritan becomes a thief. Such surprise reversals are typical of the events that follow, which foreground the ethics of how people act in response to disaster: Do they embrace cooperation or yield to exploitation? As Sandra Stanley notes, the first blind man embodies 'Patient Zero', the mythic first carrier of the enigmatic contagion and thus its 'narrative origin' (Stanley 297). An eye examination by an ophthalmologist yields no results, establishing white-blindness as a medical mystery: as the ophthalmologist concludes, 'your eyes are perfect'; 'your blindness ... defies explanation' (*Blindness* 14). The chance cross-section of society that contagion brings together on the first day of the epidemic – a small group including the first blind man and his wife, the man who stole his car, the doctor, the doctor's wife, and a handful of patients who happen to be at the doctor's office, including a girl with dark glasses (a prostitute who goes blind during sex with a customer at a hotel), a boy with a squint and an old man with a black eyepatch – form the narrative cell from which the story expands.

The events narrated in *Blindness* follow what Priscilla Wald terms the 'outbreak narrative', a genre that arose in the wake of Pasteur's discovery of microbes and the rise of microbiology in the nineteenth century.[8] Wald defines the outbreak narrative as a 'formulaic plot that begins with the identification of an emerging infection, includes discussion of the global networks throughout which it travels, and chronicles the epidemiological work that ends with its containment' (Wald 2). *Blindness* is structured around what, to adapt Propp, might be called paradigmatic actants, settings and staple events of the outbreak narrative, including Patient Zero and the local site of the first outbreak of white-blindness among the patients at the ophthalmologist's office. Similarly, the epidemic of blindness spreads beyond the site of its outbreak through the social networks (official and concealed) that connect people, which become pathways for the spread of contagion: the girl with dark glasses' customer at the hotel, the hotel maid, the policemen who respectively escort the blind thief and the girl home, and so on. (Notably, the borders of the nation mark the farthest expansion of contagion in *Blindness*. That Saramago limits the scale of contagion to the nation is implicit in the comment announcing the universalisation of blindness two-thirds through the novel: 'everyone is blind, the whole city, the entire country' [*Blindness* 222]. In this way, he brackets complicating factors such as xenophobia and racism that arise when carriers of contagion are linked to foreigners, immigrants and the global poor, as has been the case in many modern epidemics. Instead, Saramago chooses to focus on the simple dichotomy of the contaminated and the uncontaminated, and to explore the extent of apocalyptic destruction resulting from an unstoppable contagion.)

Given that a doctor is among the first cases of contamination, the medical authorities are alerted at the earliest possible time. The official public health response is the forced quarantining of everyone known to have become blind, as well as those who are suspected of being contaminated. The building designated to receive them is a decommissioned asylum. The doctor and his wife, who never loses her sight and feigns blindness so as to stay with her husband after his deportation, are the first to arrive in quarantine, where they settle in the first ward. Directly after their arrival in the asylum, they are reunited with the first blind man, two of the doctor's patients (the girl with the dark glasses and the boy with the squint), and the car thief. A few days later they are joined by the first blind man's wife and the old man with the eyepatch. Among the stream of subsequent arrivals, some of whom occupy the remaining beds in Ward One, are others involved in the initial outbreak, including the two policemen, the hotel maid, the taxi driver, the girl's customer, the pharmacist's assistant and so on. This handful of people made up by Patient Zero and the first cases of contagion, including the doctor's wife, who in the asylum becomes 'the woman who can see', form the small group of survivors whose progress Saramago's narrative tracks.

The small collective of survivors tracked in post-apocalyptic fiction is formed by the peculiar logic through which the respective catastrophes unfold, in this case the first to be quarantined. In this way, the association forged by contagion becomes the social glue that bonds the new unit of post-apocalyptic survivors. In postapocalyptic fiction, the question of how social ties are reconstituted after the catastrophe is handled in various ways. Sometimes, as in McCarthy, (the remnants of) traditional pre-apocalyptic family units are preserved, as father and son persevere on their own after the mother's suicide. But for the most part, the apocalypse entails the destruction of pre-apocalyptic social ties and the constitution of new ones, so that the particular mode of catastrophic destruction plays a key role in sorting and selecting new social contacts. In Atwood's *MaddAddam* trilogy, Snowman and the Crakers are thrown together by their common immunity to Crake's artificial virus. In *Blindness*, chance pathways of infection are sedimented when forced quarantine reunites the victims as internees of the asylum. In fact, this process evidences the central insight of actor-network theory, that the social is nothing but a type of connection between things that are not themselves social, a theory that, as Latour affirms, works best in fast-changing conditions.

The long middle section tracing events in the asylum after the initial outbreak develops *Blindness*'s central concern with the logic of the struggle for survival: What principle will gain the upper hand? The Hobbesian state of nature as war, 'the life of man, solitary, poore, nasty, brutish, and short' (Hobbes 186)? Or the principle of cooperation? As we have seen, this reflects the interest in collective life of post-apocalyptic fiction more generally. What type of relationship will govern the remaking of the social and the remaking of world after the world- end? The predator–prey dynamic? Or benevolent relations of collaboration? The quarantine episode explores the institutional biopolitical response to the outbreak of a pandemic. In this section, Saramago traces the gradual disintegration of social order into anarchy, as the quarantine degenerates into a concentration camp. As the chaos within begins to mirror the chaos on the outside, the asylum comes to represent a microcosm of events in the city and the nation as a whole. In depicting the quarantine of the infectious blind, Saramago queries the rationale of containment: the threat that the infected pose to the healthy after the outbreak of an infectious disease. In principle, this threat is purely medical, and quarantine is justified on the grounds of the need to contain the infection and protect public health. But as recent epidemics such as HIV/ AIDS have shown, the infected are easily subjected to a logic of Othering, dehumanisation and scapegoating that places their civil rights in jeopardy. No longer viewed as fully human, they are reduced to animals and internal enemies threatening the welfare of the nation. The asylum episode tracks the rapid dehumanisation of the quarantined internees by the armed guards and the public authorities.

On their arrival, the inmates are greeted by a loudspeaker

announcement, repeated daily, that communicates official orders and instructions concerning daily routines such as the provision of food and the disposal of leftovers, hygiene, and so on. More ominously, as in Bentham's panopticon prison, the lights are kept on at all times and cannot be switched off, and 'leaving the building without authorisation will mean instant death' (*Blindness* 43). The final count of rules shows that the quarantined have effectively been abandoned: 'in the event of a fire getting out of control, whether accidentally or on purpose, the firemen will not intervene'; 'the internees cannot count on any outside intervention should there be any outbreaks of illnesses, nor in the event of any disorder or aggression'; 'in the case of death, whatever the cause, the internees will bury the corpse in the yard without any formalities' (43). Among the quarantine regime's list of rules and prohibitions, one item stands out in recommending unofficial activities: 'a recommendation rather than an order, the internees must organise themselves as they see fit' (43). As we shall see, this injunction to self-organise will later become the germ of the internees' resistance against the official quarantine regime.

From the outset, it is clear that the quarantine hospital in *Blindness* is, to borrow anthropologist João Biehl's terms, a 'zone . . . of abandonment' (Biehl, *Vita* 4). Biehl's study *Vita: Life in a Zone of Social Abandonment* is an ethnography of a charity asylum for the poorest and sickest in southern Brazil. As an account of an institution that purports to serve the public health while in fact subjecting its inmates to unspeakable abjection, filth and degradation, *Vita* offers an instructive real-life parallel to the chilling events occurring in Saramago's narrative. Both narratives take place in hospital settings, which degenerate into concentration camps in both cases. Like *Blindness*, *Vita* questions the human–animal boundary: cast off by their destitute families and the neoliberal Brazilian state and interned in a 'zone of social abandonment', the inmates are reduced to a 'social death' before their actual biological death (*Vita* 5, 23). Stripped of human and citizenship rights, they become 'noncitizens' and 'ex-humans' – a coinage based on one patient's self-description, 'I am an ex' (an 'ex-wife' with an 'ex-family') (52) – who are reduced to the state of 'bare life' (Agamben). By extrapolating such real-life biomedical systems to an apocalyptic scenario triggered by a fictitious pandemic, Saramago deflects attention from the medical cause to expose these systems' inherent horror.

In *Blindness*, things begin to deteriorate rapidly as verbal and physical fights break out among the internees. Developments follow the pattern of vicious cycles, or what cybernetics calls positive or self-amplifying feedback (see Capra and Luisi 89ff.). We discussed feedback in the previous chapter in the context of post-apocalyptic ecologies in *MaddAddam*. *Blindness* depicts a classic instance of runaway feedback: violence. Delirious with pain, one injured inmate drags himself to the main entrance at night to appeal to the soldiers for help. But the guard on duty, terrified at glimpsing the 'face of a blind man' at close range, empties a blast of gunfire into his face (*Blindness* 75). In the philosophical ethics of Emmanuel Levinas, the face of the other is the summons that, in a call for help, cannot be avoided. In a face-to-face encounter, strangers are compelled to acknowledge each other's humanity: 'the epiphany of the face qua face opens humanity' (Levinas 213). But the soldiers shoot the blind man who seeks help in the face. After this incident, food, which has continually been insufficient for the growing number of internees, is dumped in the hallway, where the soldiers shoot more blind internees in panic. The blind are ordered to bury the corpses in the courtyard, but now food wars are breaking out. Within a few days quarantine conditions degenerate into mob violence. Two hundred new blind internees arrive and, at gunpoint, are herded into the facility, which now far exceeds its total capacity of one hundred and twenty. The horror reaches its climax when an armed gang of blind criminals takes control of the asylum and begins to extort money and valuables from the internees in exchange for food. The Hobbesian state of war degenerates into total apocalypse when the thugs begin to impose sexual slavery on the women. After one of the women dies from her injuries, the doctor's wife stabs the gang leader with a pair of scissors and organises an attack against the hoodlums. The next day, after the loudspeaker dies, the lights go out, food delivery ceases and the entire hospital goes up in flames. When the internees escape the building, they find that the soldiers are gone, 'they too stricken by blindness, everyone finally blind' (*Blindness* 216).

From the outset, the quarantined are plunged into degradation and filth. To find their food, the blind 'had to go down on all fours, sweeping the floor ahead with one arm outstretched, while the other served as a third paw' (65). Their lives become immersed in stench and excrement that, unable to see, the blind cannot avoid stepping into (92). As the doctor's wife reflects,

It was not just the fetid smell that came from the lavatories in gusts
that made you want to throw up, it was also the accumulated body
odour of two hundred and fifty people, whose bodies were steeped in
their own sweat, who were neither able nor knew how to wash themselves, who wore clothes that got filthier by the day, who slept in beds
where they had frequently defecated. What use would soaps, bleach,
detergents be, abandoned somewhere around the place, if many of the
showers were blocked or had become detached from the pipes, if the
drains overflowed with the dirty water that spread outside the wash-
rooms. (134–5)

Deprived of vision, the noblest of all senses, the blind are thrust
back into their bodies and their basic functions. What Stanley
calls Saramago's 'excremental gaze' reflects the cutting of the link
between human civilisation and visuality that Freud speculatively
advanced in *Civilization and Its Discontents*. In Jay's summary,

> Human civilization, Freud conjectured, only began when hominids
> raised themselves off the ground, stopped sniffing the nether regions
> of their fellows, and elevated sight to a position of superiority. With
> that elevation went a concomitant repression of sexual and aggressive
> drives and the radical separation of 'higher' spiritual and mental facul-
> ties from the 'lower' functions of the body. (Jay 222)

The internees' progressive abjection is reflected in a profusion of
animal comparisons, such as insects (*Blindness* 81), the analogy
with ants mentioned earlier (225), or, as in the passages quoted
below, dogs, pigs and crabs. As the doctor reflects as he helplessly
stumbles across other internees' excrement, '[t]here are many ways
of becoming an animal . . . this is just the first of them' (93).

Human life in quarantine in *Blindness* is lived at the brink of
extinction. The internees searching for the food containers like
'hunted animals' present a 'grotesque spectacle' for the soldiers
who openly toy with the idea of exterminating them (100):

> it was too funny for words, some of the blind internees advancing on
> all fours, their faces practically touching the ground as if they were
> pigs, one arm outstretched in mid-air, while others, perhaps afraid
> that the white space, without a roof to protect them, would swallow
> them up, clung desperately to the rope and listened attentively, expect-
> ing to hear at any minute the first exclamation of triumph once the

containers were discovered. The soldiers would have liked to aim their weapons and, without compunction, shoot down those imbeciles moving before their eyes like lame crabs, waving their unsteady pincers in search of their missing leg. They knew what had been said in the barracks that morning by the regimental commander, that the problem of these blind internees could be resolved only by physically wiping out the lot of them, those already there and those still to come, without any phoney humanitarian considerations, his very words, just as one amputates a gangrenous limb in order to save the rest of the body. The rabies of a dead dog, he said, to illustrate the point, is cured by nature. (100–1)

Reflecting on the internees' social death as 'ex-humans' (Biehl), the doctor's wife muses, 'we're so remote from the world that any day now, we shall no longer know who we are, or even remember our names, and besides, what use would names be to us, no dog recognises another dog, or knows the others by the names they have been given' (*Blindness* 57). As in McCarthy's *The Road*, whose protagonists are simply known as 'the man' and 'the boy', the absence of proper names in *Blindness* emphasises the dispossession of the afflicted. Their namelessness (the first blind man, the woman who can see, the girl with dark glasses) and the anonymity of the setting (the city) introduces an element of indeterminacy that stresses the radical break between the world that has been destroyed and the post-apocalyptic present.

This brings us to one of the principal concerns of *Blindness*: the phenomenology of blind perception. With only four of their five senses left, how do the blind perceive the world? The novel includes extensive descriptions of the first-personal experience of sightlessness. As mentioned earlier, the amputation of vision results in the elimination of the outside observer of the disembodied Cartesian *cogito*. As the passages quoted above and below show, blind perception is immersed in its embodiment. Instead of passive contemplation, it is actively exploring the world. Stripped of vision, the royal road to representation, the blind are exiled from the stance of the disembodied spectator, the *sine qua non* of the representational paradigm. The white-blind mind is clearly an 'embodied mind' in Maturana and Varela's sense, whose mode of perception is the enaction of worlds and minds in the process of knowing. Thus, Saramago's post-apocalyptic script of living on after the world-end further highlights the change of paradigm to an ontological approach that knowledge, according to the Santiago theory, requires. Like knowledge, apocalyptic thinking is onto-logical. More specifically, post-apocalyptic fiction shifts emphasis from world-destroying to world-making. The post-apocalyptic script therefore amplifies the enactivist approach to knowledge as world-making.

In more than one way, Saramago's novel is about post-individualism: first, for the blind, there is no survival as indi-viduals, but only in small groups. Secondly, the blind are also post-individuals in the sense that they are deprived of the posi-tionality of the traditional autonomous subject making objective representations of the outside world. Detached observation pre-supposes distance, which is only granted by vision. As Miriam Helen Hill observes, vision 'deals with shapes and distances; it extends the body to lengths the limbs cannot reach' (Hill 101). The remaining senses – hearing, smell, touch and taste – operate at a much shorter range than vision.

Blindness explores various answers to the question of what might be the replacement for vision. One hypothesis is touch: 'go and touch them with your hands, the hands are the eyes of the blind' (*Blindness* 318). The recurring image of blind spatial orientation with 'arms outstretched', feeling one's way along the corridors of the asylum, or later on, along the walls of buildings in the city of the blind, is among the most frequent in *Blindness*. As noted, for Noë, touch captures the actual nature of perception: perception is 'nonpictorial' (*Action in Perception* 71). Noë even speaks of the 'touch-like character of vision itself' (96). On the enactivist account, Saramago's white-blind are awakening to the occluded physicality of biological perception. Another substitute is hearing: as the doctor explains how he recognised the man with the eyepatch, 'Above all, by your voice, the voice is the sight of the person who cannot see' (*Blindness* 117). Two blind intern-ees who are arguing 'made no gestures' and 'barely moved their bodies, having quickly learned that only their voice and hearing now served any purpose' (97).

The third option, smell, is associated with waste and the unclean. Its renewed dominance after the loss of vision is also closely linked to basic instincts, as suggested by Freud's conjec-ture about the link between olfaction and sexual drive (Freud 54 n. 1). Setting out to trade their bodies to the criminals in exchange for access to food, a grotesque line-up of foul-smelling women, their clothes filthy and in tatters, it seems impossible that the animal drive for sex should be so powerful, to the point of blinding a man's sense of smell, the most delicate of the senses . . . Slowly, guided by the doctor's wife, each of them with her hand on the shoulder of the one in front, the women started walking. (*Blindness* 177)

Unlike objects defined by vision, objects defined by smell do not have clear boundaries: miserably, although the doctor and the other blind inmates perceive the 'smell of urine' (52) or excrement, they cannot tell where precisely it is coming from.

As indicated by the cognitive labour involved in orienting themselves in space without vision, the blind are reborn as new kinds of cognitive agents at the moment they are struck with the disease. Loss of sight is a transformative event, a kind of rebirth. In the language of enactivism, the sudden loss of sight severs the structural couplings with the world that are available to sighted minds. It wipes the slate clean, as it were, clearing space for new structural couplings to emerge between newly blind minds and their environments, via the remaining four senses of hearing, touch, smell and taste.

In the terms of autopoiesis, the white-blind embark on a new process of ontogeny. This new life process of blind ontogeny begins in the asylum. This is obvious even to the soldiers:

The blind no longer lose their way, with one arm held out in front and several fingers moving like the antennae of insects, they can find their way everywhere, it is even probable that in the more gifted of the blind there soon develops what is referred to as frontal vision. Take the doctor's wife, for example, it is quite extraordinary how she manages to get around and orient herself through this veritable maze of rooms, nooks and corridors, how she knows precisely where to turn the corner, how she can come to a halt before a door and open it without a moment's hesitation, how she has no need to count the beds before reaching her own. (81)

Needless to say, the observation about the development of frontal vision is loaded with irony, since the internee whom the soldiers think is a blind woman can still see. Nonetheless, despite this ironic refraction, this reference is deliberately placed to signpost the self-organising and creative activity of blind ontogenic 'development' that Maturana and Varela call 'structural drift'. Patricia Vieira makes a related point in arguing that in Saramago's narrative, '[t]urning blind is a process of individuation' or 'becoming a subject, in that it is a process that both subjects and emancipates' (Vieira 9, 7). However, as I argue, the poststructuralist theories of subjectivity as disciplinary subjection that she invokes (Althusser, Foucault) are inadequate for Saramago's novel. Instead, blind ontogeny is the reciprocal co-constitution of blind minds and worlds as a hands-on, face-to-face phenomenon that is irreducible to the logic of disciplinary structuration.

Saramago's novel suggests that the onset of white-blindness turns humans into a type of organism that is distinct from the sighted. Newly sightless, they must find a new type of cognitive organisation that allows them to know their world, a process in which neither blind minds not worlds are pre-given, but – as Maturana and Varela put it – are brought forth in the process of living. The processes of enaction of blind lifeworlds and blind ontogeny have two dimensions. The first, just discussed, is phenomenological, concerned with the co-constitution of blind minds and worlds. The second, to which I turn now, is social. It is social coupling and linguistic coupling among the blind that results in the formation of blind collectives, as well as their coordinated drift via collective ontogenies.

The final chapters of *Blindness* narrate the experiences of the small group of survivors from Ward One after their liberation from the asylum – the woman who can see, the doctor, the first blind man and his wife, the girl with the dark glasses, the old man with the eyepatch, the boy with a squint – as they wander the city, which has now become a city of the blind. The problem explored here is the potential difference between white-blindness in captivity (the horrors of quarantine) and 'free' white-blindness after sightlessness has become a universal condition. What new possibilities, if any, appear once the apparatus of biopolitical governance and the threat of administered extermination are removed? As the narrator observes sardonically, 'there is no comparison between living in a rational labyrinth, which is, by definition, a mental asylum and venturing forth, without a guiding hand or a dog-leash, into the demented labyrinth of the city, where memory will serve no purpose' (*Blindness* 217). If the blind are no longer a minority stigmatised by the sighted majority as pariahs, will this end their dehumanisation? To what extent is the white-blind's abject condition of animal-like existence an effect of biopolitical power – 'making live and letting die' (Biehl, 'People' 112)? Once the state has collapsed, and with it the entire apparatus of biopower, will the blind be able to regain access to human civilisation? Can there be a civilisation of the blind? Can the blind remake society in the absence of vision? Freud's conjecture was that upright posture and the liberation of the human mind from the dominance of the lower functions of the body were conditional on vision. Distinct from Freud's speculation about 'elevated vision' (Jay 222), Saramago's wager is that vision is not an indispensable condition of civilisation. The final chapters of *Blindness* probe the beginnings of a new society of the blind that is based on small, self-organising collectives rather than large, anonymous systems.

The chapters set after the apocalyptic collapse of the civilisation of the seeing fully unfold the promise of alternative blind modes of knowing in the condition of post-individualism. There is a shift from the privations to the rewards of white-blindness. This section traces the development and expansion of the collective self-organisation of the blind that began in the asylum. It explores what Maturana and Varela call the emergence of third-order unities via social and linguistic coupling. Significantly, the emergence of social phenomena among the blind based on mutualism and cooperation is a dynamic that runs counter to the dominant order of Darwinian survival of the fittest that motivated the biopolitical genocide of the blind by the sighted. This is the point when predator–prey dynamics recede and relations of mutualism come to the fore. *Blindness* attests to the stubborn resilience and creativity of everyday practice celebrated by Michel de Certeau and demonstrated by Biehl's ethnography of Vita. As Biehl contends:

> What is outside biopower? Traversing worlds of risk and scarcity, constrained without being totally over-determined, people create small and fleeting spaces, through and beyond classifications and apparatuses of governance and control, in which to perform a kind of *life bricolage* with the limited choices and materials at hand (including being the subjects of rights and pharmaceutical treatments made available by state and non-state actors). (Biehl, 'People' 112)

Like *Vita*, a study of an 'outsider artist' emerging from a zone of abandonment and abjection, Saramago's *Blindness* counters facile theoretical reductions of such existence: 'Whether in social abandonment, addiction, or homelessness, life that no longer has any value for society is hardly synonymous with a life that no longer has any value for the person living it' (Biehl, 'People' 114).

As the group wander the streets in search of food and shelter, they find that the urban population has reorganised itself into small groups of homeless nomads. Because they can no longer find their way home, they survive by drifting through the city looting stores and squatting in strangers' homes that they happen to find empty. By tacit consensus, the blind have accepted dispossession and nomadism as a collective condition:

> when we have to look for food, we are obliged to go together, it's the only way of not losing each other, and . . . since no-one stays behind to guard the house . . . the likelihood is that it will already be occupied by another group also unable to find their house, we're a kind of merry-go-round. (*Blindness* 222–3)

Similarly, the pedestrian traffic of the white-blind in the streets has self-organised according to the pattern of 'ants on the trail' mentioned earlier.

Notably, because the group of survivor protagonists includes the woman who can see, they are exempted from the disorientation that defines the universal condition in the city of the blind. While the doctor's wife and her group enjoy the relative safety of their real home, conditions in the entire city of the blind reach an apocalyptic state: a supermarket basement has become a mass grave of decomposing blind bodies trapped there; rubbish and the corpses of blind humans are piling up in the streets, fed on by dogs and rats as large as dogs. But just when the city seems on the brink of an outbreak of new infectious diseases such as cholera and typhoid, the blindness pandemic ends as miraculously as it began. The Ward One collective returns to key sites of the opening scenes of the narrative. The recovery of sight proceeds in a symmetrical reversal of the original spread of the epidemic. Saramago's narrative achieves closure. But what kind of closure? Narrated time in *Blindness* is extremely short: the asylum episode covers not much more than two weeks. The following episode in the city of the white-blind before the magical restoration of sight is even shorter, no more than a week. As Frank Kermode and Paul Ricoeur argue, narratives are end-determined fictions whose beginnings and middles must be understood in view of the ending.

If narrative meaning emerges retrospectively, how does the miraculous restoration of sight reconfigure the meaning of the whole?

The doctor's wife's final observation – 'I don't think we did go blind, I think we are blind, Blind but seeing, Blind people who can see, but do not see' (*Blindness* 326) – identifies the multiple paradoxes of white-blindness. White-blindness is overdetermined: its meaning is both literal (sight) and allegorical (insight). The fantastic etiology of a pandemic of white-blindness whose mysterious advent and disappearance defies medical explanation lifts the story out of the medical realm. The figure of the blind ophthalmologist, as helpless as the other victims, serves to make the point that medical science does not have the answers to solve the mystery of the disease. Further, by defining blindness as an excess of light rather than its absence, Saramago undermines the ocularcentrism of Western culture that, as Martin Jay demonstrates, equates sight with reason and civilisation, and sightlessness with irrationality and barbarism. Saramago's white-blindness is a kind of overexposure that – as noted earlier – 'swallows up' 'things and beings' (*Blindness* 6). Indeed, white-blindness occupies a third position beyond the opposition between enlightened reason and obscurantist unreason. As the doctor reflects,

> the advantage enjoyed by these blind men was what might be called the illusion of light. In fact, it made no difference to them whether it was day or night . . . these blind people were for ever surrounded by a resplendent whiteness, like the sun shining through mist. For the latter, blindness did not mean being plunged into banal darkness, but living inside a luminous halo. (89–90)

Yet this luminous blindness is tainted by abjection, as illustrated by the doctor's observation in the bathrooms of the asylum: 'for him it was all white, luminous, resplendent, he had no way of knowing whether the walls and ground were white and he came to the absurd conclusion that the light and whiteness there were giving off the awful stench' (92).

By positing the idea of a luminous blindness, Patricia Vieira contends, *Blindness* juxtaposes two kinds of reason, the 'reason of the blind' and the reason of the sighted (Vieira 4). But as the example of the blind criminals shows, like the sighted, the white-blind are neither immune from unreason nor do they have privileged access to a higher reason. In his 1998 Nobel lecture, Saramago's comments on *Blindness* invoke the dialectic of enlightenment that Horkheimer and Adorno identified as the logic by which enlightened reason turns into totalitarianism.

> Blind. The apprentice thought, 'We are blind', and he sat down and wrote *Blindness* to remind those who might read it that we pervert reason when we humiliate life, and human dignity is insulted every day by the powerful of our world, that the universal lie has replaced the plural truths, that man stopped respecting himself when he lost the respect due to his fellow creatures. Then the apprentice … [moved on to] trying to exorcise the monsters generated by the blindness of reason … (Saramago, 'Nobel Lecture' 10)

That said, Saramago also steers clear of any reductive physiological essentialisms that would replace Western instrumental reason and modern visual technologies of power, epitomised by the carceral quarantine regime, with a superior white-blind enlightenment. Further, the figure of the 'woman who can see', who chooses to live among the white-blind out of solidarity with her blind husband and who is the real protagonist of the story, shows that physiological sightedness does not preclude genuine insight either. Her existence cannot be explained by narratological needs: although a sighted narrator is essential to telling the complete story of the blindness epidemic, this function could as easily have been performed by an external narrator as by a character focaliser like the woman who can see. It is the insight of the 'woman who can see' that embodies Saramago's ideal of an alternative reason beyond the logic of domination. It suggests the triumph of the logic of cooperation and solidarity over that of domination and bloody competition. While the blindness pandemic presents the occasion of its discovery, this superior insight, Saramago suggests, is ultimately independent of physical blindness or sight. This, I argue, is the meaning of the ending that loops back to the beginning.

Saramago suggests that in contrast to sighted cognition, the defining characteristic of what Maturana and Varela might call white-blind cognition, white-blind ontogeny and 'third order' white-blind social phenomena is a greater degree of interdependence and reciprocity. As the 'ants on the trail' analogy suggests, members of societies of the blind have less autonomy than members of societies of the sighted. Mutual dependence fills the void left by the loss of access to the fiction of autonomous individualism that,

as Saramago reminds us, is predicated on the long-range perception of vision. To quote in full the emblematic observation that
appears as the epigraph to this chapter:

> the worst thing is that we are not organised, there should be an organi-
> sation in each building, in each street, in each district, A government,
> said the wife, An organisation, the human body is also an organised
> system, it lives as long as it keeps organised, and death is only the
> effect of a disorganisation, And how can a society of blind people
> organise in order to survive. By organising itself, to organise oneself is,
> in a way, to begin to have eyes. (*Blindness* 295–6)

As the woman who can see realises, the actual substitute for the
loss of vision is none of the remaining four senses. Rather, it
is a social phenomenon – the collective self-organisation of the
blind via social and linguistic coupling. It is intriguing to note
that, like Maturana and Varela, Saramago's vision is biocentric,
spanning the arc of life from the world of the macrocosm (the
individual organism) to third-order social phenomena. The beginnings of cooperative blind self-organisation are in the asylum, as
the internees in Ward One form a line to travel around the building, and coordinate the equal distribution of beds, of food, and
so on. According to the narrator, the first ward sets an example
of cooperation: 'as any rationalised regulation of hygiene would
demand, as attentive to the greatest efficiency possible in gathering
up leftovers and litter, as to the economy of effort needed to carry
out this task' (116). A more intense level of solidarity is reached
in the aftermath of the rape-death of one of the female internees.
After the escape from the asylum, social coupling among the small
group of survivors deepens as new rituals of cohabitation are
invented in the doctor's apartment.

It makes sense to consider Saramago's socialist politics in this
respect. As Stanley notes, Saramago is 'a Communist writing in
an era that has witnessed what some scholars have described as
the "epistemological ruins of Marxism"' (Stanley 294). 'Growing
up in Portugal under the repressive Salazar regime, Saramago, a
Communist and an atheist, has long been suspicious of both the
despotic gaze of the self-aggrandized individual and the surveil-
lance power of institutionalized systems – whether a dictatorship
or the Catholic Church' (Stanley 296). Might it be too far-fetched
to suggest that the post-apocalyptic laboratory of a city of the

blind, self-organising into small collectives building by building, serves as a way of projecting the utopia of a non-dogmatic, non-totalitarian type of communitarianism?

In all of this – in contrast to actual 'ants on the trail', whose association works by chemical coupling – language plays a central role. Confirming Maturana and Varela's claim that in humans, social coupling is linguistic coupling, the activity that seems most definitive of the life of Saramago's blind collective is talking and debating. One might say that the primacy of vision has been replaced by the privilege of the spoken word; unable to depend on their eyes, the blind trust the word. The place of ocularcentrism is taken by the primacy of verbal dialogue. In the asylum, the collective decisions, first, to agree to the criminals' demand for sex slaves, and next, to attack the criminals in self-defence are reached via a tense debate in each case. At this pivotal moment, the doctor asks,

> [a]re there still people here intent on discovering who killed that fellow, or are we agreed that the hand that stabbed him was the hand of all of us, or to be more precise, the hand of each one of us. No one replied. The doctor's wife said, Let's give them a little longer, if by tomorrow, the soldiers have not brought our food, then we advance. (*Blindness* 197)

As individual sacrifice and collective welfare, individual initiative vs. collective action are weighed against each other, language is enactive: rather than inspecting a pre-existing world, it brings forth the world it is describing.

At these critical moments of instability – in the terminology of self-organisation theory – language becomes social action: it is through language that the blind internees coordinate their collective actions. These events demonstrate Maturana and Varela's concluding claims in *The Tree of Knowledge* considered earlier, that '[c]onsciousness and mind belong to the realm of social coupling' (234), which in humans is enacted through linguistic coupling. It is through language that the blind bring forth a new world of reciprocal cooperation and solidarity, countering the dominator system of social organisation governed by predator–prey dynamics. In revisiting the question of 'What is Enlightenment', *Blindness* envisions a counter-enlightenment of blind insight that is post-individual, collective and dialogic, and which suggests that this collective ontogeny is facilitated by language. It is through what autopoietic theory calls linguistic coupling that the blind are able to crawl out of the ruins of modern sighted civilisation, leave behind their dehumanised condition and reclaim their humanity.

The primacy of language (rather than vision) for the new self-organising collective sheds fresh light on Freud's theory that 'elevated sight' (Jay 222) is the *sine qua non* of civilisation. Modifying Freud's claims, Saramago suggests that the prerequisite of civilisation is not sight, but language. Freud had posited that civilisation 'set in with man's adoption of an erect posture' as 'a consequence of man's raising himself from the ground' (Freud 54). Humans' upright posture led to 'the devaluation of olfactory stimuli and the isolation of the menstrual period to the time when visual stimuli were paramount and the genitals became visible, and thence to the continuity of sexual excitation, the founding of the family and so to the threshold of human civilization' (Freud 54). Indeed, the bestial conditions of the blind in the asylum are epitomised by their loss of upright posture, when they are forced 'to go down on all fours' to find their food, like animals (*Blindness* 65). As it turns out, their degradation to feeding on the ground like animals is due to the horrors of quarantine, not to their blindness. A better example for authentic degeneration is the blind criminal gang who conscript their fellow female internees into sex slavery despite their stench: here, the reassertion of the primacy of the ignoble sense of olfaction it is due to self-abasement. The blind hoodlums have lowered themselves to the status of dogs, to use Freud's example, animals that are not ashamed to practise sexual intercourse publicly and are not offended by the smell of excrement (Freud 55). With the exception of the catastrophe in the supermarket basement, 'free blind' life in the city of the blind after the collapse of quarantine is conducted in an upright posture.

Indeed, Saramago concurs with Freud that 'the axes of verticality and horizontality' are 'connected, respectively[,] with civilization and barbarism' (Jay 226). But the events of *Blindness* illustrate a different philosophical anthropology of upright posture than Freud's: that of Erwin Straus. In his essay 'The Upright Posture', Straus offers an alternative explanation of the consequences of erect posture to Freud's theory of 'the triumph of the eye over the nose' (Jay 333). Straus agrees with Freud that upright posture 'lift[s] eye and ear from the ground', that smell loses 'the right of the first-born' among the senses while seeing and hearing assume dominion (Straus 162). But its significance lies elsewhere: in the modification of the entire face, in particular the 'transformation of the animal jaws into the human mouth' via an extensive remodelling of the muscle and bone structure of 'mandible, maxilla, and teeth' (162). Straus posits that the 'transformation of the jaw into the mouth is a prerequisite for the development of language' (163). Whereas the 'mark of the jaws is brute force' (162), the evolution of the mouth that can speak depends on the substitution of the powerful chewing muscles of the jaws by 'subtle mimic and phonetic muscles' (163). In Straus's account, the development of bipedalism and upright posture prepares the ground for civilisation by producing the mouth equipped for human speech.[9]

In *Blindness*, the new primacy of the spoken word is evidenced by social life in the city of the blind, where public debates and speeches become a major form of entertainment. The apocalyptic collapse of modern technologies has an unexpected benefit: the breakdown of the culture industry leads to the restoration of the Habermasian utopia of the eighteenth-century public sphere. Spontaneous speech-making in urban squares dwells on defunct large social systems, as noted in the previous section. Not surprisingly, there are apocalyptic prophecies, 'proclaiming the end of the world, redemption through penitence, the visions of the seventh day, the advent of the angel, cosmic collisions, the death of the sun . . .' (*Blindness* 298).

In this emerging post-apocalyptic culture of the spoken word, conversations narrow down what is within the range of existential possibilities for the white-blind, whose perception is limited to what lies within earshot. In the doctor's apartment, the group of survivors collectively discover the realistic option given the situation: to return to small, face-to-face communities. As the woman who can see remarks, 'The time has come to decide what we want to do, I'm convinced the entire population is blind' (255). Any government, the doctor's wife suggests, 'will be a government of the blind trying to rule the blind, that is to say, nothingness trying to organise nothingness' (255). The doctor speculates that if 'there are organised groups of blind people . . . this means that new ways of living are being invented' (256). This prompts the old man to declare the return to small, low-tech environments characteristic of the genre of contemporary post-apocalyptic fiction: 'We're going back to primitive hordes . . . with the difference that we are not a few thousand men and women in an immense, unspoiled nature, but thousands of millions in an uprooted, exhausted world' (256).

It is the doctor's wife who expresses the white-blind survivors' new-found collaborative vision of social life: 'if we stay together we might manage to survive, if we separate we shall be swallowed up by the masses and destroyed . . . let us continue to live together' (256–7). These judgements could as easily have been uttered by the father in McCarthy's *The Road* or Lauren Oya Olamina in Butler's *Parable* series. Unlike the former, Saramago's post-apocalyptic scenario is produced through the defamiliarising device of a fantastic plague of contagious white-blindness. In this way, Saramago's novel opens a unique perspective on to the enactive character of social and mental phenomena that similarly recasts the real, embodied and embedded realism that overcomes the double quandaries of materialism on the one hand and constructivism on the other.

Notes

1. See Maturana and Varela, *Tree of Knowledge* 12–13; Maturana and Poerksen 162–3; Varela, 'Early Days' 69–73. Most scholars only cite this highly theoretical text, which was superseded by Maturana and Varela's best-selling *The Tree of Knowledge*. First published in Spanish translation (*De Maquinas y seres vivos: Una teoría de la organización biológica*, 1973), the English original of *Autopoiesis* didn't appear until 1980.

2. As Margulis points out, the most important distinction among life forms is not the one between animals and plants, but between two types of cells, cells without a nucleus ('prokaryotes') and cells with a nucleus ('eukaryotes') (Margulis and Sagan, *Microcosmos* 29). Unlike all other organisms, microbes, or bacteria, are non-nucleated cells. Yet of the 3.5 billion years of life on earth, 'for the first 2.0 billion years the living world consisted entirely of microorganisms' (Capra 215).

3. Brian Goodwin compares isolated ants with individual neurons in a nervous system: the behaviour of isolated ants is very chaotic; it is only as a collective that ants display orderly and purposeful behaviour. 'No one has succeeded in teaching ants anything; for instance, they are simply incapable of learning to discriminate one direction from another in finding a food source, always making the same random choice at a Y junction even if the food is always in the same place. However, put a bunch of ants together, and what marvels of collective activity result! Individual neurons are not very intelligent either, but

a lot of them hooked up together can result in remarkably interesting and quite unexpected behavior' (Goodwin 69). Goodwin posits that this 'is the very essence of emergent behavior' (69); ant colonies are dynamic self-organising systems that produce order – that is to say, patterns of orderly collective behaviour – out of chaos. The emergence of regular activity does not appear until the population reaches a critical density.

4. Unlike Varela, who as a militant supporter of Allende was dismissed from his post after the 1973 coup and sought by the police (Varela, 'Early Days' 74), Maturana decided to stay in Chile after the coup, where – with the exception of one inconsequential arrest in 1977 and one unsettling personal meeting with Pinochet in 1984 – he seems to have succeeded in advancing his teaching and research (see Maturana and Poerksen 167–82).

5. In one instance, Maturana resorted to theatrical gestures to protest the use of autopoiesis outside its proper biological context: in 1978 he fell to his knees and implored the astrophysicist Eric Jantsch, author of a study entitled *The Self-organization of the Universe*, 'to stop misusing his concept' (see Maturana and Poerksen 105).

6. As Maturana and Varela note, 'the so-called "language" of bees . . . is not a language', but instinctive communicative behaviour that may be ontogenically modified (*Tree of Knowledge* 208).

7. There are six basic colours, three colour dimensions (hue, saturation and brightness), and four fundamental or unique 'hues' (red, green, yellow, blue). Unique hues combine to form complex binary hues (for example, red and yellow; blue and red), but for 'each unique hue, there is another unique hue with which it cannot coexist', a phenomenon known as 'opponent hues' (for example, red cannot coexist with green, nor can yellow with blue) (*Embodied Mind* 158). In contrast to hue (chromatic colours), white and black are achromatic colours (colours with zero hue). Why, Varela et al. ask, does colour appearance 'have this structure' (*Embodied Mind* 158)?

8. Pasteur's discovery forms the subject of Latour's first book as a single author, *The Pasteurization of France* (Schmidgen 57).

9. As Straus notes, the transformation of the jaws into the mouth has not been completed in the higher primates (162). Research cited by Maturana and Varela confirms that the incapacity of the higher primates to learn human language is primarily vocal, not intellectual. Experiments to teach apes sign language rather than phonetic language have been much more successful (see *Tree of Knowledge* 213–17).

4

Apocalypse as Field of Sense: Markus Gabriel's Ontology of Fields of Sense and Octavia Butler's *Parable* Series

This chapter turns to another variety of what I call 'new ecological realisms' after poststructuralism, Markus Gabriel's new realist ontology of fields of sense. Among the new realisms discussed in this study, Gabriel's is the most programmatic in announcing the exhaustion of postmodernism and locating his new realist ontology in the post-postmodernist era: 'New realism describes a philosophical stance that designates the era after so-called postmodernity . . . new realism is nothing more than the name for the age after postmodernity' (*Why the World* 1–2). Gabriel builds on the arguments of several contemporary philosophers from both the continental and analytic traditions, including Quentin Meillassoux and Paul Boghossian, who have declared the failure of postmodern constructivism. As defined by Gabriel, constructivism is 'the assumption that "we cannot discover any fact 'in itself'" but have instead constructed all facts ourselves' (*Why the World* 39), a belief crystallised by Nietzsche's famous claim that there are 'no facts', 'only interpretations' (qtd in *Why the World* 39).

Fields of sense ontology is a major contribution to the recovery of the concept of the real as newly relevant, surpassing poststructuralist dismissals of realism as naive *tout court*. Gabriel programmatically places himself within the 'ontological turn' in contemporary philosophy after poststructuralism. He advances his position in close dialogue with the 'speculative realism' of Quentin Meillassoux, Graham Harman and Ray Brassier. Like speculative realism, Gabriel revisits the famous Kantian Copernican Revolution that effected the 'modern primacy of epistemology over ontology' (*Transcendental Ontology* 1). But Gabriel's approach to the shared goal of redeeming ontology and overthrowing the modern rule of epistemology is quite different. As noted in Chapter 1, Meillassoux's attack on what he calls the post-Kantian philosophy of human access or correlationism is an uncompromising repudiation that leads him to endorse the other extreme, naturalism. For his part, Gabriel is as adamant in his critique of Meillassoux for embracing the dominant ideal of a mind-independent reality (which Meillassoux refers to as 'the great outdoors') as he is in flagging relapses into reductionist models of the real elsewhere in contemporary theory (for example, as will be explained below, in object-oriented ontology).

In approaching the problem of rehabilitating the real after postmodernism, Gabriel's expertise on German Idealism has proven to be essential. The central insight of post-Kantian idealist philosophy (Fichte, Schelling, Hegel), according to Gabriel, is the recognition of the reality of mental phenomena.[1] The transcendental idealism of Kant was designed to defang the threat of radical doubt by changing the standard of truth. It accepts that we cannot know things-in-themselves independently of us; instead it posits that knowledge is based on how things appear to us, which can be grasped objectively according to the universal categories of human cognition such as space, time and causality. The idealist philosophers who came after Kant, however, believed that the Kantian solution was inadequate and needed improving. As Gabriel explains, they discovered the circular nature of human knowledge: investigating thought is unlike investigating things such as trees or planets. To study the mind, we have to use the mind. There is no external critical stance on knowledge: we are always already within it and must therefore approach it from the inside. Like material things, thought exists, albeit in a different way. Hence the existence of mind (conceived in whichever way) is 'methodologically prior to the analysis of the subject's access to existence' (Gabriel, *Transcendental Ontology* ix). The crucial insight of German Idealism, according to Gabriel, is that 'we cannot circumvent ontology by "modestly" sticking with epistemology, because this presupposes an ontology of knowledge. Therefore post-Kantian idealism does not simply elaborate on Kant's epistemology, but reconstructs thought's ontological conditions' (*Transcendental Ontology* 1). In a sense, Gabriel's recovery of ontology reverses the direction of Meillassoux's approach, which rejects Kant's conception of mind-dependent truth. In contrast, Gabriel affirms the reality of mind and mental phenomena.

For this reason, Gabriel's new realism stands out among new ontologies after poststructuralism as the most robust in asserting the equal claim to truth and to reality of literature, religion and the arts. One of the key concepts of German Idealism is *Geist*, a term that has no equivalent in English, and that denotes both spirit (as in *Zeitgeist*, 'spirit of the times') as well as mind, or consciousness. In German, 'den Geist aufgeben [give up]' means to die. A third sense of *Geist* is 'meaning', a notion that underlies the German term for the humanities, *Geisteswissenschaften*. As Gabriel observes, the German idealists placed *Geist*, the understanding of meaning, at the centre of philosophy, to which the German term for humanities owes its name (*Why the World* 142). For his part, Gabriel turns his expertise on the forefathers of the *Geisteswissenschaften* towards a rehabilitation of humanistic work in our own time.

Gabriel celebrates the contribution of the humanities to knowledge in the ontological pluralism he defends. He maintains that, far from being synonymous with reality as such, the natural universe studied by science is only one field of sense among many others. According to Gabriel, the central concern of ontology is not the universe, but the world. For Gabriel, the world is 'everything that is the case' (following Wittgenstein), encompassing material (things) as well as non-material entities (facts). Further, we are always already in the world (following Heidegger). The scientific universe has been demoted to the status of 'ontological province' (*Why the World* 49), where it ranks as only one among an infinite number of other fields, including humanistic ones such art, poetry, mythology or politics. As Gabriel quips, 'poetry is just as capable of truth as a well-grounded mathematical theorem' (*Why the World* 196). Or more combatively, 'it is impossible to eliminate "Geist" by calling it brain perspiration' ('Existenz' 195). As Gabriel asserts, 'countering the hasty dismissal of spirit by postmodern constructivism, it is of the utmost importance to rehabilitate spirit' (*Warum es die Welt* 173; see also *Why the World* 142).

In addition to German Idealism, Gabriel also draws on various other traditions, including analytic philosophy. Like Maturana and Varela – and unlike Latour, who rejects phenomenology for excluding non-humans[2] – Gabriel further builds on the phenomenological tradition for his new realist ontology. In Europe, Gabriel initially developed his project of 'new realism' after postmodernism in collaboration with Maurizio Ferraris.[3] In 2013 Gabriel coordinated an international conference on new realism, 'Aussichten für einen Neuen Realismus' (Prospects for a New Realism), at Bonn University, which resulted in the collection of essays, *Der Neue Realismus* (*New Realism*, 2014).

Field of sense ontology proposes a revisionary concept of existence as appearance in a context, or more precisely, as appearance in a field of sense. Fields are worlds, contexts of meaning (of which an infinite plurality exist, including physics, cooking, art and so on). There are no things without facts that are true about things: 'Things in themselves always appear only in fields of sense, and that means that they are already embedded in facts' (*Why the World* 124). To attribute existence to isolated things-in-themselves, or to a mind-independent reality more generally, are claims that Gabriel rejects as variations of the 'old realism' of the representationalist paradigm (*Fields of Sense* 10). If objects by themselves do not exist, neither do contexts by themselves: 'To exist is to appear in specific fields of sense where the fields of sense characterise what exactly it is for something to appear in them' (*Fields of Sense* 44). Gabriel's contextual definition of the real as the composite of things and facts on the one hand and specific contexts in with they appear on the other makes his new ontology a core constituent of the new ecological realisms after poststructuralism considered in this study.

There are striking correspondences between Gabriel's new realism and systems thinking, the new twentieth-century science that examines organised wholes rather than constituent parts of wholes.[4] Gabriel's new realism is also a holistic, contextual or ecological realism, a realism whose basic units are wholes rather than parts. In the language of systems theory, fields of sense ontology 'concentrates not on basic building blocks, but on basic principles of organization' (Capra 30). This effects a reversal of the mechanistic model, which understands wholes by breaking them down into their smallest parts. Like Maturana and Varela's theory of autopoiesis and enactivism, which was considered in the previous chapter and which comes out of systems theory, Gabriel's field of sense realism emphasises the irreducible nature of organised wholes: wholes are more than the sum of their parts. Parts cannot be isolated from the patterns of organisation in which they appear. In field of sense ontology, as in autopoiesis and enactivism, organised wholes (the fields) and not isolated objects or parts are the 'ontological base units' (*Warum es die Welt* 68; see also *Why the World* 50). There are no pre-given objects outside of fields of sense. Roughly analogous to systems theory's claims about emergence (properties of the whole that none of the parts have, arising from the interaction and relationships among the parts), Gabriel insists that existence is 'a property of the fields, but not of the elements appearing within them' (*Fields of Sense* 65).

Like the other new realists considered here, Gabriel seeks to navigate a middle course between the twin dangers of postmodern constructivism on the one hand and scientific reductivism on the other. As he words it in his early study, *Transcendental Ontology*, 'I hope to be able to steer a course between the Scylla of a merely epistemological approach and the Charybdis of a one-sided ontology à la Badiou' (*Transcendental Ontology* x). Notably, Gabriel – as noted earlier – shares his sense of navigating between these extremes with Maturana and Varela, who describe their 'epistemological Odyssey: sailing between the Scylla monster of representation and the Charybdis whirlpool of solipsism' (*Tree of Knowledge* 134). Similarly, Gabriel pictures what Latour calls the 'modern constitution' via the opposing notions of the mind-independent external world, the 'world without spectators' (the scientific universe), and the 'world with spectators' (human society and culture). Like Latour, Gabriel rejects this dichotomy. According to Gabriel,

> both metaphysics and constructivism fail because of an unjustified simplification of reality, in which they understand reality unilaterally either as *the world without spectators* or, equally one-sided, as *the world of spectators* ... The world is neither exclusively the world without spectators nor the world of spectators. This is the new realism. Old realism – that is, metaphyics – was only interested in the world without spectators, while constructivism quite narcissistically grounded the world and everything that is the case on our fantasies. Both theories lead to nothing. (*Why the World* 7)

In other words, the problem is a consequence of the unacceptable universalisation of the stance of the scientific observer as a disembodied eye absent from the scene of representation of reality. Much of nature can be explained by reference to mathematical laws. But it does not follow that everything that exists is in nature. As Gabriel contends, 'a scientific worldview was prematurely inferred in which humans are no longer to be found. The human being began to erase itself from the world and to turn the world into its cold home: it began to identify the world with the universe' (*Why the World* 100).

I pair Gabriel with Octavia Butler's *Parable* series because field of sense ontology offers an ideal conceptual lens through which to understand what might easily be dismissed as Butler's naivety or New Ageism. Butler's central concern is a key manifestation of *Geist* – religion. Butler's protagonist, Lauren Oya Olamina, is a spiritual leader who founds a post-apocalyptic religion named Earthseed. Like McCarthy's, Atwood's and Saramago's novels, Butler's *Parable* series is a post-apocalyptic survivor narrative: its two volumes, *Parable of the Sower* (1993) and *Parable of the Talents* (1998), narrate how Lauren, the teenage daughter of a black Baptist minister, charts a path for survival for herself and a small utopian community of survivors in the late 2020s and early 2030s during a period of apocalyptic social, environmental and economic upheaval in America that is referred to as 'the Pox'. Middle-class LA communities such as Lauren's Robledo are besieged, robbed, terrorised and eventually invaded and burned by mobs of impoverished street poor on drugs, who rape, torture and murder the residents. Inspired by the 1992 Rodney King riots, Robledo's near-future science fictional scenario emblematises a national crisis: the collapse of capitalist modernity and the breakdown of contemporary civilisation.

Parable of the Sower follows Lauren, orphaned and homeless at the age of 18, as she escapes the urban apocalypse by joining the stream of scattered nomads migrating north in quest of safety. But far surpassing the goal of bare survival in a world in ruins, her focus is on devising an alternative civilisation to the modern one that has collapsed into chaos. In the *Parable* series, the quest for a new type of community and social organisation – a quintessential feature, as we have seen, of post-apocalyptic fiction in general – takes the shape of a spiritual or religious quest: the novels of Butler's *Parable* series are post-apocalyptic novels of ideas – of *Geist* or spirit in Gabriel's terms. They are novels about matters of belief and value, in Latour's terms 'matters of concern'. By extension, this chapter's pairing of Gabriel and Butler also reflects on parallel religious and mythological references in the other post-apocalyptic novels: for example, McCarthy's adaptation of the myth of Prometheus in *The Road* ('We are carrying the fire') or the apocalyptic green religion of the Gardeners that is the subject of the second volume of Atwood's *MaddAddam* series, *The Year of the Flood*. Yet in none of the other works does religious belief play as central a role as it does in Butler's *Parable* series.

Earthseed is a survivalist metaphysic emerging from, and founded on, the experience of disaster: Lauren creates it as an adolescent while enduring the inexorable approach of the destruction of her sheltered, suburban, middle-class American lifestyle. Apocalypse – the iron fact of mutability and change – is inscribed as the key principle of Lauren's faith: 'God is Power– / Infinite, / Irresistible, / Inexorable, / Indifferent. / And yet, God is Pliable– / Trickster, / Teacher, / Chaos, / Clay. / God exists to be shaped. / God is Change' (*Sower* 25). In Gabriel's terms, the familiar idea of 'God' appears in a new field of sense, a new organised context of experience and meaning – the context of apocalypse. According to field of sense ontology, there are no isolated things-in-themselves. As the *Parable* series demonstrates, this is also true for the realm of the divine and of spirituality. Apocalypse is the field that rearranges the appearance of things and ideas within it, including the figure of 'God'. Butler asks, what does it mean for God to appear in the context of the self-destruction of modern civilisation?

Gabriel's claim about the field-dependence of objects illuminates the difference between Lauren's God-as-Change and the traditional God of Christianity, as worshipped in her minister father's Baptist church. According to Gabriel's holistic conception of reality, existence or reality is a property of the field (the world of the apocalypse) and not of the objects appearing within it (God). As we have seen, apocalyptic thinking represents a unique articulation of holistic ontology. The following will further demonstrate how the post-apocalyptic script of a 'binary time, a before and an after' (Keller 90) underpinning the *Parable* series illuminates the constitutive nature of world in ways that the abstract claims of field of sense ontology cannot.

Field of sense ontology explains why Lauren's reconceptualisation of God is not a delusion or heathen cult worship (as her 'Christian American' brother Marcus later charges). On the contrary, Earthseed is the way that divinities and mortals (to use Heidegger's terms) are newly disclosed in a post-apocalyptic world of hyper-insecurity of day-to-day living at death's door. Yet Marcus's hostility is unsurprising, for Lauren's post-apocalyptic revelation overthrows the doctrines of biblical revelation by abandoning the notion of the divine as absolute being and by dethroning the personal God who governs the Christian picture of the end of the world. Far from absolute, God is relative to the field in which he appears. When the destruction of enclaves of middle-class comfort throws her into a nomadic existence, Lauren abandons the settler mentality of conventional Christianity for a new mobile logic of survival. Earthseed is what Gabriel calls a constitutive mythology of the post-apocalypse: the Earthseed metaphor after which Lauren names her 'God-is-Change belief system' is ecological and marks the reframing of human existence within a non-anthropocentric organisation. Human life shifts to a bio-centric lifestyle shared with plants. As Lauren's journal records, '[T]oday I found the name, found it while I was weeding the back garden and thinking about the way plants seed themselves, wind-borne, animalborne, far from their parent plants. They have no ability at all to travel great distance under their own power, and yet, they do travel' (*Sower* 77–8). The seed metaphor inscribes the core properties of displacement, nomadism and diasporic dispersion that define the post-apocalyptic world of the *Parable* series. It also names the values of flexibility and mobility required to survive in it. The appearance of Earthseed in the post-apocalyptic world identifies the triumph of the logic of deterritorialisation over the logic of settlement or territorialisation. Similarly, the plant-to-seed alternation between fixed 'roots' and mobile 'routes' following new waves of displacement proves a prescient description of Earthseed's subsequent history that begins in *Parable of the Sower* and continues in *Parable of the Talents*.

Markus Gabriel's Ontology of Fields of Sense

Like Latour's actor-network theory and the theory of the factish, Gabriel's field of sense ontology may be understood as the effort to reconstitute the concept of the real on a new footing in the wake of the postmodern challenge and the science wars of the 1990s. While Maturana and Varela and Latour outline variations of post-positivist realism, ontologies that overcome the double positivist and poststructuralist challenges from within science studies, Gabriel joins the debate as a humanist and a philosopher. Gabriel's goal is to challenge scientism and to reclaim ontological territory that rightly belongs to philosophy and to the humanities more generally. For Gabriel, ontology has been unjustifiably ceded to the sciences in the false reduction of the world (unified overall totality, defined as 'everything that is the case'; *Why the World*

33) to the physical universe (the object domain of the natural sciences). (Note that Gabriel does not use the terms 'world' and 'object' in their usual sense but as having a technical philosophical meaning, which is explained below.) For too long, 'philosophers have allowed themselves to be overawed, so to speak' by the natural sciences (*Why the World* 46). This section reviews the principal characteristics of Gabriel's ontology of fields of sense.

The beginnings of fields of sense ontology are in Gabriel's expertise in the philosophy of the late Schelling and German Idealism, developed in several publications, the most important of which are his essay 'The Mythological Being of Reflection – an Essay on Hegel, Schelling, and the Contingency of Necessity' (2009) and the study *Transcendental Ontology: Essays on German Idealism* (2011). Indeed, the late Schelling, 'who introduces a much-discussed and controversial distinction between *negative philosophy* and *positive philosophy*' (*Transcendental Ontology* 63), sponsors Gabriel's own variation on this division into a 'negative ontology' and a 'positive ontology'. These rubrics are the titles of the first and second parts of *Fields of Sense: A New Realist Ontology* (2015). Gabriel describes *Fields of Sense* as the more 'detailed' philosophical 'counterpart' to his earlier best-selling *Warum es die Welt nicht gibt* (2013), translated into English as *Why the World Does Not Exist* (2015).[5] However, Schelling and German Idealism recede into the background to the extent that Gabriel develops his own system of field-of-sense realism. In both *Why the World Does Not Exist* and *Fields of Sense*, analytic philosophy and logic (Gottlob Frege, Bertrand Russell, Georg Cantor, Willard Van Orman Quine, Hilary Putnam, Thomas Nagel, Paul Boghossian, Theodore Sider, as well as Alain Badiou and Quentin Meillassoux, and so on) play a much larger part in the argument than is the case in the work on German Idealism that culminates in *Transcendental Ontology*. Nonetheless, field-of-sense ontology may be seen as updating transcendental ontology, or the 'ontology of knowledge' (*Transcendental Ontology* 1), by incorporating transcendental ontology within the broader new ontological realism of fields of sense.

The best gloss of the division between negative and positive ontology is found in *Why the World Does Not Exist*:

Main principle of negative ontology: the world [unified totality] does not exist.

1st main principle of positive ontology: there exist an infinite number of fields of sense.

2nd main principle of positive ontology: every field of sense is itself an object. From this it immediately follows that, for each field of sense, there is a field of sense in which it appears. (*Warum es die Welt* 264–5; see also *Why the World* 78–9)[6]

Negative ontology culminates in what Gabriel calls the 'no-world view': *the* 'world does not exist', which Gabriel defines as 'any kind of unrestricted or overall totality, be it the totality of existence, the totality of what there is, the totality of objects, the whole of beings, or the totality of facts or states of affairs' (*Fields of Sense* 187). Positive ontology develops ontological pluralism, reconstituting the investigation of existence in place of the crossed-out totality.

The division into negative and positive ontology is helpful insofar as it marks the transitional point from the 'old realism', postmodern constructivism and related positions that Gabriel rejects to the new realism that he defends. To begin with old realism: old realism is Gabriel's umbrella term for a cluster of three concepts of the real considered objectionable – the concept of a mind-independent external world, the subject–object dualism it is founded on, and metaphysics (unified total reality, or *the* world). As noted above, the external world (things-in- themselves, the world without spectators) is a construct of modern science that posits a pre-existing 'outside' world (nature, the scientific universe) from which humans (or more precisely, mind) have been erased. New realism counters that reality is much bigger than the scientific universe, for reality also includes, for example, the human mind of the scientist investigating the universe. As Gabriel contends, one rock on which the concept of external reality founders is the higher-order problem of the observer: insofar as the observer also exists, his or her existence cannot be accounted for in a mind-independent external world. Gabriel explains:

Every thought about the world is at the same time a thought in the world. We cannot think the world from above or from the outside and for this reason we literally cannot think about the world. Thoughts about the world 'as a whole' are not truth-apt thoughts; they do not have an object to which they refer. (*Warum es die Welt* 104; see also *Why the World* 80)

Countering the worldless *cogito* of Descartes and Kant, Gabriel holds that human thoughts are more than just mental constructs: they are themselves 'small event[s] in the world' (*Why the World* 12). For this reason, Gabriel sides with German Idealism as well as phenomenology in rejecting the Kantian transcendental ego as an 'empty logical form' (*Transcendental Ontology* xi). Kant excluded things-in-themselves from knowledge, defining a paradigm shift in the transcendental turn in modern philosophy from ontology to epistemology. However, this ignores a central fact: 'Kant did not sufficiently take account of the seemingly trivial fact that the subject exists' (*Transcendental Ontology* xi). To illustrate Gabriel's claim quoted above, the reality that appears in a photograph is not all that exists: so does the person who takes the picture. The discovery of this principle, according to Gabriel, is the achievement of German Idealism: 'While Fichte, Schelling, and Hegel each take Kant in very different directions, their common project is transcendental ontology in the form of an ontology of the transcendental subject' (*Transcendental Ontology* xix). This is also the claim advanced in the study *Mythology, Madness, and Laughter*, which Gabriel co-authored with Slavoj Žižek. By elucidating some 'widely neglected features' of post-Kantian Idealism, Gabriel and Žižek propose to show that it 'was designed to effectuate a shift from epistemology to a new ontology without simply regressing to pre-critical metaphysics' (Gabriel and Žižek, 'Introduction' 5). In his earlier project before field-of-sense ontology, *Transcendental Ontology*, Gabriel explores this problem in depth, by introducing the concept of 'transcendental ontology'. '*Transcendental ontology investigates the ontological conditions of our conditions of access to what there is*' (*Transcendental Ontology* ix). The 'thought that transcendental ontology adds to this question is *that our thoughts about the way the world is are themselves a way the world is*' (xii).

The contemporary 'ontological turn' after poststructuralism in which Gabriel participates constitutes a fresh cycle of attempts to overcome the post-Kantian restriction of modern philosophy to epistemology. For example, Latour labels the transcendental ego the 'mind-in-the-vat' (*Pandora's Hope* 6). But lest this latest 'ontological turn' be mistaken as the first, Gabriel recognises and draws on Heidegger's contribution in *Being and Time* of the foundational deconstruction of Cartesian subject–object dualism and the construct of an external world. In Heidegger's influential affirmation:

'In directing itself toward ... and in grasping something, Dasein does not first go outside of the inner sphere in which it is initially encapsulated, but, rather, in its primary kind of being, it is always already "outside" together with some being encountered in the world already discovered' (*Being and Time* 62 §13). Heidegger redefines the Cartesian observer as Dasein. As Gabriel notes, 'the world is not identical with the world without observers but includes us as participants' ('Heidegger' 46). 'Heidegger has shown that we cannot count on a grounding external world that already consists in individuated objects, to which we just need to add values or numbers' ('Heidegger' 47). Progressing further beyond the positions of German Idealism, Heidegger explicitly postulates the primordiality of being over knowledge: being (that the observer exists already in a world) precedes the epistemological problem (what her conditions of knowledge are). In Heidegger's view, this had been concealed by the 'forgetting of being' in modern philosophy. Indeed, the ontology of the late Heidegger – the philosophy of the event (*Ereignis*) – plays an important role in Gabriel's transcendental ontology.

In Gabriel's view, another rock on which the 'old realist' notion of a pre-existing external world founders is the problem of reference. Access to a pre-existing external world depends on the concept of reference. Concepts are said to be referential if they are directly linked to the 'external world'. For example, the logical positivists of the Vienna Circle focused on developing a scientific language composed of 'words that refer directly to sense data' (Polkinghorne 63). An example of such a referential statement would be 'yellow blob here'. The logical positivists were influenced by Wittgenstein's *Tractatus Logico-Philosophicus* (1921), which also maintained that 'there are some words that directly name parts of reality' (Polkinghorne 105). To expose the instability of the notion of referentiality, Gabriel draws on the work of the late nineteenth-century logician and mathematician Gottlob Frege. In his essay, 'Sense and Reference', Frege examines a form of statement known as 'identity statements' in logic, showing that 'there is no immediate access to reference' (*Transcendental Ontology* xiv). Frege used the famous example of 'morning star' and 'evening star': 'According to Frege, the proper names "evening star" and "morning star" refer to the same thing, that is, Venus. However, "Venus" is also a proper name' (*Transcendental Ontology* xiii). Frege defines 'sense' as the varying ways in which objects are given or appear, and 'reference' as the object that they refer to. Gabriel offers a simple example of an identity statement of his own: '2 + 2 = 3 + 1' (*Why the World* 68). He explains:

> Now Frege calls '2 + 2' and '3 + 1' 'modes of givenness' and equates this with the term 'sense'. The sense of terms equated in an identity statement is different, while that to which they refer is identical (i.e. . . . the number 4). Thus, in a true, informative, and coherent identity statement we learn that the same thing (the same person, the same fact) can be presented in different ways. Instead of givenness, I prefer the term 'appearance'. Thus, sense is the way in which an object appears. (*Warum es die Welt* 90–1; see also *Why the World* 68–9)

The point here is that reference is not a stand-alone (or objective) concept. Reference, as it turns out, continually refers us back to sense: 'There are no objects or facts outside of fields of sense. Everything that exists appears in a field of sense' (*Why the World* 70). Morning star and evening star both appear in the field of the everyday lifeworld. Venus appears in the scientific field of astronomy. Hence, Gabriel concludes, objects don't ground themselves: rather, 'fields ground objects' (*Fields of Sense* 167).

To Gabriel, what counts as an object is therefore not pre-given but 'theory-dependent' (*Fields of Sense* 61). Gabriel draws on Frege for the key insight that existence is not an inherent property of objects, but a property of the fields in which they appear (*Fields of Sense* 101). Objects do not pre-exist the contexts in which they appear, they only exist insofar as they appear in contexts. As the following section argues, Butler's *Parable* series holds the same view, exploring the field-dependency of objects with regard to one of the most important and contentious phenomena of all – the figure of God and the divine. Butler challenges the view that God is who he is thought to be – timeless, unchanging being. Far from being absolute (the unmoved mover), how God appears is relative to the post-apocalyptic world in which he appears. Lauren's notion of the relativity of God overthrows traditional notions of the divine as the realm of perfection. This is a revolutionary idea, which field of sense ontology helps us illuminate.

Gabriel demonstrates the field-dependence of objects by way of another example that he calls the 'allegory of the cubes' ('Neutral Realism' 189; see also *Fields of Sense* 223–4). Gabriel's allegory echoes the experiments of logical positivism with a purely descriptive language and identifies their failure:

Suppose that three cubes lie on a table: a blue, a red, and a white cube. Now we ask an unbiased passer-by how many objects there are on the table – which normally should trigger '3' as the right response. A physicist with metaphysical tendencies might on the other hand give an estimation of the elementary particles that 'lie on the table', and in doing so also give the correct response 'N', where N is considerably larger than 3. A creative response could be '1', where the cube array is viewed as a singular artwork, for example, an ironic allusion to the films by Kieslowski. And so on. Let 'sense' here refer to the description under which 3, N, and 1 turn out to be true answers to the question concerning *how many objects there are on the table*. ('Neutral Realism' 189)

As seen here, direct reference turns out to be nothing but mediated sense (object grounded by field). There is no immediate access to autonomous objects by way of 'reference'. Any reference presupposes the choice of a context, or field, or theory, or domain in which the selected object appears. But this choice is often pre-reflective. Adapting Heidegger, this might be called the 'forgetting of field'. Typically, contexts that are forgotten are contexts that are too familiar to be noticed.

Further pursuing the notion of absolute being, according to Gabriel, a third dimension of old realism to be rejected is metaphysics. In the Introduction to *Fields of Sense*, Gabriel states his intention to 'shed new light on the questions traditionally dealt with under the heading of "ontology" and "metaphysics" by giving up two ideas: first, the association of ontology and metaphysics, and second, the idea that there is or ought to be a unified totality' (*Fields of Sense* 5). He elaborates:

Metaphysics is a combination of a) an account of reality versus appearance, and b) a theory of totality, a theory I also refer to as the investigation of the world as world . . . Roughly, metaphysics originates in the desire to uncover reality as it is in itself, where this means reality independently of what we add to it by thinking about it. (*Fields of Sense* 6)

In all its various aspects, metaphysics names the belief that there is a fundamental reality beneath the phenomenal world of appearances. As Gabriel notes, the idea of an ultimate reality, a highest real or absolute truth transcending phenomenal reality, is an old European concept dating from Plato. In contrast, the metaphysics of modern times is neither God nor Plato's timeless forms but scientism, 'the belief that only the natural sciences understand the fundamental level of reality ... while all other knowledge claims are always reducible to the sciences' (*Why the World* 103). Rejecting this idea, Gabriel affirms the irreducibility of all phenomena to a higher-order reality of any kind. In our time, such fundamental entities are typically assumed to be the elementary particles, genes and neurobiology of modern scientific materialism:

> For materialism, all non-material objects exist only, as it were, as an appendage to the material. This thesis promotes itself by claiming to offer a complete explanation of the world, which states: everything that exists is material, which also includes our thoughts, which are merely material (neuronal) states of the brain. Anything seemingly non-material is only a phantom. (*Warum es die Welt* 45; see also *Why the World* 30)

In Gabriel's view, the reductionist model of a higher-order real located in a world-behind-the-world ('Hinterwelt') to which surface reality may be reduced is thoroughly flawed (*Warum es die Welt* 191; see also *Why the World* 160). Like Latour, Gabriel embraces the model of a flat ontology, noting that the 'idea of a flat ontology brings out an important feature' of his new realist ontology (*Transcendental Ontology* 253).[7] Gabriel's rejection of a higher-order real corresponds to Latour's principle of irreduction discussed in Chapter 1. Just as, for Latour, no actor-networks are reducible to other actor-networks, for Gabriel, no field is reducible to another. (To be clear, the reductive contextualisation that both Gabriel and Latour reject is the idea of absolute wholes – 'the' world, or a box-like framework – located behind or 'above' the plurality of contexts or fields of sense that Gabriel posits. In other words, Gabriel's contextual realism implies ontological pluralism, whereas higher-order realism eliminates it, endorsing ontological monism.) The rejection of the notion of a fundamental reality in turn has implications for the distinction between (surface) appearance and (hidden higher) reality posited by old realism. Gabriel's new realism demolishes this dichotomy. There is no opposition between appearance and reality: insofar as existence is defined as the appearance of objects in fields of sense, appearance *is* reality. 'Appearances are as real as it gets' (*Fields of Sense* 168).

To recapitulate: the core of Gabriel's negative ontology is the rejection of metaphysics in the specific sense of a unified overall totality: *the* world does not exist. The most systematic exposition of Gabriel's no-world view is offered in his TEDx talk.[8] In that talk, Gabriel proceeds by way of a series of propositions of what world (in the sense of totality) might be, and arrives at their falsification. The first proposition is that the world is the totality of things, with things defined as spatiotemporal objects. To complete the collection of things whose total sum would be 'the world', one would have to draw up a complete list. This might take several lifetimes. But even supposing that such an exhaustive list could be created, the project would fail, due to the higher-order problem encountered earlier in the context of thought: the world as a totality of things would have to include the list in addition to the things listed there. Gabriel observes: 'Ludwig Wittgenstein, in the first sentences of his *Tractatus Logico-Philosophicus*, was the first to call attention to this decisive point: I. The world is everything that is the case. II. The world is the totality of facts, not of things' (*Why the World* 33). Facts are defined as 'something that is true of something' (*Why the World* 33). In the example Gabriel discusses, if the moon and the sun, both spatiotemporal objects, exist, then there is also the fact that the sun is bigger than the moon. But facts are not spatiotemporal objects, since there is no location in space-time for the fact that the sun is bigger than the moon. Facts are concepts. Nonetheless, they exist, since they describe actual properties of things. 'Objects are embedded in facts' (*Fields of Sense* 167). Like thoughts, facts are not just mental constructs; they are part of the inventory of the world. For this reason, the mechanistic concept of world as a collection of spatiotemporal things fails.

Gabriel next examines the proposition that the world is the totality of facts (the hypothesis of the *Tractatus*). The experiment again is to make a list of all facts (of everything that is true about something). Once again, a higher-order ontological problem intervenes: any complete list of all facts must also include the list itself, since the list is part of the unrestricted totality of what exists. The existence of the list could be accounted for by making a meta-list. But the meta-list would in turn have to appear in any complete list of the totality of facts, so it requires yet another meta-meta-list, and so on. We are here encountering the problem of infinite regress: 'We never come to an end . . . Rather, the world is always deferred' (*Why the World* 82). Gabriel explains that

> One can imagine the unending deferral of the world as a form of fractal ontology. Fractals are geometric structures that consist of an infinite number of copies of themselves . . . The non-existent world is copied within itself an infinite number of times, so to speak; there are many worlds, which are in turn composed of many worlds. For this reason we only ever know sections of the infinite. An overview of the whole is impossible, because the whole does not exist at all. (*Why the World* 82)

In the philosophical terminology of *Fields of Sense*, Gabriel articulates his position as follows: 'I defend *meta-metaphysical nihilism*, that is, the view that metaphysics literally talks about nothing, that there is no object or domain it refers to. I will also call this the *no-world view*, that is, the view that the world does not exist' (*Fields of Sense* 7).

In proposing the no-world view, Gabriel builds on Badiou and Meillassoux, who have argued 'that the old European notion of an infinite totality must be replaced by and through the concept of an in principle untotalizable *transfinite*' (*Transcendental Ontology* 124–5; see also 'Kontingenz oder Notwendigkeit' 181–2). The claim that the Absolute or the All (in the sense of an unrestricted totality) cannot exist is made by recourse to analytic philosophy. Like Badiou and Meillassoux, Gabriel draws on Cantor's theorem and Russell's paradox. Cantor and Russell model a 'set-theoretical ontology' (*Fields of Sense* 116). Cantor's theorem holds that the set of possible subsets of a set is necessarily larger than the original set, even if the latter is infinite: 'The alleged whole is rather the transfinite dimension of infinite proliferation' (*Transcendental Ontology* 125). Gabriel endorses Badiou's and Meillassoux's attempts to do ontology without the absolute, without totalisation. He accepts Badiou's conclusion: 'giving up on totality in the sense of an all-encompassing set, a set which has absolutely everything as its members' (*Fields of Sense* 116). However, he registers a methodological objection: 'In ontology, set theory does not speak for itself' (*Fields of Sense* 117). As Gabriel points out, Badiou and Meillassoux employ a form of mathematicism, which is 'the position that everything is subject to mathematical structures' (*Fields of Sense* 222).[9] That this is unacceptable was grasped by a classical authority: 'Aristotle already pointed out against Plato's mathematicism that there are many objects we cannot think of mathematically, as they involve contingency and vagueness in forms that are not accessible to any discrete description' (*Fields of Sense* 222). Typically, this is the case in other fields of sense, such as 'love'.

Having reviewed the deficiencies of various aspects of 'old realism', we can proceed to the details of the new realism that Gabriel proposes. Given that, as negative ontology establishes, the world is neither the totality of things nor the totality of facts, how to define the world within the frame of positive ontology? In Gabriel's initial definition, 'The world is neither the totality of things nor the totality of facts, but it is that domain in which all existing domains are found. All domains that exist belong to the world' (*Why the World* 45). A unified totality – *the* world – does not exist, but it can positively be defined as follows: '*The world is the field of sense in which all other fields of sense appear*' (*Why the World* 74). The main principle of positive ontology is ontological pluralism: there is no unified totality; there are merely indefinitely many fields of sense. 'In part, some of these overlap each other, in part, others will never come into contact with each other in any way' (*Warum es die Welt* 94; see also *Why the World* 72). Thus, 'many things are connected with many other things, but it is false (in the strict sense, actually impossible!) that everything is connected' (*Why the World* 10). Day to day, each human life is lived by weaving an idiosyncratic trajectory through the labyrinth of fields of sense that include the worlds of work, poetry, nonsense, music, TV, science, and last but not least, philosophy. 'The world in which we live shows itself as a single, continuous transition from field of sense to field of sense, as an amalgamation and interlacing of fields of sense' (*Warum es die Welt* 125; see also *Why the World* 97). Like Latour, if Gabriel shares any feature with postmodernism, it is this rejection of totalisation. Yet while postmodernism is an epistemology, new realisms are ontologies.

Gabriel's concept of the world draws on the notion introduced by Heidegger of world as the 'domain of all domains' (*Why the World* 45). The crucial shift here is from a mechanistic and quantifying to a contextual or ecological paradigm of the real. For Heidegger, knowledge is always disclosed from within, on condition of a prior immersion into a world (*Umwelt*). Things always exist in a specific context, from within which they are disclosed as what they are. Space is not abstract, but relative, divided into specific contexts or domains, which must 'always already' be discovered for knowledge to occur. For example, in the well-known tool analysis in *Being and Time*, Heidegger writes: 'Something akin to a region must already be discovered if there is to be any possibility of referring and finding the places of a totality of useful things available to circumspection' (*Being and Time* 100 §22).[10] Adopting Heidegger's phenomenological concept of world and his contextual definition of existence, Gabriel posits that '[e]xisting always takes place locally, which can be identified as being-here' ('Existenz' 198). In other words, existence is always 'relative' to one or more specific fields (*Why the World* 90).

In his more technical expositions in *Fields of Sense* and his contribution to his edited collection *Der Neue Realismus*, 'Existenz, realistisch gedacht' ('Existence, conceived realistically'), Gabriel voices a strong critique of modern ontology of the analytic tradition in the wake of Russell. In Gabriel's view, contemporary ontology falls short because of its quantifying mechanistic view of existence:

> What I am attacking is the idea that existence is significantly related to quantifiable individuation, whether the objects thus counted are substances, events, or absolute processes. I reject the idea that to be is to be one, or a one, a unified object, be it unified in itself or unified by thought, language, discursive practices, the symbolic order, the neurochemistry of what we think of as intentionality or what have you. (*Fields of Sense* 105)

Gabriel rejects the 'dogma of twentieth-century ontology in the form of the notion that all we need to say about existence is identical with what we need to say about the existential quantifier: ∃' (*Fields of Sense* 91). The existential quantifier identifies existence ('there is') with 'counting as one', or being 'a unified object' (*Fields of Sense* 102). For example, apples and drops of water are very different kinds of objects. In a bowl with one apple, adding two more apples yields three apples. In a cup with one drop of water, adding two more drops of water does not yield three drops of water, but just a bigger drop of water. Because not all objects – not even spatiotemporal ones – are countable is another reason why the world cannot be a collection of objects. The mechanistic paradigm of the world as a collection of things fails because objects cannot be identified in the abstract. Therefore, existence also cannot be a property of isolated objects. There are no objects below the threshold of domains. Hence, for Gabriel, things cannot be ontological base units. Drawing on Frege and his deconstruction of direct reference to external-world objects, Gabriel maintains that '"existence" cannot be a proper property of objects' (*Transcendental Ontology* xxii). Objects are not the entities on which to found ontology.

Gabriel's rejection of unified objects as ontological base units places his new realist ontology at odds with object-oriented ontology, which claims that ontologically distinct substances are primary (see also Shaviro 144). According to Harman, 'the object in its inner life is never touched by any of the entities that bump, crush, meddle, or carouse with it' (*Guerrilla Metaphysics* 73). On the other hand, field of sense ontology and object-oriented ontology are aligned in their shared anti-reductionism with regard to scale as well as the diversity of things. Thus, Gabriel appreciates the distinction made by Harman between two tendencies of explaining away objects, 'undermining' and 'overmining' (*Fields of Sense* 144). In the allegory of the three cubes mentioned above, for example, an object underminer would claim that they are reducible to the more fundamental reality of a swirl of elementary particles. Scientific materialism typically 'undermines' objects. 'Overmining' is the contrary view that 'reduces [objects] upward rather than downward. Instead of saying that objects are too shallow to be real, it is said that they are too deep' (Harman, *Quadruple Object* 10). In the allegory of the three cubes, the art critic who sees one art object instead of three cubes is an object overminer.

At this point, let us revisit the problem of appearance vs. reality. Isn't it true – Gabriel asks, playing devil's advocate – that there are things in themselves that we construct from different perspectives, by looking at or talking about them in different ways? Gabriel's new realist response to the problem of appearances adopts the phenomenological stance: when things show themselves to an observer, they show themselves as they really are. Husserl's maxim 'To the things themselves!' referred to things as given to consciousness, to phenomena. In *Being and Time*, Heidegger technically defines phenomena as that which show themselves out of themselves as they are: 'the concept of phenomenon is understood from the very beginning as the self-showing in itself' (*Being and Time* 29 §6A). Heidegger clearly sets out the 'phenomenological concept of phenomenon' in opposition to the Platonic concept of appearance as unreal semblance: 'Phenomena are *never* appearances' (*Being and Time* 28 §7A). For phenomenology, the phenomena of art, dreams, mythology or the everyday lifeworld are not fictions that distort or misconstrue a higher objective truth that lies behind these appearances, to be revealed by the metaphysics of scientism. (Nor is it the case, as postmodern constructivism posits, that there are only deceptive appearances and no facts.) As Gabriel elucidates,

> The point is that things in themselves appear in different ways. The appearances are themselves things in themselves; they are as real as it gets. The way the appearances exist is contingent upon the field of sense in which they appear. The plurality of ways of appearing is not an illusion. Reality does not consist of hard facts that are withdrawn from appearance; instead, reality consists of both things in themselves *and* of their appearances, with appearances also being things in themselves. How my left hand appears to me is as real as my left hand in itself. (*Warum es die Welt* 154-55; see also *Why the World* 124)

Appearances *are* real: this is the gist of Gabriel's new realist definition of existence: 'Existence = appearing in a field of sense' (*Why the World* 65).

This assertion may sound like sophistry, but it is perfectly consistent with Gabriel's field-oriented or ecological concept of the real. In Gabriel's view, existence is a higher-order property of fields not of objects. As he clarifies the above definition further:

> Existence is a property, but not a property of individuals, but rather of fields of sense, namely their property that something appears within them . . . To exist is to appear in a field of sense, which I take to be a property of the fields, but not of the elements appearing within them. (*Fields of Sense* 65)

There are trolls in Norwegian mythology. But that is not to say that there are trolls in Norway (*Why the World* 88). There are electrically charged objects in electric fields. Or, to look ahead to the discussion of Butler's *Parable* series in the following section, there is a new changeable God in the post-apocalyptic world. God is no longer considered an unchanging being. The nature of the field (mythology, geography, electricity, the home – or apocalypse) determines which objects appear in them and which don't – including the nature of supreme beings, divinities. As Gabriel illustrates, the objects that appear in one's living room, such as sofa, table and TV, are not the objects that appear in the universe, such as planets. I may be watching the stars through a telescope while standing at my living room window. Nonetheless, this does not mean that planets, which appear in the universe, also appear in the field of sense that is my living room (*Why the World* 34–5). This is what Gabriel means by maintaining that fields of sense – not discrete objects – are ontological base units. There are the 'places where anything appears, if it appears at all' (*Warum es die Welt* 68; see also *Why the World* 50).

As these examples show, fields come in all varieties. Some fields are material and physical. Others are non-material. Some fields are political, some are entirely discursive or even blatantly imaginary: there are 'meerkats, local elections, the universe, and living rooms' (*Why the World* 50). But, qua fields, all possess the property of existence – ontological pluralism. Gabriel rejects any attempt to put limitations on the 'infinite number of fields of sense' (*Why the World* 78). For this reason, Gabriel dismisses 'zoontology' or anthropocentric ontology (*Fields of Sense* 33–71). Zoontology is a fallacy that 'overestimate[s] our position as special knowers in our planet "zoo"' (*Fields of Sense* 34): existence has to be thought more broadly than what is interesting or important from the point of view of zoontology. At the same time that Gabriel makes a crucial distinction between fields of sense and objects, he also maintains that this distinction is relative rather than absolute. This is stated in the second main principle of positive ontology: 'every field of sense is an object. From this it immediately follows that, for every field of sense, there is a field of sense in which it appears' (*Why the World* 79). Given this, how to tell the difference between fields and objects? 'Insofar as fields are grounded, they are objects, and insofar as they ground, they are fields' (*Fields of Sense* 167).

Fields are not Nietzschean perspectives or interpretations. Unlike the latter, fields are plural and real. This is true of all fields, not just particle physics but also mythology, poetry, art and the field of apocalypse. Gabriel's point here parallels Latour's theory of the factish, which dismantles the dichotomy between humanistic beliefs that are dismissed as 'not real' and scientific facts that are accepted as 'real'. The objective nature of the fields is also the reason why Gabriel adopts Frege's notion of fields of sense, instead of alternatives such as 'perspectives'. As Gabriel explains:

Fields are generally unconstructed, and their force is felt by the objects entering them. An electric field, for instance, can be detected by some bodies entering it, and we can detect it by using things manifesting certain properties when interacting with the field. The field provides objective structures and interacts with the objects appearing within it. It is already there, and objects can pass through it and change its properties. Fields are not horizons or perspectives; they are not epistemological entities or objects introduced to explain how we can know how things are. They are an essential part of how things are in that without fields, nothing could exist. (*Fields of Sense* 157–8)

Gabriel's image of fields exerting force on objects entering them nicely captures the gist of Lauren Olamina's development in *Parable of the Sower*: as the organisation of Lauren's suburban world falls apart, the phenomenon of the divine is revealed to her in a new, equally unstable guise. In addition to the metaphor of electric fields, Gabriel also uses the metaphor of magnetic fields to explain the difference between fields of sense and domains. Gabriel's choice of fields over domains relates to his rejection of the quantifying view of existence prevailing there (and in set-theoretical ontology), which was discussed earlier (*Fields of Sense* 157–61).[11] Domain is a concept from traditional domain ontology. Domains 'have a tendency to be neutral regarding the question concerning what is found in it' (*Why the World* 87). They are mere containers. Gabriel compares domains to rooms: rooms are still rooms even if they are empty, and no matter what objects are put in them. 'In contrast, fields of sense cannot be understood without the orientation or arrangement of the objects that appear in them. They are similar to magnetic fields: one sees magnetic fields only when one disperses certain objects over them that consequently reveal their form' (*Warum es die Welt* 113; see also *Why the World* 87). Whereas domains are indifferent to what is collected in them, identity is essential to fields: 'Fields of sense are determined by the objects that appear in them. Fields of sense and their objects belong together. Objects are closely bound up with the sense of the fields' (*Warum es die Welt* 113; *Why the World* 87). Thus, subatomic particle objects cannot appear in the field of fashion. The magnetic field illustrates the identity fit between objects and fields at all scales and in all types of fields. Yet unlike Barad's agential realism, field of sense ontology is not scale-blind: for Barad, processes in the quantum world literally define processes everywhere else; thus, human inter-action is *intra*-action. In contrast, field of sense ontology does not claim that the laws of electromagnetism explain why humans are attracted to each other. Gabriel's electromagnetic analogy is restricted to the abstract law of fit between fields and objects: fields determine the kinds of objects that appear and the processes that take place in them. What these are will vary in each case. Thus, in the *Parable* series, the changing, mutable God of Lauren's post-apocalyptic spirituality and the apocalyptic world she or he belongs to share the same nature – the principle of crisis and disaster.

It is illuminating to note that the concept of field introduced by Gabriel corresponds to developments in the history of science that he does not fully explore or make sufficiently explicit. Indeed, Gabriel's choice of examples, magnetic and electric fields, anchors his new realist ontology of fields of sense in an important moment in the history of science, the nineteenth-century discovery of electromagnetism. Michael Faraday and James Clerk Maxwell's theory of electrodynamics was one of the first steps beyond mechanism to the systems view. In electromagnetism, the active forces are not isolated objects but integrated wholes – fields. In Capra and Luisi's account, by 'replacing the concept of a force with the much subtler concept of a field, they were the first to go beyond Newtonian physics, showing that fields had their own reality and could be studied without any reference to material bodies' (Capra and Luisi 31). In contrast to Newtonian physics, an object-based physics that pictures solid objects moving through space following the laws of motion, the fundamental entities in the theory of electrodynamics are fields, or irreducible wholes.

More recently, fields as ontological units have also figured in theories of self-organisation, which was the subject of the previous chapter. Brian Goodwin conceptualises organisms as morphogenetic fields. More generally, contemporary organismic biologists, a group including Stephen Rose as well as Levins and Lewontin, seek to shift the debate from genes to organisms: organisms are not simply collections of their genes, but irreducible wholes whose ontogenic development is the result of the interaction of multiple forces, only one of which is genetic. According to Webster and Goodwin, 'the term "morphogenetic field" denotes *something* real, irrespective of the adequacy of our theories, because we can physically manipulate fields and because they cause things to happen' (Webster and Goodwin 98).

To tie this back to Gabriel's theory of fields of sense: the principle of identity fit confers an element of objectivity and realism to fields that is immanent rather than imposed from the outside. It requires being-within, the Heideggerian principle of thrownness that states that worlds disclose themselves only when accessed from the inside. In his essay on Schelling, 'The Mythological Being of Reflection', Gabriel develops this point by arguing that Schelling's late philosophy prefigures this Heideggerian insight. The key concept introduced by Schelling is unprethinkable being (*unvordenkliches Seyn*), which he identifies with mythology (Gabriel, 'Mythological Being' 20). In Schelling's view, mythology 'denominates the brute fact of existence of a logical space, which cannot be accounted for in logical terms' (20). For Schelling, in other words, 'reflection bears an indelible mythological remainder' (21): this means that thought 'cannot properly account for the fact of its own existence' (22). '*Reflection is limited precisely because it is engendered by mythology and not the other way around*' (62). According to Gabriel, Schelling's point corresponds to Heidegger's insight into the primordiality of being over knowledge. But there is an important difference: 'unlike Heidegger, Schelling locates the primordial withdrawal of the event in *mythology*' (26). 'Mythology is the brute fact of our thrownness into a meshwork of beliefs, into a belief-system which is only accessible from within' (66). Schelling's achievement, Gabriel argues, is the recognition of the centrality of constitutive mythologies: 'Constitutive mythologies open up a world' (67). As I argue in the following section, this is also the central insight of Butler's *Parable* series.

It should be evident that field of sense ontology mounts a strong defence of literature, art and religion as genuine forms of knowledge in their own right. Indeed, *Why the World Does Not Exist* concludes with two chapters, 'The Meaning of Religion' and 'The Meaning of Art', exploring the singularity of religion and art. Art demonstrates that there are no things-in-themselves, things existing in isolation. 'Art shows that objects only ever appear in fields of sense, insofar as art brings its objects to appearance by connecting them with the sense in which they appear' (*Why the World* 190). Art makes us aware that pre-reflective worlds of meaning exist as contexts in which things appear, by displacing them from 'the fields of sense in which they normally appear without our being aware of how they are doing so' (*Warum es die Welt* 215; see also *Why the World* 185). Gabriel's non-reductive approach to art and religion as fields of sense among a plurality of other fields therefore further buttresses the case made in this study – to adapt Derek Attridge's term – for the singularity of post-apocalyptic literature.

Apocalypse as Field of Sense: Octavia Butler's *Parable* Series

In an interview, Butler describes the two volumes of the *Parable* series, *Parable of the Sower* and *Parable of the Talents*, as near-future science fiction warning about the calamitous consequences of present developments. 'Robert A. Heinlein had these three categories of science-fiction stories: the "what-if" category; the "if-only" category; and the "if-this-goes-on" category', Butler told an audience at MIT in 1998. 'And I liked the idea. So this is definitely an if-this-goes-on story' (Canavan, 'Butler's Lost Parables' 2).[12] Butler's portrait of post-apocalyptic California in the aftermath of 'the Pox' extrapolates developments in Reagan-era neoliberal America: deregulation of private markets, small government, tax cuts, increasing class and racial inequality. The regalian (or representative-administrative) functions of the state still exist (local, state and federal government, police, firefighters, army).[13] However, state institutions are either ineffective or corrupt: state services are restricted to property owners, the police generally do not investigate crimes and refuse to offer protection to the destitute and the homeless. The social state has completely disappeared: the K-12 free public school system, pensions, healthcare for the elderly and the poor (medicaid) are gone. Basic literacy (reading and writing) has become a privilege.

Hazel Carby and others link the dystopian vision of the *Parable* series with a Los Angeles brand of disaster novels of the 1990s that illustrated Mike Davis's portrait of LA as a militarised and segregated 'carceral city' (*Ecology of Fear* 253).[14] Fortified walls separate gated luxury enclaves from areas in post-industrial decay. According to Davis, as in the *laissez-faire* nineteenth-century city, the late capitalist destruction of public space cedes urban space to private capital. The post-liberal carceral city wages class warfare on the poor and homeless segregated in downtown 'free-fire zones' (*Ecology of Fear* 377). Lauren's husband Taylor Bankole assesses the apocalyptic condition of Butler's early twenty-first-century America as follows:

The period of upheaval that journalists have begun to refer to as 'the Apocalypse' or more commonly, more bitterly, 'the Pox' lasted from 2015 through 2030 – a decade and a half of chaos. This is untrue. The Pox has been a much longer torment. It began well before 2015, perhaps even before the turn of the millennium. It has not ended. I have also read that the Pox was caused by accidentally coinciding climatic, economic, and sociological crises. It would be more honest to say that the Pox was caused by our own refusal to deal with obvious problems in those areas. We caused the problems: then we sat and watched as they grew into crises . . . Overall, the Pox has had the effect of an installment-plan WW III. (*Talents* 7–8)

As seen here, the if-this-goes-on variety of apocalyptic fiction is a risk-assessment narrative. Its speculative realism, as noted in Chapter 1, hinges on causal connections that tie pre-apocalyptic presents to (post-)apocalyptic futures.

Parable of the Sower relates the early history of Lauren Oya Olamina's life in the period between 2024 and 2027. The first half of the novel depicts the inexorable deterioration of conditions in Lauren's neighbourhood of Robledo, a middle-class suburb '20 miles from Los Angeles' (*Sower* 10). It narrates the destruction of Robledo by arsonists, through riots of the underdogs, and follows Lauren as she begins a new life on the road among homeless refugees migrating north to escape from the Hobbesian conditions of urban warfare of all against all.

Lauren remakes her life by gathering a small multiracial community around her from those she meets on the road. On the highway, now 'a river of the poor' (*Sower* 223), Lauren begins to proselytise refugees: 'I've come to think that I should be fishing that river even as I follow its current' (*Sower* 223). As the group of survivors from Robledo and other disasters, many of whom are escaped slaves, aggregates, Lauren becomes their spiritual leader, developing her utopian vision of Earthseed as a new spiritual and social paradigm for life in the post-apocalyptic period. The narrative ends with the settlement of the group in the coastal foothills of Humboldt County in northern California on land owned by one of the community members, Taylor Bankole, a black doctor of Lauren's father's age who becomes Lauren's husband.

Acorn, as they name their settlement, is a classic utopian enclave, 'a secession within real social space' (Jameson, *Archaeologies* 2). Acorn's organisation negates the principles of late capitalist America: 'like a foreign body within the social' (Jameson, *Archaeologies* 16), Acorn is its antithesis. A world where 'everything is made by hand' (*Sower* 288), Acorn harks back to nineteenth-century US farming settlements on the frontier. As on the historical Western frontier, it is surrounded by an alien wilderness both natural and social – except that its social dimension is not represented by indigenous people but by the barbarism of degenerated late capitalist US civilisation. However, it is clear from the start that their new wilderness home is not a safe haven. Upon their arrival, they find the burned remains of the previous settlement and its occupants, Bankole's sister's family: 'a broad black smear on the hillside; a few charred planks sticking up from the rubble, some leaning against others; and a tall brick chimney, standing black and solitary like a tombstone in a picture of an old-style graveyard. A tombstone amid the bones and ashes' (*Sower* 314). Lauren has escaped the Robledo holocaust only to build a new home on the ruins of another.

Parable of the Talents continues Lauren Olamina's story in the years from 2032 to 2035. Unlike *Parable of the Sower*, which is narrated exclusively by Lauren via dated entries from her journal 'Earthseed: The Books of the Living', *Parable of the Talents* is not a monologic but a dialogic narrative. It has four narrators instead of one: Lauren's daughter, Larkin (her given name) or Asha Vere (her Christian American name), is the editor of the overall narrative, whose bulk is composed of continued chronological entries from her mother's journal, but which also contains a small number of entries from the journals of Lauren's husband Bankole ('Memories of Other Worlds') as well as that of Lauren's brother, Marcus ('Warrior'). Having been separated from her mother only months after her birth until their reunion when she is 34, Larkin-Asha Vere's relation to her mother is painfully alienated and critical. Lauren's daughter's editorial commentaries, which begin every chapter, critically refract Lauren's own narrative that follows. The voices of mother and daughter frequently occupy contradictory positions of affirmation and negation. As in *Sower*, all chapters in *Talents* are prefaced by Earthseed verses. Similarly, both novels close on biblical parables that follow the main text: the Parable of the Sower (Luke 8:5–8) and the Parable of the Talents (Matthew 25:14–30). Through the tension between Earthseed verses and the closing references to the Bible, the meaning of both works is suspended contrapuntally between Earthseed's utopian principles and a stern Christian message about seeding and harvesting, beginnings and just outcomes.

Parable of the Talents picks up Acorn's history on 'Arrival Day', the fifth anniversary of its founding (*Talents* 9). The first half of the novel narrates its slow growth from the founding 13 members to a community of about 60 subsisting by trading agricultural products and other services with neighbouring towns. Then, in the first year of office of the newly elected Christian fundamentalist US President, former Texas senator Andrea Steele Jarret, disaster strikes again, as Acorn is attacked and invaded by Christian American crusaders, who turn Acorn into a concentration and 're-education' camp. Its residents are put into collar slavery; Acorn children are kidnapped and placed with Christian American foster families. Collar slavery is a technology that turns its victims into abject marionettes of another's will. Through collars placed around their necks, slaves can be lashed electronically without leaving visible injuries, to the point of convulsions and death. Escape is impossible: getting too far from the control unit will choke the slave. Only about a dozen of the Acorn settlers, including Lauren, are still alive after almost two years, when a massive landslide caused by the crusaders' reckless logging of the surrounding slopes buries the camp's control centre, allowing the prisoners to liberate themselves and escape 'Camp Christian'.

After the destruction of Acorn, Lauren successfully reconstitutes the Earthseed movement, turning it into a nationally recognised organisation and becoming its celebrated leader. Lauren's last entry of 2035 states: 'I've reached so many people from Eureka to Seattle to Syracuse that I believe that even if I were killed tomorrow, some of these people would find ways to go on learning and teaching, pursuing the Destiny. Earthseed will go on' (*Talents* 393). During the same years, she also – unsuccessfully – searches for her lost daughter. The public success story of Lauren's rise to national celebrity status is countered by a story of private defeat and sibling betrayal: Lauren's half-brother Marcus, whom Lauren rescues from collar slavery and brings to live at Acorn, defects to become a minister in Christian America. He withholds information about the whereabouts of Larkin from his sister, and falsely tells Larkin of her mother's death when he takes her in as a young adult. The epilogue jumps forward to the year 2090, to report Lauren's witnessing of the launching of the first Earthseed space shuttle before her death.

Earthseed as Constitutive Mythology of the Post-Apocalypse

Both *Sower* and *Talents* have two kinds of plot, a disaster narrative that traces two successive events of apocalyptic destruction, and a post-apocalyptic narrative of ideas that recounts the process of rebuilding from the ruins and the refounding of civilisation on new speculative principles. The disaster narrative covers events that destroy. Conversely, the narrative of ideas establishes new positive values, the principles of Earthseed. The disaster narrative is about the negation of established ideas and worlds: deterritorialisation. The narrative of ideas is about remaking world: reterritorialisation. Dialectical movement from territorialisation to deterritorialisation, from world-destroying to world-making, is inscribed into the metaphor of plant metamorphosis that Lauren's Earthseed is named for: its life cycle extends from mobile routes ('seed') to roots ('earth') to seed, and so on. As a whole, this makes the *Parable* series what James Clifford considers a diaspora narrative:

> Diaspora discourse articulates, or bends together, both roots *and* routes to construct . . . alternate public spheres, forms of community consciousness and solidarity that maintain identifications outside the national time/space in order to live inside, with a difference. Diaspora cultures are not separatist, though they may have separatist or irredentist moments. (Clifford 251)

As a utopian enclave that has 'seceded' from contemporary American civilisation, Acorn embodies Earthseed's separatist moment. But Acorn does not sum up Earthseed's history as a whole.

Robledo is consumed in one of the apocalyptic conflagrations set by Pyro addicts, hordes of have-nots aroused by a drug that turns them into arsonists. Members of an 'insane burn-the-rich movement' (*Sower* 163), they set neighbourhoods on fire from coast to coast 'to expose or destroy the hoards hoarded by the rich' (*Sower* 205). Gasoline, which only the rich can afford to buy, has become a weapon in the hands of the have-nots against the haves. In retrospect, Lauren's experience of Robledo's destruction confirms a prophetic nightmare of apocalyptic fire that she has on her fifteenth birthday. *Sower* opens with this vision:

> The wall before me is burning. Fire has sprung from nowhere, has eaten through the wall, has begun to reach toward me, reach for me. The fire spreads . . . I thrash and scramble and try to swim back out of it, grabbing handfuls of air and fire, kicking, burning! Darkness. (*Sower* 4)

Yet the fire of destruction is also a fire of renewal: the chapter covering the conflagration at Robledo is prefaced by an Earthseed verse referring to both destructive and renewing dimensions of fire: 'In order to rise / From its own ashes / A phoenix / First / Must / Burn' (153). Fire is a phase that must be passed through to reach the next stage of development – the negation of the negation and an early sign of Butler's dialectical twist on the topic of apocalypse.

Robledo's destruction plunges Lauren into the 'have-nots' cast out from the walled enclaves of the 'haves': 'I am one of the street poor now', says Lauren, but 'I mean to survive' (*Sower* 156, 172). Given 'the "thrownness" characteristic of our being-in-the-world' (Gabriel, 'Mythological Being' 26), the nomadic condition that the post-apocalyptic refugees are stranded in is all-important. With two other Robledo survivors, Lauren sets out on the road north through the post-apocalyptic wasteland. California's iconic freeways, once celebrated as places where speed 'obliterate[s]' space (Baudrillard 9), are now carrying masses of refugees instead of cars. On the post-apocalyptic freeways, traffic crawls at a much slower pace.

> [T]he freeway crowd is a heterogeneous mass – black and white, Asian and Latin, whole families are on the move with babies on backs or perched atop loads in carts, wagons or bicycle baskets, sometimes along with an old or handicapped person. Other old, ill, or handicapped people hobbled along as best they could with the help of sticks or fitter companions. Many were armed with sheathed knives, rifles, and, of course, visible, holstered handguns. The occasional passing cop paid no attention. (*Sower* 177)

The theme of survivors travelling on abandoned roads is a central trope of ruin in post-apocalyptic fiction.[15] It is at the core of McCarthy's *The Road*, where two survivors, a man and his son, traverse the post-apocalyptic wasteland on former state roads, pushing a shopping cart with their remaining possessions. Fleeing north towards cooler climes, Robledo's survivors in *Parable of the Sower* travel in the opposite direction to the survivors in *The Road*, who are fleeing post-apocalyptic winters for the south. Lauren's group adopts survival tactics on the road, pledging to trust and defend each other to the point of taking others' lives if necessary. It is in this context of a small collective struggling for bare survival against human and non-human predators that Lauren shares her two secrets – her hyperempathy syndrome and her fledgling religion, Earthseed. A public health repercussion of 'the Pox', hyperempathy syndrome is a birth defect in newborns caused by a drug, Paracetco, which Lauren's mother abused before her birth. An 'organic delusional syndrome' (*Sower* 12), hyperempathy causes its victims, so-called 'empaths' or 'sharers', to vicariously feel both the pain and the pleasure of others. As victims of rape, for example, sharers feel the rapist's pleasure as well as their own pain.

The apocalyptic destruction of Robledo prompts Lauren to elaborate Earthseed spirituality. By reducing modern civilisation to rubble, apocalypse opens up a new world. Finding herself thrown into this new space, Lauren formulates a post-apocalyptic utopian antithesis to vulture capitalism, as well as to the traditional Baptist belief system of her minister father, who has unsuccessfully tried to make do within that system. Earthseed principles are further refined in conversations on the road. In the founding of Acorn, the abstract ideals of Earthseed materialise as real, as they come to shape the practices of community life. In this way, Butler distinguishes between what Jameson calls 'the Utopian form and the Utopian wish' or impulse (*Archaeologies* 1): the imagining of utopian alternatives and their realisation are two separate and successive phases.

Acorn, organised around Earthseed spiritual practices, is also the antithesis of Robledo, organised around Baptist Christianity. Even so, there are ominous parallels: tellingly, the thorn fence that Acorn settlers build around their wilderness enclave harks back to the wall with which Robledo residents surrounded their urban neighbourhood. Both Robledo and Acorn are enclaves of relative safety in a Hobbesian world where life is lived in continual fear of violent death at the hands of murderous strangers. Both are also segregationist, value-based enclaves within the larger context of capitalist exploitation. As islands of privilege in a sea of desperation and structural oppression, they maintain themselves by way of a fortress mentality. Yet this strategy proves to be in vain in both cases: in the end, the contradiction between the alternative enclave and the surrounding external real space results in the enclave's annihilation by outside forces. At Robledo, Pyro addicts drive a truck through the gate, shoot the residents and torch the houses. Six years later at Acorn, Christian American crusaders drive several armoured trucks through the fence, firing riot gas into the settlers escaping into the hills to take them captive, and killing many, including Lauren's husband Bankole. As is evident, the second apocalyptic destruction at Acorn echoes the first at Robledo: both catastrophes register the antinomy between dystopian reality and utopian enclave and bring it to a head.

In the two volumes of the *Parable* series, disaster narrative and post-apocalyptic narrative of ideas form a continuing dialectical movement of thesis and antithesis, position and negation. Dialectics pictures opposites as moments of transition and becoming in a larger whole. Butler is a dialectical thinker: the post-apocalyptic religion of Earthseed is not presented as a completed and static system (being) but as a dynamic one (becoming). Earthseed evolves in a series of distinct historical stages, through an ongoing dialectical movement of apocalyptic annihilation and post-apocalyptic rebuilding, dispersal and aggregation. As a 'constitutive mythology' of the post-apocalyptic period, Earthseed internalises nomadism and its logic of mobility as well as phases of destruction and latency as constituent features of its organisational pattern.

This is the paradoxical meaning of Lauren's God-is-Change belief system: God-is-Change means, first, that there is a God. That is to say, there is a higher being representing a transcendent reality of some kind. But this is an impersonal deity, unlike the personal deity of Christianity. Most crucially, however, this transcendent entity is not eternal and unchanging, but changeable. God-is-Change means that God is 'constantly *changing*'. As a post-apocalyptic metaphysic and a social movement, Earthseed is about process rather than product. God appears as change because of the nature of the post-apocalyptic field of sense. Lauren's belief is brought about by a drastic change in the nature of the world she inhabits. Apocalyptic destruction forces her to abandon the classic notion of God as absolute being. God-as-Change is no longer absolute in the sense of existing without cause. God is a now a relative concept, a reduced force that is subject to the laws of the apocalyptic world in which he appears. Or, as Gabriel puts it in his essay on Schelling, 'the necessary is contingent' ('Mythological Being' 26). According to Gabriel, this is Schelling's central insight: 'The very contingency of a given framework transforms its starting point, its "terminus a quo", into something contingent' (59). Gabriel's comments on the meaning of religion describe the reconfiguration of the divine in the *Parable* series: 'I do not claim that God really exists – in the sense that there is a person who imposes laws … the question is merely in which field of sense he exists, how "God" appears' (*Warum es die Welt* 208; see also *Why the World* 178).

The Earthseed belief system places human existence within a biocentric frame, abandoning the anthropocentric paradigm of traditional Christianity. In the moment of discovering Earthseed, Lauren reflects: 'Whether you're a human being, an insect, a microbe, or a stone, this verse is true: *All that you touch / You Change*' (*Sower* 79). In its restless transformations, Earthseed resembles the cellular slime mould, an organism that is mentioned in passing (*Talents* 84). The slime mould switches back and forth between decentred and centred modes of existence, between the form of independent amoeba and the form of multicellular aggregate. It can 'survive the absence of food and water. When conditions recur that allow growth, the spores are released from the fruiting body and germinate' (Goodwin 47). This is another feature that distinguishes Earthseed from the traditional Christianity of Lauren's Baptist father as well as the oppressive Christian American faith of her brother Marcus. Both are modelled on the self-contained, centred model of community. In contrast, Earthseed is a decentred entity, including a diasporic 'traveling culture' (Clifford).

Earthseed denotes both a utopian ideal and its finite manifestation (such as Acorn); its dialogical logic of development unfolds through various historical manifestations. It has a historical dimension, going through a 'life process' from conception in the destruction of Robledo to later realisations. In its dialectical movement from the ideal to the real, from spiritual principles to historical manifestation and beyond, Earthseed is presented as a fallible project rather than a perfect alternative society and belief system. I am not suggesting that this is a purebred Hegelian dialectic with all the implications of Hegelianism, such as teleology towards progress and totality or the absolute (see Copleston 36, 40–1): unlike the Hegelian prototype, Butler's dialectic in the *Parable* series is an 'open system' rather than a closed totality, a system that is not closed at the end or at the top. The process of continual transformation by which Earthseed unfolds is dialectical in the broad sense that 'dialectic is at heart a mediation of historical difference' (Rosenberg qtd in Cole 815). At each point in the history of Earthseed, Butler confronts the contradictions proper to this given moment and brings them to the point where that moment is unmade and overcome.

But, one might ask, isn't it difficult to deny that Earthseed is a metaphysic? After all, it reflects on 'God', one of the concepts traditionally denoting unified totality. I suggest that Earthseed's God-as-Change belief system aligns with the main principle of Gabriel's negative ontology: the world does not exist. Earthseed's crux as a metaphysic is that it thinks beyond closure, beyond the unified whole: Earthseed is an anti-metaphysical metaphysic, a metaphysic against itself. It is a belief system that constantly undermines itself, by undermining any of its concrete realisations. As noted above, as the constitutive mythology of the post-apocalypse, Earthseed expresses the 'field imaginary' of the apocalyptic field of sense; the necessary can only appear as the relative and contingent: change. The point I want to make is that this is what it means for 'God' to appear in the field of sense that is Butler's post-apocalypse: God appears as 'change'.

As Gabriel contends, fields are real; they are objective structures rather than perspectives. As in Gabriel's example of magnetic fields, fields and the objects that appear in them are closely bound together. The post-apocalyptic world and the divinity that appears in it share the same identity: the principle of crisis and upheaval. Lauren's God-is-Change militates against totalisation. The absolute being that is supposed to ground existence is revealed as a non-ground, as contingency. Or, to use the terms coined by Badiou and Meillassoux and endorsed by Gabriel, in the place of God as the infinite, Earthseed thinks God as the 'untotalizable *transfinite*' (*Transcendental Ontology* 125; see also Meillassoux 103ff.). Perhaps there is no more poignant expression of this point than the world-endism of apocalyptic thinking. Yet Butler radicalises its meaning. In dethroning God as absolute being, Butler demolishes the Christian script of the end of the world. In Revelation, the divine script, the scroll of seven seals, literally unleashes the destruction of the world and orchestrates its remaking in the arrival of New Jerusalem (see Keller 3). In Revelation, the end of the world obeys the divine plan. In the *Parable* series, the end of the world composes a new divinity.

Like other Angelinos, Lauren Olamina finds herself thrown into an apocalyptic extrapolation of Mike Davis's carceral city at the very opening of the *Parable* series, but she is one of the very few who faces up to this fact. As the 15-year-old Lauren struggles with her minister father over the meaning of the increase in extreme violence in the city, he questions her: 'Do you think our world is coming to an end?' (*Sower* 62). Condescendingly, he lectures her, '"You've just noticed the abyss . . . The adults in this community have been balancing at the edge of it for more years than you've been alive"' (66). For some Robledo residents, this results in nihilism: for example, Mrs Sims commits suicide after the murder of her children's family in the unwalled foothills of Los Angeles (21). But this is not how Lauren interprets this strange new reality. Lauren's approach can be illuminated by another aspect of field of sense ontology. As Gabriel maintains, strictly speaking, nihilism is an incoherent view, because even if nothing has any meaning, there is still the fact that nothing has any meaning, which is something rather than nothing. This is what Gabriel refers to as the principle of facticity. This same insight also marks the beginning of Lauren's post-apocalyptic mythology: '*The only lasting truth / Is Change. / God / Is Change*' (*Sower* 79). Trying to make sense of the collapse of modern civilisation as we know it, Lauren arrives at the one positive fact that can be depended upon in an apocalyptic world of total risk of annihilation. The fact that there is no ground becomes the groundless ground to stand on. God-is-Change is a metaphysic of the society of extreme risk – a religion, as Lawrence Buell suggests, tailored for 'dwelling' in crisis ('Global Warming' 265).

Rather than nihilism, in field of sense ontology the argument from facticity helps overcome constructivism: 'Facticity means that there is something rather than nothing – that is, that there exists anything at all. The argument from facticity objects against constructivism that it overlooks this, namely that it fails to acknowledge that constructions themselves are things that really exist' (*Why the World* 133). In other words, anyone making the claim that there is no reality, only cultural and linguistic constructs, cannot ground his or her own argument as a truthful statement. For the claim that everything is constructed eventually necessitates the existence of an unconstructed fact (*Warum es die Welt* 167). The principle of facticity identifies the absurdity of absolute constructivism, for the latter eliminates 'the difference between true and false' (*Why the World* 126). Gabriel's critique of the self-consuming nature of constructivism echoes a long-standing critique of postmodernism that Peter Zima calls the 'problem of indifference' (Zima 115): there is no way to decide between better and worse among relativised truths.

In the *Parable* series, the principle of facticity inspires Lauren's revolutionary post-apocalyptic metaphysic. As Gabriel writes in his essay on Schelling, 'the threat of absolute indeterminacy is the origin of the mythological narrations of the origin of the world' ('Mythological Being' 18). He elaborates, 'the fact that language fails vis-à-vis an all-encompassing nothingness releases creative energies which eventually overturn nothingness: this is why there is something rather than nothing. Nothing becomes something in our constant activity of naming the void' (17). Facing the void, Lauren dispels the threat of nihilism to which others succumb by naming the void: God is Change. For the only means by which Lauren's constitutive mythology can truthfully express the post-apocalyptic condition is by incorporating the factor of world-destroying into its world-making mythology. This is not to say that there are no other competing belief systems: the Baptist church continues to exist after Lauren's father's disappearance on his way to work shortly before the destruction of Robledo. More sinisterly, 'the Pox' sees the rise of right-wing Christian fundamentalism, the Church of Christian America, which is Earthseed's nemesis. Neither Baptism nor Christian America, which is openly totalitarian, are beliefs that genuinely respond to the new post-apocalyptic 'rule' of contingency and finitude. This is borne out in the eventual decline of the Christian American movement with growing discontent over its totalitarian measures and President Jarret's fall from power, which takes place against the contrasting rise of the Earthseed movement to national prominence. As Lauren reflects in 2090 at the end of her life, 'some of these dissatisfied people are finding what they want and need in Earthseed' (*Talents* 393).

This is also one important reason why the *Parable* series is safe from common charges against utopianism that target either the latter's supposed naive wish-fulfilment or its darker totalitarian dimensions. This dialectical movement between the historical-real and the conceptual-ideal relates to Tom Moylan's reading of the *Parable* series as a 'critical dystopia'. According to Moylan, dystopia, the negative utopia that arose to critique the authoritarian modern state at the beginning of the twentieth century, is not equivalent to anti-utopianism as such: dystopias have always accessed both utopian as well as anti-utopian positions. Moylan maintains that a 'distinction may be made between the limit case of an open (epical) dystopia that retains the utopian commitment at the core of its formally pessimistic presentation and a closed (mythic) one that abandons the textual ambiguity of the dystopian narrative for the absolutism of an anti-utopian stance' (Moylan 156). Dystopias that offer nothing but panoramas of pessimism and despair are closed and mythic in form. On the other hand, the kind of dystopias that keep faith with the 'radical hope' of the spirit of utopia (157) warn about changes for the worse to come, but they also hold on to the possibility of emancipation and resistance. In Moylan's view, these dystopias, which are open and epic in form, are 'critical utopias'. To extend Moylan's notion of critical dystopia, the *Parable* series is a self-critical dystopia. For Butler subjects Earthseed-Acorn, Lauren's utopian counter-narrative to dystopian vulture capitalism, to a critique of its own. As we shall discuss in the following section, in part this is effected through the dialogic narrative technique in the second volume, *Parable of the Talents*, which juxtaposes Lauren's visionary voice with Asha Vere's editorial commentary and criticism.

But there is an additional dimension of the *Parable* series' self-critical dystopianism. This is played out at the level of plot, through the several iterations of the sequence of utopian world-making and apocalyptic world-destroying. In *Talents*, the utopian thesis of Acorn is annihilated in an apocalypse like its predecessor at Robledo. The apocalyptic collapse of Acorn into 'Camp Christian' in turn prompts Lauren to rethink her strategy of realising utopia. Rather than rebuild the settlement, Lauren decides not only to burn and abandon the remains, but also to abandon the type of historical materialisation of utopian desire that underpins Acorn – the model of the segregationist utopian enclave. As Peter Stillman notes, Lauren rebuilds Earthseed by making it a mainstream movement (Stillman 17). While the first Earthseed community at Acorn is composed of refugees and 'have-nots' assembled in the flight north, the second Earthseed community is formed by recruiting followers from all social strata, including the propertied classes. In the interim, and in the terms of Earthseed's metaphorical plant ecology, the life cycle of Earthseed reverts from roots – settlement ('earth') – back to routes – diasporic dispersion ('seed'). As noted, Earthseed's roots were 'routes': as Lauren comments, 'Earthseed is being born right here on Highway 101' (*Sower* 223). It is to these nomadic 'roots' that Lauren returns in the wake of the invasion of Acorn and the catastrophe of 'Camp Christian'. After the enslavement and the liberation of its survivors, Lauren reflects: 'I've done this: I sent my people away. We survived slavery together, but I didn't believe that we could survive freedom together. I broke up the Earthseed community and sent its parts in all directions' (*Talents* 266). Decades later at the close of *Talents*, mobility again gains the upper hand over settlement, after Lauren's rise to national prominence as a spiritual leader: Earthseed's futuristic Destiny, which is achieved through the first shuttle launch into space, represents a revival of Earthseed nomadism on a grander scale.

That any of the historical realisations of Earthseed are always potentially under erasure and subject to critique is further borne out by the third unwritten volume of the series, *Parable of the Trickster*. Butler's ambivalence about the third volume, which she 'started and stopped' working on 'over and over again from 1989 until her death' (Canavan, 'Butler's Lost Parables' 2), kept her from being able to complete the book. *Trickster* was intended to follow the history of Earthseed in its outer space colonies. This futuristic stage would be Earthseed's third historical manifestation, as it were – following the first, established at the end of *Sower* (Acorn, the separatist Earthseed enclave) and the second, established at the end of *Talents* (Earthseed, the mainstream nationwide religious cult). According to Gerry Canavan, 'the very first scholar to open the boxes at the Huntington that contain what Butler had written of *Trickster* before her death' in 2006 ('Butler's Lost Parables' 2), Butler's notes for *Parable of the Trickster* demonstrate how deeply ambivalent she was about Earthseed's futuristic Destiny, the project of outer space emigration. Its setting, a planet named 'Bow', is an 'alien world where . . . [the] Earthseed colonists are saddened to discover they wish they'd never left Earth in the first place' ('Butler's Lost Parables' 2). There are multiple scenarios and subplots with various disastrous outcomes including insanity and homicide. As Canavan reports,

> [W]e discover that achieving Earthseed's Destiny, despite Lauren Olamina's dreams, hasn't solved the problem of the human at all, only extended our confrontation with the very difficult problems that drove its development in the first place – only removed to some other world

where they can take some other form. The Destiny was essentially a hyperbolic delaying tactic, a strategy of avoidance; even achieved, it's worthless in its own terms. The fundamental problem is still how to make a better world with such bad building blocks as human beings. ('Butler's Lost Parables' 4)

Once again, as in the earlier demise of Acorn, the project of 'territorialising' Earthseed – now in an extraterrestrial setting – collapses because of the contradictions concealed in it. Among Butler's papers, there are even discarded plot fragments from Lauren's missing decades between the end of the history narrated in *Talents* and her death, which depict her as a 'much darker character' than ever appeared in either of the published volumes, *Sower* and *Talents*. They show her as a 'callous power-broker' and a 'zealot' and who mercilessly punishes would-be defectors from her Earthseed communities (Canavan, 'Butler's Lost Parables' 4).

The *Parable* Series as Post-Apocalyptic Neo-Slave Narrative

Most soberingly, 'the Pox' brings the return of slavery. Like McCarthy's, Atwood's and many other post-apocalyptic novels, such as Marcel Theroux's *Far North* (2009), Butler's *Parable* series depicts the reversion to slave labour of all kinds (sexual slavery, forced labour, debt slavery). In times of scarcity, the human body becomes the most valuable commodity to be exploited. Almost all of the new members of the small collective that Lauren assembles on the road travelling north from Robledo are ex-slaves. One of them had been taught by his mother to read and write by sneaking books out of their master's library: 'Slaves did that two hundred years ago' (*Sower* 218). As Lauren reflects, '"So we become the crew of a modern underground railroad" . . . Slavery again – even worse than my father thought, or, at least sooner. He thought it would take awhile' (292). She adds, 'if we can convince ex-slaves that they can have freedom with us, no one will fight harder to keep it' (292–3).

As Ingrid Thaler notes, the master–slave relationship is an important theme in *Parable of the Sower* (Thaler 15). According to Thaler, it is a key paradigm in Black Atlantic speculative fiction, which may be traced to its centrality to Black Atlantic cultures.[16] Enslavement of various kinds is a formative experience for nearly all the main protagonists of the *Parable* series; in *Talents*, the Olamina siblings Lauren (as memoirist of collar slavery at Camp Christian) and Marcus (through his personal narrative of life as a teen in collar sex slavery) both recount mini-slave narratives of enslavement and liberation. Indeed, the *Parable* series has significant overlaps with the so-called neo-slave narrative, a late twentieth- and early twenty-first-century genre encompassing works such as Toni Morrison's *Beloved* (1987) and *A Mercy* (2008), Ishmael Reed's *Flight to Canada* (1976) and Octavia Butler's own *Kindred* (1979).[17]

In part, the *Parable* series adapts several classic themes of the nineteenth-century slave narrative to its near-future post-apocalyptic scenario. One is the passage from slavery in the south to freedom in the north. The trajectory of the exodus of Lauren's Earthseed community begins in southern California, comes to a temporary halt in northern California at the end of *Sower*, and continues on to Portland, Oregon, in *Talents*. Another is the depiction of slavery as a condition of extreme physical and emotional suffering, a kind of hell on earth. In his account of his years as a teen collar sex slave, Marcus affirms that collar slavery dragged him to unimaginable depths of degradation: a collar 'makes you turn traitor against your kind, against your freedom, against yourself' (*Talents* 131). Lauren's entries in *Talents* covering collar slavery at Camp Christian recount sadistic sexual and physical abuse, including electronic lashings that, as in the days of chattel slavery, lead to the deaths of the victims. Collar slavery represents an apocalyptic variation on the theme of the slave's total submission to the master's will. Insidiously, collar technology precludes the very possibility of heroic rebellion in the model of Frederick Douglass, who reclaims his humanity through physical resistance against his master's will: 'You have seen how a man was made a slave; you shall see how a slave was made a man' (Douglass 294). There is no way for a collared slave to independently reclaim his or her freedom and self-determination. Facing the depth of their abjection and vulnerability, 'some collared people kill themselves, not because they can't stand the pain, but because they can't stand the degree of slavishness to which they find themselves descending' (*Talents* 84). When new inmates deported to Camp Christian rise in rebellion, their actions are promptly stopped in their tracks by pain. The name of their leader, 'David Turner', recalls both the militant black anti-slavery activist David Walker, author of the

Appeal (1829), and Nat Turner, the leader of the 1831 slave revolt in Virginia.

In *Parable of the Talents*, which updates the historical record of 'the Pox' with events in the early 2030s, a news entry reports that a missing person was traced to a squatter camp where he had been forced into collar slavery and prostitution. 'And with that, bingo! Slavery was discovered in Texas in 2032' (*Talents* 84). In relation to another incident of enslaving unaccompanied minors, Lauren comments that 'the Thirteenth and Fourteenth Amendments – the ones abolishing slavery and guaranteeing citizenship rights – still exist, but they've been so weakened by custom, by Congress and the various state legislatures, and by recent Supreme Court decisions that they don't much matter' (*Talents* 40). While Butler clearly places her contemporary post-apocalyptic dystopia within the historical context of American slavery, she also makes it clear that, in her speculative near-future scenario, slavery returns not as racial slavery, but as the enslavement of the 'have-nots' by corporate capital and religious fascists. Slavery has become a universal condition tied to lack of property, wealth or power rather than a specific condition such as race. This expansion of slavery across race barriers correlates to the universal appeal that Earthseed later comes to achieve. Further, Earthseed as a liberation theology clearly draws on the black anti-slavery tradition. 'I believe [Earthseed's] teachings helped me, helped all of us to survive Camp Christian. God is Change. I've lost none of my belief' (*Talents* 295). Lauren compares her experience at Camp Christian to chattel slavery:

> My ancestors in this hemisphere were, by law, chattel slaves . . . I used to think I knew what that meant. Now I realize that I can't begin to imagine the many terrible things that it must have done to them. How did they survive it all and keep their humanity? Certainly, they were never intended to keep it, just as we weren't. (*Talents* 270)

But there are further angles to be pursued. In another twist on the slave narrative, Lauren's story of enslavement at Camp Christian recovers the paradigm of the female slave narrative established by Harriet Jacobs's *Incidents in the Life of a Slave Girl* (1861). A young mother of a two-month-old daughter, Lauren is separated from her daughter during the Christian Crusaders' invasion of Acorn. Like Jacobs, she becomes a violated slave mother, subject to sexual assault. Unlike the classic male slave narrative represented by Douglass, defined by the single-minded struggle for autonomy and freedom (the 'pattern of fight-and-flight'), the female slave narrative has two goals, freedom as well as family (Smith 252). As Fagan Yellin has shown, Jacobs genders the slave narrative, creating a new kind of female heroine whose struggle is not only for freedom, but also to restore the motherhood of which she has been dispossessed by slavery. As in *Incidents*, slavery destroys Lauren's family, and like Jacobs, after regaining her freedom, Lauren labours tirelessly – if unsuccessfully – to reconstitute her motherhood by searching for her daughter. Indeed, viewing Lauren's quest in *Talents* against the backdrop of the female slave narrative and its model protagonist, the heroic slave mother, goes some way towards explaining Butler's insertion of the Olamina family drama as a subplot into the larger narrative of Lauren's quest for a post-apocalyptic religion. Gendered slavery and the dispossession of motherhood is the root of the bitterness of Lauren's lasting alienation from her daughter Asha Vere and her brother Marcus at the end of the second volume of the *Parable* series. In her last 2090 entry, Lauren writes that, despite begging her daughter to attend the launch of the first Earthseed space shuttle, 'My Larkin would not come ... How completely, how thoroughly [Marcus] has stolen my child. I have never even tried to forgive him' (*Talents* 407).

At the beginning of *Sower*, Lauren Olamina is a teenage daughter seeking independence from her family and especially from the authority of her father. One early Earthseed verse reads, 'A tree / Cannot grow / In its parents' shadows' (*Sower* 82). At the beginning of *Talents*, Lauren Olamina is a wife, a mother, and the founder of a community, a larger family made up of ex-slaves and other post-apocalyptic survivors. Both families – the biological family and the Earthseed family – are destroyed by the invasion of Acorn and the enslavement of its settlers. Lauren's goal after her liberation is a double quest to reconstitute both families, the Earthseed collective as well as the mother–daughter relationship. Lauren views her reconstitution of Earthseed and her search for her daughter Larkin as two parallel and compatible goals. In stark contrast, Asha Vere is tormented by the rivalry between her mother's two families. Accusing Lauren of preferring Earthseed over her biological family, she speculates, 'I wonder what my life would have been like if my mother had found me ... How long would it have been before she put me aside for Earthseed, her other kid?' (*Talents* 294). After her first disappointing reunion with her mother, Asha Vere painfully concludes: 'All Earthseed was her family. We never really were, Uncle Marc and I. She never really needed us, so we didn't let ourselves need her' (*Talents* 405).

On the other side of the balance sheet, Lauren's journal entries record her painstaking and heroic efforts to locate her daughter, including by begging her Christian American brother Marcus to help her find Larkin in his capacity as an insider to the Christian American movement. Yet Marcus abandons his sister, while secretly tracking Larkin and bringing her into his home as a young adult. Like the other three narrative voices in *Talents*, Asha Vere is an unreliable narrator, who reveals her pain and subjective bias in her first comments on her mother's journal: 'I've hated her, feared her, needed her. I've never trusted her' (*Talents* 2). Raised by puritanical Christian American foster parents, Larkin has a loveless childhood. She finds refuge in designing so-called Dreamask (virtual reality) scenarios, adopting a Dreamask heroine's name, Asha Vere, as her professional pen name as a Dreamask designer.

Tellingly, Asha Vere contrasts her uncle and her mother through their opposite responses to slavery:

> What Uncle Marc had been through as a slave marked him . . . What did my mother's time as a beaten, robbed, raped slave do to her? She was always a woman of obsessive purpose and great physical courage. She had always been willing to sacrifice others to what she believed was right. (*Talents* 309)

Asha Vere also blames Lauren as the one responsible for the carnage at Acorn, in refusing to abandon Acorn despite Bankole's entreaties: 'She sacrificed us for an idea' (*Talents* 138). Asha Vere's judgement is harsh and seems unjustified. Lauren's daughter is clearly the victim of her uncle Marcus's manipulation. But Asha Vere also experiences an unmistakable negative response during her first encounter with her mother, when she finds Lauren 'an overwhelming person' and feels the need 'to get away from her' (*Talents* 403).

The dissonance between mother's and daughter's testimonies in *Talents* is never resolved. Conceivably Butler employs the paradigm of the female slave narrative as a tool to critique the totalitarian aspects of Lauren's role as prophet of a post-apocalyptic religious cult. As a fictional heroine, the Lauren of *Talents* is thus a composite figure, both the heroic slave mother working to release her child from captivity in a Christian American foster family as well as the post-apocalyptic survivor and spiritual leader that she has become in the course of *Sower*. She is both an auto-biographical ex-slave heroine writing the memoir of her personal struggle for freedom and family like Harriet Jacobs, as well as a powerful public figure, the founder of an alternative religious cult. Butler cleverly employs the voice of the alienated offspring of black enslaved motherhood as a critical force that advances the dialectic of auto-critical transformation that animates the *Parable* series. It is clear that Asha Vere is resentful about having been abandoned by her mother: 'She learned from everyone and every-thing. I think if I had died at birth, she would have managed to learn something from my death that would be useful to Earthseed' (*Talents* 154). Because, unlike the nineteenth-century heroic slave mother, Lauren does not focus all her energies on gathering her children out of slavery into her free home, but divides her 'talent' between her biological child and her spiritual child and public movement, Earthseed, she is found culpable by her daughter. Lauren observes at the beginning of *Talents*, 'My "talent", going back to the parable of the talents, is Earthseed' (21). The narra-tive engine of dialectical historical transformation that, adapting Moylan, I identify as Butler's self-critical utopia is thus nourished by an early expression of the black literary tradition, the fugitive slave narrative.

Possibilities and Limits of Earthseed as Post-Apocalyptic World-Making Mythology

Earthseed is a survivors' religion. As this study argues, there is an important difference between apocalyptic and post-apocalyptic narrative. While apocalyptic narrative is about getting ready for the coming end of the world, post-apocalyptic narrative is about crawling out of the wreckage and remaking world and society from within the wasteland of ruins. Apocalyptic narratives are told by prophets who predict the future cataclysm to come, whereas post-apocalyptic narratives are told by survivors whose reflections are grounded in the facticity of a catastrophe that has already happened. The oddly hopeful quality that characterises post-apocalyptic fictions of survival derives from their focus on world-making in the wake of catastrophe. Butler's *Parable* series illustrates the difference: it is true that Lauren foresees the Robledo holocaust in her apocalyptic dream, and that the core revelation that God is change comes to her in advance. But more than a 'doomster' prophet, Lauren is an organiser and founding figure. Earthseed only begins to grow and spread after the apocalypse has happened, and Lauren does not share her belief with others until the post-apocalyptic period, at which point she no longer speaks as a prophet of the coming end, but as one survivor among many. In a word, Earthseed does not develop until the field of sense that is the post-apocalypse has arrived.

A constitutive mythology of survival, Earthseed is revealed in a moment of crisis. A defining characteristic of Earthseed is facing setbacks and calamities and converting them into strengths. As Asha Vere says of her mother: 'She was always able to draw strength from disaster' (*Talents* 154). 'It's a good thing ... that my mother's God was Change. Her life had a way of changing in abrupt, important ways' (92). Specifically, Earthseed posits two principal maxims: first, to accept God as 'change', and second, to proactively 'shape' God as change. These are enshrined in the key verse: 'God is change': 'All that you touch / You Change. / All that you Change / Changes you. / The only lasting truth / Is Change. / God / Is change' (*Sower* 79). This verse, the first in 'Earthseed: The First Book of the Living', also appears in Asha Vere's introductory editorial entry in *Talents* (3). What is more, the post-apocalyptic God-as-Change cannot be relied on as a moral principle: 'God is neither good / nor evil, / neither loving / nor hating. / God is Power. / God is Change' (*Sower* 245). The maxim that the 'only lasting truth / Is Change' names the values of flexibility and mobility required for survival. As Lauren observes, '*All successful life is / Adaptable*' (*Sower* 124). Here, it is easy to err: as resourceful as it was for Lauren to found a new community of survivors after the Robledo apocalypse, it was also a mistake for her to hold on to the Acorn settlement when it should have been disbanded in light of the deteriorating political situation.

As Thaler notes, the second maxim of 'shaping God' in turn formulates the concept of an 'active believer' (Thaler 87). How does this second doctrine follow from the first? In addition to the oscillation between roots and routes discussed earlier, there is another contradiction inherent in Earthseed mythology that Lauren refers to as a 'puzzle' 'or circular reasoning' (*Sower* 78): one the one hand, one must endure the implacable rule of absolute contingency.

But paradoxically, that same rule of change that brings annihilation also clears the path to the restoration of agency. For if there is no personal God, but only the non-ground of absolute mutability, then humans can be no exception to the rule. They must be contributing participants in the ongoing process of transformation. If everything that exists is in motion, then so are humans. Lauren writes, 'God can't be resisted or stopped, but can be shaped and focused' (*Sower* 25). 'The Self must create / Its own reasons for being. / To shape God, / Shape Self' (258). Earthseed's puzzle is the paradox of dependent agency: how to make the post-apocalyptic world habitable for the humans stranded in it. What are the practices and beliefs, different from the practices and beliefs of modern civilisation that has been destroyed, that will allow the survivors to make this post-apocalyptic wasteland their home? The central mystery of Earthseed is the transformation of passive suffering into active agency.

> God is Change, and in the end, God prevails. But God exists to be shaped. It isn't enough for us to just survive, limping along, playing business as usual while things get worse and worse. If that's the shape we give to God, then someday we must become too weak – too poor, too hungry, too sick – to defend ourselves. Then we'll be wiped out. There has to be more that we can do, a better destiny that we can shape. Another place. Another way. Something! (*Sower* 76)

What does the idea of active believership involve in practice? For one, prayers are abolished: 'God is not to be prayed to' (*Sower* 25). New members at Acorn are instructed with a verse against prayer: '*Do not worship God: / Inexorable God / Neither needs nor wants / Your worship./ Instead, / Acknowledge and attend God, / Learn from God, / With forethought and intelligence, / Imagination and industry, / Shape God*' (*Talents* 76). This is because a personal deity needs personal attention, but divinity-as-process does not. 'Prayers only help the person doing the praying, and then, only if they strengthen and focus that person's resolve' (*Sower* 25). Earthseed's no-prayer policy directs the believer's energy to resilience and perseverance, and away from passive expectation associated with traditional prayer. At Acorn, twice-weekly gatherings take the place of church service. Gatherings begin with the reading of Earthseed verses and consist of open discussion and criticism. There are no sermons, only teaching and meditation. Spiritual practice is not separate from community life, but informs its various aspects, including schooling and farming. There are birth ceremonies and funeral ceremonies accompanied by Earthseed verses. Corresponding to the biocentric master metaphor of earthseed, Earthseed's principles are 'green' in affirming the interconnectedness of ecosystems: 'God is Change– / Seed to tree, / tree to forest; / Rain to river, / river to sea; / Grubs to bees, / bees to swarm. / From one, many; / from many, one; / Forever uniting, growing, dissolving– / forever Changing. / The universe / is God's self-portrait' (*Sower* 315). Nonetheless, Butler is not indebted to the ideas of deep ecology, because 'the human remains at the center' (Thaler 84). The principal focus of the *Parable* series is the ethics of human action. I agree with Thaler's assessment as far as the dynamics of narrated events and character are concerned. It needs to be modified, however, in the light of scientific dimensions of the God-is-Change doctrine, which I address below.

It comes as no surprise that a traditional Christian such as Marcus recoils from the elimination of prayers and sermons, not to mention the idea of a personal deity. After buying Marcus's freedom from collar slavery, Lauren learns that the younger brother she had thought dead had been rescued and adopted by Baptist street preachers. At Acorn, Marcus challenges the authority of Earthseed verses by quoting the Bible: 'For I am the Lord. I change not' (*Talents* 150). His challenge in turn is countered from the floor; Zahra Moss informs him that 'Our God isn't male' (150). Soon after, Marcus leaves Acorn to join Jarret's Christian America. For Marcus as for others who vote a Christian fundamentalist president into office, Jarret is a 'potential savior' (156) who can restore the nation from 'the Pox'.

In addition to the God-as-Change doctrine, Earthseed's third principal maxim is its futuristic Destiny. The verse that enshrines the Destiny is given to Lauren early on, before the Robledo apocalypse: '*The destiny of Earthseed / Is to take root among the stars*' (*Sower* 85). On the one hand, as noted earlier, the long-term vision of solving humanity's problems through outer space emigration harks back to the nomadic origins of Earthseed as a faith for those displaced by disaster. This project of journeying into infinite space has defined Lauren's vision from the very outset: 'I think we'll have to seed ourselves farther and farther from this dying place' (*Sower* 78). From another angle, Earthseed's futuristic Destiny substitutes for the afterlife of traditional Christianity. As Asha Vere explains,

'Earthseed's heaven is literal, physical – other worlds circling other stars ... For the human species, immortality is something to be won by sowing Earthseed on other worlds' (*Talents* 47).

Related to positing a futuristic Destiny of outer space travel, Lauren also claims scientific support for Earthseed (see also Thaler 85; Stillman 28). She persuasively puts the God-as-Change doctrine on a modern scientific footing. As a science-oriented verse reads: 'Changes. / The galaxies move through space. / The stars ignite, / burn, / age, / cool, / Evolving. / God is Change' (*Sower* 224). While Lauren brings back the 'crossed-out God' (Latour), the God she brings back is not the traditional absolute Being. That Earthseed is relative to the post-apocalyptic field in which it appears aligns with contemporary science, such as relativity theory. Indeed, Lauren explicitly refers to modern post-Newtonian science in developing her doctrine of change: 'Change is ongoing. Everything changes in some way – size, position, composition, frequency, velocity, thinking, whatever. Every living thing, every bit of matter, all the energy in the universe changes in some way' (*Sower* 218). In the following description, Bankole expounds the link between Earthseed's doctrine of change and modern science:

> Olamina believes in a god that does not in the least love her. In fact, her god is a process or a combination of processes, not an entity. It is not consciously aware of her – or of anything. It is not conscious at all ... Some of the faces of her god are biological evolution, chaos theory, relativity theory, the uncertainty principle, and, of course, the second law of thermodynamics ... Yet Earthseed is not a fatalistic belief system. God can be directed, focused, speeded, slowed, shaped. All things change, but all things need not change in all ways. God is inexorable, yet malleable. Odd. Hardly religious at all ... Earthseed is Olamina's contribution to what she feels should be a species-wide effort to evade, or at least to lengthen the specialize-grow-die evolutionary cycle that humanity faces, that every species faces. (*Talents* 46)

The Earthseed verse about stars cooling alludes to the second law of thermodynamics, the law of entropy. Thermodynamics overturned classical Newtonian physics, which viewed nature as a realm of timeless and reversible processes. As Stengers elucidates, thermodynamics also introduced the 'arrow of time' into physics: unlike the Newtonian universe, a timeless world of solid things and bodies governed by the laws of mechanics, the physical universe of thermodynamics is characterised by irreversible transformation and heat loss (*Cosmopolitics I* 173ff.). Just as energy dissipates, the universe is 'running down': stars have life cycles of about eight billion years before they are consumed. The entire solar system is facing the certain prospect of extinction. Lauren mentions the coming solar apocalypse: 'the universe is cooling down, running down, dissipating its energy' (*Sower* 218). In short, in abandoning the idea of timelessness, Earthseed's God-as-Change doctrine not only rejects traditional religion, it also reflects the new science. Newtonian science used to be about permanence; today science is about change. After thermodynamics, relativity theory and the uncertainty principle took further steps in breaking with the Newtonian science of timeless permanence. With the exception of thermodynamics, Butler does not develop the scientific 'face' – in Bankole's expression – of Earthseed as clearly as one would wish.

Further pursuing the notion of instability, Asha Vere contrasts her uncle Marcus and her mother Lauren via their opposite views of chaos. Lauren 'saw chaos as natural and inevitable and as clay to be shaped and directed. As she says in one of her verses: *Chaos / is God's most dangerous face– / Amorphous, roiling, hungry. / Shape Chaos– / Shape God. / Act*' (*Talents* 110). 'My uncle Marc, on the other hand, hated the chaos. It wasn't one of the faces of his god. It was unnatural. It was demonic' (*Talents* 111). The disagreement stems from the fact that the siblings are thinking of very different kinds of chaos. Marcus has biblical chaos in mind, the antithesis of divine order. In contrast, Lauren's chaos is the scientific chaos of contemporary chaos theory.

A later chapter of the new scientific paradigm of complexity that begins with thermodynamics, chaos theory conceptualises the spontaneous emergence of order and pattern. This is captured in the notion 'order out of chaos', which gave the title to Prigogine and Stengers' book about the post-Newtonian science of change. As Prigogine and Stengers elucidate, the theory of self-organisation leads to a new view of matter in which matter 'is associated with spontaneous activity' (9). In referencing chaos theory, Butler thus also alludes to the creation of new structures from the bottom up in the self-organising process. Self-organising 'order out of chaos' in turn sheds fresh light on the Earthseed maxim of 'shaping God'. 'To shape God' describes not only the human activity of the active Earthseed believer discussed above. It also addresses the creative activity of non-human nature: 'active matter' (Prigogine and Stengers 286). As noted in Chapter 1, the notion of active matter underlies new materialisms (Karen Barad, Jane Bennett and others), a distinct branch of new ontologies after poststructuralism. From this angle, Earthseed also connects to Humberto Maturana and Francisco Varela's theory of autopoiesis, which was discussed in the previous chapter. Autopoiesis (literally, 'self-making') identifies self-making as the definition of life. Living systems are the products of their own organisation: organisms are both self-generating and self-maintaining.

In the debate with her brother Marcus over Earthseed, Lauren insists that she did not invent but discovered Earthseed. Rejecting Marcus's charge that Earthseed is 'fiction' (*Talents* 127), Lauren insists that '"all the truths of Earthseed existed somewhere before I found them and put them together. They were in the patterns of history, in science, philosophy, religion, or literature. I didn't make any of them up"' (127). In other words, the God-is-Change doctrine is more than just religious belief, or even mere belief. In terms of the distinction between scientific knowledge (*episteme*) and mere belief (*doxa*) that has informed the methodological debate in the sciences (Polkinghorne 9), Lauren claims that Earthseed is scientific knowledge. Or, to recall Latour's related discussion of the dichotomy of fact vs. value, in claiming to have discovered rather than invented Earthseed, Lauren lays claim to the traditional concept of the real as facts, as things that 'are seen as not made' (*Factish Gods* 63). Yet Lauren obviously did not find the God-is-Change belief system by the method of scientific experimentation or induction. The three principal axioms of Earthseed were formulated when Lauren was still a teenager at Robledo. They were found by deductive logic, like the truths of mathematics. Defying the modern segregation of knowledge and belief, Lauren claims that they are scientific laws *as well as* spiritual truths. As Peter Stillman observes, Earthseed surpasses 'the Enlightenment bifurcation of reason and faith' (Stillman 28). Lauren maintains that the Earthseed doctrine meets the standards of scientific knowledge; at the same time, she calls it 'God'. Thus, like Atwood's *MaddAddam* series, Butler's *Parable* series undoes the separation between scientific facts and matters of value.

Another way of appreciating the Janus-faced nature of Earthseed as a science-based religion is to recall Reinhart Koselleck's distinction between religious prophecy and rational prognosis considered in Chapter 1. Earthseed lays claim to both. The eschatological future predicted by religious apocalypticists was the religious apocalypse. In contrast, the very concept of modernity, as Koselleck sets out, is based on exchanging the closed and known future of the biblical apocalypse for the modern future, which is unknown and open. This quintessential modern future is 'change'. As noted in Chapter 1, with the return of apocalyptic thinking in the twentieth century, the classic notion of the 'open' temporality of modernity has undergone important changes. The future is no longer open, but closed: 'no future'. Contemporary post- apocalyptic fiction, as this study argues, introduces another turn to this story. It reopens the future that the twentieth-century 'doom boom' had closed. Lauren's God-is-Change doctrine formulates a unique variety of the characteristic hopeful quality of the post-apocalyptic script. It makes the experience of destruction part of the everyday reality of living. As Frederick Buell has suggested, it makes crisis 'a way of life' in which people dwell on a daily basis (*Apocalypse* 314–18). Claire Colebrook makes a similar point, contending that

> there will not be complete annihilation but a gradual witnessing of a slow end, and . . . we are already at that moment of witness, living on after the end. Indeed, this is what an ethics of extinction requires: not an apocalyptic thought of the 'beyond the human' as a radical break or dissolution, but a slow, dim, barely discerned and yet violently effective destruction. (Colebrook 40)

This in turn helps explain another peculiarity of the *Parable* series as post-apocalyptic fiction. Butler blurs a characteristic feature of the apocalyptic script, the barrier of time (Jameson) that separates the time before and the time after the world-end. There is no radical break such as Crake's bioterrorist annihilation of the majority of humans in the *MaddAddam* series, or the unspecified cataclysm that has put the planet on a seemingly irreversible spin towards extinction in *The Road*. Unlike in the above-mentioned novels, in the *Parable* series the state never entirely collapses; one of the most advanced modern technologies, space travel, even flourishes. In the *Parable* series, the apocalypse casts a permanent shadow over the 'new beginning' after the end.

In *Parable of the Talents*, the conflict between institutionalised Christianity and the grassroots movement that is Earthseed is also embodied in the personal rivalry between the two half-siblings, Marcus and Lauren Olamina. Among this personal rivalry's several sources is the sexist fear of female leadership. In dispensing with the idea of a personal deity, Earthseed also challenges patriarchy, the conventional symbol of any social system of exploitation. In this regard, it is key that Earthseed arises as a grassroots movement against traditional social authority. As the faith of the underdog, Earthseed also revisions gender: in Zahra Moss's words, 'our God isn't male'. The early phase of Earthseed's development takes place against the backdrop of a strong opposition between Earthseed as a democratic grassroots movement and the fascist authoritarianism of the Christian American movement.

Given this initial opposition, in *Parable of the Sower*, of Earthseed as the underdog's religion versus fundamentalist Christianity as the faith of the oppressor, the critical voice of Asha Vere in depicting her mother as a dictator in *Parable of the Talents* is all the more jarring. The red thread in Asha Vere's journal is the depiction of her mother as a 'dangerous' (*Talents* 381) person, strong-willed and egotistical, a propagandist and a seducer of people. In an opening salvo, she accuses the Earthseed movement of deifying their founder: 'They'll make a God of her ... And she needed large events to manipulate. All gods seem to need these things' (1). Lauren is seen as calculating: 'She worked hard at seducing people. She did it first by adopting vulnerable needy people, then by finding ways to make those people want to be part of Earthseed' (63). On the one hand, Asha Vere attributes aggressive ambition to her mother that she claims her father Bankole failed to see: 'His mistake was in seeing her as a young girl. She was already a missile, armed and targeted' (9). On the other hand, Asha Vere draws a distinction between the early phase of Earthseed and the subsequent phase of its expansion into a mass movement: 'If my mother had created only Acorn, the refuge for the homeless and the orphaned ... If she had created Acorn, but not Earthseed, then I think she would have been a wholly admirable person' (63–4). As Asha Vere's narrative reaches the final stage of Earthseed as a mainstream movement that 'financed scientific exploration and inquiry ... set up grade schools and eventually colleges' (379), 'a wealthy sect ... that owned land, schools, farms, factories, stores, banks, several whole towns' (380), the negatives prevail over the positives. She concludes that Lauren was a 'cult leader, after all. She was supposed to be seductive. But she wasn't going to seduce me' (381). One particular target of Asha Vere's sarcasm is the Destiny of space colonisation as an escapist plot that circumvents the problems on earth: 'so many diseases, so much hunger, so much poverty, such suffering, and here was a rich organization spending vast sums of money, time, and effort on nonsense' (380).

For better or worse, Asha Vere's critique as the estranged child of her biological mother, as I have argued above, makes the *Parable* series a self-critical dystopia. Overall then, Earthseed emerges as a less-than-perfect response to the post-apocalyptic condition. But this, in turn, is yet another aspect of Lauren's revolutionary rejection of the ancient notion of a transcendent world of ideals.

Notes

1. On the development from Kant to German Idealism, I have found helpful the essays collected in *The Cambridge Companion to German Idealism*, ed. Karl Ameriks, especially Frederick Beiser, 'The Enlightenment and Idealism' (18–36), Paul Guyer, 'Absolute Idealism and the Rejection of Kantian Dualism' (37–56), Terry Pinkard, 'Hegel's Phenomenology and Logic: An Overview' (161–79), Günter Zöller, 'German Realism: The Self-Limitation of Idealist Thinking in Fichte, Schelling, and Schopenhauer' (200–18), and Dieter Sturma, 'Politics and the New Mythology: The Turn to Late Romanticism' (219–38).

2. Latour writes: 'For all its claims to overcoming the distance between subject and object . . . phenomenology leaves us with the most dramatic split in this whole sad story; a world of science left entirely to itself, entirely cold, absolutely inhuman; and a rich lived world of intentional stances entirely limited to humans, absolutely divorced from what things are in and of themselves' (*Pandora's Hope* 9).

3. At the beginning of *Why the World Does Not Exist*, Gabriel explains that the new realism was 'heralded in the summer of 2011 – strictly speaking, on 23 June 2011 around 1:30 p.m. – during a lunch in Naples with the Italian philosopher Maurizio Ferraris' (*Why the World* 1). Conceived as a rebuttal of Lyotard's *Postmodern Knowledge*, Ferraris rejects the postmodern erasure of the real, which he calls 'realitism' and whose constituents he identifies as the ironisation (Nietzsche), desublimation (Deleuze/Guattari) and deobjectification (Foucault) of knowledge. Ferraris's critique of postmodernism broadly corresponds to Gabriel's critique of constructivism. Like Gabriel and Meillassoux, Ferraris posits an 'ontological turn' after postmodernism that seeks to undo the Kantian restriction of philosophy to epistemology. In Ferraris's assessment, Habermas's

charge that postmodernism amounts to a right-wing backlash against the Enlightenment – which found its legitimacy in what Ferraris calls the 'fallacy of knowledge-power' – is justified (Ferraris, *Manifesto of New Realism* 20). The strengths of Ferraris's *Manifesto* are in its succinct critique of postmodernism. His development of a new realist ontology, however, starts off on a problematic footing; Ferraris returns to the dichotomy between internal and external worlds of the representationalist paradigm. Overall, his proposal for a 'treatise toward a perpetual peace' between constructivism and realism amounts to a restatement of the problem rather than a concrete solution.

4. Jocelyn Maclure seems to share this impression, as stated in his casual observation that 'readers will also wonder to what extent Gabriel agrees with heterodox philosophers of mind, neuroscientists, and cognitive scientists who see the mind as embodied, embedded, and extended' (6).

5. Whenever possible, quotations are from the English version *Why the World Does Not Exist*. In some cases, I have modified the translation. In these cases, references are to the original German edition, *Warum es die Welt nicht gibt*. Such references are accompanied by page references to the equivalent passage in the English translation.

6. 'Let us call the thesis that the world does not exist the main principle of negative ontology. Against this stands the main principle of positive ontology, which claims that necessarily, there exist an infinite number of fields of sense' (*Why the World* 78). This is followed by the 'second main principle of positive ontology: every field of sense is an object. From this it immediately follows that, for every field of sense, there is a field of sense in which it appears' (*Why the World* 79).

7. Gabriel qualifies this point by noting that differences in the nature of fields of sense '[block] the possibility of a completely flat ontology. Some fields are flat and some fields are curved' (*Transcendental Ontology* 253).

8. Gabriel's TEDx talk is available online at <https://www.youtube.com/watch?v=hzvesGB_TIo> (accessed 12 October 2020).

9. In chapter 11 of *Fields of Sense* ('Modalities II: Necessity, Contingency, and Logical Time') and elsewhere, Gabriel offers a detailed critique of the speculative realism of Meillassoux and Brassier. Gabriel's critique addresses Meillassoux's concept of correlationism. In Gabriel's view, 'Meillassoux's critique of correlation misses the distinction between between ontic (first-order) and ontological (reflective) theorizing' ('Mythological Being' 87). Similarly, Meillassoux's notion of

ancestrality (the period anterior to the emergence of the human species) is not about physical time (the time 5 million years ago that the event of the accretion of the earth actually happened), but about logical time (the temporality of truth judgments).

> We are aware that our thoughts logically present the galaxy to us as something that has existed in ancestral times, and that still largely exists without being fully explored. The *logical* past of the galaxy, however, is not identical with the *physical* past of the galaxy . . . Meillassoux confuses logical and physical past . . . His point about ancestrality should never have been cast in terms of an actual stretch of time before the existence of intelligent beings within the universe, as the point is really about truth-conditions and not about time in the physical or rather common sense sense of 'time'. If anything, his point is about logical time, but then ancestrality is, of course, a synchronic category. (*Fields of Sense* 295)

In Gabriel's view, this objection is also valid against Ray Brassier. As Gabriel asserts, 'it is not sufficient to add post-apocalyptic facts, as Ray Brassier does, facts that will obtain when no one will be around anymore to refer to them' (287). 'That there once was a time where no one referred to anything, because no one was around to have any beliefs, and that there might sooner or later be a time in which no one will be around anymore to notice anything, is exciting from the perspective of zoontology' (288).

10. Heidegger's concept of region is more fully developed in 'Conversation on a Country Path'.

11. 'Fields do a better job in ontology than domains. They explain what domains are supposed to explain, namely how anything can exist given that existence is not a proper property, without inclining in advance in the direction of constructivism or anti-realism. Constructivism or anti-realism are more generally motivated by analyses of truth-conditions' (*Fields of Sense* 163).

12. As Lisa See observes, 'in her writing Butler has probed science fiction's three premises: what if, if only, and if this goes on. In *The Parable of the Sower* she pursues the if-this-goes-on category, once again drawing from the news – smart pills, gangs, global warming, drought, sociopathic behavior, the swallowing up of American companies by foreign conglomerates – to create a story that takes place in a desperately dry twenty-first century Southern California, a place of walled enclaves and drugged-out arsonists, where people murder for water, food, and jobs' (See 41–2).

13. I borrow the distinction between '"regalian" functions (police, courts, army, foreign affairs, general administration, and so on)' of the state and the social state from Thomas Piketty (475).

14. 'Metropolitan Los Angeles has become a dystopian symbol of Dickensian inequalities and intractable racial contradictions' (Carby 19). See also Thaler 74; Menne 725; Stillman 17.

15. Andrew Tate devotes a chapter to the post-apocalyptic road novel, considering McCarthy's *The Road* as well as Jim Crace's *The Pesthouse*.

16. Thaler explains that in 'Black Atlantic Speculative Fiction, this Black Atlantic sensibility of the past within the present is combined with speculative fiction's sensibility of the present within the future. Rather than focusing on science exclusively, or limiting speculations about time to the chronological future as in futurist fiction, speculative fictions envisions time in a "radically discontinuous" setting in the past, present, and/or future and contemplate social structures and subject positions in speculative time spaces' (Thaler 7–8).

17. Butler has pointed out parallels between the near-future dystopia of the *Parable* series and her neo-slave narrative, *Kindred*: 'The *Parable of the Sower* was probably more serious than anything I've written since *Kindred*. It was an "If this goes on ..." story. And, frankly, there isn't anything in there that can't happen if we keep on going as we have been [...] Even the things you try not to think about as part of American life. Slavery, for instance. Every now and then, it will come out that people have been held against their will and forced to work after having been seduced by lies about good salaries and that sort of thing. In this country they're usually Hispanic' (Francis 44).

5

New Phenomenologies after Poststructuralism (Jean-Luc Marion and Alphonso Lingis) and Cormac McCarthy's *The Road*

This chapter turns to 'new' phenomenologies after poststructuralism. Founded in the early twentieth century by Edmund Husserl in an attempt to overcome Cartesian dualism, phenomenology is the study of the structures of first-personal consciousness (such as perception, imagination or memory) and human experience. The rise of structuralism and later poststructuralism led to a devaluation of phenomenology and its focus on how things are given in the mode of first-person experience. In Alphonso Lingis's words, '[b]y midcentury developments in other sciences led to discrediting the phenomenological conception of subjectivity' ('First-Person Singular' 53). Or, as Richard Kearney writes, 'textuality swallowed the body and turned it into *écriture*' ('Carnal Hermeneutics' 17). With the passing of structuralism and the arrival of poststructuralism, which offered distinct avenues of critique (such as Jacques Derrida's deconstruction) of structuralism's weaknesses, nothing much changed. Thus, in his influential critique of Husserl's version of phenomenology, Derrida sought to expose in it the metaphysics of self-presence. Deconstructing phenomenology, Derrida goes beyond phenomenology, exemplifying the linguistic turn that displaced phenomenology's original focus on what is immanent to consciousness. Yet by doing so in ways that are at the same time 'deeply Heideggerian' (Moran 437), deconstruction is also a testimony to phenomenology's continued relevance.

This chapter turns to the question of who or what comes after 'the death of the subject' proclaimed by structuralism and poststructuralism. This question is explored by phenomenology, which is currently undergoing a comeback, a resurgence directly related to the more auspicious intellectual climate of the decline of poststructuralism. I will turn to the work of Jean-Luc Marion, the leading contemporary practitioner of phenomenology in Europe (alongside Michel Henry, who died in 2002), and the American phenomenologist Alphonso Lingis. Both Marion and Lingis chart new paths towards a recovery of the force of the 'first-person singular' (Lingis) that is evident in individual experience, affect and ethical commitment. Marion's project is to formulate a phenomenology of the most elementary of phenomena: givenness itself. To be human is first to receive what is given. Asking 'what comes after the poststructuralist subject?', Marion contends that it is a reduced figure of the self that he calls 'the gifted'. For his part, Lingis presents a phenomenology of the self as arising from impassioned states and passionate identification and commitment, which is marginalised in modern philosophy founded on the *cogito*. As I will show, the holistic phenomenology of givenness that Marion develops from the principle of the 'primacy of givenness', as well as Lingis's affect-based phenomenology, constitute two important contributions emerging from the discipline of phenomenology to the new ecological realisms after poststructuralism that are the subject of this study.

In fully focusing on phenomenology, this fifth and final chapter at the same time continues phenomenological threads developed in the previous chapters on Maturana and Varela's theories of autopoiesis and enactivism and Gabriel's new realism of fields of sense. As noted earlier, both Maturana and Varela as well as Gabriel draw on the phenomenological tradition in their parallel but independent projects to reconstitute realism after poststructuralism. The phenomenological realm of meaning (that things are presented or 'given' to experience, and that experience is always situated and first-personal) is thereby affirmed as an important constituent of new ontologies after poststructuralism. As we have seen in previous chapters, phenomenology is ontology. In phenomenological thought, 'the reality of the object is not located behind its appearance, as if appearance in some way or other hides the real object' (Gallagher and Zahavi 21). Appearances *are* real. Further, as Gabriel shows, reality as such ('the world' as a unified totality) does not exist; instead, the only thing that exists is an indefinite number of fields of sense. Among these, the fields of sense related to subjective experience are accessed by the phenomenological method. As Dermot Moran notes, the discovery of the irreducibility of the first-personal to scientific third-personal knowledge was the achievement of the phenomenological method: 'Husserl's central insight was that consciousness was the condition of all experience' (Moran 61).

Although contemporary neuroscience certainly offers accurate maps of the brain's neurobiology, the subjective character of experience (say, the feeling of 'being happy' or of 'being sad') is not reducible to its corresponding neuronal activity in the brain in such mental states. As neuroscientist Antonio Damasio affirms, 'there is a major gap in our current understanding of how neural patterns become mental images. The presence in the brain of dynamic neural patterns (or maps) related to an object or event is a *necessary* but not sufficient basis to explain the mental images of the said object or event' (Damasio 198). There is no known explanation for how and why physical events in the brain become non-material mental events. At the beginning of the twenty-first century, this 'explanatory gap' has not been bridged: 'we are no closer now to grasping the neural basis of experience than we were a hundred years ago' (Noë, *Out of Our Heads* x). Neurocentrism's claims that '*the self is a brain*' (Gabriel, *I Am Not a Brain*) are unfounded. Thought and mind continue to remain a mystery to contemporary brain science. For all these reasons, phenomenology ranks so prominently among the 'new realist' approaches selected in this study.

Related to the reaffirmation of first-personal experience after structuralism and poststructuralism, this chapter on 'new phenomenologies' also re-examines the question of agency, a crucial component of theories after poststructuralism. New realist reconceptualisations of agency likewise appear in Latour's actor-network theory and in Maturana and Varela's theories of autopoiesis and enactivism (as the reciprocal co-constitution of mind and world), which have been discussed in previous chapters. The new phenomenologies selected here similarly conceptualise agency – to use Latour's language – as distributed agency, agency that is borrowed, influenced, dominated and translated (Latour, *Reassembling* 46). Marion's phenomenology of givenness offers a phenomenological contribution to theories of distributed agency after poststructuralism – a new ecological realism of the first-personal, as it were. As Marion contends, 'we cannot be the source of what we experience': 'if nothing is given, we have nothing to experience' or to be conscious of (Mugerauer, 'The Double Gift' 24). The condition for there to be phenomena is that, first, something is given and, second, something is received. Givenness and response are co-constitutive (together generating what Marion calls the 'gift') as the two moments that generate phenomena – that is to say, experience and consciousness. Furthermore, because to be human and to experience is first to receive what is given, the dynamics of the gift in turn produce a new self. This new self that emerges is a non-autonomous, reduced self – recipient first ('the "unto whom"'), then agent (Marion, *Being Given* 287). Marion names it 'the gifted' (*l'adonnée*).

Important to note, being 'gifted' for Marion has the deeper – and darker – sense of 'what befalls me'. For this reason, post-apocalyptic fiction in general is an excellent match for Marion's claims. What befalls the survivor-protagonists of Atwood's, Butler's, Saramago's and McCarthy's post-apocalyptic novels is a terrible tragedy: forced to witness the destruction of modern civilisation, they face the task of surviving in the midst of a wasteland of ruins without sacrificing their humanity. The finitude of apocalyptic thinking and the post-apocalyptic script of living on after the world-end call for new models of selfhood that can account for radical breaks and transformations. Conversely, Marion's phenomenology of givenness models a post- individual and decentred self that arises in response to the experience of an overpowering event. In dismantling the mechanistic concept of things and people existing independently of worlds or contexts, Marion's phenomenology parallels the field of sense ontology considered in the previous chapter. Yet even as it – like the theories of autopoiesis and enactivism considered in Chapter 3 – dethrones the pre-existing autonomous subject, picturing self as inseparable from its responses to environmental realities, the phenomenology of givenness similarly insists that such responses are intrinsically free in that they cannot be determined by outside forces.

I pair Marion and Lingis with Cormac McCarthy because the destruction is most complete there. *The Road* is the darkest of all the post-apocalyptic novels discussed here. In *The Road*, an unnamed cataclysm has annihilated most of the human race as well as almost all animal and plant life. Nature is almost entirely dead, the climate has cooled, and some humans have resorted to banding together in marauding gangs of cannibals to hunt other humans for food. Under these conditions, McCarthy's unnamed protagonist, simply known as 'the man', has been given a terrible responsibility – to raise his son, born after the apocalypse.

The mother has abandoned the family by committing suicide, leaving father and son behind. Set in an unspecified locale in the general vicinity of the US South, *The Road* depicts the two refugees making their way south towards the coast in search of a warmer climate.[1] They traverse the post-apocalyptic wasteland on former state roads, pushing a shopping cart with their remaining possessions. As I will discuss, *The Road* portrays how the givenness of the apocalyptic event and the task of survival in the aftermath produces a new post-apocalyptic self – the 'gifted'. McCarthy's dire setting highlights the constitution of this already-present but hitherto occluded subjectivity. Rather than committing suicide like his wife, the man heeds the call of givenness and responds to it. Further illustrating Lingis's claims, *The Road* depicts the formation of new, post-apocalyptic selves emerging from passionate commitment ('I am a father') as well as identification between father and son ('We are carrying the fire').

New Phenomenologies after Poststructuralism

As stated, phenomenology centres on the intrinsically first-personal quality of consciousness and experience. In its attempt to capture the first-personal access to things, phenomenology asks about the qualitative features of experience – that is to say, the '(phenomenal) quality of "what it is like" or what it "feels" like' to have experience (Gallagher and Zahavi 49). As Gallagher and Zahavi point out, a fortuitous notion defining phenomenology's unique contribution – from outside the phenomenological tradition – the concept of 'what it is like' was formulated by the analytic philosopher Thomas Nagel (9). What-it-is-likeness names the situated point of view that characterises consciousness and subjective experience. As Nagel maintains, 'an organism has conscious mental states if and only if there is something that it is like to *be* that organism – something it is like *for* the organism. We may call this the subjective character of experience' (Nagel, 'What is it Like?' 166). 'Every subjective phenomenon is essentially connected with a single point of view' (Nagel, 'What is it Like?' 167). This is the quality of 'mineness' (Heidegger's *Jemeinigkeit*), or what Marion calls *ipseity*. The first-personal is often in the first-person singular (a perspective that Lingis explores in his study *The First Person Singular*), but it also appears in the first-person plural, as we shall see in the discussion of McCarthy's *The Road*.

Seemingly straightforward, this situated first-personal characteristic of consciousness nevertheless harbours a thorny problem. For phenomenology's goal is not 'a description of idiosyncratic experience – "here and now, this is just what I experience" – rather, it attempts to capture the invariant structures of experience' (Gallagher and Zahavi 26). In other words, it aims 'to disclose structures that are intersubjectively accessible' (26). According to Gallagher and Zahavi, 'the phenomenologist studies perception not as a purely subjective phenomenon, but as it is lived through by a perceiver who is *in the world*, and who is also an embodied agent with motivations and purposes' (8). Phenomenology aspires to the status of an objective study of first-personal experience. This is what Husserl identified in the concept of eidetic analysis (also referred to as eidetic reduction or variation): *eidos* (essence, essential structure) names the invariant structures of phenomena as they appear to consciousness (Gallagher and Zahavi 27; see also Polkinghorne 42; Moran 11). For example, what are the essential properties of a book, a ball or the activity of 'standing in line' that cannot be dropped without losing the integrity of the thing or activity intuited? *Eidos* identifies the 'whatness' of the thing or activity given to intuition (*Anschauung*), as Husserl worded it. Importantly, *eidos* is objective in a phenomenological rather than a scientific-empirical sense. Givenness is to first-personal consciousness and meaning, not to third-personal knowledge satisfying the standards of natural science. In phenomenological methodology, 'objectivity becomes a region that is constituted or built by consciousness and is not a statement about a quality of empirical realities' (Polkinghorne 42). For example, the concept and activity of 'standing in line' exists in the phenomenological realm of consciousness. As a non-material phenomenon that cannot be measured or quantified, is not accessible to the methodology of natural science. Less obviously, the same is true for a thing like a ball or a book. But this does not mean that these 'intentional objects', as Husserl called them, do not exist. They just do not exist as objects for the natural sciences, which, as we have seen in the previous chapter, Markus Gabriel rightly demoted to an 'ontological province' for this very reason.

Phenomenology was founded to overcome the dichotomy between subject and object, showing the intertwining of the subjective and the objective that has been lost in Cartesian dualism. As Merleau-Ponty puts it, 'Inside and outside are inseparable. The world is wholly inside and I am wholly outside myself' (407). Like all the other 'new ecological realist' approaches studied here, phenomenology navigates – as Maturana and Varela phrase it – the Scylla of representationalism on the one hand and the Charybdis of solipsism/idealism on the other. Husserl's clarion call 'to the things themselves' refers neither to scientific facts nor to pre-given objects, but to intentional or first-personal objects, that is to say, to things as they appear to consciousness. On the other hand, as phenomenologists like to say, consciousness is never absolute, but always 'consciousness of' something. This is what phenomenology refers to as the 'intentionality of consciousness' (Gallagher and Zahavi 107). Furthermore, and as Heidegger affirms in his overcoming of Husserl's phenomenology of intentional objects by way of his phenomenology of being, the very language of subject vs. object, subjective vs. objective, is problematic. Nonetheless, it is difficult (as seen in the quotations from Lingis and Nagel above) to avoid these terms altogether. Thus, at the outset I wish to clarify that, even if the terms subjective and objective occasionally appear in this chapter, they should be read as meaning first-personal and third-personal, in other words, stripped of their Cartesian connotations.

From Husserl's phenomenology of intentional objects through Heidegger's phenomenology of being to Levinas's phenomenology of the Other to Merleau-Ponty's phenomenology of embodied mind, phenomenology has been unabashedly anthropocentric, concerned with the perception, consciousness and experience of humans. In his influential essay 'What is it Like to be a Bat?' Nagel speculates about the phenomenology of non-humans: 'After all, what would be left of what it was like to be a bat if one removed the viewpoint of the bat?' (173). Nagel's provocative speculations about the possibilities and limits of a phenomenology of bats – as 'a fundamentally *alien* form of life' (168) – have stimulated further work among theories participating in the ontological turn after poststructuralism: Ian Bogost's *Alien Phenomenology; or, What It's Like to Be a Thing*, a study associated with object-oriented ontology. Speculative realism was founded on contesting phenomenology in particular. As noted in Chapter 1, in the polemic against correlationism – which Meillassoux defines as 'there can be no X without a givenness of X' (Meillassoux qtd in Gratton 14) – the outlook that Meillassoux attacks as correlationist is phenomenology. This is evident in his use of the term 'givenness'.

In fact, Meillassoux opposes phenomenology as 'strong . . . correlationism' (Meillassoux 41 and *passim*) – in other words, the strongest variety of the outlook that he seeks to challenge.

Rather than follow Bogost's lead, this chapter heeds Nagel's sceptical comments about the limits of access to the first-personal experience of non-human beings. The sonar world-orientation of bats and the visual world-orientation of humans are fundamentally alien and incompatible. For this reason, Nagel concludes that 'we cannot ever expect to accommodate in our language a detailed description of Martian or bat phenomenology' ('What is it Like?' 170). This is because at present 'we are completely unequipped to think about the subjective character of experience without relying on the imagination – without taking up the point of view of the experiential subject' (178). The movie *Batman* does not convey 'what it is like' to be a bat, but what it is like to be a human who imagines what it is like to be a bat. Conversely, as Nagel points out, it is conceivable that Martians might try to form an idea about 'what it is like' to be human, but the 'structure of their own minds might make it impossible for them to succeed' (170). Similarly, it is possible that advances in media technology (videogames, and so on) that simulate bat echolocation will improve dramatically, but as long as the viewer is human, this problem remains.[2]

Phenomenology's goal of overcoming the gap between subjective and objective, the first-personal and the intersubjective, presents a stiff challenge even in the case of varieties of human experience. To recall our discussion of José Saramago's *Blindness*: what does it mean to explain to a person who can see (that is, most readers of fiction) 'what it is like' to be (white-)blind? Any speculative phenomenology of non-humans runs up against the limits of what biologists Richard Lewontin and Richard Levins refer to as the sensorimotor modalities of species. As Lewontin maintains:

The common external phenomena of the physical and biotic world pass through a transforming filter created by the peculiar biology of each species, and it is the output of this transformation that reaches the organism and is relevant to it. Plato's metaphor of the cave is appropriate here. Whatever the autonomous processes of the outer world may be, they cannot be perceived by the organism. Its life is determined by the shadows on the wall, passed through a transforming medium of its own creation. (Lewontin 64)

As we saw in Chapter 3 on Maturana and Varela's theories of autopoiesis and enactivism, organisms specify reality according to their nervous system's organisation. This organisation is species-specific. Viewed from this angle, the human-centred orientation of phenomenology must be seen as directly related to its ambition to convey the first-personal – that is, situated – nature of experience. In other words, if we respond to the posthuman critique of anthropocentrism and view humans within a wider biocentric rather than a narrow anthropocentric frame, phenomenology's ties to human experience impose limits in areas that do not share significant similarities across species – such as organic vision, examined by Maturana and Varela. Indeed, as Tom Sparrow details in *The End of Phenomenology*, this is precisely the reason for object-oriented ontology's departure from phenomenology. Object-oriented ontology envisions a 'full-fledged realism', which cannot be merely human-oriented (Sparrow 122). Since the goal is to 'give an account of interobject encounters and causal interaction', phenomenology must be left behind (122). Because the situatedness of first-personal consciousness and experience is definitive for phenomenology, we are being redirected towards the human, instead of away from it and towards the non-human. As long as the first-personal is tied to the modality of species, phenomenology entails placing human experience at the centre.

Jean-Luc Marion's Phenomenology of Givenness

The phenomenological philosopher Jean-Luc Marion proposes what may be the most compelling solution to the problem of who or what comes after the poststructuralist 'subject' in his analysis of 'the gifted' – she or he to whom phenomena must be given if there are to be phenomena at all. Marion sees his project as going beyond Husserl and Heidegger in 'doing a phenomenology of the most basic of phenomena: *givenness itself*' (Mugerauer, 'The Double Gift' 23–4). Givenness is a translation of Husserl's *Gegebenheit* (*Being Given* 2). Marion's work develops by way of an extended engagement with Husserl and Heidegger, which begins with *Reduction and Givenness: Investigations of Husserl, Heidegger, and Phenomenology* (1989; 1998), the first volume of a trilogy. *Being Given: Toward a Phenomenology of Givenness* (1997; 2002) and *In Excess: Studies of Saturated Phenomena*

(2001; 2002) follow as the second and third volumes respectively. As Marion explains:

> No doubt, the possibility of a 'third reduction' was shocking – but if Husserl's transcendental reduction is indeed at play within the horizon of objectness, if Heidegger's existential reduction is deployed within the horizon of Being, shouldn't we, as soon as the reduction is no longer blocked by the object or the being, designate it specifically as the third, ordered to the pure given? (*Being Given* 2–3)

That said, *Being Given* constitutes the centrepiece of Marion's phenomenology of givenness. It is his major work, presenting a systematic exposition in five parts of the key constituents of phenomena: 'Givenness' (Book I), 'The Gift' (Book II), determinations and degrees of 'The Given' (Books III and IV) and 'The Gifted' (Book V).

For its part, *In Excess* focuses on a specific variety of phenomena that Marion calls strong or 'saturated' phenomena. Unforeseeable, unbearable, overwhelming and without comparison, 'saturated' phenomena – phenomena 'in excess' – epitomise the 'given par excellence' (*Being Given* x). Marion also refers to them as 'paradoxes'. Thematically, they may be divine (such as a revelation or a miracle), natural (such as catastrophes), social (such as revolutions or wars) or aesthetic (certain powerful works of art). Exceeding any anticipation and irrupting from beyond any horizon of expectation, saturated phenomena are spectacular instances of the given in Marion's sense of 'what befalls us'. According to Marion,

> intuition always submerges the expectation of the intention . . . givenness not only entirely invests manifestation but surpassing it, modifies its common characteristics. On account of this investment and modification, I also call saturated phenomena 'paradoxes.' The fundamental characteristic of the paradox lies in the fact that intuition sets forth a surplus that the concept cannot organize, therefore that the intention cannot foresee. As a result, intuition is not bound to and by the intention, but is freed from it, establishing itself now as a free intuition (*intuitio vaga*). Far from coming after the concept and therefore following the thread of the intention (aim, foresight, repetition), intuition subverts, therefore precedes, every intention, which it exceeds and decenters. (*Being Given* 225)

Viewed through the systematic categories of analysis deployed by Marion for that structure in *In Excess*, such phenomena 'in excess' may be temporal or historical events ('the event'), paintings ('the idol'), phenomena related to the body such as disease ('the flesh') or a type of gaze that 'no longer offers any spectacle to the gaze and tolerates no gaze from any spectator, but rather exerts its own gaze over that which meets it' ('the icon') (*Being Given* 232). According to the helpful summary in the translator's Introduction to *In Excess*,

> the focus of *In Excess* is on saturated phenomena, or paradoxes, those that so exceed the Kantian categories of quantity, quality, relation, or modality that they interrupt or even blind the intentional aim. Marion considers in each chapter in turn the saturated phenomena of the event (which saturates according to quantity, being unable to be accounted for), the idol (which saturates according to quality, being unbearable by the look), flesh (which saturates according to relation, being absolute), and the icon (which saturates according to modality, being unable to be looked at). (xiv)[3]

Among these four types of saturated phenomena, the event is defined by the quality of facticity (as having 'always already' occurred). The event is a historical phenomenon. More precisely, it is a historical phenomenon of a particular kind – the revolutionary event. As Marion explains,

> when the arising event is not limited to an instant, a place, or an empirical individual, but overflows these singularities and becomes epoch-making in time ... covers a physical space such that no gaze encompasses it with one sweep ... and encompasses a population such that none of those who belong to it can take upon themselves an absolute or even a privileged point of view, then it becomes a historical event. (*Being Given* 228)

Epoch-making, total and defying comprehension, apocalypse is a prime instance of the event intended by Marion. Marion does not mention apocalypse, referring to war as an example. But more intense than war, the time-shattering and world-destroying characteristics of apocalypse make it a prime instance of the catastrophic event in Marion's sense. The paradox of the apocalyptic temporality of finitude is that by destroying history and world, it clears the space for remaking time and world. Both destructive and generative, apocalypse initiates a transition from one epoch to another. A discontinuity that facilitates the emergence of a new continuity, apocalypse pictures the force of givenness in a narrative mode that seems uniquely suited to Marion's scheme. More generally, the type of saturated phenomenon that is exemplified by the event also epitomises phenomena as such, by encapsulating the 'eventmental character of phenomenality in general' (*In Excess* 36). As Marion notes, 'it fixes all at once the originally eventmental character of every phenomenon insofar as first it gives *itself* before showing *itself*' (*In Excess* 52). As we shall discuss below, givenness comes first, before anything else. It is primary.

This chapter argues that the phenomenology of givenness advances our understanding of apocalyptic thinking, just as apocalyptic thinking sheds fresh light on the phenomenology of givenness. Marion's category of the transformative event specifically is amenable to conceptualising the post-apocalyptic condition that has been meted out to the protagonists of McCarthy's novel. As we shall explore further in the final section on *The Road*, the apocalyptic event models Marion's concept of the 'saturated phenomenon' in general, and of the 'event' in particular. Apocalyptic ontology's world-endism translates Marion's abstract concept into a concrete scenario. Because givenness so well expresses the task of post-apocalyptic survival, Marion's phenomenology is closely aligned with post-apocalyptic fiction. Its terms are uniquely suited to illuminating the singularity of first-personal experience depicted in post-apocalyptic fiction. I have selected *The Road* because it is perhaps the darkest instance of this genre, a fact that makes the match between Marion and McCarthy especially close and fortunate. The final section will establish how McCarthy's novel in turn offers an excellent illumination of Marion's phenomenological inquiry into the dialectic of givenness and response that generates a new self, the 'gifted', 'the figure of "subjectivity" granted to and by givenness' (*Being Given* x). It will further detail how McCarthy expresses what Marion calls phenomena 'in excess' through a specific artistic form, the baroque, an aesthetics of excess.

The phenomenology of givenness may seem complicated, but in fact Marion's argument can be mapped out by way of a simple diagram (Fig. 1). I will now discuss the four positions of the diagram in turn, following Marion's conceptual order from the most basic upward: 1) givenness, which has primacy; 2) the response to the

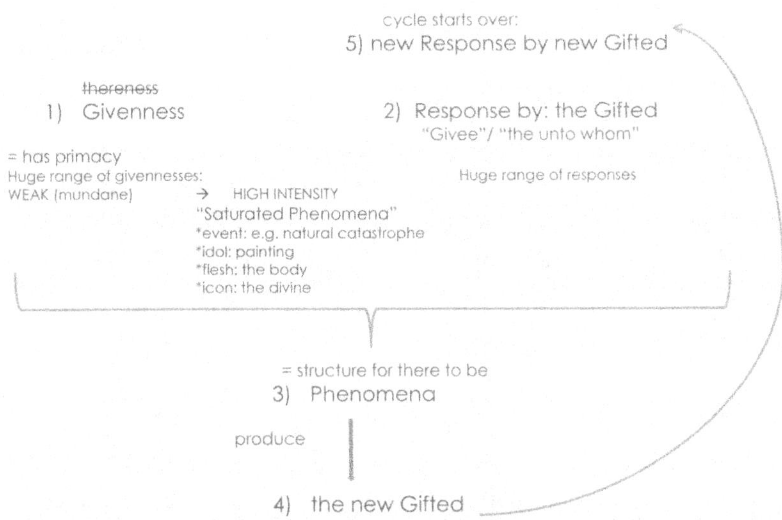

Figure 1 Jean-Luc Marion's phenomenology of givenness

given by the receiver, who, in responding, gives herself over to the given; 3) phenomena (or the 'gift'), which are co-constituted by the dialectic of givenness and response; 4) the new self that is in turn produced by phenomena ('the gifted'). After this, 5) the cycle starts again: the gifted (4), the new self that has been generated through the receiver's mode of response to the given that has befallen it, returns to the second position of the response (2), moving once again into the firing line to receive the impact of new givennesses. As for phenomena (3), there is a huge range of phenomena, because there is a huge range (from weak to moderate to overwhelming) of its two co-constitutive elements: givennesses (1) and responses (2). As discussed above, saturated phenomena are overpowering instances of the given. Notwithstanding the somewhat misleading term, saturated phenomena are not yet 'phenomenalised' (that is to say, Marion distinguishes them in principle from any response by a potential receiver).

Even so, no instance of the 'given', even a saturated phenomenon such as Marion's example of religious calling – or, for present purposes, an apocalyptic event – predetermines the response it is met with. On the contrary, it may encounter very different types of responses. In *The Road* and contemporary post-apocalyptic fiction more generally, the return to scarcity that ensues in the wake of the apocalyptic collapse of modern civilisation illustrates that givenness never elicits one uniform response, but a huge variety. In fact, as we have had occasion to note before, opposite kinds of responses among the survivors constitute the focal concern of post-apocalyptic fiction: Will the apocalyptic plague of white-blindness in Saramago's *Blindness* lead to a collapse into anarchy and extreme violence – the rule of 'blind' competition? Or will it stimulate the emergence of a new and superior kind of social order based on cooperation? Butler's *Parable* series asks: Does survival after the world-end entail the discovery of a new constitutive mythology that expresses what it is like to live in a permanent state of crisis, or does it prove the authority of the traditional God of Christianity? The protagonists of post-apocalyptic fiction make the 'right' choice, the antagonists the 'wrong' one. Character classification in post-apocalyptic fiction follows the survivors' mode of response to the catastrophe that befalls them. As elsewhere, in *The Road* the 'bad guys' revert to a Hobbesian dominator system (nature as 'state of war') by preying on fellow survivors through various kinds of slavery, even cannibalism. In stark contrast, the protagonists form alternative social units that are ethical and self-sustaining, rejecting the temptation to lapse into predator–prey relationships. In *The Road*, the 'man' and his son tell each other that 'we're the good guys' (129) and 'we wouldnt ever eat anybody' (128), a passionate affirmation that illuminates Marion's distinction between givenness, which is primary, and response, which comes second. The response is never pre-programmed by the type of givenness it encounters. For its part, the family's non-exploitative response to apocalypse in turn generates new post-apocalyptic selves (the 'gifted') for the pair, which are further tested in the course of events. As is clear, Marion offers a new version of Arendt's claim in *The Human Condition* that 'through *action* we are born into subjectivity' (Arendt 175–81).

In Marion's view, givenness has primacy because it comes first: 'a phenomenon only shows *itself* to the extent that it first gives *itself*' (*In Excess* 30). As Marion contends, 'I have but one theme: if the phenomenon is defined as what *shows itself* in and from itself (Heidegger), instead of what admits constitution (Husserl), this *self* can be attested only inasmuch as the phenomenon first *gives itself*' (*Being Given* 4). Alluding to Husserl's maxim, 'to the things themselves', Marion writes that '[o]nly a phenomenology of givenness can return to the things themselves because, in order to return to them, it is necessary first to see them, therefore to see them as they come and, in the end, to bear their unpredictable landing' (*Being Given* 4). The primacy of givenness is evident in its facticity, the shock of the given. To connect this back to the previous chapter on field of sense ontology, givenness is roughly analogous to the idea of a necessary starting point that cannot be accounted for, which Gabriel introduces via Schelling's notion of 'unprethinkable being' as well as Heidegger's thrownness. Claiming to go beyond Heidegger's phenomenology of being, Marion defends the primacy of the given as such. Givenness comes before any response, and does not imply a first-personal being 'unto whom' the given is inflicted.

Indeed, thinking Marion's phenomenology together with Gabriel's field of sense ontology shows their compatibility. For Gabriel, fields ground objects. For Marion, the dialectic of givenness grounds the gifted. Both theories are premised on a figure/ground shift from seeing individual objects to seeing interrelationships and contexts as primary. Marion's new realist figure of the self does not exist outside the field of givenness in which it arises: self is world-dependent, a law crystallising in the birth of post-apocalyptic selves in the new futures after the world-end. That said, Marion's phenomenology of givenness foregrounds temporality (the earth-shaking event, the process of becoming) more than does field of sense ontology, as do Maturana and Varela's autopoiesis and enactivism (in the phenomenon of emergence). But might not Gabriel's primacy of field problematise the 'facticity' of any 'given', since a given that appears in one field might appear very differently in another field, thus disrupting the dialectic of givenness and receiver in Marion's circuit? The answer is that extreme events themselves come out of fields: earthquakes emerge from geological fields; wars emerge from political and economic fields; environmental disasters emerge from the dynamics of ecosystems; Jesus' calling of Matthew emerges from the field of Jewish religion. Like the phenomenology of givenness, fields of sense ontology recognises overwhelming events that generate new contexts or fields though creative destruction.

As stated above, phenomenology's goal is to capture the invariant structures of first-personal experience. Husserl believed he had discovered the essence of the phenomenon in the structure of the intentional act (*noesis*) and its intentional object (*noema*). Marion cites Husserl's classic definition: 'The word "phenomenon" is ambiguous by virtue of the essential correlation between

appearing [*Erscheinen*] and *that which appears* [*Erscheinenden*]'
(Husserl qtd in Marion, *Being Given* 21). For his part, Heidegger
superseded Husserl in locating the most basic layer of the phenomenon not in objects, but in being as such. As Marion notes,
Heidegger's phenomenology of being develops from the analysis of
human Dasein in *Being and Time* to his late philosophy of *Ereignis*
(the event of appropriation or enowning). In Marion's view, while
Husserl introduces the concept (*Gegebenheit*) but 'flee[s] from
the task' of thinking givenness (*Being Given* 36), Heidegger gets
a closer glimpse; an early breakthrough in *Being and Time* ('"ça
donne" or "it gives"'; *Being Given* 33) is later recovered when
Heidegger interprets 'it gives' as *Ereignis* (*Being Given* 37). As
Marion explains,

> Heidegger and Husserl thus proceed in the same way and to the same
> point. Both in fact have recourse to givenness and espouse its function
> as ultimate principle – by which they attest it and, at the same time,
> their respective geniuses. But, one of them, in ending up at objectness,
> lets givenness escape, while the other, by assigning beingness to the
> *Ereignis*, abandons it. Both are familiar with givenness without offi-
> cially recognizing it as such. (*Being Given* 38)

Marion maintains that, superseding both Husserl and Heidegger,
what is needed is 'a new definition, at once broader and more
basic, of the phenomenon – no longer as object or being, but as
given' (*Being Given* 3). Or as he also words it, 'objectness and
beingness could thus be thought as mere variations, legitimate
but limited, quite exactly as horizons, which are outlined by and
against the background of givenness' (39).

The gist of the argument in *Being Given* is illustrated by a
reading of Caravaggio's painting *The Calling of St Matthew*, which
Marion presents in the fifth and last part of *Being Given*, entitled
'The Gifted' (283–5) (Fig. 2). The example of Caravaggio's painting is helpful in two respects: first, it illustrates the key constituents
of Marion's phenomenology of givenness described above by way
of a compelling concrete example. In addition, Marion's discussion of Caravaggio's painting is an ekphrastic reading that further
demonstrates the prominence of art in Marion's phenomenology:
painting ('the idol') is one of the modes in which phenomena
manifest themselves.[4] This core passage of Marion's reading of
The Calling of St Matthew is worth quoting at length:

Figure 2 Caravaggio, *The Calling of St Matthew*, 1598/1601, Iglesia de San Luis de los Franceses, Rome (photograph: Album / Art Resource, NY)

Let us consider what is being staged in this painting: a ray of light traverses the space on a diagonal, designating the line where two beams of opposed gazes cross. In the upper right, in the shadows, a man with his back turned (Saint Peter, perhaps) follows the gaze and gesture of another, facing forward (Christ), whose almost hidden eyes and outstretched arm point toward the left, where a group seated around a table are busy counting coins – Matthew is levying the tax on a couple of people, surveyed by two witnesses . . . [W]e only have to look for a minute at the phenomenon that Caravaggio has put into visibility to sense that Christ's gesture is not addressed generally to the indistinct group surrounding Matthew – where three out of five notice and even look at this outstretched arm – but rather to Matthew and Matthew alone, who sees in it *his* calling ... We see it – this call – appear in Matthew's gaze infinitely more than we do in Christ's gesture. For Matthew, who lifts his eyes from the table and turns away from the coins, does not perceive Christ so much as the gaze of Christ, which is intended for him. Not Christ as another spectacle to be seen, but Christ's gaze as a weight that weighs on his own gaze and holds it captive. Then – and here is the decisive moment – caught in the crossing of the gazes, Matthew, with his left hand, makes the merest suggestion of a gesture pointing to himself in silent response to the call, which is neither said nor heard, and asks or else announces: 'Me?' What makes us see the calling, that is to say the doubly invisible call, does not come from a visible signal ... but from the response itself. While around the table three (two cannot tear their attention from the coins) saw the signal, only Matthew read a call therein because he alone took it for himself – in the sense that a guest, a soldier, or a player says, each in his own way, 'The next one's mine!' He alone asked himself, 'This is mine? This is for me?' – thus he is at once given over as the 'unto whom' of what gives itself and, with this very fact, notifies him of the call ... Matthew received the call of his calling by taking it upon himself – and this taking it upon himself already constituted the first response. One could perhaps understand in this way the (at first glance redundant) function of the character (Saint Peter) who shadows Christ from behind: he would in fact respond to Matthew's response by confirming the silent question 'Me?' with a second hand sign: 'Yes, you!' – unless he is asking Christ to confirm that Matthew's first question ('Me?') indeed accomplishes the expected response ('Him?' 'Yes, him!'). In this way, without breaking the silence of the painting, Caravaggio succeeds in making visible the in itself invisible call by choosing to construct not the indistinct phenomenon of a signal (the outstretched arm), but that of a mute and singular response (Matthew designating himself with his hand). This call is painted in this response: the painter's gaze saw (and now shows us) that the call gives itself phenomenologically only by first showing itself in a response. The response that gives itself after the call nevertheless is the first to show it. (*Being Given* 284–5)

Let me address the several key points of this passage in turn. According to Marion, Caravaggio's painting presents a complete inventory of the key elements of the phenomenology of givenness:
1) Jesus' gestural calling of St Matthew exemplifies givenness. It also illustrates the primacy of givenness: the given is absolute, coming first, by way of an 'unpredictable landing' (*Being*

Given 132). There is no way that Matthew could have anticipated Jesus' call. As Marion elucidates, 'we must therefore speak of the unpredictable landings of phenomena, according to discontinuous rhythms, in fits and starts, unexpectedly, by surprise, detached from each other, in bursts, aleatory' (132). Christ's calling of Matthew is an example of the 'saturated phenomenon' of a transformative event, imperative and absolute, 'the undeniable par excellence' (283).

2) Matthew's silent gestural response to the call embodies the receiver's response to the given. If givenness is primary, the response is secondary. Marion's reading of Caravaggio's painting nicely illustrates what Marion calls the 'delay of the responsal' (*Being Given* 294), always second in order. In addition, the example of the calling of St Matthew draws out the first-personal nature of the response to the given. Evident in Matthew's question, 'This is mine? This is for me?' (285), the *ipseity* of Matthew's response contrasts with the comparative indifference of the other persons around the table.

3) Next, 'the crossing of the gazes' (*Being Given* 284) and gestures – the interactive dialogue of Christ's call and Matthew's response – together constitute what Marion calls the gift, the phenomenon of first-personal experience. This further illustrates the phenomenological concept of appearance. As we have already seen, phenomenology posits that appearances *are* real: they show themselves as they really are. In the terms of Marion's phenomenology, the phenomenon results from the interlacing of the response and the given. For phenomena to occur, two parties are required, the given and the response: 'it does not suffice, nevertheless, that the given give *itself* in order to show *itself*' (*In Excess* 49). Yet the two elements are inseparable. Although the given is primary, it takes a response for the given to be phenomenalised, to become manifest (visible, audible, perceived and so on). In other words, Christ's call would not be phenomenalised without Matthew's response; Matthew's response is needed for Christ's call to become manifest, for the 'invisible to be rendered visible' (*Being Given* 284). As Marion maintains at the close of the passage above, 'the call gives itself phenomenologically only by first showing itself in a response. The response that gives itself after the call nevertheless is the first to show it' (285). Paradoxically, even though the response comes second, the call 'is heard only in the response and to its measure' (287).

As Marion explains, 'nothing establishes that the gifted always can or wants to receive *all* that is given' (*Being Given* 310). Worse, it might be the case that 'the gifted might no longer be able or might decide not to bear the given, to no longer convey it to the visible' (313). Matthew might decide to look away instead of heeding Christ's summons. He might decide to remain a tax collector instead of becoming Christ's disciple. In *The Road*, by committing suicide, the protagonist's wife decides to reject the horrific burden of post-apocalyptic parenting and survival that has befallen her. Unlike the man, who accepts the call to survive and raise his son, the mother, who abandons the family to kill herself, illustrates the possibility of givenness failing to meet with a response. Needless to say, as the gruesome events of McCarthy's narrative unfold, the mother's choice often seems the more rational one. A genuine instance of the saturated phenomenon – characterised by being 'unforeseeable', 'unbearable', 'unconditioned (absolute of all horizon) in terms of relation', and 'irreducible to the I' (*Being Given* 218) – the post-apocalyptic condition in *The Road* constitutes givenness so much 'in excess' that is it debatable whether it ought to meet with a response at all. One might argue that it shouldn't. In *Being Given* Marion discusses the example of the 'survivor[s] of the extermination camps', who 'were affected in their (biological, therefore phenomenological) flesh by a suffering so intense, so durable, and so all-encompassing (physical, psychological, spiritual) that one can justly call it absolute – with neither comparison, competition, nor possible relation with another or with an Other – in short, a suffering become a world unto itself' (317). In *The Road*, there are humans living in conditions that rival extermination camps. Foraging for food, the man and the boy happen upon a house that has been repurposed as a cannibal mansion. In the basement, a scene of unspeakable horror awaits them – a group of naked humans kept in captivity like livestock for future slaughter and consumption. 'Huddled against the back wall were naked people, male and female, all trying to hide, shielding their faces with their hands. On the mattress lay a man with his legs gone to the hip and the stumps of them blackened and burnt. The smell was hideous' (*The Road* 110).[5] The two barely escape with their lives; it was to escape ending up as human livestock that the mother had committed suicide. In point of fact, McCarthy could have narrated the first-personal experience of the human food slaves. What would it feel like for post-apocalyptic survivors to end up as the prey of cannibals, spending their last days awaiting their slaughter? This scenario would mean phenomenalising a givenness truly abysmal – albeit perfectly realistic under the circumstances, and arguably more realistic than the story McCarthy tells.

Rather than portraying such unspeakable but realistic apocalyptic horror, McCarthy opts for a happy ending that obeys the rule of wish-fulfilment, what is desirable rather than what is probable. *The Road* closes with father and son reaching their destination on the coast, where the father succumbs to death from chronic lung disease, while the son is rescued by a family of strangers who adopt him. In the aftermath of one of their narrow escapes, the man asks himself whether his wife's decision had not been the more rational one. Whatever the case may be, had all the survivors of the unnamed catastrophe in *The Road* followed the mother's example, there would be no phenomenon at all, no first-personal experience of – or response to – the inordinate givenness of the apocalypse – and, of course, no post-apocalyptic narrative. In Marion's words, 'What gives itself (the call) becomes a phenomenon – shows itself – in and through what responds to it and thus puts it on stage (the gifted)' (*Being Given* 287).

One further clarification needs to be made: Marion's notion of the gift is completely unrelated to the concept of gift exchange in anthropology. As Marion elucidates, 'the indisputable gift is not identified with an object or with its transfer; it is accomplished solely on the occasion of its own happening, indeed without object and transfer' (*Being Given* 103). The 'gift does not consist in a transferred object, but in its *givability*' (107), by which Marion means that, even though they co-constitute the phenomenon or gift, both the given and the response are singular acts.

4) To return to Marion's reading of Caravaggio's painting, we are now ready to broach what for our purposes constitutes the central element of his phenomenology: his claim that what used to be the subject newly appears as a receiver, the recipient of the gift. Marion names this being 'the gifted' (*l'adonnée*). Having acceded to Christ's call, Matthew's response generates a new self, the 'gifted', which is granted solely by the response to the given: henceforth Matthew will be Christ's disciple. He will stop being the tax collector who originally noticed and heeded Christ's call. Marion's 'gifted' is thus a 'reduced "self"' (*In Excess* xv) – a non-autonomous, non-heroic self that is a recipient before

becoming an actor. For Marion, 'thus is born the gifted, whom the call makes the successor to the "subject", as what receives itself entirely from what it receives' (*Being Given* 268). '[D]emoting the I to a *me*' (*In Excess* xv), Marion views the self as 'the "unto whom"' (*Being Given* 269). This is a post-individualist vision of a decentred self: Matthew is not the autonomous source of his identity, but the 'begifted' one. Like the figure of the beloved, the gifted is a being who becomes who he or she is by virtue of his or her response to what has befallen him or her – which may be love, or a religious calling, or, as with the post-apocalyptic survivor, a terrible catastrophe.

Within the larger question that this study is examining of what comes after poststructuralism, Marion's figure of 'the gifted' addresses a specific sub-aspect, how to reconceptualise subjectivity or first-personal experience after poststructuralism. For Marion, '"who comes after the subject" – I call him "the gifted", with no other *subjectum* besides his capacity to receive and to receive *himself* from what he receives' (*Being Given* 4). Marion maintains that

> To have done with the 'subject', it is therefore necessary not to destroy it, but to reverse it – to overturn it. It is posited as a center: this will not be contested, but I will contest its mode of occupying and exercising the center to which it lays claim – with the title of a (thinking, constituting, resolute) 'I.' I will contest the claim that it occupies this center as an origin, an ego or first person, in transcendental 'mineness.' I will oppose it to the claim that it does not hold this center but is instead held there as a recipient where what gives itself shows itself, and that it discloses itself given to and as a pole of givenness, where all the givens come forward incessantly. At the center stands no 'subject', but a gifted, he whose function consists in receiving what is immeasurably given to him, and whose privilege is confined to the fact that he is himself received from what he receives. (*Being Given* 322)

As is clear, the decentred figure of the 'gifted' explicitly takes the place of the delegitimised concept of the subject.

It is important to clarify that even if the gifted is a decentred self, it is nonetheless not the familiar decentred self of poststructuralism – the subject of discipline, power and ideology. At first sight, Marion's account of the call/response structure might be mistaken as an echo of Althusser's theory of interpellation. One of the principal instances of the linguistic turn, Althusser's theory of interpellation exemplifies the hermeneutics of suspicion in positing a deterministic theory of the subject as the precipitate of ideology. For Althusser, the realm of first-personal consciousness – the territory of phenomenology – is nothing but the domain of ideology. Althusser's account presented in 'Ideology and Ideological State Apparatuses' is well known, but a brief gloss is helpful nonetheless. Subjectivity is premised on subjection to ideology: *'ideology has the function (which defines it) of "constituting" concrete individuals as subjects'* (Althusser 116). This is achieved through the process of what Althusser calls interpellation (or hailing) via a call/ response scenario modelled on that at birth, when a newborn child, born into a family with a pre-existing family name, is baptised with a name chosen by its parents. Likewise, *'all ideology hails or interpellates concrete individuals as concrete subjects'* (117), except that the agents here are abstract systems, which Althusser calls ISAs (Ideological State Apparatuses). Althusser's list of ISAs encompasses the church, education, family, the law, the political system and other entities. Althusser pictures the process as an everyday scenario of a policeman hailing a stranger: 'Hey, you there!' (118). In response, 'the hailed individual will turn around. By this mere one-hundred-and-eighty-degree physical conversion, he becomes a *subject*. Why? Because he has recognized that the hail was "really" addressed to him, and that "it was *really him* who was hailed" (and not someone else)' (118). In responding to the call, the individual becomes a docile subject consenting to reproducing the meaning and values of the institution that hails him. In a word, the individual's recognition 'It is (really) I!' is actually a misrecognition (121).

Marion's version of the call/response structure in the reading of Caravaggio's *The Calling of St Matthew* discussed above differs from Althusser's in several key respects. This is the case in spite of substantial parallels. Like Marion, Althusser also draws on a biblical example: Moses' calling by Yahweh (Althusser 121). Conversely, the differences illustrate the gap between structuralist and poststructuralist theories of the subject-as-subjection (to ideology, power, and so on) on the one hand, and Marion's phenomenological concept of the gifted on the other. Instead of reproducing the call as in Althusser's interpellation, for Marion, the response completes the call. While the call is primary and the response comes second, Marion's response is irreducible to the call.

McCarthy's *The Road* exemplifies this point: the man and the boy and the cannibal gangs all respond to the overwhelming event of the apocalypse, but do so in very different ways. The Althusserian call and response are arranged in a hierarchy in which the call of institutional ideologies constitutes the higher reality that manifests itself in the individual's response and self-misrecognition. (Since Althusser's essay lists a number of ISAs, it is conceivable that any individual might be interpellated by multiple competing ISAs. But this does not change the poststructuralist view, encapsulated by Althusser's account of interpellation, that consciousness, as Catherine Belsey words it, is an 'effect of signification: I owe to the big Other the meanings and differences that permit me to think at all' [Belsey 66].) In contrast, Marion's call/response structure ('the gift') is non-reductive: the response is not pre-programmed. It is an unpredictable and creative answer to the call governed by rules internal to the receiver's mental pattern. Similarly, for Maturana and Varela, the non-predictability of the response to environmental stimuli has an even larger significance. According to the theory of autopoiesis considered in Chapter 3, it distinguishes living from non-living systems more generally.

As Marion elucidates, it is only in overwhelming or saturated phenomena – such as Matthew's calling – that the dynamic of givenness and response sharpens into the urgency of call and response: 'what will happen when a phenomenon given as saturated arises? The impact will be radicalized into a *call*, and the receiver into *the gifted*' (*Being Given* 266). Such a summons leads to a loss of autonomy:

> The interloqué suffers a call so powerful and compelling that he must surrender [*s'y rendre*] to it . . . Thus he must renounce the autarchy of self-positing and self-actualizing . . . The pure and simple shock (*Anstoss*) of the summons identifies the I only by transforming it without delay into a *me 'to whom'*. (*Being Given* 268)

Yet one might object, doesn't this sound like Althusser? (Indeed, what Marion calls 'interlocution' [269] corresponds to Althusser's interpellation.)[6] If it does, this is because the parallels are close between Marion's and Althusser's varieties of the call/response structure: both posit the primacy of the call, as well as its shocking impact on the receiver, reducing the 'I' to the 'unto whom'.

As Marion elaborates, 'the gifted forever bears the marks of his delay to the call', among which is 'inauthenticity' (*Being Given* 290–1). In other words, the gifted is not an authentic self that gives birth to itself in the manner of the Cartesian *cogito*: 'The gifted turns up by extricating himself from the "I think" and its pretension to positing on principle *I=I*' (290). 'What absolutely must be contested is the originary character of authenticity as self-appropriation' (290). The crucial difference is that, for Marion, the response and the gifted – 'who comes after the subject' and who is generated by his or her response to the call – are (in Latour's helpful terms) actants who are active mediators instead of passive intermediaries or marionettes of ideological structures. As Marion maintains, 'only the response performs the call, and the gifted renders visible and audible what gives itself to it only by corresponding to it in the act of responding' (288). As noted earlier, the events of *The Road* demonstrate this point clearly. That 'performing the call' – manifesting or phenomenalising it – is a free act and not a determined one is borne out by three drastically different responses among the post-apocalyptic survivors: the non-response of suicide, the ethical response of care in the face of horror, and the exploitative response of cannibalism.

Alphonso Lingis's Phenomenology of Passionate Identification

Further clarity on how the changed understanding of first-personal experience and consciousness accounts, in large part, for why phenomenology is experiencing a revival after structuralism and poststructuralism is provided by Alphonso Lingis's late work. In principle, blurbs might not be the best authorities to quote. But the anonymous summary on the back of Lingis's *The First Person Singular* (2007) is an excellent place to start discussion of his work:

> Alphonso Lingis's unique works of philosophy are not so much written as performed . . . Lingis's topic here is the subject itself, understood not as consciousness but as an embodied, impassioned, active being. This is not the linguistic or the literary subject posited by structuralism and post-structuralism, nor the rational consciousness theorized by post-Enlightenment philosophy. Rather, it is a being embodied in passionate, intensifying activity and in the rituals and practices of a social and cultural collective . . . *The First Person Singular* is an elegant cultural

analysis of how subjectivity is differently and collectively understood, invested, and situated. (*First Person* n.p.)

Having made his reputation as a translator of key works by Merleau-Ponty and Levinas (including Merleau-Ponty's posthumous *The Visible and the Invisible*), and having authored formal phenomenological studies, Lingis developed a non-traditional, performative and lyrical style of writing in his late works (van Manen 165). On Harman's account, Lingis is a 'carnal phenomenologist' (*Guerrilla Metaphysics* 3), following Levinas and Merleau-Ponty in undoing the textualisation of philosophy. 'Carnal hermeneutics' is Kearney's related description of a school of phenomenology and hermeneutics. Featuring Levinas and Merleau-Ponty but not Lingis, carnal hermeneutics restores the cognitive subject to the physical world, as an embodied and sensate self operating, as Merleau-Ponty would claim, 'in and from the flesh of the world' (Kearney, 'Carnal Hermeneutics' 38). Many of Lingis's books also include writing and images drawn from his global travels of an anthropological orientation. One of his most recent works in this mode, *The First Person Singular* blends phenomenological analysis and philosophical reflection with expressive writing in a literary vein. In *The First Person Singular*, Lingis returns to the core domain of phenomenology, first-personal experience and consciousness. In a companion essay, 'Return of the First-Person Singular' (2012), a revised version of which appeared in *Irrevocable: A Philosophy of Mortality* (2018), Lingis defends the phenomenological investigation of first-personal experience, further illuminating the revival of phenomenology after structuralism and poststructuralism.[7]

'Return of the First Person Singular' examines three 'sectors of research that break with the postmodern conception of subjectivity' – anthropology, medical practice and creative art (55). According to Lingis, all three disciplines demonstrate the inadequacy of the postmodern philosophy of mind, informed by structural linguistics,

> [in which] meanings are articulated in the taxonomic contrasts, semantic systems, grammatical forms, and rhetorical paradigms of languages, which are social and institutional productions. The meanings of speech acts produced by individuals are determined from the specific tongue, milieu, profession, and social and practical situation in which they are uttered and from the distribution, condensations, and displacements of signifiers in the unconscious. (54)

In particular, leaving structural anthropology behind, cultural anthropology newly recognises the need to recover the first-personal perspective of the mind of the informant, as articulated in 'his or her own voice' (57): 'The mind of the informant is not simply a locus where the ideological system of his culture is inscribed; it is a force of commitment – commitment to some pieces of this system but also to his own work and his maneuvers in the network of his political and psychological relations with others' (57).

In medical practice, for example, medical anthropologists perceive the need for 'individuals . . . to take responsibility for their illness and healing' (58) in addition to and beyond their medical treatment. Towards this goal, we 'need a theoretical understanding of the first person singular', the entity that gives meaning to her suffering and aspirations (58). 'For all this, the medical discourse is of no avail' (58). As Lingis maintains, 'the sufferer has to elaborate a narrative of her aspirations and her fate, her destiny, her lifetime. The patient's narrative of that alien event in her life that is her illness will determine what treatments she will accept and may even have an effect on the efficacy of those treatments' (59). This same articulation of the creative force of meaning-making in the midst of suffering also appears in the branch of creative art that is *art brut*, works of art produced by the insane.

In *The First Person Singular*, Lingis presents these abstract claims in a different mode of writing, which blends the phenomenological and anthropological with the performative-expressive. The book is organised as a series of loosely connected vignettes grouped together under different aspects of the first-personal, including 'Being Here', 'The Voice', 'My Own Voice', and so on. 'How I Come to Be Here' (chapter 2) introduces one key claim: that sense of self (I, me, mine) arises from, and peaks in, impassioned states. Emotions, marginalised in rationalist modern Western philosophy founded on the *cogito*, need to be acknowledged as the source of the sense of self. According to Lingis,

> The I is an *I enjoy, I endure, I suffer*. (*First Person Singular* 7)
> The sense of oneself is an *I need, I want, I am contented*. (7)
> I am where my bodily and affective forces are integrated, manipulate things, and confront obstacles. The sense of oneself that arises in a body in action is an *I can*. (8)
> In impassioned states I find myself to be on my own. (10)
> The I, singularized and brought to a peak of concentration and

intensity is *I am thrilled, I am delighted, I am enraged, I am terrified.* (10)

The proclamative style of Lingis's claims about emotions as the source of the first-personal sense of 'mineness' perfectly illustrates his double-voiced method. Parallel to the affirmative- expressive mode exemplified by the quotations above runs a more formal mode of phenomenological and philosophical analysis. As Lingis affirms,

> Conscious life is not a steady state; it moves from the eclipse of consciousness in sleep to the tasks and pleasures of our everyday environment ... Impassioned encounters are lived in high intensity and with quickened and amassed energies. (*First Person Singular* 9)
>
> [In] impassioned states ... a sense of oneself is at a peak of concentration and intensity. (10)
>
> Impassioned states, seen as disruptions of the integrated and socialized individual and of the effective operation of mercantile society, have been marginalized and pathologized in the philosophy of mind. But they remain central in literature and drama ... (11)

Moving the emotions from the margins to the centre to highlight the grounding of first-personal experience in feeling, *The First Person Singular* joins current trends in the history of the emotions and affect theory. For our purposes, however, field-specific debates are less important than the affirmation of the centrality of emotion as such.[8]

In 'I am a ...' (chapter 8) Lingis revisits one of the shrines of structuralist subjectivity, the theorem of the 'I' as linguistic shifter. As linguistic shifter, the 'I' pre-exists subjectivity and determines its place in the social world; in Lacan's more forceful claim, the linguistic shifter represents the symbolic order that separates us from the real (our bodily drives). Countering the claims of structuralist subjectivity, Lingis maintains that in passionate identification, 'the word "I" has a special force. "I am on my own now." "I am a mother"' (*First Person Singular* 37). Passionate commitment trumps the structuralist doctrine that, in Barthes's famous expression, 'it is language which speaks, not the author' (Barthes 143). For Lingis,

> To say 'I am a dancer' is to commit my body to travail, injury, and pain.
> To say 'I am a mother' is to commit my body to set free the child, and

the adolescent and adult it bore, or to care for the genetically defective child it gave birth to until its death. To say 'I am a doctor' is to commit my body to total mobilization for hours and at any hour and to the daily proximity to deadly diseases. (*First Person Singular* 39)

In the following passage, Lingis critiques structuralist subjectivity – such as Althusser's interpellation – even more focally:

The words with which others identify us – 'Jean is a man', 'She is the mother', 'He is a pilot' – may function simply to identify us with a category, situate us in a class or social function. But in pronouncing inwardly or out loud the words 'I am a man', 'I am a dancer', 'I am a mother', I stand forth. Fixed in myself, these commonest of words generate visions of things not yet seen, of open roads and wilderness beyond the corporate post at which we are stationed, of dances never yet seen or danced ... In our visionary body, the word we put on ourselves in saying 'as for me', 'I, a mother', 'I am young still', is an oracular word. (50)

Far from reducing individuals to the rule of interpellation, the 'I am' of passionate identification is a mode that dares to imagine otherwise. It opens up a counter-reality to the reality of the status quo – an imaginary, utopian reality. This is precisely the function of such passionate affirmations in *The Road*, which the man and the boy intone like mantras: 'We are the good guys'; 'We are carrying the fire.' As we shall see in the following section, such watchphrases affirm the principle of life against the entropic world of the post-apocalypse. Constructing a counter-wasteland, that these are 'oracular words' in Lingis's sense is underscored by the many references to the sacred in McCarthy's novel, to which I now turn.

Post-Apocalyptic Baroque and Post-Apocalyptic Selves in Cormac McCarthy's *The Road*

Like Atwood's *MaddAddam* trilogy and many other post-apocalyptic novels, narration in *The Road* is organised by a dual-time structure. Focalised through the first-personal consciousness of a survivor shipwrecked among the ruins of late capitalist civilisation, narration alternates between the post-apocalyptic present and the survivor's memories of the catastrophe and the time before it occurred. In *The Road*, the chasm between the pre-apocalyptic past and the post- apocalyptic present is deepest, because the destruction of life wrought by the cataclysm is near-total. Like Atwood and Butler, McCarthy confronts the question of whether there is hope for a redeemed future 'after the end'. Yet while Atwood explores the prospects for long-term alternative ecological futures after the destruction of fossil-fuelled modern civilisation and Butler investigates the post-apocalyptic reconfiguration of the divine, McCarthy's *The Road* all but destroys such hopes.

In McCarthy's novel, the future of life as such is in question. The post-apocalyptic world in *The Road* is an entropic universe in rapid tailspin towards the complete extinction of all life – human as well as non-human. In the wake of an unspecified catastrophe, the sun is permanently obscured, the landscape is covered with ash from the conflagration and the charred remains of plants and things, and the climate is cooling. What has been 'given to' – or rather, inflicted on – the human survivors in McCarthy's novel is more extreme than in any of the other novels discussed here. The collapse of modern political, social and technological systems (the state, supply infrastructure and so on) and the degradation of humans to a pre-technological nomadic lifestyle of scavenging among the ruins for food and shelter are standard for the genre. But no other work pictures such complete post-collapse resource scarcity, and humans so close to extinction, as *The Road*. The apocalypse in *The Road* has wound the clock forward, as it were, to a speculative future scenario involving the extinction of almost all non-human life, leaving the human survivors stranded on a dying planet without warmth or renewable food sources. The only things to eat (save for other humans) are the diminishing stores of food (in the houses and supermarkets of abandoned cities) left over from before the cataclysm.

In depicting the struggle of the man and the boy for survival in the darkening wasteland of ruins littered with the detritus and corpses of the extinct modern world, *The Road* stages an archetypal battle between 'two diametrically opposed views of evolutionary change' (Capra 48): entropy and evolution. Entropy projects a grim picture of cosmic development as the inexorable dissipation of energy resulting in heat death, whereas evolution tells a hopeful story of the emergence, preservation and reproduction of living organisms. In the most general of terms, *The Road* dramatises the conflict between two scientific views of cosmic evolution, the grim picture of increasing entropy enshrined in the second law of thermodynamics on the one hand, and the hopeful picture of the emergence and development of life on the other. Entropy and evolution articulate two contrasting models of cosmic history – the no-future of the coming solar apocalypse and the positive growth of life.

According to Fritjof Capra, these two opposing views picture 'a living world unfolding toward increasing order and complexity and that of an engine running down, a world of ever-increasing disorder' (Capra 48). Placing the principles of entropy and evolution within a unified framework, systems theory posits that life may be pictured as

> islands of order in a sea of disorder, maintaining and even increasing their order at the expense of greater disorder in their environment. For example, living organisms take in ordered structures (food) from their environment, use them as resources for their metabolism, and dissipate structures of lower order (waste). In this way, order 'floats in disorder', as [Ilya] Prigogine . . . puts it, while the overall entropy keeps increasing in accordance with the second law. (Capra and Luisi 160)

Indeed, the claim that living organisms 'exist in [a] boundary region near the "edge of chaos"' is the central hypothesis of evolutionary biologist Stuart Kauffman of the Santa Fe Institute in New Mexico, a cross-disciplinary research centre dedicated to developing complexity theory (Capra 204). Since 2001 McCarthy has been associated with the Santa Fe Institute as a Fellow.[9] As Kevin Kearney speculates, McCarthy 'most likely drew from some of his colleagues' research' ('Cormac McCarthy's *The Road*' 166) for the depiction of post-apocalyptic extinction in *The Road*. In an interview, McCarthy remarks that the only research he did for *The Road* was to 'talk to people about what things might look like under various catastrophic situations' (see Jurgensen). What then are the catastrophic events in cosmological evolution that McCarthy may have drawn on for *The Road*?

The centrepiece of McCarthy's post-collapse ecology is the permanent obscuring of the sun: the man observes 'the dull sun moving unseen beyond the murk' (*The Road* 14); 'the unseen sun cast no shadow' (69). There are analogies with various catastrophic crises in the earth's prehistory. As Lynn Margulis has shown, the evolution of life from the emergence of the microcosm to the appearance of visible life forms, the macrocosm and its animals, plants and fungi, experienced repeated catastrophes, triggered either by the scarcity of essential nutrients or the surplus of toxic pollutants and wastes (Margulis, *Microcosmos*). The hydrogen crisis (the depletion of hydrogen in the atmosphere) and the oxygen crisis (the excess of oxygen in the atmosphere), both occurring during the age of the microcosm that extended for two billion years, were landmark instances of such planetary 'bifurcation points'. Bifurcation points are critical thresholds at which a dynamic system 'may either break down or break through to one of several new states of order' (Capra 191). In each case, the threat of extinction was fended off when organisms found new metabolic pathways for extracting food and energy from the environment. That is to say, catastrophe was averted through innovation, when blue-green algae twice invented new biotechnologies that are the foundation of terrestrial life today: photosynthesis (the extraction of hydrogen from water) and oxygen-breathing (the absorption of excess oxygen from the atmosphere). In the resulting pattern of evolutionary development, the threat of extinction was therefore followed by intense periods of biological growth and innovation. These irregular global catastrophic events, whose lethal challenge was overcome by creative evolutionary responses, probably form the precedent for McCarthy's speculative post-collapse scenario.

For this reason, as Margulis and Sagan note, physicists have recently 'invented the word "negentropy" for life, which, in its tendency to increase information and certainty, seems to contradict the second law' (*What Is Life?* 15–16). While the underlying analogy is flawed (the second law holds even as evolution contravenes it [16]), the larger point is well taken: life as the autopoietic creation of self-maintaining organic systems is a creative response to opposed tendencies towards disorganisation and death. Negentropy, the struggle to negate entropy, is a great metaphor for *The Road*. In McCarthy's post-apocalyptic scenario, it is difficult to imagine such a creative response occurring ever again, mainly because access to solar energy on earth is shutting down. The biosphere – the 'twenty kilometers thick' layer of life surrounding earth, from the atmosphere at the top to the bottom of the ocean (*What is Life?* 5) – has been cut off from solar energy by ash from the conflagration that has turned the sky grey and blotted out the sun. Towards the end of *The Road*, the father muses:

for all he knew the world grew darker daily. He'd once found a light-meter in a camera store that he thought he might use to average out readings for a few months, and he carried it around with him for a long time thinking he might find some batteries for it but he never did. (*The Road* 213)

This comment evokes the environmental catastrophe that led to the extinction of the dinosaurs at the end of the Cretaceous period about 65 million years ago.[10] Multiple causes, including meteor impact and volcanic eruption, obscured the sun for long periods, depriving vegetation of sunlight. Plants, then herbivores, then carnivores died. Death advanced through the food chain, and the extinction of half of the plant and animal species, including dinosaurs, ensued. Replace carnivorous dinosaurs with humans, and we have the scenario of *The Road*: a countdown to the looming extinction of humans because of the planet's parallel cataclysmic plunge into barrenness and sterility. *The Road* is animated by the temporality of a ticking clock relentlessly approaching extinction.

In the remainder of this chapter, I will discuss *The Road* through the lens of Marion's phenomenology of the given and Lingis's phenomenology of passionate identification. I will connect these to McCarthy's stylistic experiments in combining two antithetical styles, the baroque and minimalism, to express the horror of apocalyptic givenness and the response to it through strategies of post-apocalyptic survival. McCarthy uses two different dialects, one to express the horror of world-destruction (the neo-baroque), the other to articulate post-apocalyptic world-making (minimalism). As I will show, *The Road*'s double-voiced narration further illustrates the singularity of post-apocalyptic literature vis-à-vis new realist critical theory.

McCarthy's narrative is set about 8–10 years after the cataclysm, the age of the boy born in the immediate aftermath of the apocalypse. Given the atrocities that have occurred in the interim, the future extinction of humans seems a reasonable prospect in another decade or two. The cause of the disaster is unspecified: 'The clocks stopped at 1:17. A long shear of light and then a series of low concussions.' 'A dull rose glow in the windowglass' (*The Road* 52). Some critics speculate that the explosion must have been of nuclear origin, plunging the planet into a 'nuclear winter' (see Ashford). But the meteor impact that led to mass extinction at the end of the Cretaceous period also triggered infernal explosions and firestorms of the magnitude of millions of atomic bombs.[11] The man's memory of the following years records the gradual dying of plants and animals:

> Once in those early years he'd wakened in a barren wood and lay listening to the flocks of migratory birds overhead in that bitter dark. Their half muted crankings miles above where they circled the earth as senselessly as insects trooping the rim of a bowl. He wished them godspeed till they were gone. He never heard them again. (*The Road* 53)

By the time of the narrative present, the only signs of non-human life are a patch of edible mushrooms found in the woods (40) and the sound of a dog barking, which is never heard again (83). The post-apocalyptic wasteland registers the advanced degree of extinction of natural life:

> A raw hill country. Aluminum houses. At times they could see stretches of the interstate highway below them through the bare stands of secondgrowth timber. Cold and growing colder. Just beyond the high gap in the mountains they stood and looked out over the great gulf to the south where the country as far as they could see was burned away, the blackened shapes of rock standing out of the shoals of ash and billows of ash rising up and blowing downcountry through the waste. The track of the dull sun moving unseen beyond the murk. (*The Road* 14)

The reference to 'secondgrowth timber' indicates that trees still reproduce, but the question is for how much longer. On an abandoned farm, the man finds dried apples in the orchard and 'a lingering odor of cows in the barn' (120). Yet when 'thinking about cows', the man realises 'they were extinct' (120), just like birds and trout in the river. Interspersed throughout are passages memorialising lost animals and plant species.

In *The Road*, the stylistic form employed to depict post-apocalyptic ruin and extinction is the neo-baroque. The neo-baroque refers to a broad, inter-artistic, twentieth- and twenty-first-century trend in visual and word-based media that recovers seventeenth-century baroque cultural forms, works and writers. Many of the narrative reflections on ruin, mortality, finitude, the coming extinction of humanity and inexorable entropy in *The Road* are written in the ornate baroque style – often associated with Faulkner – that had also been noted in McCarthy's early work, most centrally *Blood Meridian*. Although *The Road* has received much critical attention, this connection has not yet been thoroughly explored.[12] As the man reflects,

> In that long ago somewhere very near this place he'd watched a falcon fall down the long blue wall of the mountain and break with the keel of its breastbone the midmost from a flight of cranes and take it to the river below all gangly and wrecked and trailing its loose and blowsy plumage in the still autumn air. (*The Road* 20)

This and similar passages memorialising extinct animals and plants, like other passages describing the post-apocalyptic waste-land of ruins, dead objects and corpses, are focalised through the father's memories – as is the entire narrative. The boy, born after the cataclysm, has no first-personal experience of the pre-apocalyptic period. Indeed, the father's knowledge advantage over his son in *The Road* parallels that of Jimmy over the Crakers in Atwood's *Oryx and Crake*: a survivor communicates memories of the vanished pre-apocalyptic world to interlocutors who belong entirely to the post-apocalyptic period.

The disappearance of trout in particular, mentioned three times, epitomises the death of nature (*The Road* 30, 41, 286; see also Gwinner 154ff.). *The Road* also ends in this baroque mode, with the closing paragraph looking back to mourn the living earth irretrievably lost:

> Once there were brook trout in the streams in the mountains. You could see them standing in the amber current where the white edges of their fins wimpled softly in the flow. They smelled of moss in your hand. Polished and muscular and torsional. On their back were ver-miculate patterns that were maps of the world in its becoming. Maps and mazes. Of a thing which could not be put back. Not be made right again. In the deep glens where they lived all things were older than man and they hummed of mystery. (*The Road* 286–7)

Gwinner raises an interesting question about the focaliser of this passage. At this point, the father is dead (Gwinner 155). The son cannot be the focaliser, because of his lack of first-personal memories of the time before. Clearly, McCarthy is breaking with the psychological realism characteristic of focalisation and narra-tion in *The Road* up to this point. Separating consciousness from embodied experience, the dead father's first-personal memories are voiced from beyond the grave as it were.[13] Elevated to a timeless realm, the man's disembodied memories haunt the end of the narrative. McCarthy may be emulating a similar device in William Faulkner's novel *As I Lay Dying*, where Addie Bundren's section narrating her first-person consciousness comes after her actual death, in the manner of a posthumous address.

Baroque style is characterised by the principle of abundance and excess. It is the antithesis of minimalism: not 'less is more' but 'more is more' or 'more is not less'. Paradoxically, however, baroque excess is a symptom of its opposite, as suggested by the baroque byword, 'horror of the void'. As the Mexican novelist Carlos Fuentes explains:

> The Baroque, language of abundance, is also the language of insufficiency. Only those who possess nothing can include everything. The *horror vacui* of the Baroque is not gratuitous – it is because the vacuum exists that nothing is certain. The verbal abundance of . . . Faulkner's *Absalom, Absalom!* represents a desperate invocation of language to fill the absences left by the banishment of reason and faith. (Fuentes 543)

Fuentes's observation about the baroque as the rhetoric of loss explains the baroque's affinity with Marion's phenomenology of givenness. More than superficial, these parallels are deeply structural. As noted earlier, 'saturated' phenomena 'set forth a surplus that the concept cannot organize' (Marion, *Being Given* 225). They 'exceed and decenter' (225) every intention. The baroque rhetoric of abundance – words to fill the painful void – is an artistic strategy to cope – to respond – that incorporates the challenge (disruption) into the fabric of its response (the new aesthetic order). This is exactly how Marion pictures phenomena – 'the gift' – as co-constituted by givenness and response. The unsayable is brought into the said; McCarthy's baroque phenomenalises the unspeakable horror of the post-apocalyptic wasteland in *The Road*. Baroque compositions are disorderly structures or stable instabilities, the product of early modern religious schisms as well as social and intellectual upheavals such as the scientific revolution. At the higher-order level of narrative strategy, McCarthy's baroque narrative form thus manifests a deformation that mirrors that which marks the post-apocalyptic decentred self, an 'I' 'demoted' to an 'unto whom'.

In literature, the baroque's hallmarks include digressive and lofty rhetoric, slow-paced narration laden with descriptive detail, labyrinthine, hypotactical sentences, arresting images in the manner of metaphysical conceits presenting ingenious, far-fetched analogies, and a learned vocabulary of rare and obscure words. Only the first of the two passages above is baroque at the sentence level, a situation that is representative throughout *The Road*, whose preference for short sentences, sentence fragments and brief dialogue has been noted, as I shall discuss below. But word choices such as 'torsional' and 'vermiculate' do not fit this pattern; they exemplify erudite baroque diction. The metaphors likening a falcon's breastbone to a ship's keel and a trout's dorsal patterns to maps of the world are conceits. Phrases such as 'wimpled softly', 'all gangly and wrecked and trailing its loose and blowsy plumage' evince the lofty tone and proliferation of descriptive naming that are characteristic of baroque style.

From seventeenth-century baroque works such as Robert Burton's *The Anatomy of Melancholy* (1621) and Sir Thomas Browne's *Hydriotaphia, Urne-Buriall* (1658) to twentieth-century neo-baroque works such as Djuna Barnes's *Nightwood* (1936), William Faulkner's *Absalom, Absalom!* (1936) and W. G. Sebald's *The Rings of Saturn* (1995), baroque style has been associated with melancholic reflection on transience and mortality of all stripes, religious and secular. It is no surprise that in *The Road*, McCarthy should employ it to memorialise destruction at the grandest scale: the apocalyptic annihilation of most humans and the coming extinction of life on earth.

Melancholy, the mood of irretrievable loss and trauma, is closely associated with the baroque, the dynamic rhetoric of excess and theatrical display. This link can be traced in a wide variety of expressions across the visual and word-based arts in the historical baroque and the neo-baroque. One is the Catholic religious baroque's cult of *memento mori*, represented by devotional images and their iconography of saints and martyrs contemplating skulls, tombs, expiring candles and other symbols of the transience of earthly life. Another is Renaissance melancholia, embodied by the figure of the melancholic scholar, the 'tortured but creative male genius' (Schiesari 16). As Juliana Schiesari explains, the latter's suffering – unlike that of his twentieth-century feminised counterpart, the abject and unproductive Freudian melancholic – comes with the compensations of learning and knowledge. The early modern figure of the melancholic scholar-intellectual who appears in the works of Burton and Browne has been recuperated by twentieth-century writers such as Barnes and Sebald to forge the voices of their melancholic narrators contemplating ruin, death and catastrophe, as I have discussed elsewhere.[14] I argue that *The Road* is a new addition to Anglophone neo-baroque fiction that revives baroque melancholia and transposes it into a modern setting. Note that these comments are specific to the baroque thread in *The Road*, not the novel as a whole, which also includes a minimalist thread that I will address below. As such, *The Road* joins forces with *Nightwood, Absalom, Absalom!* and McCarthy's own *Blood Meridian*.

The Road, to the best of my knowledge, is the only work among contemporary post-apocalyptic fiction that connects scenarios of ecological holocaust to the baroque. Yet McCarthy's choice is completely natural: apocalyptic narrative and its prediction of coming destruction has long been the domain of the baroque in the religious apocalypse of Christian eschatology. McCarthy's speculative near-future apocalypse is scientific, not religious. However, both scientific and religious types display the definitive traits of apocalyptic narrative: the revelation of a coming annihilation on a global scale. In McCarthy's twenty-first-century environmental apocalypse, religious prophecy gives way to scientific prognosis, but the grim prospect of global destruction remains the same.

McCarthy's narrator contemplates the apocalyptic scenario of a dying biosphere caused by the blocking out of the sun by an enormous cloud of ash in language that alternates between scientific sobriety and baroque flourishes. A reflection that begins poetically with an alliterative sound effect ('the world grew *darker daily*'; *The Road* 213, my italics) veers towards scientific fact in the next sentence. This is the statement about measuring the darkening of the planet with a light meter quoted above. Earlier, the same subject of the loss of solar energy is again treated in alliterative and lofty baroque rhetoric: 'the dull *s*un moving *uns*een beyond the murk' (14, my italics). This blend of the scientific with the apocalyptic and poetic is reminiscent of the prose of the English baroque writer and physician Sir Thomas Browne, in particular his treatises *Hydriotaphia, Urne-Buriall* and *The Garden of Cyrus*. Published together in 1648, these two works complement each other: whereas *Urne-Buriall* is about impermanence, dissolution and death, *The Garden of Cyrus* is about renewal, resurrection and the restoration of order via the cosmic pattern of the quincunx. Rather than direct quotation, McCarthy's recovery of Browne works through indirect reminiscence. *The Road* mirrors Browne's grand baroque style together with Browne's themes – mortality and the hope of renewal. It is worth noting the millenarian dimension of *The Garden of Cyrus*. As Frank Huntley points out, Browne's prophetic vision appears on the last page: 'All things begin in order, and so shall they end, and so shall they begin again; according to the ordainer of order and mystical Mathematicks of the City of Heaven' (*Garden of Cyrus* 387; see Huntley 133).

The link that connects McCarthy's neo-baroque with Browne's baroque prose leads primarily to *Urne-Buriall*. Written upon the occasion of the discovery of some sepulchral urns in Norfolk, *Urne-Buriall*, Browne's most popular work, is a wide-ranging, learned meditation on funerary practices across times and cultures, mortality, time itself, and the possibilities and limits of human knowledge. The description of a specific object (an urn, names on a gravestone) triggers abstract meditations on death, transience and decay. As Browne observes,

> There is no antidote against the *Opium* of time, which temporally considereth all things . . . Graves-stones tell truth scarce fourty years; Generations passe while some trees stand, and old Families last not three Oaks.
> The number of the dead long exceedeth all that shall live. The night of time far surpasseth the day, and who knows when was the Equinox? (*Urne-Buriall* 309, 310–11)

Browne's tone is melancholic; the fifth chapter contains a number of well-known passages reflecting on the coming end of history that evoke similar musings in *The Road*.

As in Browne's works, interspersed throughout *The Road* are baroque epiphanies on mortality, philosophical meditations that plumb the meaning of the post-apocalyptic world. *The Road* employs the (neo-)baroque – the rhetoric of excess – to take stock of a phenomenon in excess – the unbearable fate of being ship-wrecked on a dying planet. One such epiphany comes after an episode when the father and son find a group of humans kept in captivity like livestock in the basement of a mansion occupied by a gang of cannibals. The passage reflects on the dehumanisation of the human food slaves to the abject status of prey hunted by predators (other dehumanised humans):

> [H]e saw for a brief moment the absolute truth of the world. The cold relentless circling of the intestate earth. Darkness implacable. The blind dogs of the sun in their running. The crushing black vacuum of the universe. And somewhere two hunted animals trembling like groundfoxes in their cover. Borrowed time and borrowed world and borrowed eyes with which to sorrow it. (*The Road* 130)

In Marion's phenomenology of givenness, these baroque epiphanies constitute the 'response' to the given on the part of this particular receiver. This passage depicts two isolated humans surrounded by an all-encompassing darkness. The man and the boy are like lights in the dark, two living beings shipwrecked in a wasteland of death. Similarly, the man's revelation ('the absolute truth of the world') flares up briefly only to be lost the next moment. This figure of a light in the darkness also appears as a leitmotif in *Urne-Buriall*. Laurence Breiner observes that knowledge, according to Browne, is like a 'light in the dark' (Breiner 269). Like the discovery of the Norfolk urns, buried and long-forgotten, human knowledge is only a small spot in the 'dark matrix that surrounds us in space and time' (264). As Browne states: 'That great Antiquity *America* lay buried for a thousand years; and a large part of the earth is still in the Urne to us' (*Urne-Buriall* 267). Browne associates the figure of light-surrounded-by-darkness with the uncovering of subterranean treasures. In picturing the 'earth' 'circling' in the 'black vacuum of the universe', McCarthy places the same image in an apocalyptic cosmological frame.

The post-apocalyptic landscape that the state road leads through is 'cauterized terrain' (*The Road* 14). Large swathes of it are burned, barren land littered with the cadavers of animals and the corpses of humans: the 'bones of dead creatures sprawled in the washes', which in turn are lined by 'a jungle of dead kudzu' adjoining a 'marsh where the dead reeds lay over the water' (177). Imported to the US from Japan in the late nineteenth century, kudzu turned out to be an invasive species whose spread displaced native plants. Like raccoons, kudzu counts among the few species with the potential to thrive in the increasingly connected eco-systems around the world that worst-case scenarios project may replace existing local species. Hence the elimination of the hardy kudzu attests to the severity of the ecological disaster in *The Road* (see also Kollin 159). Along with living nature, colours have disappeared: the landscape is monochromatic, the dominant colour is grey. Burned to ashes, things have taken on the colour of ash and soot: snowfall comes as 'wet gray flakes', melting into '[g]ray slush by the roadside' and '[b]lack water running from under the sodden drifts of ash' (*The Road* 16). Instead of daylight, there is 'gunmetal light' (6). The father and son hope to see the blue of the ocean (182), but are disappointed upon reaching their destination at the 'gray beach': 'I'm sorry it's not blue' (215).

Regarding the extinction and sterility of the natural world in *The Road*, it is instructive to point out a contrast with Atwood's *MaddAddam* series. Unlike McCarthy's, Atwood's post- apocalyptic landscape is hyper-fertile: with a tropical climate arriving in New England, lush vegetation is fast overgrowing the abandoned urban settlements. As we saw in Chapter 2, in Atwood's trilogy, artificial species (such as Pigoons and Crakers) thrive in the manufactured wilderness on post-collapse Eaarth, forming new ecosystems as they interact with natural species as well as the small number of human survivors. Relatedly, Crake's bioterrorism is targeted specifically at humans, while sparing animals and plants, which it was intended to liberate from human control and exploitation. The post-apocalyptic scenario in *The Road* is the reverse: the death of nature is matched against a large number of surviving humans. Thus, McCarthy's and Atwood's visions of the near future pursue different agendas. One insight this implies is that the notion of posthumanism – a concept applicable to the *MaddAddam* trilogy – is insufficient as an explanation for *The Road*. For McCarthy's novel places humans at the centre of its post-apocalyptic scenario, which further underscores the compatibility of phenomenology as a critical approach, for its parallel focus on human experience. *The Road* is about what befalls humans alone and how those humans respond to the shock of the saturated phenomenon – the terrain of Marion's phenomenology of the given.

The post-apocalyptic wasteland is littered with the broken objects of the shattered modern world. There are burned cities, ruined houses, a train wreck and a wrecked ship. The irredeemable loss of the pre-collapse past is illustrated by a stopover at an abandoned house that used to be the father's childhood home. Decaying and stripped bare by previous refugees passing through, the home has become uncanny, a ghostly reminder of the home-lessness of the refugees stranded in the post-apocalyptic world. The father's guided tour ('This is where we used to have Christmas when I was a boy' [26]) elicits no response from the boy, who just wants to leave. In these and similar efforts to transmit memories of the dead past, the father realises the futility of his attempts to communicate a world that is alien to his son: 'Sometimes the child would ask him questions about the world that for him was not even a memory. He thought hard how to answer. There is no past. What would you like?' (52–4).

> Maybe he understood for the first time that to the boy he was himself an alien. A being from a planet that no longer existed. The tales of which were suspect. He could not construct for the child's pleasure the world he'd lost without constructing the loss as well and he thought perhaps the child had known this better then he . . . That he could not enkindle in the heart of the child what was ashes in his own. (153–4)

The road itself is a junkyard of countless car wrecks and aban-doned objects, consumer commodities now useless:

> Odd things scattered by the side of the road. Electrical appliances, fur-niture. Things abandoned long ago by pilgrims enroute to their several and collective deaths. Even a year ago the boy might sometimes pick up something and carry it with him for a while but he didnt do that any more. (199–200)

Accepting the futility of keeping such possessions, which have become meaningless in the post-apocalyptic lifeworld organised around bare survival, the man finally disposes of his wallet:

> He'd carried his billfold about till it wore a cornershaped hole in his trousers. Then one day he sat by the roadside and took it out and went through the contents. Some money, credit cards. His driver's license. A picture of his wife. He spread everything out on the blacktop. Like gambling cards. He pitched the sweatblackened piece of leather into the woods and sat holding the photograph. The he laid it down in the road also and then he stood and they went on. (51)

This is an especially good example of the loss of conventional subjectivity that McCarthy explores, setting the stage for the creation of new modalities of the self. I will discuss these strategies of self-making through what Lingis calls passionate commitment and identification below. Indeed, the decentring of the self illustrated by the man's dispossession in *The Road* corresponds to the decentring of the divine in Butler's *Parable* series. In both cases, entities assumed to be sovereign or absolute (God, the subject) are shown to be context-dependent, attached to a relativistic framework.

One object in particular, a roadside advertisement in 'ten-foot letters' – 'See Rock City' (*The Road* 21) – absurdly surviving the destruction of its purpose, epitomises the ruin of capitalist modernity. The state roads that the man and the boy travel on, guided by a 'tattered oilcompany roadmap' (42), point to abstract social, technological and economic systems – government, state law, the market economy, transportation and so on. But these have vanished, for 'there's not any more states' (43). As in Saramago's *Blindness* and Atwood's *MaddAddam* trilogy, society shrinks to localised, self-organising, small groups and face-to-face communities. As in Atwood and Saramago, McCarthy's post-apocalyptic castaways are immersed in an object world of absolute immanence – stranded on the wasteland amid the rubble of the destroyed modern civilisation. The road and the map ('These are our roads, the black lines on the map. The state roads' [*The Road* 42]) are nothing but the debris of modern social systems – in this case, the American high-speed transportation system – that have been destroyed.

As discussed in previous chapters, narrative perspective is an important feature in apocalyptic narrative. How do humans gain access to knowledge about the future? As David Leigh observes, religious apocalyptic narrative discloses a 'transcendent reality' otherwise occluded to humans (Leigh 5). Unlike John in Revelation who is lifted into the heavenly throne room but returns to earth to prophesy the coming world-end, McCarthy's survivor protagonist surveys the same panorama of ruin, but from the opposite side of the apocalyptic divide. The following tableau of the remains – objects and corpses – of a conflagration upon which father and son stumble may serve as an example:

Beyond a crossroads in that wilderness they began to come upon the possessions of travelers abandoned in the road years ago. Boxes and bags. Everything melted and black. Old plastic suitcases curled shapeless in the heat. Here and there the imprint of things wrested out of the tar by scavengers. A mile on and they began to come upon the dead. Figures half mired in the blacktop, clutching themselves, mouths howling. (*The Road* 190)

Unlike the biblical prophet, McCarthy's post-apocalyptic narrator looks backward to the residues of the cataclysm rather than forward to its future arrival. As accomplished fact rather than foretold future, the post-apocalyptic rendering of the world-end is retrospective, a mode that emphasises aftermaths. A refugee stranded on a dying planet, McCarthy's protagonist evidences the striking affinity of post-apocalyptic narrative with Marion's picture of a reduced self in the throes of givenness.

The seventeenth-century baroque arose as the expression of cultural crisis. The dominant concept of history it encodes is tragic: transience, impermanence, decay and destruction. In his study of German seventeenth-century tragedies, *The Origin of German Tragic Drama* (1928), Walter Benjamin examines what he calls 'the baroque cult of the ruin' (178). Considering the spatial settings of baroque plays, Benjamin points out the centrality of spatial panoramas of decay ('The Ruin', 'Setting') (*Origin* 177–82, 91–5). A shattered object world of dead things is the staple of baroque plays, which tend to take stock of the historical process of destruction by way of panoramic displays of the debris left in its wake. Benjamin describes this device as the spatialisation of time: 'History merges into the setting'; 'chronological movement is grasped and analysed in a spatial image' (*Origin* 92). Benjamin's theory of baroque allegory offers further insight into the literary poetics of post-apocalyptic givenness in McCarthy's novel. In baroque allegory, the material remains of destruction – rubble, shattered objects, dead bodies – are summoned to testify to the process of destruction. As Benjamin elaborates, '*in the ruin* history has physically merged into the setting' (*Origin* 177–8, my emphasis). For Benjamin, the historian's task is 'to brush history against the grain' ('Theses' 257). The goal is to unmask false harmonies, forcing the reader to confront the truth of destruction otherwise concealed beneath a veneer of false harmony. Baroque allegories are demystifying, critical compositions:

Whereas in the symbol destruction is idealized and the transfigured face of nature is fleetingly revealed in the light of redemption, in allegory the observer is confronted with the *facies hippocratica* of history as a petrified, primordial landscape. Everything about history that, from the very beginning, has been untimely, sorrowful, unsuccessful, is expressed in a face – or rather a death's head. (Benjamin, *Origin* 166)

This strategy of thinking from the ruins that is at work in seventeenth-century baroque plays also models the post-apocalyptic poetics of *The Road*, which similarly presents a series of baroque panoramas and static tableaux of apocalyptic ruin in which (post-apocalyptic) history has physically merged into the setting. We have already seen several instances in the passages describing the extinction of falcons and trout, the degradation of humans to prey, and the incinerated remains of the holocaust in the passage above. In *The Road*, almost everything that is known about the apocalypse and its immediate aftermath is presented retrospectively and indirectly, via spatial tableaux that decipher the material remains of annihilation. In adopting this technique, *The Road* becomes a textual museum of sorts, albeit a museum of apocalyptic destruction. Its exhibits are Benjaminian allegorical ruins left behind by the cataclysm, augmented by the subsequent carnage of gangs of degenerate assassins.

I shall close this discussion of McCarthy's post-apocalyptic neo-baroque by considering the most important tableau of apocalyptic destruction in *The Road*. It comes shortly before the pair's second encounter with cannibalism. The man and the boy discover the remains of a newborn infant in a still-smoking campfire. As the man reflects,

The world soon to be largely populated by men who would eat your children in front of your eyes and the cities themselves held by cores of blackened looters who tunneled among the ruins and crawled from the rubble white of tooth and eye carrying charred and anonymous tins of food in nylon nets like shoppers in the commissaries of hell. The soft black talc blew through the streets like squid ink uncoiling along a sea floor and the cold crept down and the dark came early and the scavengers passing down the steep canyons with their torches trod silky holes in the drifted ash that closed behind them silently as eyes. Out on the roads the pilgrims sank down and fell over and died and the bleak and shrouded earth went trundling past the sun and returned again as trackless and as unremarked as the path of any nameless sisterworld in the ancient dark beyond. (*The Road* 181)

Beginning in the future tense, this passage sketches an apocalyptic vision of the devolution of humans into cannibals. Through its rare diction, complex syntax and the solemn rhetoric of a requiem, McCarthy's baroque rhetoric of excess responds to what Marion calls a phenomenon so much in excess that it *'cannot be borne'* (*In Excess* 202).

Style is widely commented on in criticism of *The Road*. Indeed, my reading of the neo-baroque dimension in *The Road* departs from the critical consensus that its stylistic tendency is minimalism, the antithesis of baroque stylistic excess. For many, *The Road* marks a turning point in McCarthy's fiction, abandoning the earlier Faulknerian baroque maximalism that characterised his novel *Blood Meridian* (1985) for Hemingwayan minimalism. As Ashley Kunsa observes, 'We cannot traverse *The Road* without a startling awareness of its departure from McCarthy's previous style' (Kunsa 68). She notes that *Blood Meridian* is 'often allusive and baroque to the breaking point, prose frequently likened to that of William Faulkner. The style of *The Road*, on the contrary, is pared down, elemental' (Kunsa 58). Andrew Hoborek similarly views McCarthy's post-apocalyptic novel as turning away from Faulkner towards Hemingway, or from 'maximalism' to 'minimalism' (Hoborek 492). These rubrics denote the 'stylistic dialectic instituted in creative writing programs and, through them, post-World War II fiction more generally', and for which in '*The Program Era*, Mark McGurl employs Hemingway and Faulkner as names' (Hoborek 492).[15]

Critics are unanimous in noting the lack of detailed information regarding the nature and cause of the cataclysm in *The Road*. McCarthy's refusal to name people, settings and the precise cause of the catastrophe creates structural indeterminacies (Kearney, 'Cormac McCarthy's *The Road*' 161). A detailed account of minimalist strategies in *The Road* would include the absence of proper names for all the characters, the nameless protagonists ('the man', 'the boy', 'the woman') as well as all the nameless strangers the father and son encounter on the road, dangerous predators as well as helpless victims. All are equally anonymised: the 'roadrat' (*The Road* 66) from the caravan of 'roadagents' (172) who grabs the boy and is shot by the man; 'the burned man' who has been struck by lightning; the 'naked people' (111) who are the food slaves in the cannibal mansion, and the 'four bearded men and two women' (112) who are their captors; the 'pilgrims' (181) who collapse on the road and die; the 'thief' who steals the pair's possessions on the beach and who is 'an outcast from the communes' (255); and last but not least, the 'veteran of old skirmishes' (281) who adopts the boy after the man's death. As Kunsa notes, the moral refrain that divides good from evil ('we are the good guys' vs. 'they were the bad guys' [*The Road* 140, 92 and *passim*]) carries the work of abstraction to the 'simple and essential' even further (Kunsa 59).

In addition to McCarthy's refusal to name people, settings and the precise cause of the catastrophe, minimalism in *The Road* also includes syntactical phenomena such as the 'fractured narrative structure, proliferation of sentence fragments, and brief, repetitive dialogue' (Kunsa 68). Much of the novel is made up of brief dialogue and fragmented sentences. What motivates all this, Kunsa contends, is that 'the proper place names of the pre-apocalyptic world have become obsolete' (63). McCarthy's strategy of omitting the proper names of people and places highlights the 'binary time' (Keller) of post-apocalyptic fiction. Set on the far side of the apocalyptic upheaval that divides the time before from the time after, the indeterminate post- collapse world consigns the ruined civilisation to the past (see also Kunsa 64). The namelessness of the post-apocalyptic world, which *The Road* shares with Saramago's *Blindness*, contrasts with *Oryx and Crake*, where Jimmy renames himself 'Snowman', as well as Butler's *Parable* series, which also begins with a baptism of sorts, though not of a person but of a religion (Earthseed). This difference in marking ontological transformation is symptomatic of McCarthy's overall focus on the horror of post-apocalyptic givenness.

I agree that these minimalist tendencies exist, but contend that they represent only one of the *The Road*'s two narrative threads, alongside the neo-baroque.[16] Turning now to the minimalist thread, how should it be conceptualised in relation to *The Road*'s neo-baroque aspect? How does the novel's baroque rhetoric of excess connect to its minimalist terseness and structural indeterminacies? Kunsa, who does not recognise the baroque trend in *The Road*, constructs a simple opposition between a minimalist *The Road* and a baroque *Blood Meridian*. He suggests that while both novels 'are chockfull of unforgettable horrors', the language of *Blood Meridian* memorialises slaughter, whereas *The Road*'s minimalism signals towards hope, seeding the novel's 'unexpectedly optimistic worldview' (Kunsa 58). For Kunsa, stylistic economy is a way of controlling the horror of the post-apocalyptic condition.

I agree with Kunsa's diagnosis of *The Road*'s latent optimism, which, as this study demonstrates, is actually a structural feature of contemporary post-apocalyptic fiction as a whole. It appears even in this, the darkest of these works. But I argue that while the baroque thread is linked to the novel's backward-looking commemoration of catastrophe and loss, the minimalist style correlates with the depiction of everyday practices of 'making-do' and post-apocalyptic survival: staying mobile by walking the roads, repurposing useless commodities for new post-apocalyptic uses, scavenging for food and clothing. These are post-apocalyptic variations of the tactics of everyday life that Michel de Certeau examines in *The Practice of Everyday Life*: walking, cooking, dwelling, reading, storytelling – the arts of appropriation of those who lack a proper space and who depend on bricolage and other ruses to survive. The man customises a shopping cart to transport their possessions as the homeless do today. He attaches a motorcycle mirror as a rearview mirror to watch out for marauding gangs, and 'two old brooms . . . to clear the limbs from the road in front of the wheels' (*The Road* 19) of ash and snow. The refugees wear face masks made from sheets (156). Making-do includes leisure activities: the man 'carve[s] the boy a flute from a piece of roadside cane' (77). As de Certeau contends, such '"ways of operating" or doing things' (de Certeau xi) serve to 'mak[e] habitable' structured spaces: 'The space of a tactic is the space of the other' (de Certeau 37). Practice strips use of its connotation of passive consumption, bringing to light its rebellious creativity: use is a mode of second-hand creation by way of recycling.

Such unofficial tactics of making-do are the mainstay of daily life in post-apocalyptic novels: the self-organising practices of survival of the white-blind in Saramago's *Blindness*, the daily routines of post-apocalyptic homemaking and cross-species social life in Atwood's *MaddAddam* series, and the invention of post-apocalyptic spirituality and community in Butler. They bespeak the constructive world-making orientation of post-apocalyptic fiction that distinguishes it from the world-destroying emphasis of apocalyptic narrative as such. *The Road* stands out among these works by stylistically marking the distinction between forward-looking practices of 'crawl[ing] out of the wreckage' (Irr 170) and backward-looking contemplation of the horror of the wreckage through double-voiced narration: neo-baroque panoramas of the ruins of the world-end sit side-by-side with minimalist accounts of post-apocalyptic self- and world-making.

According to Marion, for phenomena to occur, two parties are required, givenness as well as the response of the receiver, and the phenomena thus constituted ('the gift') in turn produce a new self ('the gifted'). In an interview, McCarthy makes the point that the cause of the catastrophe is insignificant; what is significant instead is the response of the survivor:

> I don't have an opinion. At the Santa Fe Institute I'm with scientists of all disciplines, and some of them in geology said it looked like a meteor to them. But it could be anything – volcanic activity or it could be nuclear war. It is not really important. The whole thing now is, what do you do? (McCarthy qtd in Jurgensen)

The remainder of this section discusses the making of new post-apocalyptic selves through everyday practice. Among the practices of survival of 'the gifted', walking features centrally in *The Road*, which – like Butler's *Parable* series and similar post-apocalyptic novels – rewrites the frontier narrative as well as the American road story (Kollin 167; Kearney, 'Cormac McCarthy's *The Road*' 163). According to de Certeau, walking in the city constitutes a 'pedestrian speech act' (de Certeau 98) that rearticulates the modern urban system: *'space is a practiced place'* (117). In *The Road* – as in Butler's *Parable* series – post-apocalyptic refugees crowd on to the state roads and interstate highways, adopting a nomadic lifestyle to avoid starvation and death. As an old man, Ely – the only named character in the novel and a post-apocalyptic prophet of sorts – remarks: 'I was always in the road. You cant stay in one place' (*The Road* 168).

A junkyard littered with the debris of consumer culture and a graveyard strewn with corpses, the American road has become the 'practiced place' of the post-apocalyptic refugees. De Certeau 'insists on the analogy' of everyday practice 'as an *act*' (Highmore 107): walking actualises the ruined road in the same way that speech 'actualises' the system of language. The itinerary of the family's walk on the road across the burned terrain is an attempt to make the ruined world habitable. Yet in making the ruined road the mobile home, as it were, of its nomad protagonists, McCarthy's novel elevates this quintessential icon of post-apocalyptic ruin to a spiritual symbol. McCarthy writes, 'they set out upon the road again . . . cowled and shivering in their rags like mendicant friars' (*The Road* 126). Through the practice of walking, the road is transformed into a counter-principle to the wasteland. In this light, *The Road*'s policy of refusal of naming acquires yet another dimension. That '*the* man and *the* boy are always accompanied by the definitive [*sic*] article' (Kearney, 'Cormac McCarthy's *The Road*' 164) might be extended to mean that McCarthy updates the archetype of the 'ordinary man' to whom de Certeau's study is dedicated. On Marion's account, this corresponds to the figure of 'the gifted', a reduced self who nonetheless generates a creative – rather than pre-programmed – response to what has befallen him or her.

Critics have noted the religious rhetoric in *The Road*: the references to God, tabernacle, prophets, post-apocalyptic survivors as pilgrims (see Ashford 186; Kunsa 60; Kearney, 'Cormac McCarthy's *The Road*' 173; Gwinner 149; Monk). Indeed, the working title of the novel was 'the Grail' (Josephs 139). The man thinks of himself as 'appointed . . . by God' (*The Road* 77) to take care of the boy. The boy represents a 'messianic' figure (Kearney, 'Cormac McCarthy's *The Road*' 173; Clark, *American Literary Minimalism* 135). As the man reflects, 'he knew only that the child was his warrant. He said: If he is not the word of God God never spoke' (*The Road* 5). The man responds to the saturated event of the apocalypse by passionately committing himself to raising his son, born after the cataclysm. In *Oryx and Crake*, the responsibility of taking care of the Crakers is inflicted on Jimmy. Rather than commit suicide like Crake, Jimmy decides to heed the call, renaming himself 'Snowman' as a token of his acceptance. His old self ('Jimmy') is dead; Snowman is 'the gifted', a reduced self that, in Marion's words, 'receives itself entirely from what it receives' (*Being Given* 268).

Like Jimmy, the man also receives a call of parenting after the cataclysm. Like Jimmy – and unlike his wife – he heeds the call. Giving himself over to the task of raising a child in the post-apocalyptic world, the man becomes 'the gifted', in other words, a father. The man's passionate commitment to fatherhood is as extreme as the circumstances: he views it as a religious mission ('appointed by God'), and he drives his body to the point of collapse to carry his son to safety. *The Road* confirms Lingis's claim that sense of self peaks in passionate commitment and passionate identification. The affirmation of identity through which the man and the boy bring forth their solidarity is, in Lingis's terms, an 'oracular word' (*First Person Singular* 50). These are phrases that father and son recite like mantras: 'Because we're the good guys. Yes. And we're carrying the fire' (*The Road* 129). This further demonstrates de Certeau's claims about the importance of storytelling – the 'art of speaking' (de Certeau 77) – as an everyday practice. Like physical practices, the symbolic practice of narration makes the post-apocalyptic world habitable. The slogans of being the bearers of goodness and fire constitute the seeds of a post-apocalyptic mythology of a kind that is more fully fleshed out in Butler's *Parable* series. Even so, like Earthseed, it is a 'counter-factual imagination of things' (Hoborek 496) that is thrust against the void.

Children are rare in *The Road*; other than the boy and the two children in the boy's new foster family, the only glimpse of children is of boys enslaved as 'catamites' (*The Road* 92) among a gang of marauders passing by. In *The Road*'s entropic universe slouching towards extinction, the child, the embodiment of the reproductive future, acquires an elevated status representing the renewal and regeneration of life. As he is approaching death, the man has a vision of the boy looking at him 'from some unimaginable future, glowing in that waste like a tabernacle' (273). Life, manifest in the symbol of fire, functions as a counter-wasteland, the antithesis of apocalypse and death. As noted, fire burning in the midst of darkness and ash is a leitmotif in *The Road*. It represents the 'opposition between the life fire and endless entropy' (Kearney, 'Cormac McCarthy's *The Road*' 162) that, along with the stylistic dialectic between minimalism and the neo-baroque, structures the novel. Just like the material fire that father and son kindle most days 'to light the long gray dusks, the long gray dawns' (*The Road* 7), they carry the spiritual fire of 'goodness' in a Hobbesian world of evil. The messianic figure of the boy is its earthly incarnation. Approaching death, the man tells the boy that the fire is 'inside' him: 'It was always there. I can see it' (279). He adds, 'There is no prophet in the earth's long chronicle who's not honored here today' (277). The man's deathbed affirmation negates an earlier statement by Ely, who says 'There is no God and we are his prophets' (170). Ely, who 'knew' the cataclysm 'was coming' (168), is actually an advocate of nihilism. But like the fire glowing in the waste, the 'gifted' who gives himself over to the call of fatherhood in the post-apocalypse – speaking on the brink of death – has the last word.

Notes

1. Given that the man and the boy are both 'moving south' (*The Road* 4) headed for the coast, the two possible regional settings are the US South and California. Rare references to specific southern locations such as a former plantation home where '[c]hattel slaves had once trod those boards bearing food and drink on silver trays' (106) and 'a town in the piedmont' (183) decide the matter in favour of the South. Following these and other textual clues (such as the heights of passes crossed), Wesley Morgan has reconstructed a detailed travel route for the father and son's journey from the Kentucky–Tennessee border to the North Carolina coast, filling in the geographical blanks deliberately placed in the novel by the author.

2. Developing an object-oriented ontology that places things at the centre of attention, Bogost claims that, like humans, things of the material world also act upon each other. In Graham Harman's example, fire ignores colour when it burns cotton of any colour (Harman, *Quadruple Object* 44). There is no question that an investigation of the interaction between things without humans may be a valid focus of research. Thus, accepting Nagel's point about the fundamental alienness of bats and other non-human beings, Bogost proposes an 'alien phenomenology [that] accepts that the subjective character of experiences cannot be fully recuperated objectively, even if it remains wholly real. In a literal sense, *the only way to perform alien phenomenology is by analogy*: the bat, for example, operates like a submarine' (Bogost 64). Under the label of 'metaphorism', he moves on to a fascinating discussion of what it is like for a non-human actant, a photographic sensor, to 'see'. Metaphors aside, what I would question is whether the concept of phenomenology is appropriate for this kind of inquiry, because of phenomenology's focus on the first-personal experience of living beings.

3. Marion writes: 'To introduce the concept of the saturated phenomenon into phenomenology, I just described it as *invisable* (unforeseeable) in terms of quantity, unbearable in terms of quality, unconditioned (absolute of all horizon) in terms of relation, and finally irreducible to the I (irregardable) in terms of modality' (*Being Given* 218).

4. In the chapter entitled 'What Gives' in *The Crossing of the Visible*, Marion explores givenness with regard to painting: 'The painter sees and so gives to be seen what without him would forever remain banished from the visible. The painting does not manage the organi-

zation of the visible by otherwise combining what is already seen: it adds to the mass of the already-seen or possibly anticipated phenomena an absolutely new phenomenon, still not seen . . . The painting – at least one that is authentic – imposes in front of every gaze an absolutely new phenomenon, increasing by force the quantity of the visible. The painting – the authentic one – exposes an absolutely original phenomenon, newly discovered, without precondition or genealogy, suddenly appearing with such a violence that it explores the limits of the visible identified to that point' (*Crossing* 25).

5. As Hoborek points out, the 'ominous "heap of clothing" in the mansion's foyer likewise hints at the Holocaust' (489). Francesca Haig explores Holocaust resonances in *The Road*, noting a number of parallels with Elie Wiesel's Holocaust memoir, *Night*: the heaps of ash, the burned bodies of victims, the desperate invocation of God and the question of suicide, the father's wish to shelter his son from the horrors surrounding them.

6. As Marion explains, 'The gifted is late ever since his birth precisely because he is born; he is late from birth precisely because he must first be born. There is none among the living who did not first have to be born, that is to say, arise belatedly from his parents in the attentive circle of waiting for words that summoned him before he could understand them or guess their meaning' (*Being Given* 289).

7. I am citing the revised 2018 version of this essay.

8. A key debate concerns the distinction between non-signifying, non-conscious, corporeal affect versus signifying, conscious, meaning-laden emotion and how they relate to each other (see Leys).

9. See Frye, 'Chronology' xxi. The home page of the Santa Fe Institute lists McCarthy as a member of the Board of Trustees: <https://www.santafe.edu/people/profile/cormac-mccarthy> (accessed 15 October 2020).

10. As discussed below, the cause of the catastrophe in *The Road* is intentionally left undetermined. David Kushner notes that during the composition phase of the novel McCarthy sought out the opinion of Santa Fe Institute palaeobiologist Doug Erwin on the extinction of the dinosaurs during the Cretaceous period.

11. Marco Evers, 'Funzel am Himmel', *Der Spiegel* [Hamburg], 28 January 2017, 5.

12. As discussed in more detail below, brief references to baroque style in McCarthy can be found in Kunsa and Hoborek.

13. Gwinner argues that in 'the paradoxical narrative perspective of the last paragraph', 'the narrator addresses actual readers as if we were

survivors in the novel, like the boy, who know firsthand the post-apocalyptic world but have no experience with the preapocalyptic world' (156, 155).

14. See Kaup, *Neobaroque in the Americas*, and 'The Neobaroque in W. G. Sebald's *The Rings of Saturn*'.

15. McCarthy's work has been linked to his mastery of this stylistic dialectic, as shown in Phillip Snyder and Delys Snyder's comment that 'McCarthy's stylistic range and virtuosity – from the rich rococo of *Suttree* to the austere restraint of *The Road* creates a unique signature among contemporary writers' (Snyder and Snyder 36). Julian Murphet and Mark Steven likewise note the stylistic disparity between minimalism and an alternative marked 'style' that they, however, fail to define further (Murphet and Steven 5–6). Robert C. Clark's is the most recent reading of *The Road* within the tradition of what he calls 'American literary minimalism', defined as a stylistic principle of austerity ('less is more'). The Introduction traces a history of this tradition from its roots in the late nineteenth century through Imagism and Hemingway to the new minimalist fiction in the 1980s (Raymond Carver and others), the focus of the study. The book concludes with a chapter on McCarthy's *The Road* following chapters on Jay McInerney's *Bright Lights, Big City*, Susan Minot's *Monkeys* and Sandra Cisneros's *Caramelo*. Clark discusses *The Road*'s efficiency, laconic dialogue, 'terse, poetic style characteristic of works of American Minimalism', and Imagist direct treatment of things (*American Literary Minimalism* 123). Overly formulaic, Clark's strong claims about *The Road*'s Imagist principles sit oddly with some quoted passages in baroque style.

16. Hoborek acknowledges that 'amidst the terse Hemingwayesque sentences', 'Faulknerian resonances' peek out in some passages (Hoborek 491).

Abberley, Will. 'Language Decay and Creation in Postapocalyptic Fiction'. In Germanà and Mousoutzanis, eds., *Apocalyptic Discourse*. 193–205.

Alaimo, Stacy, and Susan Hekman. 'Introduction: Emerging Models of Materiality in Feminist Theory'. In Alaimo and Hekman, eds., *Material Feminisms*. 1–19.

—, eds. *Material Feminisms*. Bloomington: Indiana University Press, 2008.

Ameriks, Karl, ed. *The Cambridge Companion to German Idealism*. Cambridge: Cambridge University Press, 2000.

Althusser, Louis. 'Ideology and Ideological State Apparatus (Notes Towards an Investigation)'. In *Lenin and Philosophy and Other Essays*. New York: Monthly Review Press, 2001. 85–126.

Arendt, Hannah. *The Human Condition*. Chicago: University of Chicago Press, 1958.

Ashford, Joan Anderson. 'Sophia's Table and Nuclear Narrative in Cormac McCarthy's *The Road*'. In *Ecocritical Theology: Neo-Pastoral Themes in American Fiction from 1960 to the Present*. Jefferson, NC: McFarland, 2012. 175–97.

Attridge, Derek. *The Singularity of Literature*. London: Routledge, 2004.

Atwood, Margaret. *MaddAddam*. 2013; New York: Random House, 2014.

—. *Oryx and Crake*. 2003; New York: Random House, 2004.

—. 'Writing *Oryx and Crake*'. In *Writing with Intent: Essays, Reviews, Personal Prose, 1983–2005*. New York: Carroll and Graf, 2005.

—. *The Year of the Flood*. 2009; New York: Random House, 2010.

Barad, Karen. *Meeting the Universe Halfway: Quantum Physics and the*

Entanglement of Matter and Meaning. Durham, NC: Duke University Press, 2007.

—. 'Posthumanist Performativity: Toward an Understanding of How Matter Comes to Matter'. In Alaimo and Hekman, eds., *Materialist Feminisms*. 120–47.

Barthes, Roland. 'The Death of the Author'. In *Image/Music/Text*. Trans. Stephen Heath. New York: Hill and Wang, 1977. 142–8.

Baudrillard, Jean. *America*. Trans. Chris Turner. New York: Verso, 1988.

Beck, Ulrich. *World Risk Society*. Cambridge: Polity, 1999.

Belsey, Catherine. *Poststructuralism: A Very Short Introduction*. Oxford: Oxford University Press, 2002.

Benjamin, Walter. *The Origin of German Tragic Drama*. 1928. Trans. John Osborne. London: Verso, 1985.

Bennett, Jane. *Vibrant Matter: A Political Ecology of Things*. Durham, NC: Duke University Press, 2010.

Benoist, Jocelyn. *Elemente einer realistischen Philosophie*. 2011. Trans. David Espinet. Frankfurt: Suhrkamp, 2014.

—. 'Realismus ohne Metaphysik'. In Gabriel, ed., *Der Neue Realismus*. 133–53.

Berger, James. *After the End: Representations of Post-Apocalypse*. Minneapolis: University of Minnesota Press, 1999.

Best, Stephen, and Sharon Marcus. 'Surface Reading: An Introduction'. *Representations* 108.1 (2009): 1–21.

Biehl, João. *Vita: Life in a Zone of Social Abandonment. Photographs by Torben Eskerol*. Berkeley: University of California Press, 2005.

—. 'When People Come First: Beyond Technical and Theoretical Quick-Fixes in Global Health'. In *Global Political Ecology*, ed. Richard Peet et al. London: Routledge, 2011. 102–28.

Bode, Christoph, and Rainer Dietrich. *Future Narratives: Theory, Poetics, and Media-Historical Moment*. Berlin: de Gruyter, 2013.

Boghossian, Paul A. *Fear of Knowledge: Against Relativism and Constructivism*. Oxford: Clarendon Press, 2006.

Bogost, Ian. *Alien Phenomenology; or, What It's Like to Be a Thing*. Minneapolis: University of Minnesota Press, 2012.

Bosco, Mark. 'The Apocalyptic Imagination in *Oryx and Crake*'. In Bouson, ed., *Margaret Atwood*. 156–71.

Bouson, J. Brooks, ed. *Margaret Atwood: The Robber Bride, The Blind Assassin, Oryx and Crake*. London: Continuum, 2010.

Brassier, Ray. *Nihil Unbound: Enlightenment and Extinction*. New York: Palgrave, 2007.

Brockmeier, Kevin. *The Brief History of the Dead*. New York: Random House, 2006.

Brooks, Peter. *Reading for the Plot: Design and Intention in Narrative*. Cambridge, MA: Harvard University Press, 1984.

Brown, Bill. *A Sense of Things: The Object Matter of American Literature*. Chicago: University of Chicago Press, 2003.

—. 'Thing Theory'. In Brown, ed., *Things*. 1–16.

—, ed. *Things*. Chicago: University of Chicago Press, 2004.

Browne, Sir Thomas. *The Garden of Cyrus; or, The Quincunciall, Lozenge, or Network Plantations of the Ancients, Artificially, Naturally, Mystically Considered*. In *The Major Works*, ed. C. A. Patrides. London: Penguin, 1977. 317–88.

—. *Hydriotaphia, Urne-Buriall; or, A Brief Discourse of the Sepulchrall Urnes Lately Found in Norfolk*. In *The Major Works*, ed. C. A. Patrides. London: Penguin, 1977. 261–315.

Buell, Frederick. *From Apocalypse to Way of Life: Environmental Crisis in the American Century*. New York: Routledge, 2004.

—. 'Global Warming as Literary Narrative'. *Philological Quarterly* 93.3 (2014): 261–94.

Butler, Octavia E. *Parable of the Sower*. New York: Grand Central Publishing, 2000.

—. *Parable of the Talents*. New York: Grand Central Publishing, 2000.

Canavan, Gerry. '"There's Nothing New / Under the Sun, / But There Are New Suns": Octavia Butler's Lost Parables'. *Los Angeles Review of Books*, 9 June 2014. https://lareviewofbooks.org/essay/theres-nothing-new-sun-new-suns-recovering-octavia-e-butlers-lost-parables. Accessed 12 October 2020.

—. 'Hope, but Not for Us: Ecological Science Fiction and the End of the World in Margaret Atwood's *Oryx and Crake* and *The Year of the Flood*'. *Literature Interpretation Theory* 23.2 (2012): 138–59. https://doi.org/10.1080/10436928.2012.676914

Capra, Fritjof. *The Web of Life: A New Scientific Understanding of Living Systems*. New York: Random House, 1997.

Capra, Fritjof, and Pier Luigo Luisi. *The Systems View of Life: A Unifying Vision*. Cambridge: Cambridge University Press, 2014.

Carby, Hazel V. 'Figuring the Future in Los(t) Angeles'. *Comparative American Studies* 1.1 (2003): 19–34.

Chakrabarty, Dipesh. 'The Climate of History: Four Theses'. *Critical Inquiry* 35.2 (2009): 197–222.

Chang, Hui-Chuan. 'Critical Dystopia Reconsidered: Octavia Butler's

Parable Series and Margaret Atwood's *Oryx & Crake* as Post-Apocalyptic Dystopias'. *Tamkang Review* 41.2 (2011): 3–20.

Clark, Robert C. *American Literary Minimalism*. Tuscaloosa: University of Alabama Press, 2015.

Clark, Timothy. *Ecocriticism on the Edge: The Anthropocene as a Threshold Concept*. London: Bloomsbury, 2015.

Clarke, Bruce, and Mark B. N. Hansen. 'Introduction: Neocybernetic Emergence'. In Clarke and Hansen, eds., *Emergence and Embodiment*. 1–25.

—, eds. *Emergence and Embodiment: New Essays on Second-Order Systems Theory*. Durham, NC: Duke University Press, 2009.

Claviez, Thomas. 'Introduction: Neo-Realism and How to "Make It New"'. *Amerikastudien/American Studies* 49.1 (2004): 5–18.

Clifford, James. *Routes: Travel and Translation in the Late Twentieth Century*. Cambridge, MA: Harvard University Press, 1997.

Cole, Andrew. 'The Function of Theory at the Present Time'. *PMLA* 130.3 (2015): 809–18.

Colebrook, Claire. *Death of the Posthuman: Essays on Extinction*, Vol. 1. Ann Arbor: Open Humanities Press, 2014.

Coole, Diana, and Samantha Frost, eds. *New Materialisms: Ontology, Agency, and Politics*. Durham, NC: Duke University Press, 2010.

Copleston, Frederick. *A History of Philosophy. Vol. 7, Modern Philosophy; Part 1, Fichte to Hegel*. Garden City, NY: Image Books, 1965.

Crace, Jim. *The Pesthouse*. New York: Random House, 2007.

Damasio, Antonio. *Looking for Spinoza: Joy, Sorrow, and the Feeling Brain*. New York: Harcourt, 2003.

Danowski, Déborah, and Eduardo Viveiros de Castro. *The Ends of the World*. Trans. Rodrigo Nunes. Cambridge: Polity, 2017.

Davis, Mike. *City of Quartz: Excavating the Future in Los Angeles*. New York: Random House, 1992.

—. *Ecology of Fear: Los Angeles and the Imagination of Disaster*. New York: Random House, 1998.

de Certeau, Michel. *The Practice of Everyday Life*. Vol. 1. Berkeley: University of California Press, 1984.

DeLanda, Manuel. *Assemblage Theory*. Edinburgh: Edinburgh University Press, 2016.

DeLanda, Manuel, and Graham Harman. *The Rise of Realism*. Cambridge: Polity, 2017.

Dellamora, Richard, ed. *Postmodern Apocalypse: Theory and Cultural Practice at the End*. Philadelphia: University of Pennsylvania Press, 1995.

Di Leo, Jeffrey R. 'Introduction'. In Di Leo, ed., *Criticism after Critique*. 1–11.

—, ed. *Criticism after Critique: Aesthetics, Literature, and the Political*. New York: Palgrave Macmillan, 2014.

Douglass, Frederick, 'Narrative of the Life of Frederick Douglass, An American Slave, Written By Himself'. In *The Classic Slave Narratives*, ed. Henry Louis Gates, Jr. New York: Penguin, 1987. 243–331.

Felski, Rita. 'Context Stinks!' *New Literary History* 42.4 (2011): 573–91.

—. 'Introduction'. *New Literary History* 47.2–3 (2016): 215–29.

—. *The Limits of Critique*. Chicago: University of Chicago Press, 2015.

—. *Uses of Literature*. Oxford: Blackwell, 2008.

Ferraris, Maurizio. *Introduction to New Realism*. London: Bloomsbury, 2015.

—. *Manifesto of New Realism*. Trans. Sarah de Sanctis. Albany: State University of New York Press, 2012.

Fluck, Winfried. 'Surface Knowledge and "Deep" Knowledge: The New Realism in American Fiction'. In Versluys, ed., *Neo-Realism in Contemporary American Fiction*. 65–85.

Francis, Consuela, ed. *Conversations with Octavia Butler*. Jackson: University Press of Mississippi, 2010.

Freud, Sigmund. *Civilization and Its Discontents*. Trans. James Strachey. New York: Norton, 1961.

Frye, Steven. 'Chronology of McCarthy's Life and Works'. In Frye, ed., *The Cambridge Companion to Cormac McCarthy*. xvii–xxii.

—, ed. *The Cambridge Companion to Cormac McCarthy*. Cambridge: Cambridge University Press, 2013.

Fuentes, Carlos. 'The Novel as Tragedy: William Faulkner'. In Zamora and Kaup, eds., *Baroque New Worlds*. 531–53.

Gabriel, Markus. *Der Mensch im Mythos: Untersuchungen über Ontotheologie, Anthropologie und Selbstbewusstseinsgeschichte in Schellings Philosophie der Mythologie*. Berlin: Walter de Gruyter, 2005.

—. 'Existenz, realistisch gedacht'. In Gabriel, ed., *Der Neue Realismus*. 171–99.

—. *Fields of Sense: A New Realist Ontology*. Edinburgh: Edinburgh University Press, 2015.

—. *I Am Not a Brain: Philosophy of Mind for the Twenty-First Century*. Trans. Christopher Turner. Cambridge: Polity, 2017.

—. 'Introduction'. In Gabriel, ed., *Der Neue Realismus*. 8–18.

—. 'Is Heidegger's "Turn" a Realist Project?' *Meta: Research in Hermeneutics, Phenomenology, and Practical Philosophy* 6 (2014), special issue: 44–73. http://www.metajournal.org//articles_pdf/44-73-gabriel-meta-special-2014.pdf. Accessed 12 October 2020.

—. 'Kontingenz oder Notwendigkeit: Schelling und Hegel über den modalen Status des logischen Raums'. *Deutsches Jahrbuch Philosophie* 2 (2011): 178–93.

—. 'The Mythological Being of Reflection: An Essay on Hegel, Schelling, and the Contingency of Necessity'. In Gabriel and Žižek, *Mythology, Madness, and Laughter.* 15–92.

—. *Neo-Existentialism: How to Conceive of the Human Mind after Naturalism's Failure.* Ed. Jocelyn Maclure. Cambridge: Polity, 2018.

—. 'Neutral Realism'. *The Monist* 98.2 (2015): 181–96.

—. *Transcendental Ontology: Essays in German Idealism.* London: Bloomsbury, 2011.

—. *Warum es die Welt nicht gibt.* Berlin: Ullstein, 2013.

—. *Why the World Does Not Exist.* Trans. Gregory Moss. Cambridge: Polity, 2015.

—. 'Why the World Does Not Exist'. TEDx Studio Munich. https://www.youtube.com/watch?v=hzvesGB_TIo. Accessed 12 October 2020.

—, ed. *Der Neue Realismus.* Berlin: Suhrkamp, 2014.

Gabriel, Markus, and Slavoj Žižek. 'Introduction'. In Gabriel and Žižek, *Mythology, Madness, and Laughter.* 1–14.

—. *Mythology, Madness, and Laughter: Subjectivity in German Idealism.* New York: Continuum, 2009.

Gallagher, Catherine. 'The Rise of Fictionality'. In *The Novel, Volume I: History, Geography, and Culture*, ed. Franco Moretti. Princeton: Princeton University Press, 2006. 336–63.

Gallagher, Shaun, and Dan Zahavi. *The Phenomenological Mind: An Introduction to Philosophy of Mind and Cognitive Science.* London: Routledge, 2008.

García Márquez, Gabriel. *One Hundred Years of Solitude.* Trans. Gregory Rabassa. New York: Harper Perennial, 1970.

Garrard, Greg. *Ecocriticism.* New York: Routledge, 2012.

Germanà, Monica, and Aris Mousoutzanis, 'Introduction: After the End?' In Germanà and Mousoutzanis, eds., *Apocalyptic Discourse.* 1–13.

—, eds. *Apocalyptic Discourse in Contemporary Culture: Post-Millennial Perspectives on the End of the World.* London: Routledge, 2014.

Gomel, Elana. 'The Plague of Utopias: Pestilence and the Apocalyptic Body'. *Twentieth Century Literature* 46.4 (2000): 405–33.

Goodwin, Brian. *How the Leopard Changed Its Spots: The Evolution of Complexity*. Princeton: Princeton University Press, 2001.

Gratton, Peter. *Speculative Realism: Problems and Prospects*. London: Bloomsbury, 2014.

Gwinner, Donovan. '"Everything Uncoupled from Its Shoring": Quandaries of Epistemology and Ethics in *The Road*'. In Spurgeon, ed., *Cormac McCarthy*. 137–56.

Haig, Francesca. '"Billows of Ash": Cormac McCarthy's Road Back to Auschwitz'. In Germanà and Mousoutzanis, eds., *Apocalyptic Discourse*. 162–74.

Hall, John R. *Apocalypse: From Antiquity to the Empire of Modernity*. Cambridge: Polity, 2009.

Hames-García, Michael. 'How Real is Race?' In Alaimo and Hekman, eds., *Material Feminisms*. 308–39.

Hanson, Rick, with Richard Mendius. *Buddha's Brain: The Practical Neuroscience of Happiness, Love, and Wisdom*. Oakland: New Harbinger Publications, 2009.

Haraway, Donna J. *Staying with the Trouble: Making Kin in the Chthulucene*. Durham, NC: Duke University Press, 2016.

Harman, Graham. *Guerrilla Metaphysics: Phenomenology and the Carpentry of Things*. Chicago: Open Court, 2005.

—. *Object-Oriented Ontology: A New Theory of Everything*. London: Pelican, 2018.

—. 'Object-Oriented Philosophy'. In *Prince of Networks*. 151–228.

—. *Prince of Networks: Bruno Latour and Metaphysics*. Melbourne: re.press, 2009.

—. *The Quadruple Object*. Winchester: Zero Books, 2011.

—. *Speculative Realism: An Introduction*. Cambridge: Polity, 2018.

—. *Tool-Being: Heidegger and the Metaphysics of Objects*. Chicago: Open Court, 2002.

Harris, Wendell, ed. *Beyond Poststructuralism: The Speculations of Theory and the Experience of Reading*. University Park: Pennsylvania State University Press, 1996.

Hayles, N. Katherine. *How We Became Posthuman: Virtual Bodies in Cybernetics, Literature, and Informatics*. Chicago: University of Chicago Press, 1999.

Heffernan, Teresa. *Post-Apocalyptic Culture: Modernism, Postmodernism, and the Twentieth- Century Novel*. Toronto: University of Toronto Press, 2008.

Heidegger, Martin. *Being and Time*. Trans. Joan Stambaugh. Ed. Dennis J. Schmidt. Albany: State University of New York Press, 2010.

—. 'Conversation on a Country Path'. In *Discourse on Thinking: A Translation of Gelassenheit*. Trans. John M. Anderson and E. Hans Freund. New York: Harper and Row, 1966. 58–90.

Heise, Ursula. *Sense of Place, Sense of Planet: The Environmental Imagination of the Global*. Oxford: Oxford University Press, 2008.

Hengen, Shannon. 'Moral/Environmental Debt in *Payback* and *Oryx and Crake*'. In Bouson, ed., *Margaret Atwood*. 129–40.

Herman, David. 'Stories as a Tool for Thinking'. In *Narrative Theory and the Cognitive Sciences*, ed. David Herman. Stanford: CSLI Publications, 2003. 163–92.

Hicks, Heather J. 'Apocalyptic Fiction, 1950–2015'. *Oxford Research Encyclopedia of Literature*. Oxford: Oxford University Press, 2017. http://literature.oxfordre.com/view/10.1093/acrefore/97801902010 98.001.0001/acrefore-9780190201098-e-190. Accessed 12 October 2020.

—. *The Post-Apocalyptic Novel in the Twenty-First Century: Modernity Beyond Salvage*. Basingstoke: Palgrave Macmillan, 2016.

Highmore, Ben. *Michel de Certeau: Analysing Culture*. New York: Continuum, 2006.

Hill, Miriam Helen. 'Bound to the Environment: Towards a Phenomenology of Sightlessness'. In *Dwelling, Place, and Environment: Towards a Phenomenology of Person and World*, ed. David Seamon and Robert W. Mugerauer. Dordrecht: M. Nijhoff, 1985. 99–111.

Hoban, Russell. *Riddley Walker*. London: Jonathan Cape, 1980.

Hobbes, Thomas. *Leviathan*. 1651. Ed. C. B. Macpherson. Harmondsworth: Penguin, 1981.

Hoborek, Andrew. 'Cormac McCarthy and the Aesthetics of Exhaustion'. *American Literary History* 23.3 (2011): 483–99.

—. 'Living with PASD'. *Contemporary Literature* 53.2 (2012): 406–13.

Howells, Coral Ann. 'Margaret Atwood's Dystopian Visions: *The Handmaid's Tale* and *Oryx and Crake*'. In *The Cambridge Companion to Margaret Atwood*, ed. Coral Ann Howells. Cambridge: Cambridge University Press, 2006. 161–75.

Huntley, Frank. 'The Garden of Cyrus as Prophecy'. In *Approaches to Sir Thomas Browne: The Ann Arbor Tercentenary Lectures and Essays*, ed. C. A. Patrides. Columbia: University of Missouri Press, 1982. 132–42.

Irr, Caren. *Toward the Geopolitical Novel: U.S. Fiction in the Twenty-First Century*. New York: Columbia University Press, 2004.

Jacobs, Harriet A. *Incidents in the Life of a Slave Girl, Written By Herself*. Ed. Jean Fagan Yellin. Cambridge, MA: Harvard University Press, 1987.

Jameson, Fredric. *The Antinomies of Realism*. London: Verso, 2013.

—. *Archaeologies of the Future: The Desire Called Utopia and Other Fictions*. New York: Verso, 2005.

Jay, Martin. *Downcast Eyes: The Denigration of Vision in Twentieth-Century French Thought*. Berkeley: University of California Press, 1993.

Josephs, Allen. 'The Quest for God in *The Road*'. In Frye, ed., *The Cambridge Companion to Cormac McCarthy*. 133–45.

Jurgensen, John. 'Hollywood's Favorite Cowboy: Interview with Cormac McCarthy'. *The Wall Street Journal*, 20 November 2009.

Kaplan, David M. *Ricoeur's Critical Theory*. Albany: State University of New York Press, 2003.

Kaup, Monika. *Neobaroque in the Americas: Alternative Modernities in Literature, Visual Art, and Film*. Charlottesville: University of Virginia Press, 2012.

—. 'The Neobaroque in W.G. Sebald's *The Rings of Saturn*: The Recovery of Open Totality Countering Poststructuralism'. *Contemporary Literature* 54.4 (2013): 683–719.

Kearney, Kevin. 'Cormac McCarthy's *The Road* and the Frontier of the Human'. *Literature Interpretation Theory* 23.2 (2012): 160–78. https://doi.org/10.1080/10436928.2012.676986.

Kearney, Richard. 'Introduction: Carnal Hermeneutics from Head to Foot'. In Kearney and Treanor, eds., *Carnal Hermeneutics*. 15–56.

Kearney, Richard, and Brian Treanor, eds. *Carnal Hermeneutics*. New York: Fordham University Press, 2015.

Keller, Catherine. *Apocalypse Now and Then: A Feminist Guide to the End of the World*. Minneapolis: Fortress Press, 2005.

Kermode, Frank. *The Sense of an Ending: Studies in the Theory of Fiction*. Oxford: Oxford University Press, 1967.

Kollin, Susan. '"Barren, Silent, Godless": Ecodisaster and the Post-Abundant Landscape in *The Road*'. In Spurgeon, ed., *Cormac McCarthy*. 157–71.

Koselleck, Reinhart. *Futures Past: On the Semantics of Historical Time*. Trans. Keith Tribe. Cambridge, MA: MIT Press, 1985.

Kunsa, Ashley. '"Maps of the World in Its Becoming": Post-Apocalyptic Naming in Cormac McCarthy's *The Road*'. *Journal of Modern Literature* 33.1 (2009): 57–74.

Kunstler, James Howard. *World Made by Hand*. New York: Atlantic Monthly Press, 2008.

Kushner, David. 'Cormac McCarthy's Apocalypse'. *Rolling Stone*, 27 December 2008.

Latour, Bruno. 'An Attempt at a "Compositionist Manifesto"'. *New Literary History* 41.3 (2010): 471–90.

—. 'The Enlightenment without the Critique: A Word on Michel Serres' Philosophy'. In *Contemporary French Philosophy*, ed. A. Phillips Griffiths. Cambridge: Cambridge University Press, 1987. 83–97.

—. *An Inquiry into Modes of Existence: An Anthropology of the Moderns*. Trans. Catherine Porter. Cambridge, MA: Harvard University Press, 2013.

—. *On the Modern Cult of the Factish Gods*. Trans. Catherine Porter and Heather MacLean. Durham, NC: Duke University Press, 2010.

—. *Pandora's Hope: Essays on the Reality of Science Studies*. Cambridge, MA: Harvard University Press, 1999.

—. *The Pasteurization of France*. Trans. Alan Sheridan and John Law. Cambridge, MA: Harvard University Press, 1988.

—. *Politics of Nature: How to Bring the Sciences into Democracy*. Trans. Catherine Porter. Cambridge, MA: Harvard University Press, 2004.

—. *Reassembling the Social: An Introduction to Actor-Network Theory*. Oxford: Oxford University Press, 2005.

—. *We Have Never Been Modern*. Trans. Catherine Porter. Cambridge, MA: Harvard University Press, 1993.

—. 'Why Has Critique Run Out of Steam? From Matters of Fact to Matters of Concern'. In Brown, ed., *Things*. 151–73.

Leigh, David J. *Apocalyptic Patterns in Twentieth-Century Fiction*. Notre Dame: University of Notre Dame Press, 2008.

Levinas, Emmanuel. *Totality and Infinity: An Essay on Exteriority*. Trans. Alphonso Lingis. Pittsburgh: Duquesne University Press, 1969.

Lewontin, Richard. *The Triple Helix: Gene, Organism, and Environment*. Cambridge, MA: Harvard University Press, 2000.

Lewontin, Richard, and Richard Levins. *Biology under the Influence: Dialectical Essays on Ecology, Agriculture, and Health*. New York: Monthly Review Press, 2007.

Leypoldt, Günter. 'Recent Realist Fiction and the Idea of Writing "After Postmodernism"'. *Amerikastudien/American Studies* 49.1 (2004): 19–34.

Lingis, Alphonso. *The First Person Singular*. Evanston: Northwestern University Press, 2007.

—. 'Return of the First-Person Singular'. In *Irrevocable: A Philosophy of Mortality*. Chicago: University of Chicago Press, 2018. 53–61.

Livingston, Ira. *Between Science and Literature: An Introduction to Autopoietics*. Urbana: University of Illinois Press, 2006.

Love, Heather. 'Close Reading and Thin Description'. *Public Culture* 25.3 (2013): 401–34.

Luhmann, Niklas. 'The Autopoiesis of Social Systems'. In *Essays on Self-Reference*. New York: Columbia University Press, 1990. 1–20.

Maclure, Jocelyn. 'Introduction: Reasonable Naturalism and the Humanistic Resistance to Reductionism'. In Gabriel, *Neo-Existentialism*. 1–7.

Margulis, Lynn, and Dorion Sagan. *Microcosmos: Four Billion Years of Microbial Evolution*. Berkeley: University of California Press, 1986.

—. *What Is Life?* Berkeley: University of California Press, 1995.

Marion, Jean-Luc. *Being Given: Toward a Phenomenology of Givenness*. 1997. Trans. Jeffrey L. Kosky. Stanford: Stanford University Press, 2002.

—. *The Crossing of the Visible*. Trans. James K. A. Smith. Stanford: Stanford University Press, 2004.

—. *In Excess: Studies of Saturated Phenomena*. 2001. Trans. Robyn Horner and Vincent Berraud. New York: Fordham University Press, 2002.

—. *Reduction and Givenness: Investigations of Husserl, Heidegger, and Phenomenology*. 1989. Trans. Thomas A. Carlson. Evanston: Northwestern University Press, 1998.

Martin, Theodore. *Contemporary Drift: Genre, Historicism, and the Problem of the Present*. New York: Columbia University Press, 2017.

Maturana, Humberto R., and Bernhard Poerksen. *From Being to Doing: The Origins of the Biology of Cognition*. Trans. Wolfram Karl Koeck and Alison Rosemary Koeck. Heidelberg: Carl-Auer Verlag, 2004.

Maturana, Humberto R., and Francisco J. Varela. *Autopoiesis and Cognition: The Realization of the Living*. Dordrecht: Reidel, 1980.

—. *The Tree of Knowledge: The Biological Roots of Human Understanding*. 1987; Boston, MA: Shambhala Press, 1998.

McCarthy, Cormac. *The Road*. New York: Random House, 2006.

McKibben, Bill. *The End of Nature*. New York: Random House, 2006.

Meillassoux, Quentin. *After Finitude: An Essay on the Necessity of Contingency*. Trans. Ray Brassier. London: Bloomsbury, 2008.

Menne, Jeff. '"I Live in this World, Too": Octavia Butler and the State of Realism'. *Modern Fiction Studies* 57.4 (2011): 715–37.

Merleau-Ponty, Maurice. *Phenomenology of Perception*. Trans. Colin Smith. London: Routledge and Kegan Paul, 1962.

Miller, Walter M. *A Canticle for Leibowitz*. Philadelphia: Lippincott, 1960.

Moran, Dermot. *Introduction to Phenomenology*. London: Routledge, 2000.

Morgan, Wesley. 'The Route and Roots of *The Road*'. *The Cormac McCarthy Journal* 6 (Autumn 2008): 39–47.

Morton, Timothy. *Dark Ecology: For a Logic of Future Coexistence*. New York: Columbia University Press, 2016.

—. *The Ecological Thought*. Cambridge, MA: Harvard University Press, 2010.

—. *Ecology without Nature: Rethinking Environmental Aesthetics*. Cambridge, MA: Harvard University Press, 2007.

—. *Hyperobjects: Philosophy and Ecology after the End of the World*. Minneapolis: University of Minnesota Press, 2013.

Moya, Paula. 'Introduction: Reclaiming Identity'. In *Reclaiming Identity: Realist Theory and the Predicament of Postmodernism*, ed. Paula Moya and Michael R. Hames-García. Berkeley: University of California Press, 2000. 1–26.

Moylan, Tom. *Scraps of the Untainted Sky: Science Fiction, Utopia, Dystopia*. Boulder: Westview Press, 2000.

Mugerauer, Robert. 'Maturana and Varela: From Autopoiesis to Systems Applications'. In *Traditions of Systems Theory*, ed. Darrell Arnold and Robert King. New York: Routledge, 2013. 158–78.

—. 'The Double Gift: Place and Identity'. In *Place and Phenomenology*, ed. Janet Donahue. New York: Rowman and Littlefield International, 2017. 17–38.

Murphet, Julian, and Mark Steven. 'Introduction: "The Charred Ruins of a Library"'. In Murphet and Steven, eds., *Styles of Extinction*. 1–8.

—, eds. *Styles of Extinction: Cormac McCarthy's The Road*. New York: Continuum, 2012.

Nagel, Thomas. *Mind and Cosmos: Why the Materialist Neo-Darwinian Conception of Nature is Almost Certainly False*. Oxford: Oxford University Press, 2012.

—. 'What is it Like to be a Bat?' In *Mortal Questions*. Cambridge: Cambridge University Press, 1979. 165–80.

Nicol, Brian. *The Cambridge Introduction to Postmodern Fiction*. Cambridge: Cambridge University Press, 2009.

Noë, Alva. *Action in Perception*. Cambridge, MA: MIT Press, 2004.

—. *Out of Our Heads: Why You Are Not Your Brain, and Other Lessons from the Biology of Consciousness*. New York: Farrar, Straus and Giroux, 2009.

Pavelich, Andrew. 'After the End of the World: Critiques of Technology in Post-Apocalypse Literature'. In *SciFi in the Mind's Eye: Reading*

Science through Science Fiction, ed. Margret Grebowicz. Chicago: Open Court, 2007. 185–98.

Phillips, Dana. '"He Ought Not Have Done It": McCarthy and Apocalypse'. In Spurgeon, ed., *Cormac McCarthy*. 172–88.

Piketty, Thomas. *Capital in the Twenty-First Century*. Trans. Arthur Goldhammer. Cambridge, MA: Harvard University Press, 2014.

Polkinghorne, Donald. *Methodology for the Human Sciences: Systems of Inquiry*. Albany: State University of New York Press, 1983.

Prigogine, Ilya, and Isabelle Stengers. *Order Out of Chaos: Man's New Dialogue with Nature*. New York: Bantam, 1984.

Rebein, Robert. 'Contemporary Realism'. In *American Fiction after 1945*, ed. John N. Duvall. Cambridge: Cambridge University Press, 2012. 30–43.

Ricoeur, Paul. *Time and Narrative*. Vol. 1. Trans. Kathleen McLaughlin and David Pellauer. Chicago: University of Chicago Press, 1984.

—. *Time and Narrative*. Vol. 2. Trans. Kathleen McLaughlin and David Pellauer. Chicago: University of Chicago Press, 1985.

—. *Time and Narrative*. Vol. 3. Trans. Kathleen McLaughlin and David Pellauer. Chicago: University of Chicago Press, 1988.

Rimmon-Kenan, Shlomith. *Narrative Fiction: Contemporary Poetics*. London: Routledge, 2002.

Rose, Stephen. *Lifelines: Life Beyond the Gene*. Oxford: Oxford University Press, 1997.

Rosen, Elizabeth. *Apocalyptic Transformation: Apocalypse and the Postmodern Imagination*. Lanham, MD: Lexington Books, 2008.

Saramago, José. *Blindness*. Trans. Giovanni Pontiero. 1995; New York: Harcourt Brace, 1999.

—. 'The 1998 Nobel Lecture'. *World Literature Today* 73.1 (1999): 5–10.

Schiesari, Juliana. *The Gendering of Melancholia: Feminism, Psychoanalysis, and the Symbolics of Loss in Renaissance Literature*. Ithaca: Cornell University Press, 1992.

Schmidgen, Henning. *Bruno Latour in Pieces: An Intellectual Biography*. Trans. Gloria Custance. New York: Fordham University Press, 2015.

Searle, John. 'Aussichten fuer einen neuen Realismus'. In Gabriel, ed., *Der Neue Realismus*. 292–307.

See, Lisa. 'PW Interviews: Octavia Butler'. In Francis, ed., *Conversations with Octavia Butler*. 41–2.

Serres, Michel, and Bruno Latour. *Conversations on Science, Culture, and Time*. Trans. Roxanne Lapidus. Ann Arbor: University of Michigan Press, 1995.

Shaviro, Steven. *The Universe of Things: On Speculative Realism.* Minneapolis: University of Minnesota Press, 2014.

Shechner, Mark. 'American Realisms, American Realities'. In Versluys, ed., *Neo-Realism in Contemporary American Fiction.* 27–50.

Shumway, David R. 'Criticism and Critique: A Genealogy'. In Di Leo, ed., *Criticism after Critique.* 15–25.

Simms, Karl. *Paul Ricoeur.* London: Routledge, 2003.

Smith, Stephanie A. 'The Tender of Memory: Restructuring Value in Harriet Jacobs's *Incidents in the Life of a Slave Girl*'. In *Harriet Jacobs and Incidents in the Life of a Slave Girl: New Critical Essays,* ed. Deborah M. Garfield and Rafia Zafar. Cambridge: Cambridge University Press, 1996. 251–74.

Snyder, Phillip A., and Delys W. Snyder. 'Modernism, Postmodernism, and Language: McCarthy's Style'. In Frye, ed., *The Cambridge Companion to Cormac McCarthy.* 27–38.

Sparrow, Tom. *The End of Phenomenology: Metaphysics and the New Realism.* Edinburgh: Edinburgh University Press, 2014.

Spinoza, Benedict de. *Ethics.* Ed. James Gutmann. New York: Hafner Publishing, 1949.

Spurgeon, Sara L., ed. *Cormac McCarthy: All the Pretty Horses, No Country for Old Men, The Road.* London: Continuum, 2011.

Stanley, Sandra Kumamoto. 'The Excremental Gaze: Saramago's *Blindness* and the Disintegration of the Panoptic Vision'. *Critique* 45.3 (2004): 293–307.

Stein, Karen F. 'Problematic Paradice in *Oryx and Crake*'. In Bouson, ed., *Margaret Atwood.* 141–55.

Stengers, Isabelle. *Cosmopolitics I.* Trans. Robert Bononno. Minneapolis: University of Minnesota Press, 2010.

Sterling, Bruce. *Distraction.* New York: Bantam, 1998.

Stillman, Peter G. 'Dystopian Critiques, Utopian Possibilities, and Human Purposes in Octavia Butler's *Parables*'. *Utopian Studies* 14.1 (2003): 15–35.

Straus, Erwin W. 'The Upright Posture'. In *Phenomenological Anthropology: The Selected Papers of Erwin W. Straus.* Trans. Erling Eng. New York: Basic Books, 1966. 137–65.

Suvin, Darko. *Metamorphoses of Science Fiction: On the Poetics and History of a Literary Genre.* New Haven: Yale University Press, 1979.

Szendy, Peter. *Apocalypse-Cinema: 2012 and Other Ends of the World.* Trans. Will Bishop. New York: Fordham University Press, 2015.

Tate, Andrew. *Apocalyptic Fiction.* London: Bloomsbury, 2017.

Thaler, Ingrid. *Black Atlantic Speculative Fictions: Octavia E. Butler, Jewelle Gomez, and Nalo Hopkinson*. New York: Routledge, 2010.

Theroux, Marcel. *Far North*. New York: Farrar, Straus, and Giroux, 2009.

Thielemann, Werner. 'Sehende Blinde–Parádoxon oder Erkenntnisprinzip: Gedanken zu José Saramagos *Ensaio sobre a cegueira* (Die Stadt der Blinden)'. *Lusorama: Zeitschrift für Lusanistik/Revista de Estudos sobre os Países de Língua Portuguesa* 38 (March 1999): 6–17.

Thompson, Evan. *Mind in Life: Biology, Phenomenology, and the Sciences of Mind*. Cambridge, MA: Harvard University Press, 2007.

Thompson, Evan, and Diego Cosmelli. 'Brain in a Vat or Body in a World? Brainbound versus Enactive Views of Experience'. *Philosophical Topics* 39.1 (2011): 163–80.

Todorov, Tzvetan. *The Fantastic: A Structural Approach to a Literary Genre*. Trans. Richard Howard. Ithaca: Cornell University Press, 1975.

Treanor, Brian. 'Mind the Gap: The Challenge of Matter'. In Kearney and Treanor, eds., *Carnal Hermeneutics*. 57-73.

Tresch, John. 'Another Turn after ANT: An Interview with Bruno Latour'. *Social Studies of Science* 43.2 (2013): 302–13.

Trexler, Adam. *Anthropocene Fictions: The Novel in a Time of Climate Change*. Charlottesville: University of Virginia Press, 2015.

Van Manen, Max. *Phenomenology of Practice: Meaning-Giving Methods in Phenomenological Research and Writing*. Walnut Creek, CA: Left Coast Press, 2014.

Varela, Francisco J. 'The Early Days of Autopoiesis'. In Clarke and Hansen, eds., *Emergence and Embodiment*. 62–76.

Varela, Francisco J., Evan Thompson and Eleanor Rosch. *The Embodied Mind: Cognitive Science and Human Experience*. Cambridge, MA: MIT Press, 1993.

Versluys, Kristiaan, ed. *Neo-Realism in Contemporary American Fiction*. Amsterdam: Rodopi, 1992.

Vieira, Patricia I. 'The Reason of Vision: Variations on Subjectivity in José Saramago's *Ensaio sobre a cegueira*'. *Luso-Brazilian Review* 46.2 (2009): 1–21.

Wald, Priscilla. *Contagious: Cultures, Carriers, and the Outbreak Narrative*. Durham, NC: Duke University Press, 2008.

Watt, Ian. *The Rise of the Novel*. Berkeley: University of California Press, 1957.

Webster, Gerry, and Brian Goodwin. *Form and Transformation: Generative and Relational Principles in Biology*. Cambridge: Cambridge University Press, 1996.

Whitehead, Colson. *Zone One*. New York: Doubleday, 2011.

Wolfe, Cary. *What Is Posthumanism?* Minneapolis: University of Minnesota Press, 2010.

Yellin, Jean Fagan. 'Introduction'. In Jacobs, *Incidents in the Life of a Slave Girl*. Cambridge, MA: Harvard University Press, 1987. xiii–xxxiii.

Zamora, Lois Parkinson. *Writing the Apocalypse: Historical Visions in Contemporary U.S. and Latin American Fiction*. Cambridge: Cambridge University Press, 1989.

Zamora, Lois Parkinson, and Monika Kaup, eds. *Baroque New Worlds: Representation, Transculturation, and Counterconquest*. Durham, NC: Duke University Press, 2010.

Zima, Peter V. *Moderne/Postmoderne: Gesellschaft, Philosophie, Literatur*. 2nd edn. Tübingen: A. Francke, 2001.

Index